Arabella's thoughts were in turmoil. Adam St Just was the last man— absolutely the *last*—she'd ever thought would offer for her.

She twisted the towel in her hands. *What do I do?*

His offer was astonishingly flattering. One of the great prizes on the Marriage Mart, a man who'd had caps past counting set at him… *And he chooses me?* Why?

He'd said that he admired her, that he respected her, that he had affection for her. She knew what he meant by that last word: affection. St Just didn't leer at her like Lord Dalrymple did, but she recognised the warmth in his eyes. He wanted her, as a man wants a woman.

Arabella shuddered.

Her instinctive response to St Just's offer had been *no*—it still was. Because if she married him she'd have to share his bed.

ACKNOWLEDGEMENTS

This book started its life while I was travelling in Canada. I'd like to thank the various public libraries in and around Victoria on Vancouver Island (in particular the Esquimalt branch) where I figured out the plot. And thanks to the public library in Prince Rupert (a town where the bald eagles are as plentiful as sparrows), where the second chapter was written. But the biggest thanks go to the owners of the backpackers' hostel on Denman Island, on whose veranda the first chapter was written. I wish I could have written the whole book there!

THE UNMASKING OF A LADY

Emily May

First published in Great Britain 2010
Harlequin Mills & Boon Limited,
Eton House, 18-24 Paradise Road, Richmond, Surrey TW9 1SR

© Emily May 2010

ISBN: 978 0 263 21468 0

Harlequin Mills & Boon policy is to use papers that are natural,
renewable and recyclable products and made from wood grown in
sustainable forests. The logging and manufacturing process conform
to the legal environmental regulations of the country of origin.

Printed and bound in Great Britain
by CPI Antony Rowe, Chippenham, Wiltshire

Emily May grew up in a house full of books—her mother worked as a proof-reader and librarian, and her father is a well-known New Zealand novelist. Emily has studied a wide number of subjects, including Geology and Geophysics, Canine Behaviour and Ancient Greek. Her varied career includes stints as a field assistant in Antarctica and a waitress on the Isle of Skye. Most recently she has worked in the wine industry in Marlborough, New Zealand.

Emily loves to travel, and has lived in Sweden, backpacked in Europe, and travelled overland in the Middle East, China and North Africa. She enjoys climbing hills, yoga workouts, watching reruns of *Buffy the Vampire Slayer*, and reading. She is especially fond of Georgette Heyer's Regency and Georgian novels.

Emily writes Regency romances as Emily May, and dark, romantic fantasy novels as Emily Gee (www.emilygee.com).

A previous novel by this author:

THE EARL'S DILEMMA

This book is for Margareta and Maurice,
for their very generous hospitality.

I can't thank you enough!

Chapter One

The thief stood in front of Lady Bicknell's dressing table and looked with disapproval at the objects strewn across it: glass vials of perfume, discarded handkerchiefs, a clutter of pots and jars of cosmetics—rouge, *maquillage*—many gaping open, their contents drying, two silver-backed hairbrushes with strands of hair caught among the bristles, a messy pile of earrings, the faceted jewels glinting dully in the candlelight.

The thief stirred the earrings with a fingertip. Gaudy. Tasteless. In need of cleaning.

The dressing table, the mess, offended the thief's tidy soul. She pursed her lips and examined the earrings again, more slowly. The diamonds were paste, the sapphires nothing more than coloured glass, the rubies... She picked up a ruby earring and looked at it closely. Real, but such a garish, vulgar setting. The thief grimaced and put the earring back, more neatly than its owner had done. There was nothing on the dressing table that interested her.

She turned to the mahogany dresser. It stood in the corner, crouching on bowed legs like a large toad. Three wide drawers and at the top, three small ones, side by side, beneath a frowning mirror. The thief quietly opened the drawers and let her fingers sift through the contents, stirring the woman's scent from the garments: perspiration, perfume.

The topmost drawer on the left, filled with a tangle of silk stockings and garters, wasn't as deep as the others.

For a moment the thief stood motionless, listening for footsteps in the corridor, listening to the breeze stir the curtains at the open window, then she pulled the drawer out and laid it on the floor.

Behind the drawer of stockings was another drawer, small and discreet, and inside that…

The thief grinned as she lifted out the bracelet. Pearls gleamed in the candlelight, exquisite, expensive.

The drawer contained—besides the bracelet—a matching pair of pearl earrings and four letters. The thief took the earrings and replaced the letters. She was easing the drawer back into its slot when a name caught her eye. *St Just.*

St Just. The name brought with it memory of a handsome face and grey eyes, memory of humiliation—and a surge of hatred.

She hesitated for a second, and then reached for the letters.

The first one was brief and to the point. *Here, as requested, is my pearl bracelet. In exchange, I must ask for the return of my letter.* It was signed Grace St Just.

The thief frowned and unfolded the second letter. It was written in the same girlish hand as the first. The date made her pause—November 6th, 1817. The day Princess Charlotte had died, although the letter writer wouldn't have known that at the time.

Dearest Reginald, the letter started. The thief skimmed over a passionate declaration of love and slowed to read the final paragraph. *I miss you unbearably. Every minute seems like an hour, every day a year. The thought of being parted from you is unendurable. If it must be elopement, then so be it.* A tearstain marked the ink. *Your loving Grace.*

The thief picked up the third letter. It was a draft, some words crossed out, others scribbled in the margins.

~~My dear~~ Miss St Just, ~~I have~~ a letter ~~of yours~~ you wrote to a Mr Reginald Plunkett of Birmingham has come into my possession. ~~If you want it back. In exchange for its return.~~ I should like to return this letter to you. In exchange I ~~want~~ ask nothing more than your pearl bracelet. You may leave ~~it~~ the bracelet ~~for me~~ in the Dutch garden in the Kensington Palace Gardens. ~~Place it~~ Hide it in the urn at the north-eastern corner of the pond.

The thief thinned her lips. She stopped reading and picked up the final letter. Another draft.

Dear Miss St Just, thank you for the bracelet. I find, however, that I ~~want~~ *require* ~~the necklace~~ *the earrings as well. You may leave them in the same place. Do not worry about the your letter;* ~~I have it~~ *it is safe in my keeping.*

The thief slowly refolded the piece of paper. Blackmail. There was a sour taste in her mouth. She looked down at the bracelet and earrings, at the love letter, and bit her lower lip. What to do?

St Just. Memory flooded through her: the smothered laughter of the *ton,* the sniggers and the sideways glances, the gleeful whispers.

The thief tightened her lips. Resentment burned in her breast and heated her cheeks. Adam St Just could rot in hell for all she cared, but Grace St Just…Grace St Just didn't deserve this.

Her decision made, the thief gathered the contents of the hidden drawer—letters and jewels—and tucked them into the pouch she wore around her waist, hidden beneath shirt and trousers. Swiftly she replaced both drawers. Crossing the room, she plucked the ruby earrings from the objects littering Lady Bicknell's dressing table. The rubies went into the pouch, nestling alongside the pearls. The thief propped an elegant square of card among the remaining earrings. The message inscribed on it was brief: *Should payment be made for a spiteful tongue? Tom thinks so.* There was no signature; a drawing of a lean alley cat adorned the bottom of the note.

The thief gave a satisfied nod. Justice done. She glanced at the mirror. In the candlelight her eyes were black. Her face was soot-smudged and unrecognisable. For a moment she stared at herself, unsettled, then she lifted a finger to touch the faint cleft in her chin. That, at least, was recognisable, whether she wore silk dresses or boys' clothing in rough, dark fabric.

The thief turned away from her image in the mirror. She trod quietly towards the open window.

Adam St Just found his half-sister in the morning room, reading a letter. Her hair gleamed like spun gold in the sunlight. 'Grace?'

His sister gave a convulsive start and clutched the letter to her breast. A bundle of items on her lap slid to the floor. Something landed with a light thud. Adam saw the glimmer of pearls.

'Is that your bracelet? I thought you'd lost—' He focused on her face. 'What's wrong?'

'Nothing.' Grace hastily wiped her cheek. 'Just something in my eye.' She bent and hurriedly gathered several pieces of paper and the bracelet.

A pearl earring lay stranded on the carpet. Adam nudged it with the toe of his boot. 'And this?' He picked up the earring and held it out.

Grace flushed. She took the earring.

Adam frowned at her. 'Grace, what is it?'

'Nothing.' Her smile was bright, but her eyes slid away from his.

Adam sat down on the sofa alongside her. 'Grace…' he said, and then stopped, at a loss to know how to proceed. The physical distance between them—a few inches of rose-pink damask—might as well have been a chasm. The twelve years that separated them, the difference in their genders, seemed insurmountable barriers. He felt a familiar sense of helplessness, a familiar knowledge that he was failing in his guardianship of her.

He looked at his sister's downcast eyes, the curve of her cheek, the slender fingers clutching the pearl earring. *I love you, Grace.* He cleared his throat and tried to say the words aloud. 'Grace, I hope you know that I…care about you and that I want you to be happy.'

It was apparently the wrong thing to say. Grace began to cry.

Adam hesitated for a moment, dismayed, and then put his arm around her. To his relief, Grace didn't pull away. She turned towards him, burying her face in his shoulder.

It hurt to hear her cry. Adam swallowed and tightened his grip on her. She'd grown thinner since their arrival in London, paler, quieter. *I should take her home. To hell with the Season.*

The storm of tears lessened. Adam stroked his sister's hair. 'What is it, Grace?'

'I didn't want to disappoint you again,' she sobbed.

'You've never disappointed me.'

Grace shook her head against his shoulder. 'Last year…' She didn't need to say more; they both knew to what she was referring.

'I was angry—but not with you.' He'd been more than angry: he'd been furious. Furious at Reginald Plunkett, furious at the school for hiring the man, but mostly furious at himself for not visiting Grace more often, for not realising how lonely she was, how vulnerable to the smiles and compliments of her music teacher.

The anger stirred again, tightening in his chest as if a fist was clenched there. *I should have horsewhipped him. I should have broken every bone in his body.*

Adam dug in his pocket for a handkerchief. Grace had come perilously close to ruin. Even now, six months later, he woke in a cold sweat from dreams—nightmares—in which he'd delayed his journey by one day, and arrived in Bath to find her gone. 'Here,' he said, handing her the handkerchief.

Grace dried her cheeks.

Adam smiled at her. 'Now, tell me what's wrong.'

Grace looked down at her lap, at the papers and the pearls. She extracted a sheet of paper and handed it to him.

~~My dear~~ Miss St Just, ~~I have~~ a letter ~~of yours~~ you wrote to a Mr Reginald Plunkett of Birmingham has come into my possession. ~~If you want it back. In exchange for its return.~~ I should like to return this letter to you. In exchange I ~~want~~ ask nothing more than your pearl bracelet.

'What!' He stared at his sister. 'Someone's blackmailing you?'

Grace bit her lip.

Adam's fingers tightened on the sheet of paper. 'Why didn't you tell me?'

Her gaze fell.

Because you were afraid I'd be angry at you, disappointed in you. Adam swallowed. He looked back at the blackmail letter without seeing it. He rubbed his face with one hand. 'Grace…'

'Here.' She handed him another piece of paper. The writing was the same as the first, the intent as ugly.

'You did what this person asked? You gave them your pearls?' His rage made the sunlight seem as sharp-edged as a knife. The room swung around him for a moment, vivid with anger. He focused on a chair. The rose-pink damask had become the deep crimson of blood, the gilded wood was as bright as flames. *How dared anyone do this to her?* The sheet of paper crumpled in his fist. *I'll kill them—*

'Yes.' Grace gathered the bracelet and the earrings within the curve of her palm.

Adam blinked. His anger fell away, replaced by confusion. 'Then why—?'

'Tom returned them to me.'

'Tom?'

He blinked again at the elegant piece of paper she handed him, at the brief message, at the signature and the cat drawn in black ink at the bottom of the page. His interest sharpened. That Tom.

I believe these belong to you, Tom had written. *I found them in Lady Bicknell's possession.*

'And the letter to Reginald Plunkett?'

Grace touched a folded piece of paper in her lap.

Adam read the note again. *Tom.* 'The devil,' he said, under his breath. He fastened his gaze on his sister. 'Was there anything else? Anything that might identify him?'

Grace shook her head.

Adam touched the ink-drawn cat with a fingertip. It stared back at him, sitting with its tail curled across its paws, unblinking, calm.

He lifted his eyes to the signature, and above that to the message. 'Lady Bicknell,' he said aloud, and the rage came back.

'Apparently,' Grace said.

The blackmail letters were clearly drafts. 'You have the ones she sent you?'

Grace shook her head. 'I burned them.'

Adam re-read Lady Bicknell's letters, letting his eyes rest on each and every word, scored out or not. 'She'll pay for this,' he said grimly. 'By God, if she thinks she can—!' He recollected himself, glanced at his sister's face and forced himself to sit back on the sofa, to form his mouth into a smile. 'Forget this, Grace. It's over.'

'Yes,' said Grace, but her expression was familiar: pale, miserable. She'd worn it four years ago when her mother died, and she'd worn it last November when she'd learned the truth about Reginald Plunkett.

Adam reached for her hand. 'How odd, that we must be grateful to a thief.' He laughed, tried to make a joke of it.

Grace smiled dutifully.

Adam looked at her, noting the paleness of her cheeks, the faint shadows beneath the blue eyes. 'Grace, would you like to go home?' Away from the press of buildings and people and the sly whispers of gossip.

Her face lit up, as if the sun had come from behind a cloud. 'Oh, yes!'

'Then I'll arrange it.'

'Thank you!' She pulled her hand free from his grasp and embraced him, swift and wholly unexpected.

Adam experienced a throat-tightening rush of emotion. He folded his sister briefly in his arms and then released her. *How did we become so distant?* He cleared his throat. 'Have you any engagements today? Would you like to ride out to Richmond?'

'Oh, yes! I should like that of all things!' She rose, and the pearls tumbled from her lap on to the damask-covered sofa. A much-creased letter fluttered down alongside them. It was addressed to Reginald Plunkett in Grace's handwriting.

The delight faded from his sister's face, leaving it miserable once more.

Adam gestured to the letter. 'Do you want to keep it?'

Grace shook her head.

'Shall I burn it for you? Or would you prefer—?'

'I don't want to touch it!' Her voice was low and fierce.

Adam nodded. He scooped up the pearls and placed them in Grace's palm, curling her fingers around them, holding her hand, holding her gaze. 'Forget about this, Grace. It's over.'

Grace nodded, but the happiness that had briefly lit her face was gone.

Adam stood. He kissed her cheek. 'Go and change,' he said, releasing her hand.

When she'd gone, he picked up the pieces of paper: Grace's love letter, Tom's note, Lady Bicknell's blackmail drafts. He allowed his rage to flare again. Lady Bicknell would pay for the distress she'd caused Grace. She'd pay deeply.

But some of the blame was his. The distance between them was his fault: he'd been his sister's guardian, not her friend. She'd been too afraid of his disappointment, his anger, to ask for help.

Adam strode from the morning room. His shame was a physical thing; he felt it in his chest as if a knife blade was buried there.

He had failed Grace. Somehow, without realising it, he'd become to her what their father had been to him: disapproving and unapproachable.

But no more, he vowed silently as he entered his study. *No more.*

Adam grimly placed the letters in the top drawer of his desk. He put Tom's note in last and let his gaze dwell on the signature. 'I would like to know who you are,' he said under his breath. And then he locked the drawer and put the key in his pocket.

Arabella Knightley, granddaughter of the fifth Earl of Westcote, paused alongside a potted palm and surveyed the ballroom. Lord and Lady Halliwell were launching their eldest daughter in style: hundreds of candles blazed in the chandeliers, a profusion of flowers scented the air, and yards of shimmering pink silk swathed the walls. An orchestra played on a dais and dancing couples filled the floor, performing the intricate steps of the quadrille. The débutantes were distinguishable by their self-consciousness as much as by their pale gowns.

Grace St Just wasn't on the dance floor. Arabella looked at the ladies seated around the perimeter of the ballroom, scanning their faces as she sipped her lemonade. Her lip lifted slightly in contempt as she recognised Lady Bicknell.

The woman's appearance—the tasteless, gaudy trinkets, the heavy application of cosmetics—was reminiscent of her dressing table. Her earrings… Arabella narrowed her eyes. Yes, Lady Bicknell was wearing the diamond earrings she herself had discarded as worthless.

If the woman's appearance was in keeping with her dressing table, her figure brought to mind the mahogany dresser: broad and squat. *Like a frog,* Arabella thought, watching as Lady Bicknell's wide, flat mouth opened and shut. She was disclaiming forcefully, her heavy face flushed with outrage. One of the ladies seated alongside her hid a smile behind her fan; the other, a dowager wearing a purple turban, listened with round-eyed interest.

Telling the tale of Tom's thieving, Arabella thought, with another curl of her lip. The woman certainly wouldn't mention the other items that had gone missing last night: the pearl bracelet and earrings, the blackmail letters.

Arabella dismissed Lady Bicknell from her thoughts. She continued her search of the ballroom, looking for Grace St Just.

She found her finally, seated alongside a St Just aunt. The girl wore a white satin gown sewn with seed pearls. More pearls gleamed at her earlobes and around her pale throat. She was astonishingly lovely, and yet she was sitting in a corner as if she didn't want anyone to notice her.

Arabella was reminded, vividly, of her own first Season. It was no easy thing to make one's début surrounded by whispers and conjecture and sidelong glances.

And I had advantages that Grace does not. She'd had the armour her childhood had given her—armour a girl as gently reared as Grace St Just couldn't possibly have. And she'd had advice—advice it appeared no one had given Grace.

Arabella chewed on her lower lip. She glanced at the dance floor, trying to decide what to do. Her eyes fastened on one of the dancers, a tall man with a patrician cast to his features. Adam St Just, cousin to the Duke of Frew.

She eyed him with resentment. St Just's manner was as aloof, as proud, as if it was he who held the dukedom, not his cousin. *How could I have been such a fool as to believe he liked me?* She should be grateful to St Just; he'd taught her never to trust a member of the *ton*—a valuable lesson. But it was impossible to be grateful while she still had memory of the *beau monde*'s gleeful delight in her humiliation.

Arabella watched him dance, hoping he'd misstep or trample on his partner's toes. It was a futile hope; St Just had the natural grace of a sportsman. His partner, a young débutante, lacked that grace. The girl danced stiffly, her manner awkward and admiring.

Arabella's lips tightened. No doubt St Just accepted the admiration as his due; for years he'd been one of the biggest prizes on the marriage market, courted for his wealth, his bloodline, his handsome face.

She looked again at Grace St Just. The girl bore little resemblance to her half-brother. Adam St Just's arrogance was stamped on him—the way he carried himself, the tilt of his chin, the set of his mouth. Everything about him said *I am better than you.* Grace had none of that. She sat looking down at her hands, her shoulders slightly hunched as if she wished to hide.

I really should help her.

Arabella looked at St Just again. As she watched, he cast a swift, frowning glance in the direction of his sister.

He's worried about her.

It was disconcerting to find herself in agreement with him.

Arabella swallowed the last of her lemonade, not tasting it, and handed her empty glass to a passing servant. No one snubbed her as she made her way through the crush of guests, her smiles were politely returned,

and yet everyone in the ballroom—herself included—knew that she
didn't belong. The satin gown, the fan of pierced ivory, the jewelled
combs in her hair, couldn't disguise what she was: an outsider.

Music swirled around her, and beneath that was the rustle of silk and
satin and gauze, the hum of voices. Her ears caught snippets of conversation. Much of tonight's gossip seemed to be about Lady Bicknell.
Opinion was divided: some sympathised with Lady Bicknell, others
thought it served her right.

There was no doubt why Tom had paid her a visit last night.

'That tongue of hers,' stated a florid gentleman in a waistcoat that was
too tight for him.

'Most likely,' his wife said, glancing up and meeting Arabella's eyes.
For a brief second the woman's smile stiffened, then she inclined her head
in a polite nod.

Six years ago that momentary hesitation would have hurt; now she no
longer cared. Arabella smiled cheerfully back at the woman. *Only four
more weeks of this.* Four more weeks of ball gowns and false smiles, of
pretending to belong, and then she could turn her back on society. *But
first, I must help Grace St Just.*

The girl looked up as Arabella approached. She was fairer than her
half-brother, her hair golden instead of brown, her eyes a clear shade of
blue. She was breathtakingly lovely—and quite clearly miserable.

'Miss St Just.' Arabella smiled and extended her hand. 'I don't believe
we've met. My name is Arabella Knightley.'

Grace St Just flushed faintly. She hesitated a moment, then held out
her hand. *Her brother has warned her about me.*

Arabella sat, ignoring the St Just aunt who frowned at her, lips pursed
in disapproval, from her position alongside Grace. 'How are you finding
your first Season?'

'Oh,' said Grace. She sent a darting glance in the direction of the dance
floor. 'It's very…that is to say—'

'I hated mine,' Arabella said frankly. 'Everyone staring and whispering behind their hands. It's not pleasant to be gossiped about, is it?'

Grace St Just stopped searching the dance floor for her brother. She
stared at Arabella. 'No. It isn't.'

'Someone gave me some advice,' Arabella said, 'when I was in a similar position to you. If you don't think it impertinent of me, I should like to pass it on.'

She had the girl's full attention now. Those sky-blue eyes were focused on her face with an almost painful intensity. 'Please,' Grace St Just said. Even the aunt leaned slightly forwards in her chair.

'It was given to me by Mr Brummell,' Arabella said. 'If he were still in England, I'm certain he'd impart it to you himself.'

'The Beau?' Grace breathed. 'Truly?'

Arabella nodded. 'He said…' She paused for a moment, remembering. The Beau's voice had been cool and suave, and oddly kind. 'He said I must ignore it, and more than that, I must ignore it *well.*'

It was the only time Beau Brummell had spoken to her. But he had always nodded to her most politely after that, his manner one of faint approval.

'And so I did as he suggested,' Arabella said. 'I gave the appearance of enjoying myself. I smiled at every opportunity, and when I couldn't smile, I laughed.' She smoothed a wrinkle in one of her long gloves, remembering. A slight smile tugged at her lips. 'I believe some people found it very annoying.'

She looked up and held Grace St Just's eyes. 'So that's my advice. However difficult it may seem, you must ignore what people are saying, the way they look at you. And you must ignore it *well.*'

'Ignore it?' Tears filled the girl's eyes. 'How *can* I?'

'It isn't easy,' Arabella said firmly. 'But it can be done.'

Grace shook her head. She hunted in her reticule for a handkerchief. 'I would much rather go home.' Her voice wobbled on the last word.

'Certainly you may do that, but if I may be so bold, Miss St Just…the rumours are just rumours. Speculation and conjecture. If you shrug your shoulders, London will find a new target. But if you leave now, the rumours will be confirmed.'

Grace looked stricken. She sat with the handkerchief clutched in her hand and tears trembling on her eyelashes.

'It doesn't matter whether you committed whatever indiscretion London thinks you did,' Arabella said matter-of-factly. 'What matters is whether London *believes* it or not.'

Grace St Just bit her lip. She looked down at the handkerchief and twisted it between her fingers.

'Be bold,' Arabella said softly.

'Bold?' The girl's laugh was shaky. 'I'm not a bold person, Miss Knightley.'

'I think you can be anything you want.'

Arabella's voice was quiet, but it made the girl look up. For a moment they matched gazes, and then Grace St Just gave a little nod. She blew her nose and put the handkerchief away. 'Tell me…how you did it, Miss Knightley, if you please?'

Arabella was conscious of a sense of relief. She sat back in her chair and glanced at the dance floor. Adam St Just was watching them. She could see his outrage, even though half a ballroom separated them.

It was tempting to smile at him and give a mocking little wave. Arabella did neither. She turned her attention back to Grace St Just.

Adam relinquished Miss Hornby to the care of her mother. He turned and grimly surveyed the far corner of the ballroom. His sister sat alongside Arabella Knightley, as she had for the past fifteen minutes.

They made a pleasing tableau, dark and fair, their heads bent together as they talked, Miss Knightley's gown of deep rose-pink perfectly complementing his sister's white satin.

Adam gritted his teeth. He strode around the ballroom, watching as Grace said something and Miss Knightley replied—and his aunt, Seraphina Mexted, sat placidly alongside, nodding and smiling and making no attempt to shoo Miss Knightley away.

Grace lifted her head and laughed.

Adam's stride faltered. Arabella Knightley had made Grace *laugh.* In fact, now that he observed more closely, his sister's face was bright with amusement.

She looks happy.

Arabella Knightley had accomplished, in fifteen minutes, what he had been trying—and failing—to do for months. How in Hades had she done it? And far more importantly, *why?*

Miss Knightley looked up as he approached. Her colouring showed her French blood—hair and eyes so dark they were almost black—but the soft dent in her chin, as if someone had laid a fingertip there at her birth, proclaimed her as coming from a long line of Knightleys.

His eyes catalogued her features—the elegant cheekbones, the dark eyes, the soft mouth—and his pulse gave a kick. It was one of the things that annoyed him about Arabella Knightley: that he was so strongly attracted to her. The second annoying thing was the stab of guilt—as familiar as the attraction—that always accompanied sight of her.

Adam bowed. 'Miss Knightley, what a pleasure to see you here this evening.'

Her eyebrows rose. 'Truly?' Her voice was light and amused, disbelieving.

Adam clenched his jaw. This was the third thing that annoyed him about Miss Knightley: her manner.

Arabella Knightley turned to Grace and smiled. 'I must go. My grandmother will be wanting supper soon.'

Adam stepped back as she took leave of his sister and aunt. The rose-pink gown made her skin appear creamier and the dark ringlets more glossily black. A striking young woman, Miss Knightley, with her high cheekbones and dark eyes. And an extremely wealthy one, too. But no man of birth and breeding would choose to marry her—unless his need for a fortune outweighed everything else.

She turned to him. 'Good evening, Mr St Just.' Cool amusement still glimmered in her eyes.

Adam gritted his teeth and bowed again. His gaze followed her. Miss Knightley's figure was slender and her height scarcely more than five foot—and yet she had presence. It was in her carriage, in the way she held her head. She was perfectly at home in the crowded ballroom, utterly confident, unconcerned by the glances she drew.

Adam turned to his aunt. 'Aunt Seraphina, how could you allow—?'

'I like her,' Aunt Seraphina said placidly. 'Seems a very intelligent girl.'

Adam blinked, slightly taken aback.

'I like her too,' Grace said. 'Adam, may I invite her—?'

'No. Being seen in her company will harm your reputation. Miss Knightley is not good *ton*.'

'I know,' said Grace. 'She spent part of her childhood in the slums. Her mother was a…a…' She groped for a euphemism, and then gave up. 'But I *like* her. I want to be friends with her.'

Over my dead body.

'Shall we leave?' he said, changing the subject. 'It's almost midnight and we've a long journey tomorrow.' To Sussex, where there'd be no Arabella Knightley.

He began to feel more cheerful.

'I've decided to stay in London,' Grace said.

Adam raised his eyebrows. 'You have?'

'Yes,' Grace said. 'This is my first Season, and I'm going to *enjoy* it!'

Chapter Two

Adam rode out the next morning under a grey sky. London's roads were damp from a night's rain. He passed through the gate into Hyde Park, inhaling the scents of wet grass and wet earth and the rich, fresh smell of horse manure. The Row was relatively empty. Adam urged Goliath into a canter. He liked mornings like this, when the *ton* stayed abed and he could almost pretend he was at home, exercising Goliath on the Downs, not surrounded by the sprawl and clamour of London.

His thoughts turned to Grace as he rode up and down the strip of tan. Last night she'd smiled, danced, even laughed. The Season, which had begun to look like a disaster, could be saved. He'd find a husband for Grace, a man of good birth and character, a man who'd take care of her.

Adam was conscious of a feeling of lightness, as if a weight that had been sitting on his shoulders had suddenly lifted. He began to whistle beneath his breath.

Another rider entered the Row. The black mare and the claret-red riding habit were familiar, as were the rider's elegant seat and her jaunty, plumed hat.

Adam's good mood evaporated abruptly. This was one of the irritations of London: that Arabella Knightley should choose to exercise her horse at the same time as him. He pretended not to see her, but it was impossible to maintain the pretence for long with the Row so thin of riders. The third time they passed he nodded stiffly. She returned the gesture. The amusement in her smile, the slightly mocking glint in her dark eyes, as if she was laughing at him, made his hands tighten on the reins. Goliath snorted and tossed his head.

Adam loosened his grip. 'Tomorrow we'll come earlier,' he told the horse, and then he pushed all thought of Arabella Knightley out of his head, focusing instead on the far more interesting subject of Tom the burglar's identity.

That subject occupied him as he trotted back through rain-damp streets to Berkeley Square, as he gave Goliath to his groom and walked around from the mews, as he entered the cool entrance hall and handed hat, whip and gloves to the butler. 'A pot of tea, Fiscus,' he said, and walked down the hallway to his study.

Adam sat down at his desk with the letters spread before him and a teacup at his elbow. The blackmail notes were so foul, so ugly, that they seemed to taint the air he breathed, as if they gave off an odour of rankness and decay, of rot.

The notes gave no clue of the writer's identity. The paper was plain, the handwriting ordinary. Anyone could have written them. Lady Bicknell, Tom claimed.

Adam pondered this. Lady Bicknell was a widow of long-standing who possessed a disagreeably sharp tongue. An unpleasant woman, certainly. But was she a blackmailer?

Tom said so. But Tom was a thief and therefore not to be trusted. *I need proof.* Something in Lady Bicknell's hand, with her named signed in ink, for all to see. But how?

Adam sat for a long time, thinking, and then smiled. *Yes, that will work very well.* Reaching for the teacup, he took a mouthful, grimaced and swallowed the cold liquid. He pushed the cup away, pushed the blackmail notes aside and studied the piece of paper that really interested him: Tom's note.

Who are you? he asked silently, staring at the black cat.

The cat stared back at him, giving nothing away. Its gaze was fixed, inanimate and yet almost insolent. A challenge.

'I'm going to find out who you are,' Adam said aloud.

He felt a spurt of cheerfulness. Proving that Lady Bicknell was a blackmailer, finding a husband for Grace, his own search for a bride—those were things he *had* to do. Discovering Tom's identity was something altogether different. Not only would it take his mind off worrying about Grace, it would be *fun*.

Adam pulled a blank sheet of paper towards him and uncapped his inkpot.

Look for a thief? Such behaviour is hardly worthy of a St Just! The voice was his father's, ringing in his ears, even though the old man had been dead these past three years. The cold disapproval was as loud, as clear, as if his father stood at his shoulder. *You may not be the duke, but I expect you to behave as if you are!*

Adam hissed between his teeth. He pushed any thought of his father aside, dipped his quill in ink and began to write.

Adam St Just's town house was as elegantly appointed as Arabella had expected; no one could accuse St Just of lacking either money or taste. The parlour was decorated in blue and cream, the furniture was in the Grecian style, with clean lines and scrolled ends, and a pretty frieze of acanthus leaves ran around the room.

Grace St Just was every bit as beautiful as her surroundings. Her face was flower-like, open and innocent—and also fierce. The glint in her eyes, the set of her chin, were those of a woman prepared to fight.

'Advice?' Arabella said, echoing the girl's question. 'I can only tell you how I do it.'

'Please.' Grace sat forwards eagerly.

Arabella smiled wryly. 'It sounds foolish, but…when I dress, I imagine I'm putting on armour.'

The girl blinked. 'Armour?'

'Yes.' Arabella touched her gown. 'You see muslin; I see armour.'

'Oh.'

Arabella picked up her teacup. 'And then I imagine that each disapproving stare, each sneer, each whispered remark, is a tiny arrow.' She sipped her tea. 'The arrows fly at me, but they can't hurt me.' The delicate porcelain cup made a noise as she replaced it in its saucer. *Clink.* Like an arrow striking armour. 'It makes me want to laugh when I imagine the arrows lying helpless on the ground at my feet.' She grinned at the girl. 'And my amusement annoys my detractors—which amuses me even more.'

'Oh,' said Grace again. Her expression was uncertain.

Arabella eyed her for a moment. 'If the image is too martial for you, perhaps you'd like to try something else? Oilskin repelling drops of water, or…or…have you ever seen how water rolls off a duck's back?'

'Yes.' Grace's face brightened. 'Water off a duck's back! I'll do that.'

Arabella returned the girl's smile. She picked up a macaroon and bit into it. The flavours of sugar and coconut mingled on her tongue.

Grace St Just busied herself pouring another cup of tea. 'I can't thank you enough, Miss Knightley. I'm very much in your debt—'

'Bella,' she said. 'Please call me Bella.'

The girl's smile was shy. 'Then you must call me Grace.'

Arabella took another bite of macaroon. She chewed slowly, imagining St Just's reaction when he discovered that his sister was on first-name terms with her. Laughter rose in her throat.

Grace's smile faded as she sipped her tea. Her expression became pensive.

Arabella dismissed Adam St Just from her thoughts. 'You've had an unfortunate introduction into society, but there's some usefulness to be had from it.'

'Usefulness?' Grace put down her teacup.

'It's given you the opportunity to see people for who they are. It's shown you what's beneath the surface.'

Grace looked as if she'd rather not know.

'You'd prefer the shallow, empty flattery of those who admire your name and your fortune?' Arabella asked softly.

The girl flushed and shook her head.

'Then you may look upon this experience as fortunate.'

Grace looked down at her lap. She pleated a fold of sprigged muslin between her fingers. 'Three girls who were at school with me are making their débuts this Season.' She bit her lip and glanced up. 'It must be one of them who…' Tears shone in her eyes. 'I thought they were my friends.'

Arabella handed her a handkerchief. She watched in quiet sympathy as Grace wiped her eyes and blew her nose.

The girl folded the square of linen. 'He was my music master.'

'Grace, you don't need to tell me anything. It's no concern of mine—or anyone else's—what did or didn't happen.'

'Nothing happened,' Grace said bitterly. 'Although I almost…I almost—'

'You don't have to tell me,' Arabella said softly.

Grace didn't seem to hear. 'I thought I loved him,' she said. 'I was going to run away with him. And then my brother came.' Her fingers twisted on the handkerchief, wringing it. 'And it turned out that…that *he*…that my music master was married.'

Arabella refilled Grace's teacup and handed it to her. 'A valuable experience,' she said, and smiled at the girl's look of shock. 'You've gained insight into the male character, have you not? You won't fall for blandishments and flattery again.'

Grace shook her head, still looking taken aback.

'I was courted by a fortune hunter during my first Season,' Arabella told her. 'Although I didn't realise it until afterwards. It was a useful lesson.'

'Oh?' Grace's eyes sharpened with interest.

'His name was George Dysart. He was very handsome!' Arabella smiled wryly, remembering. 'He seemed so desperately in love with me that for a time I fancied myself in love with him.' He'd made her feel precious. He'd told her that her background didn't matter to him; her fortune and her family were unimportant—it was her he loved.

She had believed him, had even begun to reconsider her decision not to marry—

'What happened?' Grace asked.

Arabella was silent as memory returned: George embracing her, trying to kiss her, and her instinctive recoil. 'I was…too slow, and so he turned his attention elsewhere. Another heiress.'

Grace's eyebrows rose. 'She married him?'

'Yes. Poor Helen.'

'You're friends with her?'

Arabella smiled at the girl's startled expression. 'You think I should resent her?' She shook her head. 'No. We've become close friends. Helen's had a dreadful marriage. I pity her sincerely.' She pulled a face. 'To think I fancied myself in love with George!'

Grace looked down at her hands. It took no particular insight to know what she was thinking about.

Arabella picked up her cup again. 'That's why I say your experience was useful. It's taught you to see men more clearly. When you come to choose a husband, it will stand you in good stead.'

'Adam's going to choose my husband for me.'

Arabella's eyebrows arched. 'Is he?' she said drily. 'And you'll have no say in the matter?'

'Oh, well…' Grace flushed. 'If I *dislike* him, then Adam won't…'

'When is this happy event to take place?'

'This Season,' the girl said. 'Only…it will be more difficult now that…the rumours—'

'Hmm.' Arabella settled back in her chair. 'How old are you?'

'Seventeen.'

'Seventeen.' All her dislike of Adam St Just rushed back in force. Grace was still a child, and he wanted to marry her off. 'If your brother wishes for a marriage this Season, let it be his own!' she said tartly.

Grace nodded. 'Yes, that's what he intends.'

Arabella blinked in surprise. 'Your brother's looking for a bride?'

'He says it's time. He's nearly thirty.'

Arabella bit her upper lip to stop it curling in a sneer. What St Just thought timely for his sister was very different from what he thought timely for himself. 'I wish him luck,' she said with polite mendacity.

'Oh, Adam's not worried.'

'I'm sure he's not,' Arabella said drily. St Just was one of the most eligible bachelors in England. He might not have a title, but he had everything else a fastidious bride required: excellent lineage, substantial wealth, good looks.

She reached for another macaroon, and found herself wishing that St Just would suffer a rebuff in his suit.

Adam laid down his quill and read through the list.

Well-heeled
Educated

Those he'd inferred from Tom's note—the quality of the paper, the elegance of the handwriting, the lack of spelling mistakes.

An artist

Well, everyone knew that. The black cat, drawn in various poses, was as famous as the thief's name.

Moral

An odd attribute for a thief, but one that went without saying—Tom always chose victims who'd harmed others.

Young

A guess, this. But Tom must be youthful to accomplish such feats as scaling walls and climbing in windows.

A member of the ton.

This was the most startling of his inferences, based not on who Tom's victims were, but *how* they were chosen. Would a servant have witnessed all the acts that had roused Tom's ire? His instinct said no.

Adam pulled a fresh sheet of paper towards him and started a new list. *Lady Bicknell, May 1818.* The first of this Season's victims, presumably punished for the malicious remarks that had reduced poor Mrs Findley to tears at the Parnells' ball.

He rolled the quill between his fingers. Who had drawn Tom's attentions last year?

Ah, yes. Lord Randall, who'd fallen off his horse in Hyde Park and, in a fury of embarrassment, whipped the poor beast until he drew blood.

Adam grimaced in memory. Without doubt, Randall had deserved Tom's visit.

He dipped the quill in ink and wrote *Lord Randall, 1817,* and then beneath that, a third name and date: *The Honourable Miss Smidley, 1817.*

Miss Smidley had stumbled upon exiting the Chapel Royal, tripping the prettiest of last year's débutantes and breaking the girl's ankle. No one who'd seen the look of triumph on Miss Smidley's face would ever think it an accident.

Adam re-read what he'd written. The Parnells' ball. Hyde Park. The Chapel Royal. Too many different places for one servant to be.

Tom was a member of the *ton.*

It was an astonishing conclusion. It was...

Adam tried to identify the sensation he was feeling. Exhilaration. It was exhilarating to think that Tom was a member of the *ton,* someone he'd spoken to, perhaps played cards with. He felt a hunter's flare of excitement. *I'll find out who you are.*

He heard his father's voice again: *I expect better behaviour of you than this. You're a St Just!*

Adam pushed memory of his father irritably aside. He dipped the quill in ink. What else did he know about the thief?

1813, Tom appears, he wrote, the quill scratching lightly across the paper. The thief had been active every year since, apart from…*1816, Tom absent.* Why? Had Tom undertaken the Grand Tour?

Adam laid the quill down. He'd find the answer to that question when he discovered the thief's identity.

He read his notes one more time before folding them with Tom's message—the cat still challenging him with its stare—and placing them in his desk drawer. He stood and stretched, aware that he was hungry.

Aunt Seraphina was in the morning room, her head bent over her needlework.

'Where's Grace?'

'In the parlour, with a visitor.'

Adam whistled lightly under his breath as he walked along the corridor. The door to the blue parlour was ajar. He heard the sound of female voices and his mood brightened still further. This was what he'd wanted for Grace: friends, gaiety. Her Season had had shaky start, to be sure, but things were looking up now and—

Grace and her friend turned their heads at his entrance. Adam froze. His face stiffened in shock.

Arabella Knightley put down her teacup. She appeared to be suppressing a smile.

Adam shut the door with a snap and advanced into the room. 'Miss Knightley. What a…pleasant surprise.'

Her eyebrows arched in amusement. She knew his opinion of her—all London knew that.

Marry Arabella Knightley? Certainly, if one wishes to live with the smell of the gutter.

The words seemed to hang between them in the air, words he'd uttered six years ago. Words the *ton* had taken up with glee.

Adam felt a swift rush of shame. He bowed stiffly.

'Would you care to join us, Mr St Just?' Miss Knightley's voice was smooth and amused.

Do you think I'll leave my sister alone with you? Adam chose a lyre-backed chair at a distance from her and sat. His eyes lighted on a silver platter of macaroons. His stomach almost rumbled.

'Bella and I have been talking about…oh, so many things!'

Bella? Adam jerked his attention from the macaroons. His sister was calling Miss Knightley, Bella?

Not for long, he promised grimly. This was one friendship he was going to terminate.

He glanced at Miss Knightley. She was watching him. Her face was composed into an expression of politeness, but there was something in those dark eyes that made him uncomfortable.

Adam looked away, at her teacup and saucer, at her plate, and tried to identify what it was he'd glimpsed. Not amusement or laughter this time. Something darker, something—

Loathing.

He shifted uncomfortably in the chair and stared at her plate. Crumbs lay on it, golden and delicious. His mouth began to water.

'We've been discussing the subject of marriage. Grace says you're going to choose a husband for her.'

His gaze jerked up. 'Yes,' he said, a short, clipped word with a silent message: *And it's none of your business.*

Arabella Knightley smiled. She turned her attention to Grace. 'I'm certain your brother will choose a man of impeccable breeding and handsome fortune—but there are more important things to a husband than that.'

Adam narrowed his eyes. He opened his mouth.

'Do you want a husband who's kind?' Miss Knightley asked. 'A man who prefers to laugh, or frown? An impatient man? A proud man?'

Grace's brow creased thoughtfully. 'Oh.'

'I shall take into account the man's character,' Adam said stiffly. The note of censure in his voice was clearer this time.

Again, Miss Knightley didn't hear it. 'Of course you will,' she said affably. 'But are the characteristics you're looking for the same ones that Grace wants?' Her expression was friendly, but there was a disconcerting gleam in her dark eyes, something…adversarial.

She's baiting me, Adam realised.

Miss Knightley turned to Grace again. 'It's *you* who'll have to live with this man, not your brother, so you must be certain he's someone who'll make you happy.'

'But…how shall I know?'

'By observation over a period of time. Which is another reason why I suggest you not be in a hurry to marry.'

Adam frowned. 'Miss Knightley—'

'You're not on the shelf,' Arabella Knightley said to Grace, ignoring him. 'Far from it! Don't allow yourself to be rushed into something you must live with for ever.'

'Miss Knightley,' Adam said curtly, 'the subject of my sister's marriage is none—'

'You have your own marriage to consider.' Arabella Knightley turned her smile to him. 'Don't you, Mr St Just?'

Adam blinked. 'I beg your pardon?' he said, retreating into hauteur, looking down his nose at her.

Miss Knightley's smile sharpened. 'Grace tells me you're looking for a bride. Do choose wisely, Mr St Just. Think how *tragic* it would be if you married someone who made your life miserable.'

Adam looked at her in dislike.

'Adam…?' Grace said uncertainly. 'You won't—'

'Of course not,' he said.

Miss Knightley abandoned her needling of him. 'Enough of marriage!' she said to Grace. Her smile became more natural. 'Shall we talk about books? Which do you prefer? *The Mysteries of Udolpho* or *The Italian*?'

'Oh, *Udolpho!*' Grace said. 'And you?'

Adam glowered at Miss Knightley. She looked the perfect lady, dressed in white muslin, dark ringlets clustered about her shapely head, but there was a vixen buried beneath that enchanting exterior.

His eyes lingered on her face, taking unwilling note of her features: the creamy skin, the soft mouth, the tantalising indentation in her chin. He was aware of a traitorous flare of attraction—

Adam wrenched his gaze away. He frowned down at the table. The golden crumbs on Miss Knightley's plate caught his eye again.

'Are you hungry, Mr St Just? Would you like a macaroon?'

'Yes, do have some, Adam.' Grace held the silver platter out to him. 'They're delicious.'

His stomach threatened to rumble. Adam reached out and took two. Chewing, he listened as Miss Knightley and Grace discussed Mrs Radcliffe's novels. He ate six macaroons, wincing each time his sister uttered the name *Bella,* before Miss Knightley rose. 'So soon?' he said insincerely, brushing crumbs from his fingertips. 'You must come again. It's been a pleasure.'

The glint in Arabella Knightley's eyes, the faint edge to her smile, told him she knew he was lying.

Adam bowed over her hand, and then turned to watch her leave the room. His eyes lingered in unwilling appreciation on her figure. Miss Knightley's ankles, glimpsed beneath the flounced hem of her gown, were very fine.

He cleared his throat and turned to Grace. 'I thought I made it *quite* clear last night that I don't want you associating with Miss Knightley.'

Grace glanced at him. 'You did.'

'Then what was she doing here—?'

'I like her,' Grace said. 'And so does Aunt Seraphina.'

Adam inhaled slowly. 'Grace, I utterly forbid you to have anything to do—'

'You sound exactly like Father.'

His head jerked slightly back. He blinked, offended. 'I beg your pardon?'

'If I want to be friends with Bella, I will!'

Bella. Adam gritted his teeth at the sound of the name on his sister's tongue. He inhaled another slow breath and tried to speak calmly. 'Grace, you're being unreasonable. I really must insist. Miss Knightley is *not* someone you should associate with.'

'Her birth is noble.'

'Yes, but—'

'She's not base-born. Is she?'

'No, but—'

'So what has she done?'

'Her mother—'

'What has *Bella* done that deserves censure?'

Adam looked at his sister in silence. 'Nothing,' he said after a long moment. He sighed, and sat down beside her. 'Grace, I'd prefer not to go into the details—'

'I wish you would!'

Adam looked at his sister. Her eyes were wide and interested.

He shifted uneasily on the sofa. Not for the first time he realised how ill equipped he was for the role of guardian. How much should he tell a girl of Grace's age? 'Ask your Aunt Seraphina,' he said cravenly.

'I have,' Grace said. 'She was very vague.'

Adam made a show of looking at his watch. 'Is that the time? I really must be going.'

The expression on Grace's face, the sceptical lift of her eyebrows, was wholly adult.

Adam ignored it. He rose and started for the door.

'Then I shall ask Bella,' Grace said to his back.

Adam halted. He turned around and stared at her.

Grace clasped her hands in her lap and stared back at him. Her whole attitude was one of hopefulness.

Better I tell her than Miss Knightley does. Who knew the sordid details Arabella Knightley would include in her recital?

Adam walked back to the sofa and sat. He straightened his cuffs and flicked a piece of lint off his sleeve, wondering what exactly to say. *Keep it brief.* He cleared his throat and spoke. 'Miss Knightley's father was the second son of the Earl of Westcote. Her mother was the daughter of a French *comte*. They met in France before the Terror and married without the permission of either of their families.' He glanced at Grace. 'She was a Catholic, you understand.'

Grace nodded, wide-eyed. 'They were disowned?'

'He was; Westcote was notoriously bad-tempered. As for her...' Adam shrugged. 'The Terror was starting. I understand her family were among the first victims.'

'Oh.'

'Knightley brought his wife to England and they lived in Kent for a number of years—in reduced circumstances, I believe, but quite respectably—and then he died.'

'How old was Bella?'

'Five, or so.' Adam shrugged again. 'Knightley left his widow no income, so she approached Westcote, asking for help. The earl refused to let her set foot inside his house. He said he'd take the child, but not her.'

'And she chose—'

'She chose to keep her daughter.'

Grace moistened her lips. 'What happened then?'

Adam looked at the silver platter and the last macaroon, stranded amid a sea of crumbs. 'Mrs Knightley went to live with a friend of her husband's, a nobleman. After a time, she became his mistress. By all accounts she was a very beautiful woman.'

'And Bella?'

'Was with her.'

Grace was silent for a moment. 'But that's not so bad, is it?' she ventured. 'Quite a number of married ladies have…have *affaires* and are still received everywhere.'

He glanced at her. Where had she learned that? 'True, but Mrs Knightley had more than one protector over a number of years, and then, when her beauty failed her, she descended into London's slums—taking her daughter with her.'

Grace plucked at a thread on the arm of the sofa. 'Was Mrs Knightley a…a fallen woman in the slums?'

'Yes,' Adam said.

Grace bit her lip. She pulled the piece of thread free and wound it around her fingertip. 'How long was Bella there?' she asked, not looking at him.

'Until her mother died. Three or four years, I think. She was twelve when Westcote took her in.'

'Twelve?' Grace said, glancing at him.

Adam nodded, remembering the twelve-year-old Grace had been: shy, eager, innocent.

'How horrible for Bella,' his sister said, her expression sober.

Adam shrugged. 'Westcote educated her, made her heir to his fortune when his sons died without issue, launched her into society—'

'No,' Grace said. 'I meant, how horrible for Bella to lose both her parents.' She bit her lip and then smiled crookedly at him. 'She was younger than I was when Mother died—and she didn't have a brother.'

Adam had no memory of his own mother's death—he'd been in swaddling clothes—but he had vivid recollection of Grace's mother dying.

He looked at his sister, remembering the lost, dazed expression in her eyes, the bleakness in her face, her silent grief as she'd clung to him—

and remembering, too, the surge of love he'd felt for her, the fierce need to protect her.

He cleared his throat. 'No,' he said. 'Miss Knightley didn't have a brother.'

Grace was silent for a moment. 'I want to be friends with her.'

Adam rubbed his brow. 'Grace,' he said. 'Miss Knightley isn't good *ton.*' He hesitated, reluctant to tell her. 'In London she's known as—'

'Miss Smell O'Gutters. Yes, I know.'

Adam winced. Shame heated his face. Miss Smell O'Gutters. A name that could be laid at his door. *No wonder she hates me.*

'I don't care about that—or about any of it! Any more than Bella cares about what happened between me and Reginald.'

Adam stared at her helplessly. 'Grace—' One of his father's favourite sayings pushed into his mouth: *For heaven's sake, try to behave as a St Just!* He bit it back.

His sister stood, brushing crumbs from her lap. 'Thank you for telling me about Bella.' She bent and kissed his cheek. 'I must go. Aunt Seraphina is taking me shopping.' A smile, a swirl of sprigged muslin and golden ringlets, and she was gone.

Adam sat for a moment, staring at the empty doorway. He lifted a hand to his cheek and lightly rubbed where Grace had kissed him. What had happened to the sister he knew? The tractable, biddable girl? The girl who looked to him for guidance and acquiesced obediently to his wishes?

She's growing up. She has a mind of her own.

It was a thought that filled him with foreboding. The world was suddenly a dangerous place, full of traps for innocent and headstrong young girls.

I need to find her a husband. Fast.

He muttered a curse beneath his breath. And then he ate the last of the macaroons.

Chapter Three

That afternoon Arabella took her maid, Polly, her sketchbook and pencils, and the stolen ruby earrings, to Kensington Gardens. 'Come back in three hours,' she told the coachman.

She strolled with Polly for ten minutes and then exited the gardens. The carriage, with the Westcote coat of arms glinting within its widow's lozenge, was nowhere in sight.

Polly hailed a hackney coach. 'Rosemary Lane,' she told the jarvey as they climbed inside.

Rosemary Lane was only a few miles from Kensington Gardens, but the slums of Whitechapel were as far from the grand squares of Mayfair as heaven was from hell. Arabella climbed down from the hackney and stepped over an open gutter, while Polly negotiated with the reluctant jarvey to return for them in an hour.

Their destination was just off Rosemary Lane, a narrow old-clothes shop with cracked and boarded-over windows. Hinges squealed as Arabella pushed the door open, a bell jangled harshly overhead, and the smell of musty, unwashed clothes invaded her nose. The scents of stale sweat, old perfume, spilled alcohol and tallow candles mingled sickeningly together. For a moment she had to pause, quelling the nausea that pushed up her throat.

The shop was dimly lit, full of mounds of used clothing. Coats hung from door mantels and hooks in the ceiling, their cuffs shiny with wear. Racks crowded the room: worn shirts and faded flannel waistcoats, stained trousers, frayed dresses and yellowing petticoats. Scuffed shoes and boots with cracked soles lay in piles on the floor.

Polly bustled in behind her and shut the door with another squeal of the hinges. 'Sally,' she called out. 'It's us.'

They changed in a small, cramped backroom, unbuttoning each other's gowns and swiftly unlacing the short stays. Arabella hung her clothes—French muslin gown, linen chemise, cambric petticoat—carefully on hooks, and then stripped off her silk stockings and laid them over the back of a chair. The only item she didn't remove was the pocket containing Lady Bicknell's earrings, tied around her waist.

Having undressed, they dressed hurriedly again, in the clothes of the poor. Arabella pulled on a coarse chemise, a discoloured blue dress that was too large for her, rough woollen stockings, a battered pair of men's lace-up boots, and a stained apron. She wrapped a ragged shawl around her head and shoulders. 'Ready?'

Polly rolled up sleeves that were too long for her and reached for her own shawl. 'Yes.'

They left the old-clothes shop through the back door, stepping into a dark, malodorous alley. Arabella linked her arm with Polly's and set off briskly in the direction of Berner Street.

The scuttling rats, the stinking piles of refuse, the rivulets of foul water running down the middle of the streets, were familiar. They didn't frighten her, but they brought back memories of the three years she'd lived in Whitechapel. The deeper they penetrated the warren of small, dark streets, the stronger the memories became. These were the sounds she remembered from her childhood: drunken shouts, the slurred singing of an inebriated woman, crying children, the yelp of a kicked dog.

'Nice to be back,' Polly said, tightening her grip on Arabella's arm. 'Ain't it?' She no longer spoke like a lady's maid; her accent was pure Cockney.

Arabella glanced at her. Polly's jaw was grimly clenched.

She felt a stab of shame. What had happened to Polly in these filthy streets was far worse than anything she'd experienced. She halted. 'Polly, if you want to return to the shop—'

'And let you walk by yourself?' Polly snorted. 'Not likely! And besides—' she took a step, tugging Arabella with her '—I want to see me brother.'

Arabella bit her lip and allowed Polly to pull her along. No one paid them any attention, two women in ragged, shapeless clothes. She scanned the street, taking care not to catch anyone's eyes. Her gaze slid over men's faces, unshaven and defeated, over the sunken cheeks and de-spairing eyes of women. *You can't help them all,* she repeated in her head. *Not all of them.*

But she could help some of them, and it was the children her eyes lingered on: grubby and half-naked, some running and shouting and playing with each other, others sitting listlessly on filthy doorsteps. *I can help some of them.* And her fingers strayed to her waist and the hidden rubies.

In Berner Street, with its soot-stained brick buildings crammed closely together, she glanced again at Polly. The grimness was gone from her maid's face. Polly's step quickened as they approached the third house from the corner and her knock on the battered door was loud and cheerful. 'Harry?' she called, pushing open the door. 'It's me, Polly.'

Arabella followed her into a narrow hallway and shut the door. She blinked, letting her eyes adjust to the dimness, hearing a shout of 'Pol!' and the clatter of boots on a wooden floor.

Arabella grinned as a burly, broken-nosed man swept Polly up in a rib-cracking embrace and kissed her soundly on each cheek. More than fifteen years had passed since she'd made Harry's acquaintance in a rat-infested alley off Dorset Street, but the boy he'd been was still stamped on his face. He had the same crooked nose and broad grin, the same shrewd eyes beneath a shock of unruly hair.

'Bella's here, too,' Polly said, and it was Arabella's turn for a hug that left her breathless.

'I'm glad you're 'ere,' Harry said. 'I picked up a new girl t'day. You can meet 'er, if you like.'

'Please,' Arabella said, and her fingers strayed to the hidden pocket again.

Harry shepherded them into the parlour, a small and sparsely furnished room, and stuck his head out into the hallway. 'Tess!' he bellowed. 'Our Pol and Bella are 'ere! They'd like to meet Aggie!'

Arabella sat on a lumpy sofa with frayed upholstery and splitting seams. Compared to her grandmother's parlour in Mayfair the room was a hovel; compared to where Polly and Harry had grown up—a cramped room in the most dilapidated of Whitechapel's rookeries—it was a palace. 'I have some earrings,' she told Harry. 'Rubies.'

'Good,' he said. 'I picked up two more girls last week, and I 'ave me eye on another.'

The rush of gratitude was so strong that Arabella's throat tightened and for a moment she couldn't speak. She looked away from his broad, plain face and busied herself extracting the earrings from the hidden pocket, fumbling her fingers through the narrow slits in her gown and petticoat. 'Here.' She held them out to him.

In these surroundings the earrings didn't look so garish. Harry held one up and examined it. 'Needs cleanin',' he said. 'But they'll fetch a good price—'

He slid the earrings into a pocket as the door opened.

A young woman stood in the doorway, her belly rounded in pregnancy. Her smile showed two missing teeth, but her face was pretty and dimpled. Holding her hand was a scrawny, waif-like girl.

The girl's gaze flicked from Harry's face to Polly's, and then to Arabella's. For a long moment they stared at each other. Arabella saw a pale, too-thin face and wide, wary eyes beneath a crooked fringe of fair hair. She smiled at the girl. 'I'm very pleased to meet you, Aggie.' She held out her hand. 'Come and sit here beside me.'

Aggie hesitated, and then released Tess's hand and crossed the room. Her dress was filthy, her bare feet almost black with dirt, but her face was clean.

'Did Tess make you wash your face?' Arabella asked, as the girl sat beside her on the sofa.

Aggie nodded. 'And me 'ands.'

Arabella looked down at the girl's hands. Her nails were ragged and dirty, but the skin was clean. Dark bruises ringed Aggie's left wrist. 'How did you get those bruises?'

'Me ma,' the girl said.

Arabella glanced at Harry.

'Trying to sell 'er for a bottle o' gin,' he said with a grimace. 'Weren't she, Aggie?'

The girl nodded.

'But Aggie ran away. And I found 'er.' Harry grinned at the girl, who smiled shyly back.

'It was very clever of you to run away,' Arabella said. 'Very brave.'

Aggie bit her lip and nodded. She looked down at her lap and twisted a fold of dirty fabric between her fingers.

'How old are you, Aggie?'

'I dunno, miss.'

Somewhere between ten and twelve, Arabella guessed. Dirty and half-starved, but with eyes that were bright with intelligence. 'Have Harry and Tess told you what's going to happen to you now?'

The girl's head lifted. Her thin face split into a grin. 'I'm gonna go t' school!'

Arabella laughed. 'You want to go to school?'

The girl nodded.

'Did Harry tell you about the school, Aggie?'

'Missus did.' The girl's gaze flicked to Harry's wife, Tess. 'She says it's in the country.'

'A place called Swanley,' Arabella said, smiling. 'Not far from London.'

'She says it's for girls like me.'

'It is.' Girls like Polly and Tess had been, girls like Aggie was now: with lives of poverty and prostitution ahead of them.

'I'll learn 'ow to read an' write, and t' speak proper,' Aggie said. 'And I'll 'ave me own bed!'

'Yes, you will.' Aggie would have her own bed, new clothes, and three good meals a day. She'd have encouragement and kindness—and most importantly, she'd have a future.

Arabella glanced at Harry, standing with an arm around Tess. 'We must be going.' She stood and held out her hand to Aggie. After a moment's hesitation the girl placed her own hand it in.

'I'm glad to have met you, Aggie. I hope you'll be very happy at school.'

Aggie nodded shyly.

Arabella released the girl's hand and turned to embrace Tess. 'Thank you,' she said.

Tess blushed and shook her head.

Harry accompanied them into the dark hallway. He hugged his sister again and opened the front door.

Arabella paused on the doorstep. 'You said you'd seen another girl?'

Harry nodded. 'In Thrawl Street.' His gaze flicked briefly to his sister. 'She's older 'n Aggie. Been on the game a few months.'

Polly's mouth tightened. She looked away.

'I'll talk to 'er tomorrow,' Harry said. 'See if she wants t' leave Whitechapel.'

Arabella nodded. 'Thank you.'

'No,' Harry said, his eyes on his sister. 'Thank you.' He glanced back at Arabella. 'Want me t' walk with you?'

She shook her head. 'We'll be fine.' She knew these streets as well as she knew the streets of Belgravia and Mayfair.

Harry nodded farewell and closed the door.

Arabella pulled the shawl forwards over her face. She linked her arm with Polly. 'Back to Rosemary Lane.' And then Kensington Gardens. And then the Fothergills' ball.

The incongruity of it made her dizzy for a moment: she stood in Whitechapel, in a street that was little more than an open sewer, and yet in a few hours' time she'd be in a ballroom, wearing a dress of midnight-blue satin and with pearls in her hair. There'd be music and the scents of mingled perfumes, the shimmer of rich fabrics and the gleam of jewels. Crystal drops would dangle from the chandeliers, glittering as brightly as diamonds.

Arabella blinked and shook her head, dispelling the momentary dizziness. She stepped forwards firmly in the direction of Rosemary Lane.

Adam sipped from his champagne glass and scanned the ballroom again. A quadrille was playing. Grace was in one of the sets, a brave smile on her face.

Miss Knightley's advice on that score had been unerring, but her other advice—

His fingers tightened on the stem of the glass. *Damned impertinence, is what it is.*

He scanned the ballroom again, searching for dark curls.

A familiar face caught his attention. The lady had dark hair and pale skin, but there the resemblance to Miss Knightley ended. Lady Vane's height was above average, her figure ample, her manner gracefully languid.

Adam relaxed his grip on the champagne glass. His mood lightened. He swallowed another mouthful of champagne and set off towards his former mistress.

'Darling!' Mary Vane's smile was both delighted and sleepy at the same time. She held out her hand to him.

Adam bowed over her gloved fingers, inhaling the faint, familiar fragrance of her perfume. 'I have a favour I'd like to ask of you.'

'A favour?' Mary waved her fan in a leisurely, graceful movement. 'For you, anything.'

Adam lowered his voice. 'I'd like you to write to Lady Bicknell, inviting her to your next charity function.'

'Lady Bicknell?' Mary wrinkled her nose. 'Why on earth would I want to do that? If the woman has any interest in soldiers' widows, I've yet to hear of it!'

Adam hesitated, then bent his head and spoke into her ear. 'I believe she's been dabbling in a little blackmail. I need to see a specimen of her handwriting.'

'Blackmail!' Mary stepped back a pace. The sleepiness was gone from her eyes. 'Is everything all right, Adam?'

'Perfectly,' he said. 'I just need to prove something.'

Mary chewed on her lower lip for a moment, surveying him, and then nodded. 'Very well, I'll write to her.'

'Thank you.' Adam took her hand again. 'You're an angel.' He bowed and kissed her fingertips.

Mary uttered an unladylike snort. 'Hardly.'

Adam grinned at her. Their affair was over—Mary no longer a widow, but once again a wife—but the fondness remained. 'Would you care to dance?'

'Far too fatiguing!' Mary hid a yawn behind her fan.

Adam laughed and took his leave of her. He retreated to an embrasure, where he leaned against the wall and sipped champagne and thought about what *precisely* he would say to Arabella Knightley. How *dared* she have the effrontery to discuss marriage with Grace—

There she was.

He experienced a moment of *déjà vu,* brief and dizzying. He'd stood like this once before: leaning against a wall, a glass dangling from his fingers, and watched as a young lady with sable-dark hair and an elegant face and eyes that looked almost black entered a ballroom. He'd been six years younger, half-foxed—and he'd stared at her and thought *I want her.*

Adam straightened away from the wall. This time it wasn't with appreciation that he watched Arabella Knightley across the ballroom. No one could deny she had style; it was in the way she moved, the way she held her head. Her beauty—the lustre of her hair, the darkness of her eyes, the pale glow of her skin—was merely fuel to his anger. He lifted his glass again, swallowed the last of the champagne, and set the glass down on a mahogany side table with a sharp *clunk*. He began to walk around the perimeter of the ballroom, pushing his way through the other guests.

He had a bone to pick with Miss Arabella Knightley.

Arabella escorted her grandmother to the card room. Playing cards— a pastime the fifth Earl of Westcote had thought unseemly for a lady— was his relict's favourite activity in her widowhood.

'Supper at midnight,' Lady Westcote said, reaching for a pack of cards. Her hair gleamed like silver in the light falling from the chandeliers.

'Yes, Grandmother.'

Arabella turned her back on the card room and its elderly inhabitants. On the threshold of the ballroom she paused, squaring her shoulders and lifting her chin. *Armour,* she told herself, touching a light fingertip to her gown. Then she took a deep breath and stepped into the ballroom again.

Someone spoke her name quietly, 'Arabella.'

'Helen!' Arabella turned, smiling. 'How lovely to see you. Are you well?'

'Very well, thank you,' Helen Dysart said.

As always, Arabella had to stop herself from hugging Helen. That silent misery could so well have been her own.

'Ah, the lovely Miss Knightley,' drawled a voice.

Arabella's smile stiffened. 'George.'

George Dysart pushed a glass of champagne into his wife's hand, not caring that it slopped over her gloved fingers. He raised a second glass in Arabella's direction, as if toasting her, and swallowed a large mouthful. His face was flushed and he swayed slightly as he stood. *Nine-tenths drunk.*

Little was left of the man who'd courted her six years ago. George's hair still fell in golden waves over his brow, but the blue eyes were now bloodshot. His figure had lost its slenderness and his face—which she'd once thought angelic—was almost unrecognisable beneath a layer of fat. He looked precisely what he was: a man given to dissipation.

George raised his glass again, this time towards his wife. 'Helen,' he said. 'Named after the most beautiful woman in the world.' He hooted with laughter, making heads turn, ended on a hiccup, and swayed slightly. 'Her parents made a mistake there, didn't they? Should have called her Medu—'

'George, would you mind getting me something to drink?' Arabella said. 'Lemonade, please.'

George Dysart shut his mouth. His hand clenched. Arabella saw Helen tense, as if expecting a blow.

George's gaze lifted, catching on the faces still turned in their direction. He seemed to swallow his rage. 'A drink? Certainly.' He brushed past Arabella, buffeting her deliberately with his shoulder.

'I apologise,' Helen said quietly. 'George has had a little too much to drink.'

'Would you like to go home?'

Helen's eyes followed her husband's progress. She shook her head. 'It's best if I stay.'

Arabella reached out and touched the back of her friend's hand lightly. 'Helen, if I can help in any way…'

Helen shook her head again.

Arabella bit her lip, wishing she could pay George a visit as Tom. It wasn't possible; everything George Dysart owned came from his wife. 'Come riding with me tomorrow.'

'Thank you.' Helen's smile reached her eyes. 'That would be lovely.'

Arabella surveyed her. Helen wasn't beautiful—her nose was too aquiline for that—but her face had character. There was quiet strength in her eyes, courage in the way she held her chin. George Dysart was a fool not to realise the value of his wife. *The sooner he drinks himself into the grave, the better.*

The quadrille came to its end. There was a surge of movement off the dance floor. 'I'd best leave before George returns,' Arabella said.

'I apologise for my husband's behaviour—'

'Don't,' Arabella said, swiftly clasping her friend's hand. She turned from Helen, halting as a man stepped into her path and bowed.

'Miss Knightley.'

Arabella gritted her teeth and smiled. 'Lord Dalrymple.'

During her first Season, her admirers—what few there'd been—had fallen into two categories: men who were prepared to ignore her mother's reputation for the sake of the Westcote fortune, and men who courted her *because* of her mother's reputation.

Lord Dalrymple fell into the latter category. She'd recognised it the first time they'd met, and she recognised it now: the look in his eyes, the slow, speculative smile, as if he were undressing her in his mind. She willed herself not to stiffen and said politely, 'How do you do?'

'Very well, Miss Knightley. Very well indeed.' Lord Dalrymple was a large man with a fleshy face, greying ginger hair, and a receding hairline. 'Are you engaged for the next dance?'

It was a familiar question, one she hated. Lord Dalrymple's touch—always slightly too familiar, too lingering—made her skin crawl.

The musicians picked up their bows again. The first strains of music were audible above the hum of conversation.

A waltz. For a moment she felt sick. No *contredanse,* where the steps would part them from each other; instead, her hand in his for the entire dance, his arm around her.

Arabella touched her gown lightly. *Armour.* 'Engaged?'

Lord Dalrymple's smile widened. His teeth glinted, large and horse-like. 'May I have this dance?'

'Miss Knightley has promised the waltz to me.'

Arabella turned towards the smooth male voice—and found herself staring at Adam St Just.

'You?' Dalrymple said, his disbelief clearly audible.

'Unless she wishes to change her mind.' St Just's voice was cool, almost bored. 'It is a lady's prerogative, after all.'

Dislike welled inside her. Arabella quashed it; she knew which was the lesser of two evils. 'Yes,' she lied, turning back to Lord Dalrymple with a smile. 'I've already promised this dance to Mr St Just.'

It was the first time in six years that Arabella had walked on to a dance floor with Adam St Just. She was aware of heads turning and sidelong glances of astonishment. She was equally astonished. Why had St Just asked her to dance?

The answer came as she glanced at him. St Just's jaw was tight, his mouth a thin line. *He's going to tell me off.*

Arabella lifted her chin. *Let him try!*

They made their bows to each other. As always, the opening notes of the waltz filled her with dread. She took a deep breath and forced herself not to tense as St Just took her hand, as his arm came around her.

They began to dance. The feeling of being trapped was strong. *A man is holding me.* Panic rose sharply in her. All her instincts told her to break free. Arabella concentrated on breathing calmly, on keeping a slight smile on her face.

'I would appreciate it, Miss Knightley, if you'd refrain from giving my sister advice about matters that are none of your concern.' St Just spoke the words coldly.

Arabella met his eyes. There was nothing of the lover about him; on the contrary, his animosity was clearly visible.

Her panic began to fade. She raised her eyebrows. 'Oh? Would you?'

St Just's jaw clenched.

Arabella observed this—and began to feel quite cheerful. 'I was only trying to help,' she said, widening her eyes.

His grip tightened. 'It is *none* of your business who my sister does— or doesn't—marry.'

Arabella ignored this remark. 'Why do you wish Grace to marry so young?'

'That's none of your business!'

'Grace is little more than a child. She has no idea what she wants in a marriage—'

'*I* shall decide what she wants!' St Just snapped.

Arabella laughed, as much from amusement as to annoy him. The sense of being trapped had evaporated. For the first time in her life, she was finding pleasure in a waltz. Each sign of St Just's irritation—the narrowing of his eyes and tightening of his jaw, the gritting of his teeth— was something to be noted and enjoyed.

'You find that amusing?'

'Yes. Grace is still learning who she is. Until she knows that, how can she—or you—have any idea what will suit her in a husband?'

'A man of good breeding.' He swung her into an abrupt turn. 'A man of respectable fortune and—'

'No,' Arabella said. 'I'm talking about a man's character.'

St Just looked down his nose at her. 'If you imagine that I'd allow Grace to marry a man of unsavoury character—'

'You misunderstand me again, Mr St Just. I'm talking about those qualities that are more particular to a person. Qualities that have nothing to do with one's bloodline or fortune, or even with one's public character.' Her smile was edged. 'Let us take, as an example, your search for a wife.'

St Just stiffened. He almost missed a step. 'I beg your pardon,' he said in a frigid tone.

'Look around you, Mr St Just. This room is filled with young women of excellent birth and breeding. The question is, which one should you choose?'

Chapter Four

'The subject of my marriage is none of your concern,' Adam said, biting the words off with his teeth.

Arabella Knightley showed her ill breeding by ignoring him. 'If bloodline is your sole criterion, then Miss Swindon would suit you perfectly. Her fortune is respectable and—like yourself—she claims a duke as her grandfather. Her manners are impeccable and her appearance pleasing.'

Adam wasn't fooled by the artless, innocent manner. Miss Knightley was deliberately trying to annoy him.

'What more could you want?' she asked, looking up at him.

Adam felt his pulse give a kick and then speed up. Such dark eyes.

He looked away and cleared his throat.

'However,' Miss Knightley continued, 'if you wish for a wife who'll be a good *mother,* then you should direct your attention towards Miss Fforbes-Brown.'

His attention jerked back to her. 'I beg your pardon?'

'What kind of mother do you want for your children, Mr St Just?'

The question was more than impertinent; it was insolent. Adam retreated into hauteur. 'I must repeat myself, Miss Knightley: that is none of your concern!'

She ignored him again. 'But then, that also depends on what kind of father you want to be, doesn't it? Do you wish to see your children's first steps and hear their first words—or are such things not important to you?' There was censure in her eyes, in her voice. 'Do you intend for your children to be brought up by a succession of nursemaids, Mr St Just, or—?'

'No,' Adam said, blurting out the word. 'I don't.' *I want what I didn't have. I want my children to know their parents. I want them to know they're loved.*

Arabella Knightley regarded him for a long moment, as if doubting the truth of his words. 'In that case, may I suggest you make Miss Fforbes-Brown your choice of bride? She's very fond of children.'

Adam glanced around the ballroom. It was better than looking at Miss Knightley, at her eyes, at that indentation in her chin, at that soft mouth. His gaze came to rest on Miss Eustacia Swindon. She was tall and fair-haired, with aristocratic features and a proud manner—and high on his list of potential brides.

Sophia Fforbes-Brown was also on the dance floor. Adam observed her for several seconds. Miss Fforbes-Brown's breeding was genteel, her fortune small, her manners undeniably warmer and more open than Miss Swindon's. True, her figure was plumper than was fashionable, but she had a pretty, laughing face.

He concentrated on pondering Arabella Knightley's suggestion—anything rather than let his attention stray to the slenderness and warmth of gloved fingers, to her—

Adam wrenched his mind back to her question. *What kind of mother do you want for your children?*

The answer was easy: Someone who'd delight in her children. Mentally he shifted Miss Swindon to the bottom of his list, and placed Miss Fforbes-Brown near the top.

The lilting strains of the waltz crept into his consciousness, and with that, a traitorous awareness of the pleasure of dancing with Miss Knightley. She was a superb dancer, light on her feet, following his lead with apparent effortlessness.

Adam glanced at her face. She was watching him.

God, she's beautiful. The rich shine of her hair, the eyes as dark as midnight. He looked at her smooth, milk-white skin, the delicate indentation in her chin, the soft curve of her mouth—and desire clenched in his chest. *I want her.*

'Mr St Just, why do you wish Grace to marry this year?'

So that someone else may have the responsibility of her—and perhaps not fail as miserably as I have.

'Because…I thought it would be best for her.'

Miss Knightley's eyebrows rose fractionally. 'You thought?'

Adam opened his mouth, and then closed it again. Had he changed his mind?

'May I suggest that you allow Grace to find her feet this Season, and not think of marriage?'

He tried to be offended by the impertinence of Miss Knightley's suggestion, but all he could think of was how incredibly tempting her mouth was. Ripe, yet demure. If he bent his head and kissed her, what would she taste of?

To his relief he heard the orchestra play the final notes of the waltz. Adam hurriedly released her hand. He stepped back a pace and bowed. And then he escorted her from the dance floor as fast as could be considered polite.

After a supper of white soup and lobster patties in the company of her grandmother, Arabella returned to the ballroom. A cotillion was playing. She watched the dancers and sipped lemonade, wishing the drink wasn't quite so sweet.

'—Miss Wootton.'

'Madness in the family?'

Arabella glanced sideways, identifying the speakers: Mrs Harpenden and Lady Clouston, their heads bent close together. Miss Harpenden, a diffident young woman in her second Season, hovered alongside her mother.

'I have it on good authority,' Mrs Harpenden said in a carrying whisper. 'They say the girl is showing signs of it already.'

'Mother,' Miss Harpenden said hesitantly, 'you can't be certain—'

'Of course they'll deny it. Who wouldn't!' Mrs Harpenden nodded sagely. 'But it must be said, they're in a rush to marry her off.'

'Mother—'

'Someone should warn the poor girl's suitors,' Mrs Harpenden said, her expression pious.

'But, Mother—' Miss Harpenden said, a note of desperation in her voice. 'You don't know that—'

'Hush,' her mother rebuked her. 'I'm talking to Lady Clouston.'

Miss Harpenden bit her lip and was obediently silent.

Arabella bit her lip too. She turned her attention to the dance floor, searching for Miss Wootton. She found her in a set near the orchestra, a pretty, vivacious girl with brown curls and rosy cheeks.

Arabella sipped her lemonade and watched Miss Wootton dance. Beside her, Mrs Harpenden's voice sank to a low whisper, audible but unintelligible.

The cotillion came to its conclusion, the dancers made their bows to each other and the dance floor emptied. Mrs Harpenden and Lady Clouston bid each other farewell. Mrs Harpenden's smile was smug as she watched Lady Clouston push her way through the throng of guests. 'Come along,' she said, turning to her daughter. 'We must find you a partner for the next dance.' She set off across the ballroom.

Miss Harpenden followed, her expression miserable.

Arabella stayed where she was. She looked again for Miss Wootton.

The girl stood on the far side of the ballroom. She was undeniably the most sought-after of this Season's débutantes, a young woman in happy possession of wealth, beauty, and a good bloodline. Young men clustered about her like bees around a honey pot.

It was the kind of popularity Grace would be enjoying if rumours weren't circulating about her.

Arabella waited until the next dance began, then made her way around the perimeter of the ballroom.

'That's Miss Knightley,' she heard a young debutante whisper as she approached. 'Have you heard what they call her? Miss Smell O'Gutters.'

The girl was hastily shushed by her companion.

Arabella's step didn't falter. In her imagination the words scrabbled to find purchase on her satin gown, failed and slid harmlessly to the floor.

She smiled cordially at the girl, who turned deep pink.

Grace St Just was seated alongside her aunt, Mrs Seraphina Mexted. Her smile was bright and fixed. Mrs Mexted caught Arabella's enquiring glance and said, 'Heard someone whispering about her.'

'Never a pleasant experience.' Arabella sat next to Grace. 'Who was it?'

'Miss Brook,' Grace said.

'Oh, yes. I know who she is. Looks like a pug dog.'

The aunt snorted, and turned the sound into a cough.

'A pug dog?' Grace said, her brow creasing.

'Yes. Poor girl, she has a very unfortunate nose.'

Grace turned her attention to the dance floor. After a moment she said, 'Oh, so she does.' Her expression became more cheerful.

Arabella smoothed the dark blue folds of her gown over her lap. 'Your aunt may disagree with me, but I believe that if a person says something about you, and they're not someone you hold in respect, then you should feel free to ignore their opinion.'

Mrs Mexted thought for a moment, and then nodded.

Grace looked doubtful. 'Are you saying I shouldn't respect Miss Brook because of her nose?'

Arabella couldn't help laughing. 'No,' she said. 'This has nothing to do with Miss Brook's nose. What I'm saying is that if someone behaves in a manner that makes it impossible for you to respect them—such as gossiping, or passing on slander—then you should give no weight to their opinion of you.' She paused for a few seconds, holding Grace's gaze. 'So my question is, do you respect Miss Brook's opinion?'

'But I don't know her,' Grace protested.

'Precisely. You don't know each other—and yet she's talking about you.'

Grace flushed. She looked down at her lap and began to pleat folds of satin between her fingers.

'Do you hold Miss Brook in respect?' Arabella asked quietly.

'Not any more.'

'Then her opinion of you shouldn't matter.'

Grace bit her lip. After a moment she said, 'That's easier said than done.'

'What is?'

Arabella glanced up. Adam St Just, looking his most supercilious, stood before them.

'Ignoring people's opinions,' Grace said, accepting the glass of orgeat he handed her. 'Bella says that's what she does.'

'Does she?' There was censure in St Just's voice. The glance he cast Arabella was chilly with disapproval. 'Everyone's opinion?'

'Oh, no,' Grace said, sipping from the glass. 'Only those people one doesn't respect.'

'And who might they be?' St Just asked, still frowning.

'People who gossip and spread rumours,' Grace said. 'Or who say nasty things about people they don't know.'

Adam St Just stopped frowning. He flushed faintly and raised a hand to straighten the folds of his neck cloth.

'Do you agree?' Grace asked.

'Er…yes,' he said.

Arabella's lip curled slightly.

Grace nodded, and sipped her orgeat. Her expression was less miserable than it had been.

St Just glanced at the dance floor, where a *contredanse* was drawing towards its conclusion. 'Excuse me,' he said. 'I'm engaged for the next dance.'

Arabella watched him move off through the crowd. Despite his wealth, St Just eschewed such adornments as fobs and seals and quizzing glasses. In his dress, he was very like Beau Brummell had been—elegant and understated, each garment cut perfectly to fit him. His build was athletic; neither his shoulders nor his calves required padding.

An attractive man—until one noticed the way he had of looking down his nose at the world.

Arabella turned to Grace. 'Do you know Miss Harpenden?'

'Elizabeth Harpenden? Her sister Charlotte was at school with me in Bath.'

'Charlotte isn't in London?'

Grace shook her head. 'She's still in Bath. Her parents won't let her come out until Elizabeth has married.'

Arabella tapped her fan against her knee and considered this information. 'And Miss Wootton?' she asked. 'Do you know her?'

'No. She's from Yorkshire, I believe.' Grace glanced to where Miss Wootton stood, attended by a number of admiring young gentlemen. 'She looks like she's enjoying herself.' Her voice was wistful and slightly envious.

'Yes.' Arabella scanned the ballroom, looking for Elizabeth Harpenden. The girl was being escorted from the dance floor by a heavy-set young man with pretensions to dandyism.

Arabella felt a moment's sympathy for Miss Harpenden. Her face was almost pretty, her figure almost graceful. In a smaller and more restricted setting she might have had a chance to shine; in London she was practically invisible.

Of course, if this Season's beauties were discredited, Elizabeth Harpenden would be more visible.

Arabella tapped her fan against her knee and watched as Mrs Harpenden received her daughter. The woman's manner was slightly bullying. *A mother who scolds, rather than praises.*

'Are you engaged for the next d-d-dance, Miss St Just?'

Arabella looked up to see Viscount Mayroyd make his bow to Grace.

'No,' Grace said, blushing prettily. 'I'm not.'

'Then may I have the p-p-pleasure?' The young man's eyes were as blue as Grace's. He had a very engaging smile.

Grace nodded. She gave her glass to her aunt and stood.

'I like him,' Mrs Mexted said, with a nod in the young viscount's direction, once he was out of earshot.

'So do I.' Perhaps because of his stutter, young Mayroyd had a kind-heartedness that many of his peers lacked.

Arabella returned to her observation of Miss Wootton. The girl was clearly enjoying herself. *But not for long, if Mrs Harpenden has her way.*

Did the woman deserve a visit from Tom?

She tapped the fan against her knee and resolved to wait a day or so before deciding.

Adam woke reluctantly. He heard his valet, Perkins, draw back the curtains and closed his eyes more tightly, trying to burrow back into the dream, to recapture the pleasures of a soft mouth and fragrant skin, of dark ringlets gleaming in candlelight—

Dark ringlets?

Adam's eyes snapped open. *It was Mary,* he told himself. But Mary had always been leisurely in bed; the woman in his dream had been eager and passionate—and as slender as Mary was voluptuous.

The last, sensual wisps of the dream vanished abruptly. Adam uttered a curse and pushed back his bedclothes.

A ride in the park on Goliath, under a sky heavy with clouds, did little to improve his mood. An hour spent sparring in Jackson's Saloon was much more successful. Adam walked around to St James's Street whistling under his breath and took the steps up to White's two at a time.

The ground-floor parlour was pleasantly empty. Lord Alvanley sat at the bow window, where Brummell had liked to sit. He looked up from a newspaper. 'Afternoon, St Just.'

'Alvanley.' Adam strolled across to the bow window. 'What's new?'

His lordship folded the newspaper and put it aside. 'Have you heard about the Wootton chit?'

Adam shook his head. He sat and reached for the newspaper. 'A bottle of claret,' he said to the waiter.

'Madness in the family,' Alvanley declared, stretching out his legs.

Adam glanced at him. 'What? The Wootton heiress?'

His lordship nodded. 'It's the latest *on dit.*'

Adam grunted, and removed Miss Wootton from his list of possible brides.

Another newcomer entered the room, his step jaunty. 'Afternoon, Alvanley,' he said cheerfully. 'St Just.'

Adam looked around. Jeremy Allen, Marquis of Revelstoke, trod towards the bow window, resplendent in a dark blue coat with extravagantly long tails, cream-coloured pantaloons and gold-tasselled hessians. The folds of his neckcloth were so intricate, the points of his collar so high, that he had no hope of turning his head. The most arresting aspect of his appearance was his waistcoat, an exotic garment featuring dazzling golden suns against a celestial blue background.

'Good God,' Alvanley said, involuntarily.

Adam uttered a laugh. He put the newspaper down and shaded his eyes with one hand. 'Go away, Jeremy. You're blinding me.'

His friend grinned and paid no attention to the request. He took the third chair in the alcove and sat, crossing his legs. His boots were polished to a mirror-like gleam. The scent of Steek's lavender water wafted gently from him. His hair was curled in the cherubim style, beneath which his eyes gleamed with mischief.

Alvanley lifted his quizzing glass and examined the glittering suns on Jeremy's waistcoat. 'Is that gold thread?'

'Of course,' Jeremy said. He produced a snuff box in sky-blue enamel that matched his waistcoat and opened it with the elegant flick of a fingertip. 'Snuff?'

'Have you heard about the Wootton chit?' Lord Alvanley asked, taking a pinch.

'Mad as a hatter,' Jeremy said. 'About to be committed to Bedlam.'

Adam raised his eyebrows. 'Surely you jest!'

'Me?' Jeremy said, grinning, swinging one leg. 'When do I jest?'

Adam, acquainted with Jeremy since their first day at Eton, chose to ignore that question. He picked up the newspaper again.

'Your name's in the betting book,' Jeremy said in an extremely innocent voice.

Adam didn't look up from the newspaper. 'No, it's not.'

'Actually, it is,' Lord Alvanley said.

Adam glanced up sharply. Alvanley was grinning widely. Alongside him, Jeremy sat examining his nails, an expression of demure innocence on his face.

Adam was familiar with that expression. He eyed his friend with misgiving. After a moment he pushed up out of his chair and went in search of the betting book. Jeremy trailed after him.

'The devil,' Adam said, as he read the latest entry. *Adam St Just, to marry Miss Knightley before the end of the year, 500 guineas.*

'Well?' Jeremy said, sly humour in his voice. 'Am I right?'

'What you are,' Adam said, closing the book with more violence than was necessary, 'is a cod's head!'

'I say,' Jeremy protested, half-laughing, following Adam as he strode back to the bow window. 'That's not very nice.'

'If you think I'm going to marry Miss Knightley, then you *are* a cod's head!' Adam said severely. His claret had arrived. He poured himself a glass and swallowed half of it in one gulp.

'You danced with her last night,' Jeremy said, sitting.

'If I married every woman I danced with, I'd be a bigamist a hundred times over!' Adam said, refilling his glass. 'You may as well pay Charlton that money now, for you've lost it!'

Jeremy swung one leg and smiled, his expression as cherubic as his curls. 'I believe I'll wait,' he said.

Adam, aware of Alvanley sitting, grinning, alongside them, retreated into a dignified silence. He reached for the newspaper again and opened it with a crackle of pages.

* * *

That night, the *ton* arrived en masse at the Pinkhursts' dress ball. The first person Adam saw, as he entered the ballroom, was Arabella Knightley in a dress of ivory-white tiffany silk shot through with gold thread and a golden fillet in her dark hair. *God, she's lovely,* was his involuntary thought. He hastily averted his gaze.

The second person he saw was Jeremy Allen, magnificent in a long-tailed coat of peacock blue, a luxuriantly embroidered waistcoat, black satin knee breeches and silk stockings. Jewels glittered in the folds of Jeremy's neckcloth and on each of his long fingers. His hair was brushed into the careful dishevelment of the Brutus.

Adam escorted Grace and his Aunt Seraphina to seats, and strolled across to greet his friend. 'Jeremy,' he said, 'you look prettier than any of the ladies here.'

Jeremy was unoffended. He laughed. He raised his quizzing glass and observed Adam through it. 'And you look very plain.'

Adam grinned.

'I see that the delectable Miss Knightley is here,' Jeremy said in a tone of sly innocence.

'Dance with her yourself, if you like her that much.' A servant in livery and a powdered wig proffered a tray. Adam took a glass of champagne.

Jeremy lowered the quizzing glass with a sigh. 'It's much more entertaining when you rise to the bait.'

Adam smiled and sipped the champagne.

'I believe I shall,' Jeremy declared.

'Shall what?'

'Ask her to dance. Excellent dancer, Miss Knightley.' He wandered off in the direction of Arabella Knightley.

Adam thrust Miss Knightley out of his thoughts and concentrated on his task for the night: interviewing potential brides. He danced with each of the young ladies on his shortlist, asked a number of questions and listened carefully to the answers.

The hour advanced past midnight. The air was heavy with the scents of perfume, pomade and perspiration. Ladies with flushed cheeks waved their fans, starched collar points drooped in the heat, and even the candles in the chandeliers seemed to wilt.

Adam found an empty alcove and a glass of chilled champagne and mentally reviewed his list of brides. He removed Miss Swindon from it entirely, and placed Miss Fforbes-Brown at the top.

His gaze strayed to Miss Knightley. She looked very French as she waited for her turn in the quadrille, slender and dark-eyed, dark-haired.

He felt a stir of attraction and wrenched his gaze from her. He drained the champagne glass. When the quadrille was over, he headed purposefully for Miss Fforbes-Brown and solicited her hand for the next waltz. It was a most agreeable dance; there was none of the discomfort of waltzing with Arabella Knightley, the barbed comments, the *frisson* of desire. He was so pleased with Miss Fforbes-Brown's plump prettiness, her common sense and cheerfulness, her enthusiasm for children, that he resolved to seek an interview with her father.

He relinquished Miss Fforbes-Brown to her next partner, a Sir Humphrey Holbrook, and retreated to the alcove again. Grace was sitting out the cotillion. Adam watched her from across the ballroom, conscious of a sharp pang of regret. Grace's début should have been a triumph; instead it was close to being a disaster.

He glanced at Miss Wootton. Like Grace, she wasn't dancing. No crowd of young men clustered around the heiress tonight, competing for her attention. She sat out the cotillion, wearing an expression of miserable bewilderment. Her mother, seated beside her, had a tight-lipped smile on her face.

Adam stood up for a quadrille next. He was waiting for his turn in the figure when he noticed that Sir Humphrey Holbrook was dancing with Miss Fforbes-Brown for a second time. This discovery so disconcerted him that he almost missed his cue for the *glissade*. He concentrated carefully on his steps and then watched the baronet escort Miss Fforbes-Brown from the dance floor. Had Sir Humphrey also realised that she'd be a good wife?

Adam frowned, and resolved to keep a closer eye on Humphrey Holbrook. He went in search of a glass of champagne and then strolled across to where his Aunt Seraphina sat. His footsteps faltered when he saw his aunt's companion. The familiar sensations swept through him— shame and guilt, the stir of attraction—and he almost turned and headed in the opposite direction.

Craven, he chided himself, and stepped forwards. 'Good evening, Miss Knightley.' He bowed, and turned to his aunt. 'Where's Grace?'

'Talking to Miss Wootton.'

Adam swung on his heel and looked across the ballroom. His sister sat alongside Miss Wootton. Grace was talking, her expression animated; Miss Wootton listened intently.

Adam turned to Miss Knightley. 'Your doing?'

She shook her head. The golden ribbon threaded through her dark hair glinted in the candlelight. 'Grace felt sorry for her. She's a very kind-hearted girl.'

'In this instance her kindness is misplaced. If Miss Wootton has some…instability, then I'd prefer that Grace didn't become friends—'

'Miss Wootton is no more unstable than you or I!' Miss Knightley said tartly. 'It's a rumour set about to discredit her.'

Adam frowned. 'Rumour? Are you certain?'

'Yes.' Her nod was emphatic. 'I overheard it being started two nights ago.'

'You did?' Adam put up his brows. 'By whom?'

'By a mother with a daughter to marry off.'

Adam sipped his champagne thoughtfully, digesting this fact. 'Does this mother have any connection with the seminary Grace attended in Bath?'

Miss Knightley glanced at him. Her eyes were almost black in the candlelight. 'Yes.'

'Do you think she's responsible for the rumours about Grace?'

'I think it likely.' Arabella Knightley lifted her shoulders in an expressive, Gallic shrug. 'But since I wasn't present when *those* particular rumours started, I have no way of knowing.'

Adam's fingers tightened on the stem of the glass. 'Who is this woman?'

Miss Knightley's eyebrows arched. 'Mr St Just, surely you don't expect me to tell you that?'

'The devil I don't—'

'Adam,' his aunt reproved.

Adam clenched his jaw and glared at Miss Knightley. She seemed unoffended by his language. A dimple appeared in her cheek, as if she was trying not to laugh, and her eyes were suspiciously bright.

'You refuse to tell me?'

'Of course,' she said. 'There's absolutely no proof that this woman spread any rumours about Grace—'

'But you think she did—'

'Precisely, Mr St Just. I *think;* I don't *know.* They're two very different things.'

Adam gripped his glass tightly. 'I should like to speak with this woman.'

'I'm sure you would,' Miss Knightley said. 'But in all conscience, I can't name her. Think how remiss it would be of me if you upbraided her for something she didn't do!'

'I shouldn't upbraid her,' he said with stiff dignity.

Her eyebrows rose again. Disbelief was eloquent on her face.

Adam flushed.

'Mr St Just, if I were to pass on information that I don't *know* to be true, I should be as worthy of blame as any scandalmonger.'

Aunt Seraphina nodded. 'Miss Knightley is correct.'

He knew she was, but being told that didn't improve his temper. Adam glared at his aunt.

She smiled placidly and patted the chair alongside her. 'Do sit down, dear. It's very fatiguing to have you *towering* over one.'

He swung his glare back to Miss Knightley. Laughter glimmered in her dark eyes. 'Mr St Just, I fear you're about to break that glass.'

Adam hurriedly unclenched his hand.

Miss Knightley looked past him. Her smile became warmer.

Adam turned his head. 'Grace.'

Grace sat beside Aunt Seraphina in a soft flurry of satin and gauze. 'I told Letty what Mr Brummell said to Bella. And she's going to do it too!'

Aunt Seraphina gave an approving nod.

Grace smoothed her skirt and turned to Miss Knightley. 'And I told her what you said, Bella, about it being useful experience, and how she has the opportunity to see people for who they truly are—and Letty *perfectly* understood what you meant!' Her face was alight with enthusiasm. 'We've decided that we're going to do it together!'

Adam couldn't help smiling at Grace's animation. The knot of anger in his chest began to unravel. 'Are you?'

Grace nodded. 'Yes! And then I told her what you said, Bella, about…'

Her brow creased in concentration. 'How one has to respect someone in order to care what their opinion of you is.'

Adam lost his smile. He glanced at Miss Knightley, remembering the words he'd spoken six years ago, feeling the familiar stab of guilt, of shame. *I wish I'd never uttered them.*

The façade Arabella Knightley presented to the world was one of resilience, insouciance, toughness, and yet, as his gaze rested on her, all he saw was the softness of her mouth, the smooth translucency of her skin, the delicacy of her bone structure—her femininity and her vulnerability.

'And I told her, oh, everything you said!'

'I had no idea my words were such pearls of wisdom,' Miss Knightley said, her tone light and ironic.

Grace didn't appear to hear the irony. She nodded. 'Oh, yes, they *are!*'

To his astonishment, Adam found himself silently agreeing. Arabella Knightley was the last friend he'd choose for Grace—but her advice had been invaluable.

'Letty and I have decided we're going to be bosom friends!' Grace announced.

Miss Knightley laughed. 'Every girl needs a bosom friend,' she said. 'Please excuse me, I see my grandmother looking for me.'

Adam stepped back. He bowed silently and watched her leave. Her words echoed in his ears: *Every girl needs a bosom friend.* Miss Knightley had no bosom friend. She had no friends that he was aware of, other than Helen Dysart.

She must be very lonely.

'Polly,' Arabella said to her maid as she climbed out of bed the following morning. 'I'm going to have a headache this afternoon.'

Polly looked up from laying out Arabella's riding habit. She grinned. 'How unfortunate.'

Warm water steamed in the porcelain bowl in the washstand. Arabella washed her face thoroughly. There was no way of knowing whether Mrs Harpenden's tongue had spread the rumours about Grace St Just, but the woman was, without doubt, the instigator of Miss Wootton's fall from grace. *And as such, she deserves a visit from Tom.*

She reached for a towel and turned to Polly.

Her maid's expression was bright and expectant.

'I shan't be attending the Pentictons' musicale tonight,' Arabella said, drying her face. 'Instead, I shall be at Half Moon Street. Number 23.'

'Number 23, Half Moon Street,' Polly repeated, with a nod. 'I'll check it out this afternoon.'

'Thank you.' Arabella laid the towel aside and began to dress. Long hours stretched until she could don Tom's shirt and trousers, but already anticipation was beginning to build inside her. She felt it tingling in her fingertips, in her toes.

Arabella blew out a breath. The waiting would be hard today.

She rode out on Merrylegs and expended some of her restless energy cantering around the Row. To her disappointment, there was no sign of Adam St Just. The mood she was in, she would have enjoyed needling him.

The afternoon was spent in her bedchamber, pretending to have a headache. She lay in bed and stared up at the ceiling, thinking about her birthday. Twenty-five days remained until that date—twenty-five days of London and the *ton*, of living a narrow, pampered life. But on the twenty-sixth day her fortune became her own and she'd no longer be bound by the promise she'd made her mother. She'd never have to set foot in a ballroom again, never have to exchange polite greetings and smiles with people who despised her as much as she despised them. She'd be free to be herself—and to spend her inheritance as she saw fit.

Arabella hugged herself tightly. The sunbeams streaming in through the window matched her mood. She stared at the shafts of light, imagining the properties she'd purchase, the staff she'd hire, the children she'd rescue from the slums.

Her grandmother looked in on her once, and recommended that she draw the curtains and dab Hungary Water at her temples.

'Where's your maid?'

'Hatchards,' Arabella said. 'Buying a book for me.'

Her grandmother sniffed, a disapproving sound. 'A footman could have done that,' she said, and departed to pay a call on one of her numerous friends.

Arabella didn't close the curtains; instead she pulled out her drawing materials. She laid a tray across her lap, selected several pieces of card, and opened her inkpot.

She'd drawn four cats in different poses by the time Polly returned, carrying a parcel wrapped in paper and string.

Arabella laid down her quill. 'Well?'

'Looks fairly easy,' Polly said, handing her the parcel. 'From the mews, that is. Not from the front.' She untied her bonnet and sat on the end of Arabella's bed. 'There's this wall, see, and from the top you can reach the first row of windows.'

'Good,' said Arabella, setting the parcel to one side. 'We'll leave at ten.'

Polly nodded. She stood. 'I'll check Tom's clothes.'

'Thank you.' Arabella returned to her work. She studied the four cats, hesitated for a moment, and then selected one. Writing carefully she inscribed a message to Mrs Harpenden. Then she capped the inkpot.

A glance at the ormolu clock on the mantelpiece showed that it was nearly six o'clock.

Arabella grimaced. Four more hours to wait.

Chapter Five

Polly had been correct—it was easy to gain entry to the rented house on Half Moon Street. A heave—and a push from Polly—had her on top of the brick wall, and in a few seconds she was crouching beneath one of the windows. It was the work of less than a minute to break one of the diamond-shaped panes, extract the glass from the leading, slip her hand inside, and open the window.

Arabella glanced back at Polly. She gave a little wave.

Polly nodded and moved into the shadows, vanishing from sight.

Arabella took a deep breath. Her senses felt heightened—sight, smell, touch, hearing—as if the world had suddenly come into clearer focus: the sharp outline of the rooftops against the night sky, the acrid smell of coal smoke, the clatter of a hackney in Half Moon Street, the grittiness of the bricks beneath her fingers.

She took another breath and eased herself over the window sill and into the room, pushing past heavy velvet curtains. For a moment she crouched in darkness, and then her eyes adjusted to the gloom. A bedroom, furnished with bed and dresser, but unoccupied; no linens covered the mattress.

Arabella crossed the room. She opened the door and peered into the corridor. A lamp stood on a marble-topped table, casting light and shadows.

She stood listening for a long moment, and then slipped into the corridor. She opened three doors before she found what she was looking for: Mrs Harpenden's room.

Arabella stepped inside and closed the door quietly behind her. She stood with her back to the door, straining to hear past the rapid beating of her heart. Silence. A candle was lit in a holder on the bedside table, its flame flickering slightly in the breeze from her entry, but no maid moved in the dressing room.

Arabella locked the door. She hurried to the window and cautiously parted the curtains, released the latch, and opened the window slightly. Then she checked the dressing room, locking the door that opened into the corridor. That done, she turned and surveyed the bedchamber. Her heart beat loudly in her ears and she had the sensation that seconds were rushing past too rapidly to be counted.

Swiftly she crossed to the satinwood dresser. Unlike Lady Bicknell's dresser, the items were neatly arranged: a hairbrush, a pot of Denmark Lotion and one of Olympian Dew, two vials of perfume—and a lacquered jewellery box.

Arabella glanced at the locked door. No sound came from the corridor.

The jewellery box opened smoothly. Earrings and brooches nestled in silk-lined compartments. Arabella lifted out the tray. Beneath it was a second tray, also lined with silk, holding bracelets and hair combs.

Arabella studied the contents of both trays. These were small things. Mrs Harpenden's necklaces, her tiara—if she owned one— were somewhere else. She glanced at the dressing room, tempted to search further, and then looked back at the open jewellery box. The smooth lustre of pearls and the gleam of gold met her eyes. *Don't be greedy,* she told herself. The longer she stayed, the greater the risk of being caught.

Two of the smaller compartments were empty, and a gap in the lower tray showed that something was missing. Arabella examined the jewellery that remained. It was all of good quality.

Her fingers trailed over pearls, over rubies, over diamonds. *That one.* She plucked the sapphire brooch from its silken nest, extracted the matching earrings and hair combs, and slid them into the pouch tied around her waist.

Swiftly she replaced the topmost tray and closed the jewellery box. She propped the card she'd made that afternoon on top. *Should payment be made for starting malicious rumours? Tom thinks so.* The cat she'd drawn at the bottom sat upright, staring down its nose with haughty disapproval.

Rather like Adam St Just.

The thought surprised her. It almost made her laugh—and with the laughter came a prickling of nervousness. She was suddenly aware of the enormity of what she was doing: entering the Harpendens' house, stealing jewellery. If she was caught, she'd be hanged—and Polly and Harry and Tess with her.

Arabella bit her lip. She hurried across to the door, leaned her ear against the wooden panels for a few seconds, then unlocked it and opened it a cautious crack.

Silence.

Arabella slipped out of the bedchamber. In less than a minute she was crouching on top of the brick wall, peering down into the shadowy mews.

'Our notorious thief has struck again.'

Adam looked up from his newspaper. 'What?'

Jeremy, Marquis of Revelstoke, settled into the chair alongside him and examined his boots. He rubbed a speck of moisture from one gleaming toe and nodded at St James's Street, visible through the bow window. 'Starting to rain.'

'What thief?'

Jeremy examined his Hessians. 'Smudged,' he said, and extracted a handkerchief from his pocket.

'What thief?' Adam said. 'Tom?'

Jeremy wiped the smudge carefully. 'The one and only.'

Excitement kindled inside him. 'Where?' Adam hastily folded the newspaper and put it aside. 'And when?'

Jeremy signalled to one of the waiters. 'Claret.' Then he settled back in the chair and looked out the bow window. 'Is that Mountford?' He raised his quizzing glass. 'Man's got a dashed odd way of tying his neckcloth, don't you think?'

Adam ignored this gambit. 'Tom,' he repeated. 'When and where?'

Jeremy lowered the quizzing glass. 'Last night. In Half Moon Street.'

'Who?'

Jeremy shrugged. 'Someone named Harpenden. Don't know 'em myself.'

'Harpenden?' Adam turned the name over in his head, trying to place it.

'Mrs Harpenden, to be precise.'

Adam frowned as he made the connection. Mrs Harpenden had a daughter on the Marriage Mart.

I wonder...

Adam pushed to his feet and gave Jeremy a curt nod of farewell.

'Hey!' his friend protested. 'Where are you off to?'

'Business.'

He'd intended to call on Mr Fforbes-Brown this afternoon, but instead he turned left when he came out of White's. His offer for Miss Fforbes-Brown's hand could wait a day—this couldn't.

Adam strode up St James's Street, oblivious to the rain. In a few minutes he was climbing the steps to his house in Berkeley Square. 'Where's my sister?' he asked the butler, Fiscus.

'Upstairs, sir. In the blue parlour.'

Adam took the stairs two at a time. 'Grace,' he said as he pushed open the door. 'Do you know a—?' He halted. 'I beg your pardon. I didn't realise you had a guest.'

He bowed to Miss Wootton and made his escape—and spent the next hour in his study, going over the lists he'd made about Tom.

He lifted his head at a soft knock. Grace opened the door. 'You wanted to speak with me?'

'Yes.' Adam hastily covered the lists. 'Do you know a family by the name of Harpenden?'

'How odd.' Grace closed the door and came to stand beside his desk. 'Bella asked me that a few days ago.'

His interest sharpened. 'Did she?'

Grace nodded.

'And...?' he prompted.

'I know Charlotte Harpenden,' Grace said. 'But she's not in London. She hasn't come out yet.'

'Was she at school with you in Bath?'

Grace nodded.

Adam was conscious of a surge of excitement. The person Arabella had refused to name, the one who'd started the rumours about Miss Wootton—and quite possibly about Grace—had to be Mrs Harpenden.

'Why?' Grace asked.

'Oh…' Adam said. 'I'm just curious. It's not important.'

Grace accepted this with a nod.

When she was gone, Adam walked over to the sideboard. He poured himself a glass of brandy and sipped thoughtfully.

How much would Charlotte Harpenden have known about Grace's planned elopement with Mr Plunkett?

As much any of the pupils at Miss Widdecombe's Select Seminary for Girls: that Mr Plunkett had been dismissed from his position and Grace removed from the school—two events that might or might not have been connected. Enough to speculate about, enough to conjecture on.

Speculation and conjecture—the foundations from which gossip and rumours were born.

Adam grimaced. *I should have left Grace at the school.* That was easy to see in hindsight. At the time…Grace had been so distressed he'd thought it best to take her home.

Adam walked back to his desk. He uncovered the lists, dipped his quill in ink, and wrote: *Mrs Harpenden, May 1818. For starting rumours.*

He read what he'd written and frowned. How had Tom known Mrs Harpenden was the culprit?

The same way as Arabella Knightley had known: by overhearing the woman.

Adam rolled the quill between his fingers. Who else, other than Miss Knightley, had heard Mrs Harpenden start the rumour about Miss Wootton?

For the answer to that question, he'd have to ask Arabella Knightley.

Adam escorted his aunt and his sister to the theatre that evening. At Grace's request, an invitation had been extended to Letty Wootton and her parents. As host, Adam's attention was on his guests; it wasn't until the curtain rose that he was at leisure to scan the boxes.

His gaze flicked from face to face—and then paused. Miss Fforbes-Brown was attending the performance, along with her parents and—

Adam's eyes narrowed. He leaned slightly forwards in his seat.

Miss Fforbes-Brown was attending the performance along with her parents and Sir Humphrey Holbrook.

Adam sat back, conscious of a feeling of extreme disquiet. *I should have called on her father today.*

In the first interval talk turned to Tom's latest theft. 'Why did he choose Mrs Harpenden?' Letty Wootton asked, wide-eyed. 'What can she have done?'

'It's unlikely she'll tell anyone,' her father said drily.

'No,' Letty said. 'But one can't help but wonder. I'd like to know what she did!'

'I'd like to know who he is,' Mr Wootton said.

So should I, Adam thought.

When the curtain lifted for the second act, he turned his attention to the audience. It took him several minutes to find Miss Knightley. She wore a dress of deep, rich red with a square neckline. Her hair was dressed in a coronet of braids. She looked… He searched for a word, rejected *severe,* and settled on *regal.* Quite a feat for a girl who'd lived in the slums.

He wished he could interview her tonight. Impatience ate at him. He had to stop himself from fidgeting while the play progressed through several acts towards its end. He watched Miss Knightley surreptitiously, anticipating the questions he'd ask. She rarely spoke to her grandmother. Her demeanour, when she did, was courteous and respectful, but not warm.

Adam turned this over in his mind while the play reached its climax. The fifth Earl of Westcote had been a proud man, very high in the instep. What had he thought of Arabella? The granddaughter he can hardly have wanted—and yet, his only direct descendant.

An awkward relationship at best, Adam decided, glancing at Miss Knightley again. And yet, awkward or not, the earl had bequeathed his wealth to her. The title and estates had gone to a distant cousin—a cousin the late earl had often been heard to call an ill-bred buffoon.

The audience broke into applause. Belatedly Adam started clapping.

'Wasn't that marvellous!' Grace said.

'Er, yes,' he said.

Miss Knightley and her grandmother left before the farce. Adam watched as they gathered their wraps and reticules.

Lady Westcote was a bird-like woman, her stature as diminutive as

Miss Knightley's, her posture erect. She wasn't the dowager countess; none of her sons had lived to be Earl of Westcote. The youngest had died in the Peninsular War, the eldest on the hunting field, and her middle son—Miss Knightley's father—had succumbed to a fever.

Adam grimaced. Three sons dead. A terrible thing for a mother to bear.

He turned his attention to the stage, frowning at the antics of the actors and trying to imagine what it had been like for Arabella Knightley—arriving as an orphan at Westcote Hall, being clothed, fed, educated, launched into society. Would she have loved her grandparents—or resented them? Seen them as her saviours—or laid the death of her mother at their feet?

Unarguably, Arabella Knightley's childhood would have been very different if the late Earl of Westcote had accepted his son's bride. There would have been no descent into the slums. Her mother would still be alive, her reputation unsullied. Quite possibly her father would be alive too.

Adam glanced at the vacated box. Did Arabella Knightley blame her grandparents for what had happened?

He thought the answer was probably *yes*.

The next morning Adam timed his ride in Hyde Park to coincide with Miss Knightley's. She was cantering along the strip of tan when he arrived. The high-spirited black mare was as easy to recognise as her rider.

Adam touched his heels lightly to Goliath's flanks. 'Come on, boy. Let's find out what she knows.'

They completed one circuit of the park some distance behind Miss Knightley, then Adam urged the big grey to come up alongside her.

She glanced at him. Her eyebrows arched in surprise. 'Mr St Just.'

'Good morning, Miss Knightley.' Adam dipped his head to her. 'May I have a word?'

The mare slowed to a walk.

Miss Knightley's hat was tilted at a jaunty angle. Beneath the brim, her dark eyes already seemed to hold a glint of mocking amusement. 'Mr St Just?'

Now that the moment had come, he suddenly felt foolish. On the heels of foolishness came annoyance with himself. Let Arabella

Knightley laugh at his question. As long as she answered it, he didn't care what her opinion of him was.

'It was Mrs Harpenden you overheard, wasn't it? Starting the rumour about Miss Wootton.'

The glint of amusement vanished. 'Mr St Just, I've already told you that I won't—'

'I know it was her,' Adam said. 'That's why she received a visit from our quixotic thief.'

Miss Knightley said nothing, she merely looked at him, her expression closed and unforthcoming.

'I'm not interested in Mrs Harpenden.' Adam shifted his weight in the saddle, leaning slightly towards her. 'It's Tom I want to know about.'

Miss Knightley blinked. 'Tom?'

'Yes,' he said. 'Who else was nearby? Who else could have overheard Mrs Harpenden—'

'You want to find *Tom?*' Her voice was as astonished as her face.

Adam felt himself flush. 'Yes.'

Miss Knightley didn't laugh at him; instead, she frowned. 'Why?'

Because it gives me something to do other than worry about Grace. Adam shrugged. 'Don't you want to know who he is?'

'No.'

'Well, I do,' Adam said. 'And I'd be grateful if you could tell me who was nearby when you heard Mrs Harpenden talking.'

Miss Knightley's expression was as eloquent as a shrug. He didn't need to see her lift her shoulders to know that she didn't remember. 'I have no idea, Mr St Just. I pay no attention to servants.'

'I don't think Tom is a servant.'

Her eyebrows arched again. 'You don't?'

'No.' Adam looked at her in frustration. 'Who was with you when you overheard Mrs Harpenden?'

'I was by myself.'

'But surely there were people nearby—'

'Dozens,' Miss Knightley said. The amusement, the mockery, had crept back into her eyes, into her voice. 'But I haven't the faintest recollection who they were.'

'If you should remember—'

'I doubt I'll recall anything more than I've already told you.' Her smile was contrite and insincere. 'Good day, Mr St Just.' The black mare surged forwards.

Adam held Goliath at a walk, conscious of a sense of frustration. 'God damn it,' he said.

The frustration was still with him when he sat down with the *Morning Post* in the bow window at White's later that day. Alongside it was a healthy dose of nervousness. Adam glanced at his fob watch. It was still too early to pay a visit to Mr Fforbes-Brown.

He swallowed a mouthful of claret and resisted the urge to loosen his neck cloth. His nervousness annoyed him. He might lack a title, but both his lineage and fortune were superior to Sir Humphrey's. There was no reason for either Mr Fforbes-Brown or his daughter to reject his offer.

Adam opened the *Morning Post*. It was unnerving to think that within few hours he'd be engaged. He felt a flicker of uneasiness. Was he being too hasty?

A moment's reflection assured him he wasn't. Miss Fforbes-Brown was the best of this year's crop of débutantes. Others surpassed her in terms of beauty and fortune, but she possessed the qualities of a fine mother: she was cheerful, sensible and extremely fond of children.

His eyes skimmed the columns—and stopped halfway down the page, arrested by an announcement.

Mr Fforbes-Brown of Upper Helmsley, Yorkshire, announces the engagement of his eldest daughter, Sophia, to Sir Humphrey Holbrook of Holbrook Manor, Derbyshire.

'God *damn* it,' Adam said. He closed the newspaper violently and reached for his wine glass.

His mood, as he entered the Thornycrofts' ballroom that evening, was dour. Grace clasped her hands together and looked around in delight. 'How beautiful! It's like a fairy bower.'

Adam looked at the flowers and the ferns and the gauzy draperies and wished he was at his club. The trill of pan flutes was an irritant.

Servants circulated among the assembled guests. Instead of livery and powdered wigs, they were dressed as ancient Greeks. Adam's lip curled in disbelief as a footman wearing a toga and a laurel wreath came towards them. The man's expression was wooden. He clearly felt as ridiculous as he looked.

'Pink champagne!' Grace said, enchanted. 'May I?'

At Aunt Seraphina's nod, she took a glass from the tray the footman offered.

Adam's disgruntlement faded as he watched his sister. Her cheeks were flushed with pleasure and delight sparkled in her eyes. *I haven't seen her look this happy in weeks.* Not since the Cranbrooks' soirée, when they'd walked into the salon to the accompaniment of whispers and sidelong glances. Grace had been nervous, eager, delighted to be attending her first London party. The delight hadn't lasted long; she'd left early and almost in tears.

'Can you see Letty?' Grace asked, looking around. 'She said she'd meet me here.'

To Adam's relief, the pan flutes were superseded by an orchestra. Letty Wootton arrived as the opening bars of the minuet were being played. The two girls departed, arm in arm, to the row of giltwood chairs that lined the wall and fell immediately into conversation. They were indisputably the most beautiful girls in the room. Grace's pale loveliness, her golden hair and blue eyes, contrasted very nicely with Letty Wootton's more robust prettiness, her nut-brown curls and rosy cheeks.

Their beauty and the animation with which they conversed, the laughter lighting their faces, drew a number of glances, but neither girl showed awareness of the interest they were attracting.

His father would have disapproved of so animated a conversation— *It's vulgar to display emotion, and St Justs are never vulgar!*—but Adam gave a nod of approval. He went in search of something to drink that wasn't pink. By the time he found it, a cluster of young men had begun to form around Letty and Grace. To his satisfaction, not all of them were fortune hunters.

'The only thing more pleasing to the eye than one Beauty,' a familiar voice drawled in his ear, 'is *two* Beauties.'

'Evening, Jeremy,' Adam said, without looking around. A face on the dance floor caught his eye: Miss Fforbes-Brown. His disgruntlement returned.

'Very clever,' Jeremy said. 'They set each other off to perfection.'

Adam grunted. He glanced at his friend. 'Good Lord,' he said, as he took in the Marquis of Revelstoke's splendour. 'Couldn't you find bigger buttons?'

Jeremy took a sip of pink champagne. 'I like 'em,' he said.

'They're the size of dinner plates.'

Jeremy smiled, unruffled by the criticism. He raised his quizzing glass and examined one of the dancers more closely.

Adam followed his gaze. He saw dark ringlets and softly indented chin. The familiar emotions flooded through him: guilt and shame, and a silent surge of desire. He looked away and gulped a mouthful of wine.

Jeremy lowered his quizzing glass. 'I hear you were riding in Hyde Park this morning.'

Adam's fingers tightened on the wine glass. 'I ride there every morning,' he said shortly.

Jeremy didn't appear to hear the warning. He swung the quizzing glass and smiled. 'With Miss Smell O'Gutters?'

Adam stiffened. 'Don't call her that.'

Laughter gleamed in Jeremy's eyes. 'Touchy, touchy.'

With difficulty, Adam restrained himself from snarling at his friend. He turned his attention to the dance floor again.

'Riding in the park with Miss Knightley,' Jeremy said musingly. 'One wonders what you were talking about…?'

Adam didn't reply. He preserved a stiff and dignified silence.

Unfortunately Jeremy was unsnubbed. 'Marriage settlements, perhaps?'

Adam swung around. 'Damn it, Jeremy—!'

Jeremy laughed.

Adam glared at him, exasperated. 'Heaven only knows why I put up with you!'

'Because I don't bore you.' Jeremy swung the quizzing glass again. 'Think how tedious London would be without me.'

The marquis waited for a moment, with an air of hopeful expectancy. When Adam made no rejoinder he released the quizzing glass with a sigh. 'You're very dull tonight,' he said, plaintively. 'I'll have to find someone else to amuse me.'

Adam watched him stroll off, and then returned his attention to the dance floor. He followed Miss Knightley's progress with his eyes. Her gown of ivory-white silk was unadorned by rouleaux, festoons of flowers, or lavish trimmings of lace. Its simplicity suited the elegance of her face.

Miss Smell O'Gutters.

The name was so ugly, so vulgar and offensive. And she had it because of him.

Adam grimaced and looked away. *I wish I'd never uttered those words.*

In fact, he wished he could consign that whole day to oblivion. It had begun with the interview with his father, the old man's icy fury. *You've been in town less than a day, and what do you do? Two dances with the daughter of a French whore! How dare you shame our name like that?*

It had been useless to protest that he hadn't known who Miss Knightley was, that he'd danced with her because of her face, not her name. His father hadn't bothered to listen. *You're to pay a visit to my brother, the Duke. You leave for Lisbon tomorrow.* The old man had looked at him contemptuously. *Dismissed.*

Adam's mouth tightened. Packed off to the continent like an errant child. He felt a surge of remembered bitterness, of impotent rage.

He'd spent the rest of the day getting drunk. He should have curbed his spleen, instead he'd vented it. *Marry Arabella Knightley?* he'd said through a haze of alcohol at his club. *Certainly, if one wishes to live with the smell of the gutter.* The target had been his father—how dared the old man think him capable of forgetting what he owed the St Just name!—but the victim had been Miss Knightley.

It wasn't until his return to England, months later, that he'd realised the *ton* had taken up his words, that a name had been coined for her: Miss Smell O'Gutters.

He grimaced again and looked for Miss Knightley. The dance had come to its conclusion; it took him some time to find her among the crush of guests. She was in conversation with Lord Dalrymple.

Adam's eyes narrowed as Dalrymple leaned towards her. Miss Knightley showed no sign of discomfort. She looked as she always did—perfectly composed, slightly amused—and yet something in her smile, in the way she held her glass like a barrier in front of her, told him she was uncomfortable.

Adam glanced around the ballroom. Where was Miss Knightley's grandmother? This was precisely the type of encounter a chaperon was supposed to prevent.

Lord Dalrymple sidled closer to Arabella Knightley. Adam hesitated a moment, and then set off across the dance floor.

'Dalrymple,' he said, as he approached. 'Miss Knightley.'

Lord Dalrymple stepped back. 'St Just.'

Adam favoured him with the slightest of nods. He turned and bowed to Miss Knightley. 'I trust you haven't forgotten our engagement?'

She surveyed him coolly. 'Which engagement is that, Mr St Just?'

'The waltz,' Adam said, and watched as her eyes widened.

'I asked Miss Knightley first!' Lord Dalrymple protested.

Adam turned to him with an insincere smile. 'My request was made this morning, when we were riding in the park.'

'Then I shall have the second waltz,' Dalrymple said, a flush of annoyance rising in his heavy cheeks.

'Our engagement was for both waltzes,' Adam said blandly. 'Perhaps Miss Knightley can give you one of the country dances?'

Dalrymple's face grew even more florid.

'I'm not engaged for this dance,' Arabella Knightley said, as the orchestra struck up another tune. 'Unless you prefer a quadrille, Lord Dalrymple?'

Dalrymple accepted the offer with bad grace. His manner, as he proffered Miss Knightley his arm, was disgruntled.

'My glass,' she said, glancing around. 'Let me find a table—'

'I'll take it,' Adam said, holding out his hand.

After a moment's hesitation Miss Knightley gave him the glass. Lord Dalrymple escorted her onto the dance floor.

'I don't think I've ever seen you play the knight errant before,' an amused voice said in his ear.

Adam stiffened. 'Hardly the knight errant.'

'Rescuing a damsel in distress?' Jeremy said. 'I believe that qualifies as a chivalrous deed.'

Adam glanced at him. 'I wouldn't call Dalrymple a dragon.'

'Merely an old goat,' Jeremy said and grinned.

Adam didn't grin; instead he frowned. 'If you thought Miss Knightley needed rescuing, why didn't you do it yourself?'

'Because it's much more amusing to watch you do it!'

Adam grunted. He returned his gaze to the dance floor, where Miss Knightley and Lord Dalrymple had found their places in a set.

'Lovely, ain't she?' Jeremy said in his ear. 'Quite the most graceful dancer I've seen.'

'Trying to marry her off?' Adam asked, his voice sarcastic.

'Only to you.' Jeremy met his sharp glance with a bland smile. 'I have an investment to protect, after all.'

'Much you care about five hundred guineas!'

'Oh, but I do,' Jeremy protested, his eyes wide and his tone earnest.

Adam snorted. 'You're as rich as Croesus.'

'No,' Jeremy said, sighing. 'That would be you. I'm but a pauper in comparison.'

Adam's snort was louder this time. 'Doing it *much* too brown, Jeremy.'

The marquis looked wounded.

'You know, Jeremy, it's a dashed shame you were born a nobleman. You should be on the stage.'

Jeremy sighed again. 'I know,' he said, in a melancholy voice. 'It's the great sorrow of my life.' He drifted away, looking as frail as possible for a man possessed of robust good health.

Adam uttered a half-laugh under his breath and returned his attention to the dance floor. Miss Knightley and Lord Dalrymple were going down the set. He watched for a moment. Jeremy was right: Arabella Knightley was a superb dancer. There was elegance and grace in each step she took.

In this Grecian-themed ballroom, the simile was easy to find: she was the goddess Artemis, the huntress, lithe and graceful, lissom.

And I have two waltzes with her tonight.

Heat flared inside him. His throat tightened.

Adam tore his gaze from Arabella Knightley. He looked down at the glass she'd given him. Pink lemonade. Ugh.

He went in search of a table to place it on.

Chapter Six

Half an hour later Adam escorted Miss Knightley on to the dance floor. He'd spent the intervening time regretting his decision to rescue her from Dalrymple. He regretted it even more as they took their places, aware of the number of glances being cast in their direction.

Adam gritted his teeth. The staring would be even more marked when he danced a second waltz with her tonight. *I was a fool to do this.*

One good thing—the only good thing—was that his cousin, the new Duke of Frew, wasn't in town to witness this. Frew's strictures were even harder to stomach than his father's had been.

Adam took hold of her hand. Heat stirred inside him, increasing his discomfort.

Arabella Knightley showed no signs of discomfort. As far as he could tell, her manner was the same as when she'd danced with Lord Dalrymple: distant, slightly amused and utterly composed. She seemed unaware of the interest they were attracting.

But then, Miss Knightley was used to stares and whispers. For her, it was always like this.

Miss Smell O'Gutters. For a moment he heard the name in his ears as clearly as if someone had uttered it aloud. It caused a sense of discordance inside him, as if the musicians played out of tune.

He'd been wrong to speak his opinion of her aloud—that went without saying—but now, for the first time, Adam found himself wondering if his opinion itself had been wrong. Miss Knightley had spent part of her childhood in the slums, but no one ignorant of her past would guess the truth;

he certainly hadn't six years ago. She brought nothing of the gutters into the ballroom with her—nothing except a name he'd inadvertently given her.

Arabella Knightley's poise, her graceful performance on the dance floor, were those of a lady of quality. There was no vulgarity in her appearance, none of the ostentatious display of jewellery seen in the *nouveau riche*. The shining cleanness of her hair, the faint scent of orange blossom that accompanied her, spoke of privilege and wealth, not London's slums.

Adam was intensely aware of her gloved hand in his, of the closeness of their bodies. There was nothing sensual about dancing in a crowded ballroom under the glare of hundreds of candles—and yet it *was* sensual. Abruptly, he wondered what it would be like to make love to Arabella Knightley. Heat flooded his body. It was suddenly difficult to breathe.

Adam cleared his throat. He concentrated on the waltz—but it only made him more aware of her responsiveness to each step he took, the natural grace of her body as she followed his lead.

Did Dalrymple think about sex when he danced with Miss Knightley?

It was disgusting to think of the man imagining her in his bed—and yet Adam knew instinctively and with utmost certainty that Dalrymple did precisely that.

Revulsion and rage rose inside him. He glanced at Miss Knightley's face. Did she know, too? Was that why she'd chosen him over Dalrymple?

His gaze rested for a moment on skin as smooth and pale as alabaster, on the dark sweep of her eyelashes, on soft lips the colour of rose petals. She glanced at him. For a breathless second he stared into eyes that were almost black—and then he wrenched his gaze away from her.

Adam concentrated on breathing, on placing his feet in time with the music. It was surprisingly difficult; the sound of his heartbeat almost drowned out the strains of the waltz.

A familiar face caught his attention: Grace, dancing with Viscount Mayroyd.

Adam focused on her. Grace didn't have Arabella Knightley's grace as a dancer, nor her composure, but she acquitted herself well.

The sound of his heartbeat faded; he could hear the music more clearly. He watched as the viscount said something to Grace, as his sister blushed and answered with a shy smile. He changed direction, leading Miss

Knightley into a sweeping curve, so as to see Mayroyd's face. The young viscount's expression was appreciative.

Adam began to feel more cheerful. Unless he was mistaken, Grace had an admirer who wasn't a fortune hunter.

Of course, Grace wouldn't be on the dance floor, waltzing and smiling, capturing the interest of young viscounts, if not for Arabella Knightley. Her shrewd advice had been invaluable.

We owe her.

He risked a glance at Miss Knightley. She was watching him.

His cheerfulness evaporated—along with his awareness of the other dancers. The music was inaudible again. The only two people in the ballroom were himself and Arabella Knightley. Familiar emotions flooded through him—shame and guilt, desire—and with them was a new one: gratitude.

His steps faltered. He was out of time with the music.

Miss Knightley's eyebrows rose fractionally. 'Mr St Just?'

Adam wrenched his attention back to the waltz. When his steps were once more in time with the music he said, 'I wish to thank you, Miss Knightley.'

Her expression became slightly wary, as if she suspected him of mocking her. 'For what?'

'For your kindness to Grace. For your advice to her.' Advice that had been given with no motive other than a desire to help. His guilt intensi-fied. 'Because of you, Grace found the courage to remain in London.'

Miss Knightley blinked. He saw her astonishment. After a moment she said, 'There's no need to thank me, Mr St Just. I didn't do it for you.'

Adam felt himself flush. 'I am aware of that,' he said stiffly, and looked away from her.

They danced in an awkward silence for several minutes. Words of apology gathered on Adam's tongue. He stole a glance at her. Miss Knightley was gazing past his shoulder. If she found their silence awkward, she gave no sign of it. She seemed perfectly at ease. A slight smile sat on her mouth, as if she observed—and was amused by—the other dancers.

She hadn't always possessed such poise, such confidence. The first time he'd danced with her, six years ago, there'd been shyness in her eyes, not amusement. She'd been as vulnerable as Grace. *And I harmed her.*

'I apologise, Miss Knightley,' he blurted.

Her attention shifted to him. He watched her eyebrows rise. 'For dancing with me?'

'No, for…for what I said about you six years ago.'

Her face stiffened. She looked away.

'You must believe that it wasn't deliberate,' Adam said. 'I was in my cups and…and I never—for one second!—thought my words would be repeated.'

Miss Knightley's gaze returned to his face. 'It was six years ago, Mr St Just.' Her voice matched her eyes: cool and distant. 'Consider it forgotten.'

The reply should have assuaged his guilt. It didn't.

'I'm sorry,' he said quietly, holding her gaze. 'It was never my intention to cause you distress.'

This time Arabella Knightley seemed to hear his sincerity. Her expression became less stiff. She observed him for several seconds in silence. 'You surprise me, Mr St Just,' she said finally. 'I never thought to hear you refer to this subject.'

'When I returned to London and discovered that everyone—' He flushed, feeling his shame anew. 'So many months had passed that it seemed…wisest to ignore it. I thought—I *hoped*—that if I pretended I'd forgotten, London would forget too.'

Miss Knightley's lips twisted wryly. 'London has a long memory.'

'Yes,' he said. 'Unfortunately.'

The waltz reached its conclusion. Adam released her hand reluctantly. They had been on the brink of something—accord, an understanding—but now the moment was lost.

He glanced at the matrons and dowagers clustering the edges of the dance floor. 'Where's your grandmother?'

'In the card room.'

He frowned. 'She takes her chaperoning duties far too lightly.'

His censure appeared to amuse Miss Knightley. 'I'm perfectly capable of looking after myself.'

'And what of Lord Dalrymple?'

Miss Knightley looked away. 'My grandmother would be delighted to see me waltz with Lord Dalrymple—and even more delighted to see me marry him.' Her voice was light, but beneath the lightness was a faint undertone that Adam recognised: contempt.

Adam's frown deepened. 'She's not encouraging Dalrymple to—'

'No, she knows my views on that subject.' Miss Knightley looked at him, and once again he saw her amusement. It hovered at the edges of her mouth and gleamed in the darkness of her eyes. 'I don't need rescuing, Mr St Just. I'm perfectly capable of looking after myself.'

Adam disagreed, but he didn't say so aloud. Instead he escorted her from the dance floor, conscious of the interest they were attracting.

It was easy to imagine his father's outrage if he could see them now, his icy fury. The old man's words still rang in his ears after all these years, burned into his memory: *A slut from the stews? If your taste runs to the gutters, find yourself a lightskirt, not a trollop you'll have to marry.*

His father had been wrong. Arabella Knightley was neither a trollop nor a slut; there was nothing flirtatious about her manner. But the old man had been right about one thing: such a marriage was doomed to failure.

However much he was attracted to Miss Knightley, however much he admired her aplomb, her poise, her kindness to Grace, she was not a woman he could ever marry.

Adam escorted her to a seat alongside his aunt. 'May I bring you something to drink? Champagne? Punch?'

'Lemonade, please.'

The refreshment room was almost as crowded as the ballroom. A queue had formed of gentlemen with wilting collar points.

Adam glanced down at the signet ring on his finger as he waited. The gold gleamed in the candlelight. He could see the ridges of the St Just crest, the words inscribed beneath the lion rampant: *Optimus Superbia.* Noble Pride.

As a St Just, pride was his birthright. *A St Just knows his worth,* his father had been used to say. Pride had been bred into him. It was in his blood, in his bones.

The shadow of Miss Knightley's mother hovered over her. Even if he'd never uttered those drunken, angry words six years ago, the whispers and the sidelong glances would still have followed her. Through no fault of her own, Arabella Knightley's reputation was tarnished. It would always be tarnished.

If I married Arabella Knightley I would be ashamed of her—and ashamed of myself for being ashamed of her.

Arabella's second waltz with Adam St Just came after supper, which she ate with her grandmother. Lady Westcote talked of her success at the card table while devouring buttered lobster, asparagus spears and a serving of syllabub in a fluted glass bowl. Arabella picked at her food while her grandmother's words flowed over her. Her thoughts were in a tumult. She couldn't believe—simply *could not* believe—that Adam St Just had apologised to her.

She speared a piece of lobster on her fork and chewed without tasting. What on earth had possessed him to do such a thing?

Arabella swallowed the lobster and reached for her glass. It was as unfathomable as his behaviour six years ago. She sipped the pink lemonade, remembering. St Just had danced with her twice, the warm admiration in his eyes unmistakable. She'd been flustered by his attention, flattered, and at the same time alarmed by her response to him, by the dangerous stirring in her blood. She'd lain awake that night in a turmoil of indecision. Adam St Just, wealthy and well born, unnervingly attractive, was interested in her. Should she encourage his attentions— or stand by her decision never to marry and rebuff him?

The choice had been made for her. Adam St Just departed London, and his words were on everyone's lips. That hateful label—Miss Smell O'Gutters—had been coined a few days later and the Season, already a gauntlet of sidelong glances and whispered comments, of silent disdain, had become a nightmare.

Pride had enabled her to smile and pretend to ignore the stifled laughter. She'd smiled and planned her revenge: something that would humiliate him, that would *hurt*.

Revenge was very well in theory, but horrifying in practice. She'd learned her lesson from Lord Crowe: she avenged other people, not herself.

Arabella speared another piece of lobster on her fork.

'—three hands in a row!' her grandmother said. 'Mrs Davenport said she'd never seen anything like it!'

Arabella gave a murmur of agreement as her thoughts swung to Lord Crowe, to her moment of triumph—and from there, to his death.

The lobster tasted like dust in her mouth. Arabella took a mouthful of lemonade and forced herself to swallow. She looked at her plate, at the uneaten food, and laid down her fork.

She'd been right to punish Lord Crowe—she still believed that—but she would never avenge herself again. The guilt wasn't worth it.

She sighed as she looked at the wilted asparagus on her plate, at the congealing butter. She'd hated Adam St Just for six years. It seemed churlish to continue hating him after his apology, but if she wasn't to hate him, what was she to do?

Arabella sipped her lemonade and pondered the question.

She couldn't possibly *like* him, could she?

No, that was impossible.

'Lady Endicott tells me that you danced the waltz with St Just tonight.'

Arabella looked up from her contemplation of her plate. 'Er…yes, that's correct.'

'I was very alarmed to hear it,' her grandmother said. She touched the brooch fastened to the stiff purple satin of her bodice in a nervous gesture. 'I'm certain your grandfather wouldn't approve.'

Arabella looked away from the brooch. It was a mourning piece, her grandfather's eye painted on ivory, surrounded by seed pearls and black jet.

'And I understand that St Just danced with you several days ago.'

'Yes.'

Her grandmother began to pleat her napkin. 'It's very worrying,' she said. 'You will remember what happened last time, won't you?'

'I'm not likely to forget,' Arabella said drily.

The hurt, the humiliation, the absurd sense of betrayal, weren't easily forgotten—although why she'd felt betrayed, she had no idea. It wasn't as if St Just had declared an interest in her; all he'd done was dance twice with her. And smile with his eyes.

'Do be careful, won't you, my dear? I should hate to see you hurt again.'

Arabella glanced at her grandmother in surprise. She blinked, taken aback by the concern on Lady Westcote's face. 'I'll be careful.'

Her grandmother resumed pleating the napkin. 'It's very worrying,' she said again.

No, Arabella thought, *it's not worrying—but it is certainly disconcerting.*

What *was* worrying was St Just's declared interest in Tom—and his conviction that Tom was a member of the *ton*.

Her grandmother was back in the card room and engrossed in a hand of whist when the second waltz was called. Arabella was aware of an undercurrent of whispers as Adam St Just escorted her on to the dance floor, of eyes watching with bright interest behind the cover of *brisé* fans.

She tried not to stiffen as St Just drew her into his hold. The touch of his hand at her waist was light, but it gave her a sense of being trapped.

Even so, it was a thousand times better than waltzing with Lord Dalrymple. She repressed a shiver. 'I should thank you.'

St Just's eyebrows rose in silent query.

'Lord Dalrymple,' Arabella said.

A fleeting expression of distaste crossed his face. 'It was my pleasure.'

Liar. Arabella couldn't help smiling. 'You enjoy being stared at, Mr St Just?'

He grimaced slightly. 'I have to confess…no.' There was something in his expression as he looked at her, in his grey eyes—

Arabella's smile faded. She looked away. She concentrated on the music, on the flow of notes and the harmony of the chords, on finding the pleasure in the waltz, not the discomfort. Adam St Just was a superb dancer. Their progress was an effortless glide over the dance floor. Even so, an uncomfortable awareness of him intruded: his closeness, the warmth of his hand at her waist, the strength of his fingers holding hers. There was a quiet sense of power in his movements.

Arabella repressed another shiver. Being this close to a man, his arm around her—

Waltzing with Lord Dalrymple was deeply unpleasant. The way his hand strayed across her back, the sly innuendos, the smell of his perspiration—not as rank as the men who'd visited her mother, but reminding her of them all the same—all were distasteful.

Dancing with St Just wasn't distasteful—but it was disturbing. Discomfort prickled over her skin. She began to feel slightly too warm.

Arabella risked a glance at him. He was watching her. His face was expressionless, but there was something in his eyes—

To her horror Arabella felt herself blush. She looked hurriedly away and concentrated on her steps, feeling as flustered and nervous as if she was a débutante. She didn't want Adam St Just to look at her like that. The heat she felt, the frisson of awareness, were frightening.

For a long, tortuous minute she followed his lead, her mind blank with panic. Then common sense returned. It was easy to stop St Just looking at her so warmly.

Arabella raised her gaze to him. 'Miss Fforbes-Brown is engaged to Sir Humphrey Holbrook.'

His face stiffened. 'Yes.'

'Such a shame,' she observed. 'Miss Fforbes-Brown would have made you an excellent wife.'

The warmth vanished from St Just's eyes. His expression became disapproving.

'Have you considered Letty Wootton? The field is relatively clear at the moment—and she does have such a *tempting* fortune.'

St Just looked down his nose at her.

Arabella began to relax—and to enjoy herself. 'She's very pretty, too. Don't you think, Mr St Just?'

'My opinion of Miss Wootton is none of your business, Miss Knightley.' Disdain was cold in his voice.

I know. Arabella almost grinned.

St Just's eyes narrowed. She had the impression he nearly missed a step.

Arabella carefully stifled the grin. 'Miss Wootton's friendship with your sister must make her an attractive candidate. The approval of one's family is *so* important in a marriage, don't you think?'

St Just made no reply. His jaw tightened, as did his grip on her hand.

Her tone became low and confiding. 'May I suggest, Mr St Just, that as a sign of affection for your new wife, you redecorate in the style of the Prince Regent? There is something so elegant about crimson and gold!'

St Just's lips thinned.

'Oh! And you should have a stream flowing down the centre of your dining table, with goldfish in it, as the Prince Regent once did. Such a charming idea, don't you think?' Arabella widened her eyes. 'Or were you one of those who thought it vulgar?'

She thought St Just gritted his teeth. After a moment he said stiffly,

'As I did not attend that dinner, I have no opinion on that particular style of decoration.'

Arabella almost grinned again. Of course he thought it vulgar; anyone with a modicum of taste must.

'It was before my come-out,' she said. The regret in her voice was unfeigned: she would have loved to have seen such an outlandish centrepiece. 'But I urge you to emulate the Prince. Perhaps at your wedding breakfast? Your bride would find it charming, I'm sure!'

St Just looked as if he'd swallowed something unpleasant.

'To have a stream running down one's table is indicative of true elegance of mind.' Her voice quivered on the last few words and she bit her lip.

Adam St Just's eyes narrowed again in suspicion. Fortunately the waltz ended at that moment.

Arabella stepped back and made a pretty curtsy. 'Thank you, Mr St Just,' she said. 'That was extremely pleasant. We must do it again.'

St Just gave a thin, pained smile. There was nothing appreciative in his gaze as he made his bow to her; the expression in his eyes was one of dislike.

Chapter Seven

Artemis was asleep in his bed. Her hair lay in dark coils across the pillowcase. Adam gazed at her, letting his eyes dwell on the elegant bones of her face, the fullness of her lips, the delicately indented chin.

A pulse beat in the hollow of her throat, and one hand lay on the sheet, palm up, the fingers curled loosely. The fragility of those slender fingers, the vulnerability of that beating pulse, made his heart ache.

Adam reached out to lightly stroke her arm. At his touch her eyes opened, dark and mysterious.

For long seconds they stared at each other, and then her lips curved in a slow smile. She stretched, cat-like, and pushed aside the sheet. In the darkened bedroom her body was silken and shadowy. He saw the soft roundness of breasts, the slender flare of hips, the dark and enticing triangle of hair at the junction of her thighs.

The muscles in his throat, in his groin, tightened. Heat flooded him.

Artemis laughed softly.

Adam's heart began to beat faster. He reached out and touched the tantalising indentation in her chin. Above his finger, her lips curved up in a smile.

Adam swallowed. He removed his finger and bent his head and kissed lightly where it had been. Her skin smelled of orange blossom.

He kissed her chin, and then her mouth. The soft lips parted with a murmur of pleasure.

Time blurred into a tangle of sensation: his fingers sliding through silken coils of hair, the taste of her mouth, the intoxicating fragrance of her skin. She was moonlight and shadows, she was fierce yet tender, her skin was as cool as his was hot. Pleasure spiralled tightly inside him. The touch of her mouth was searing—

'Good morning, sir.'

Adam jerked abruptly awake.

For a moment he stared at his valet, seeing darkly mysterious eyes, tousled black hair, a bewitching mouth. He blinked, and the man's face came into focus: narrow jaw and hazel eyes and neatly brushed brown hair. He had a cleft in his chin, like Artemis in his dream.

'Goliath is ordered around from the stables in an hour,' Perkins said. He turned away from the bed and began to lay out the shaving accoutrements.

Adam blew out a shaky breath. His heart was still beating far too fast. He raised himself on one elbow. Perkins had drawn back the curtains. Sunlight streamed in through the window panes, so bright it made him squint.

The dream dispersed—wisps of moonlight, of dark silken hair, of intense pleasure. In its place came dismay, swift and sharp.

There was nothing unusual in dreaming about sex, Adam told himself as he threw back the covers. It happened frequently.

He strode across to the washstand and cupped his hands in the steaming water. Nor was it strange that his dream lover had been Artemis. He had, after all, been to a Grecian-themed ball last night.

He washed and dried his face, avoiding his eyes in the mirror. If he didn't look at himself, then perhaps he wouldn't have to acknowledge the truth.

But the truth was there, as real as the rasp of the towel across his cheeks, as real as the sound of Perkins briskly sharpening a razor on the leather strop.

It wasn't Artemis he'd been making love to. It was Arabella Knightley.

'God *damn* it,' Adam said.

That afternoon Adam took Grace to Hatchard's bookshop on Picadilly, so she could buy a birthday gift for Aunt Seraphina. 'Do you think she'd like this?' Grace asked, fingering a copy of *The Prisoner of Chillon*.

Adam grimaced. 'How about something more cheerful?' He reached for another work by Byron, *Childe Harold's Pilgrimage*.

'I think she has that.'

'Sir Walter Scott?' Adam suggested. 'The Lady of the Lake?'

Grace bit her lip. 'I think she has that, too.'

Adam looked at the volumes of poetry, bound in calfskin of various shades and with gilt lettering on their spines. He had his own favourites, but he suspected Aunt Seraphina's tastes were more romantic than his own. 'It's your gift,' he said. 'I'll let you decide.' And he beat a prudent retreat to the shelves where the novels were displayed.

Browsing brought him to four volumes bound with blue-grey boards. *Northanger Abbey,* the title on the spines read. Adam pulled the first book from the shelf and turned to the title page.

'I've heard that's very entertaining,' a cool female voice said beside him.

Adam glanced sharply to his right. He saw dark eyes, elegant cheekbones and a softly indented chin.

He looked swiftly away and thrust the volume back into place on the shelf. Memory of the dream was vivid in his mind: he could smell the fragrance of her skin, feel the silken strands of hair tangling around his fingers. To his horror he felt a stir of arousal.

'Bella! What are you doing here?'

'Buying a book,' Miss Knightley said, turning to greet Grace.

'Oh! May I see?'

Miss Knightley handed her the book she was holding.

'*Orlando Furioso,*' Grace read aloud. 'By Ludovico Ariosto. You read Italian?' Her tone was slightly awed.

'My mother taught me,' Miss Knightley said, with a smile. 'What are you buying?'

Grace proffered a single volume bound in tan calf. Adam read the spine. *The Lay of the Last Minstrel.* 'Scott?'

Grace glanced at him and nodded.

'I'm sure Aunt Seraphina will enjoy it,' Adam said. He stepped away from Miss Knightley and cupped his hand under Grace's elbow. 'If you'll excuse us, we must go.'

His haste seemed to amuse Miss Knightley. A smile lit her eyes. 'Of course.'

But despite his best efforts, they ended up departing Hatchard's at the same time as Miss Knightley and her maid. Grace paused on Piccadilly Street. 'Shall I see you at the Mallorys' tonight?'

'Yes,' Miss Knightley said. Her bonnet was trimmed with clusters of small pink silk flowers. Matching flowers were embroidered along the hem of her muslin walking dress. Beneath the scalloped flounces, Adam caught a glimpse of shapely ankles. He looked hurriedly away. Above the bustle of Piccadilly Street, the sky was a pale, clear blue.

'Excuse me.'

He glanced around and stepped aside for Sir Arnold Gorrie to exit Hatchard's.

'St Just,' the man said as he passed, with an inclination of his head.

Adam favoured him with the slightest of nods.

Sir Arnold began to saunter along Piccadilly. It was obvious the man hadn't been born to his title; he made the mistake, common among those bred in the middle classes, of confusing elegance with opulence. Adam's lip curled in disdain. He turned back to Grace. 'Shall we be going? We don't wish to detain Miss—'

'Sir Arnold!'

Adam stopped in mid-sentence and watched as a young woman in a ragged, dirty dress hurried across the street and reached out to take Sir Arnold Gorrie's arm. She was quite obviously pregnant.

Sir Arnold pushed the woman away from him. 'Get away!' he said, raising his cane.

'But it's yours,' the woman said, reaching towards him again.

The gesture was clearly imploring, not threatening, but Sir Arnold struck her hand away with his cane.

'Please, Sir Arnold…' The woman's voice was high and desperate. 'It's yours. You know it's yours!'

Sir Arnold raised his cane again.

'Gorrie!' Adam said sharply.

Sir Arnold glanced at him. His expression was livid. He lowered the cane, took a step towards the woman, and spoke in a low, fierce voice, 'Stay away from me, you stupid slut!' And then he shoved her aside, so hard that she stumbled and fell into the gutter.

Behind him, Adam heard Grace gasp.

Sir Arnold hurried down Piccadilly without a backwards glance, almost scurrying. The woman stayed on her knees where she'd fallen, weeping.

Adam glanced at his sister. Her face was white with horror. 'Stay here,' he said, and strode to the woman's side. 'Madam?' He crouched. 'Allow me to assist you.'

The woman turned her face to him. 'The baby's his.' Her hands cradled her swollen belly. 'He knows it is!'

He'd been mistaken: she wasn't a woman, but a girl. No older than Grace, and most likely younger. Her face was thin and dirty, her eyes swollen from crying.

Adam held out his hand to her. After a moment's hesitation, the girl put her hand in his. Her fingers were as thin and dirty as her face. They trembled slightly.

Adam helped her stand and step up on to the pavement again. 'I'll hail a hackney for you,' he said, giving her his handkerchief. 'To take you home.'

'I don't have nowhere to go,' the girl said, beginning to weep again. 'Sir Arnold turned me off.'

'You were in his employ?' Adam felt a flash of rage. This, if anything, showed Gorrie's ill breeding. The man had bedded a servant—and then turned her into the streets to starve.

'Housemaid,' she said, sobbing into the handkerchief.

What should he do with her? For a fleeting instant he wished he could hurry down the street like Sir Arnold, turn the corner and ignore the girl's distress. 'Your family—?'

The girl's face twisted. 'They won't 'ave me back. Not like this.'

His rage increased. How *dare* Gorrie—

Arabella Knightley was suddenly at his side. 'See to your sister,' she said in an undertone. 'She's feeling faint.'

Adam glanced around. Grace was looking very pale. 'But—'

'My maid knows somewhere you can stay,' Miss Knightley said, speaking to the girl. 'We'll take you there now.'

'I 'aven't any money—'

'Don't worry about that,' Miss Knightley said, with a reassuring smile. She laid her hand lightly on the girl's arm. 'Come now, my maid has a hackney waiting.'

'Where will you take her?' Adam asked, annoyed by her calm assumption of authority.

'A boarding house in Camden Town,' Miss Knightley said, not looking at him. 'What's your name, my dear?'

'Eliza,' the girl said, sniffing into the handkerchief. She yielded to the pressure of Miss Knightley's hand and began to walk towards the waiting hackney cab.

'*I* shall take her there,' Adam said, firmly. 'There's no need for you to be involved, Miss Knightley.'

Arabella Knightley turned back to him. 'I'm perfectly capable—'

'I doubt your grandmother would be pleased if you involve yourself in this,' he said, with a glance at the pregnant housemaid. The girl was climbing clumsily into the hackney, helped by Miss Knightley's maid.

'And I'm certain that *you* would rather not be involved either,' she said tartly.

'Better me than you,' Adam said. 'This is not something for a lady to be involved in.'

Miss Knightley's expression became annoyed. She opened her mouth.

'No,' Adam said, in a tone that brooked no argument. 'I must insist, Miss Knightley.'

She closed her mouth and observed him for a moment. 'Very well.' Her voice told him she wasn't pleased.

Adam ignored it. He glanced at his sister. 'May I leave Grace in your care?'

'Of course.'

He walked across to where Grace stood. 'Are you all right?'

'That poor girl!'

'Yes,' Adam said, wishing she hadn't witnessed such an ugly scene. 'Miss Knightley will see you safely home.' He glanced at Arabella Knightley. She stood with her maid, having a hurried, low-voiced conversation. 'Take a hackney.'

'I'd rather walk,' Grace said.

Adam looked at her closely. Her face was still pale. 'Are you certain you're up to it?'

Grace nodded.

Miss Knightley joined them. 'Eliza needs food.' She opened her reticule and took out some bank notes. 'And perhaps she should see a doctor—'

Adam looked down his nose at her, offended she could even *think* he needed her money. 'I'll take care of it.'

'But—'

'I do not need your money, Miss Knightley,' he said stiffly.

Miss Knightley looked as if she'd like to argue. She exchanged a glance with her maid beneath the broad brim of her bonnet, and then nodded. 'If you insist.'

'I do.' He looked at the maid. 'Have you given the jarvey the address of the boarding establishment?'

'Yes, sir.' She looked a competent female, sturdy, with a plain face and a scattering of freckles across her nose.

'Good.' Adam nodded farewell to Miss Knightley and his sister, climbed into the hackney, and pulled the door closed behind him.

He settled back on the seat. Eliza watched him from the opposite corner. Her eyes were wary, her face smeared with tears. His handkerchief was clutched in one hand; with the other she cradled her belly. A livid mark on her thin arm showed where Gorrie had struck her.

Adam flexed his hands and wished he had the pleasure of beating Sir Arnold with his own cane. And then he turned his mind to the problem of what on earth to do with a pregnant, unwed housemaid.

When Arabella entered the Mallorys' ballroom that evening, the first person she looked for was Sir Arnold Gorrie. He was strolling around the perimeter of the room. His appearance was as eyecatching as the Marquis of Revelstoke's—the long-tailed coat in a shade of brown that was almost orange, the large golden buttons, the excess of jewellery adorning his person—but whereas the marquis always managed to look elegant, Sir Arnold was merely vulgar. He didn't have Revelstoke's careless charm, nor his height and elegant figure. Sir Arnold was a short, top-heavy man. His calves in their white stockings were clearly padded and not even a corset could conceal the girth of his waist.

She took note of Sir Arnold's jewellery: the showy rings, the tie pins nestling in the folds of his cravat, the glittering buckles on his shoes. A very *generous* man, Sir Arnold Gorrie, although he didn't yet know it. Very generous indeed.

Arabella escorted her grandmother to the card room, saw her seated at a table with Mrs Davenport, and returned to the ballroom. A *contredanse* was playing. Grace St Just was on the dance floor, in the same set as her friend Letty Wootton. Arabella watched for a moment. The smile on Grace's face, her unselfconscious enjoyment in the dance, were perfect. No one would guess, looking at the girl, that the Season was more an ordeal for her than a delight.

Good girl. She gave a nod of approval.

Arabella walked around the dance floor, exchanging smiles and polite, insincere greetings with the other guests. *Only three more weeks,* she told herself. *And then freedom.*

She chose a seat alongside Grace's aunt, Seraphina Mexted, whose smile of welcome seemed genuine. Grace joined them when the *contredanse* was over. She leaned close. 'Bella,' she whispered, 'guess who's here! Sir Arnold Gorrie.'

Arabella wrinkled her nose. 'I saw.' The colour of the man's tailcoat—neither brown nor orange, but a shade unattractively between the two—made him easy to spot. 'He looks like a cockerel, don't you think?'

'A cockerel?'

'Yes. Strutting around a hen yard with his chest puffed out.'

'Oh…' Grace said, and then, after a moment, 'I see what you mean!'

'And have you noticed the way his hair stands up like a cockscomb?'

Grace bit her lip. 'It's not a good hairstyle for him.'

'His tailor should have talked him out of that coat,' Arabella grimaced. 'A very *cockerel* shade of brown, don't you think?'

Grace uttered a little crow of laughter, and immediately clapped her hand over her mouth. 'Bella!'

Arabella grinned at her, unrepentant.

Grace lowered her hand. The laughter faded from her face. 'What's going to happen to that poor girl?'

Arabella looked across the ballroom at Gorrie. 'Sir Arnold must be persuaded to support her.'

Grace looked doubtful. 'Do you think that's possible?'

'Yes.' *Tom is very persuasive.* She watched as Sir Arnold, in his perambulation of the ballroom, neared the refreshment room. How many of those sparkling jewels would Gorrie donate to Tom?

Adam St Just exited the refreshment room, a glass of champagne held negligently in his hand. The two men came face to face.

Sir Arnold hesitated, and then inclined his head politely.

St Just didn't return the greeting. He stood and looked down his nose at the man, his expression one of utter contempt. Deliberately, disdainfully, he turned his back on the man.

'Oh!' Grace exclaimed, clapping her hands together. 'A direct cut!'

Arabella nodded, reluctantly impressed.

The encounter hadn't gone unnoticed. She saw a stir of interest among those close enough to have witnessed it.

Sir Arnold Gorrie's face was scarlet, a colour that didn't go well with the orange-brown hue of his coat.

'He looks even more like a cockerel now,' Arabella observed, with quiet satisfaction.

Grace gave a choke of laughter. 'Doesn't he just!'

Arabella watched as St Just walked towards them. His behaviour this afternoon had been surprising. She'd expected him to turn tail and flee like Sir Arnold Gorrie. Instead, he'd done the opposite.

She chewed on her lower lip and observed him obliquely as he greeted his aunt.

St Just turned to her. 'Miss Knightley,' he said politely. 'How do you do?'

'Adam!' Grace leaned forwards, her face alight with adoration. 'That was marvellous!'

'Er…what was?'

'A direct cut!'

To Arabella's amusement, his sister's admiration seemed to embarrass St Just. He flushed slightly. 'Oh. You saw that?'

'Yes!' Grace said. 'It was magnificent! Wasn't it, Arabella?'

Thus adjured to, Arabella nodded. 'Worthy of Beau Brummell himself.'

St Just glanced sharply at her, as if he suspected the sincerity of her praise.

'It made him look even more like a cockerel!' Grace said with satisfaction.

St Just's forehead creased slightly. 'A cockerel?'

'Yes, look at him. He's a cockerel.'

St Just swung on his heel and stared across the ballroom. His eyebrows rose. 'So he is.'

'Bella saw it,' Grace said, as smugly as if the observation had been her own.

St Just turned and looked at her. His eyes narrowed slightly. 'A talent of yours, Miss Knightley?'

'Yes,' Grace said. 'She saw that Miss Brook looks like a pug dog.'

Arabella blinked. She'd forgotten that conversation.

'A pug dog?' St Just turned on his heel again and scanned the ballroom. 'Oh, yes, I suppose she does. An unfortunate nose.' His expression, when he looked at her, was tinged with suspicion. 'Who else have you applied this…er, talent to, Miss Knightley?'

Arabella shrugged. 'The comparison isn't always easy to make.' But often it was. Adam St Just was definitely a stag. It was easy to imagine him standing on the crest of a hill, handsome and arrogant, looking down that long nose of his, aware of his superiority over all other creatures. He carried his pride with him the way a stag carried its antlers. It was in the way he held his head. She could almost see them in the air above his carefully tousled hair, branching invisibly upwards, heavy with the weight of his lineage, his breeding, his bloodline.

'But who else?' Grace persisted.

Arabella shrugged again. 'Some people are easy. Your friend Miss Wootton, for example. She reminds me of a robin; her cheeks are so rosy and her eyes so bright.'

'Oh, yes!' cried Grace. 'She does!'

'And the Marquis of Revelstoke is clearly a—'

'Peacock,' St Just said.

Arabella glanced at him, slightly disconcerted by his swiftness and accuracy. 'Yes, a peacock.'

'Who else?' Grace asked.

'Well…' Arabella scanned the ballroom. 'Lady Bicknell. I know it's not very polite, but she reminds me of a—'

'Toad,' St Just said.

Arabella turned her head and stared at him, her mouth still partly open. How had he known? She'd been going to say frog, but even so—'Er, yes,' she said.

Grace clapped her hands together. 'How clever you both are! What am I?'

'A kitten,' Arabella said promptly. 'A fluffy white kitten with big blue eyes.'

Grace blushed in delight. 'And Adam?'

'A stag,' Arabella said, looking up at him. His eyebrows rose slightly. Did he take it as a compliment? It wasn't.

'And Aunt Seraphina?'

Arabella checked that Grace's aunt was in conversation with the lady seated alongside her. She lowered her voice slightly. 'Your aunt reminds me of a beautiful Jersey cow, placid and gentle.'

Adam St Just uttered a crack of laughter. 'So she does!' He hastily straightened his face as his aunt looked around.

Arabella bit her lip and tried not to laugh too—not *at* him, but with him. She looked down at her hands, clasped in her lap, and gently pinched the tip of one gloved finger. It was disturbing to find herself wanting to laugh with St Just.

'And what about you, Bella? What are you?'

She glanced up and shrugged. 'I've never given it any thought.'

Grace pursed her lips. 'I think…a doe.'

A doe? She had an instant image of one—slender and shy, peering from the green fringes of a forest with large, dark eyes. *Is that what I seem like to others?*

'No,' St Just said drily. 'Miss Knightley has claws.'

Arabella looked sharply at him. His expression was utterly impassive, but his eyes—

He was laughing silently. There was no mockery in his grey eyes, but rather friendliness, as if he invited her to share the joke.

She was so taken aback by this observation that she couldn't think of anything to say.

'Adam!' Grace protested. 'That's not very nice.'

St Just shrugged. 'You disagree, Miss Knightley?'

'No,' Arabella said, slightly flustered. 'I think it very accurate.'

'Well, I don't think Bella has claws!'

'That's because she hasn't sharpened them on you,' St Just said, in the same dry voice. He raised his champagne glass to his lips and paused, listening to the orchestra. 'The quadrille's finishing. Excuse me, I'm engaged for the next dance.'

Arabella watched him walk away, more than a little disconcerted. Had they come close to laughing together, she and Adam St Just?

'I'm engaged for this dance, too,' Grace said. 'With Viscount

Mayroyd.' She smoothed her glove up her arm and said with an attempt at nonchalance, 'What do you think of him?'

'He seems a very nice young man.'

'He stutters,' Grace said, studying the seam of her glove.

'Does it bother you?'

Grace looked up. She shook her head firmly. 'No. But…' Her brow creased for a few seconds, as if she sought words. 'I think people have laughed at him because of it.'

'I'm certain they have.' Arabella hesitated, and then said softly, 'Grace, be careful not to confuse pity with a…a warmer emotion.'

'I don't pity him,' Grace said. She looked down at her lap and began pleating folds of cream-coloured satin. 'But I do like him.' She glanced up suddenly. 'What animal does he remind you of?'

'Viscount Mayroyd?' Arabella smiled. 'He reminds me of a puppy. Gangly and friendly and eager to please.' She paused. 'He seems very kind.'

'He is.' Grace's eyes focused on someone to Arabella's right. Viscount Mayroyd, she guessed as the girl blushed shyly.

The young viscount made his bow. His likeable manner and engaging smile only reinforced Arabella's opinion of him: an appealing young pup, awkward and eager and practically wagging his tail in an effort to please Grace.

Arabella watched with amusement as the young pair took their places on the dance floor, but when the music started her thoughts turned to Adam St Just. Her amusement faded. Had she and St Just almost laughed *with* each other?

It didn't seem possible—and yet she thought that was exactly what had happened.

Arabella chewed on her lower lip, slightly disturbed. Whatever animal she resembled, right now, she knew it had ruffled fur.

Chapter Eight

Arabella danced an energetic *contredanse* with the Marquis of Revelstoke, enjoying his banter and his resplendent appearance equally. Afterwards he went off to procure a drink for her—and returned with a glass, and Adam St Just.

'You know each other, don't you?' he said innocently, as he handed Arabella her lemonade.

'Coyness doesn't suit you, Jeremy,' St Just told him.

Revelstoke laid a hand on his breast. His eyes opened wide, blue and guileless. 'Coy? Me?'

St Just snorted.

The marquis looked extremely wounded. Arabella bit her lip to hide a smile, and sipped her lemonade.

'Are you engaged for the next dance, Adam?' the marquis asked.

St Just hesitated for a second, and then shook his head.

Revelstoke turned to her. His eyes were very blue, and very limpid. He radiated innocence. 'And you, Miss Knightley?'

'No,' Arabella said, torn between wanting to laugh at the marquis and irritation.

'Then you must dance with each other!' Revelstoke exclaimed. 'What could be more perfect?'

'Jeremy…' St Just's voice held a note of warning.

The marquis pretended not to hear it. 'Oh!' he said brightly. 'The musicians are about to start. Give me your drinks.'

Arabella bit her lip again and handed back the glass of lemonade. She avoided looking at St Just; she thought his expression might make her laugh.

St Just held out his arm to her. 'Miss Knightley?'

Arabella laid her hand on his sleeve. She glanced back as St Just led her on to the dance floor. Revelstoke's expression was smug.

The smugness made no sense. She puzzled over it for a moment, and then asked St Just, 'Why did Revelstoke want us to dance together?'

'Because he has a bet in the book at White's that we shall marry,' St Just said, exasperation clearly audible in his voice.

'A bet!' Her gaze flew to his face.

'Yes.' St Just met her eyes. To her amusement he flushed slightly.

The amusement evaporated abruptly as the musicians began to play the opening notes to a waltz. She almost balked—a hesitation St Just noticed. He glanced at her. 'Miss Knightley?'

Arabella bit her lip again—with chagrin this time, not amusement. A waltz! With Adam St Just. The very thing she'd been hoping to avoid.

'Miss Knightley?' he asked again. 'Is something wrong?'

'Nothing,' she said quickly. 'It's nothing.' What could she talk about while they danced? Hastily she cast about for a subject.

'Don't be offended by Jeremy,' St Just said, as his arm came around her. 'His sense of humour sometimes gets the better of him.'

'Yes,' Arabella said, distracted. He was holding her, one hand at her waist, the other clasping her right hand. It felt far too intimate, far too dangerous.

'Are you interested in hearing about the welfare of Gorrie's house-maid?' St Just asked. 'I understand, of course, if you don't wish to discuss so indelicate a subject…'

Her thoughts steadied. 'Eliza? Oh, yes. I wanted to talk with you about her.' She found herself able to look up and meet his eyes. 'My maid tells me you paid the landlady for a week's lodging.'

'Your maid?' His eyebrows rose. 'How does she know?'

'I sent her to the boarding house to make sure that Eliza was all right.'

She felt him stiffen. 'You thought I might have turned her out of the hackney and abandoned her?'

'No,' Arabella said. 'But I wasn't certain you'd think of everything she required.'

St Just looked at her for several seconds without speaking. Clearly he was unused to being doubted. 'And what did your maid report?' he said finally. 'Was there something I overlooked?'

'No.' Not only had St Just paid for Eliza's bed and board, he'd sent for a doctor to examine her and had—through a mixture of polite bullying and bribery—persuaded the landlady to provide Eliza with a steaming bath and fresh clothes to change into.

'I'm glad my actions met with your approval,' St Just said, his tone somewhat dry.

His actions *had* met with her approval—and that was astonishing. As astonishing as their moment of shared amusement earlier this evening. After six years of hating Adam St Just, she now found herself almost in charity with him. It made her feel slightly off balance, as if the world had shifted slightly on its axis. She didn't *want* to like him.

With that thought came an uncomfortable awareness of his proximity. The way he held her was almost an embrace. Heat shivered through her— and with the heat, fear. She wanted to turn and run, to flee this almost-embrace, this frightening awareness of him.

'Why were you so kind to Eliza?' she blurted.

St Just blinked. 'Kind?' It was clear from his voice that he hadn't seen himself in that light.

His reaction steadied her. *Not* a philanthropist, then. 'If it wasn't kindness, why did you help her?'

His expression became grim. 'A man of honour doesn't behave as Gorrie did.'

Arabella's lip curled slightly. Did he think she was that naïve? 'It's a fairly common practice among gentlemen to take advantage of their female servants.'

'Perhaps,' St Just said stiffly. 'But a man of honour takes respon-sibility for his…er, his—'

'For his by-blows,' Arabella said. Here was the perfect opportunity to needle him, to take her attention from the disturbing intimacy of his hand at her waist. She widened her eyes, as the Marquis of Revelstoke had done. 'Do you have any by-blows yourself, Mr St Just?'

Adam St Just eyed her with dislike. After a moment he said, with extreme politeness, 'Shall we change the subject, Miss Knightley?'

'By all means,' Arabella said. She cast about for another way to annoy him. 'Are you a gambling man, Mr St Just?'

Surprise crossed his face, followed by wariness, as if he suspected her intentions. 'I like to roll the dice,' he said.

'And do you win often?'

St Just shrugged, still eyeing her warily. 'Often enough.'

'And when you don't win, you lose,' Arabella said cordially.

'That's what tends to happen,' he said in a dry voice.

'How much would you lose in a night?' she asked. 'Five hundred guineas? A thousand?'

St Just looked down his nose at her. 'How much I win or lose is no one's business but my own, Miss Knightley.'

'No, it's not, is it?' she agreed. 'But money is such an interesting subject! Do you know, Mr St Just, that for the price of a pair of boots from Hoby, a poor family could eat for a year?'

'And for the price of that gown you're wearing, *two* families could eat for a year,' St Just retorted.

'Yes,' said Arabella affably, as he swung her into a turn that was too abrupt to be graceful. 'Silk is an expensive fabric.' She smiled at him, a challenge in her voice. 'I know precisely how much my clothing costs, Mr St Just, and I give an identical sum to charity. Can you say the same?'

Judging from his glare, he couldn't. 'What I choose to do with my own money is no one's concern but mine,' he said haughtily.

'Of course it isn't,' Arabella agreed. 'But do tell me, Mr St Just, how did you earn your money?'

'Earn it?' He looked as outraged as if she'd accused him of treason.

'Oh,' Arabella said in a tone of enlightenment, widening her eyes at him again. 'You did nothing to *earn* your wealth, you were *born* to it.'

St Just said nothing, he merely looked down his nose at her, his mouth tight with dislike. His grip on her hand was equally tight, pinching her fingers.

'Tell me, Mr St Just, do you believe that you're *better* than a man who earns his own money, or merely *luckier?*'

He made no reply. Arabella answered for him. 'Better, of course. Your blood should always mark you as a gentleman, even if you'd been switched at birth with a street-sweeper's son—'

His fingers flexed on her hand, tightening until the grip was almost painful. Arabella ignored it, warming to her topic. 'Suppose you'd grown up without the benefit of an education or the tender nurture of a wealthy family? Suppose you were half-starved and illiterate and dressed in rags and sweeping a street crossing?' She raised her eyebrows at him, enjoying herself. His attention was grimly fixed on her face. 'Despite all these disadvantages, something in your bearing, in your nobility of character, should *instantly* mark you as superior to those around you. It would be obvious to all who saw you that you were a gentleman. Whereas a street-sweeper's son, growing up in your place, receiving all the advantages of wealth and education, should always be vulgar.'

She smiled at him. 'Don't you agree, Mr St Just?'

He made no answer. His jaw was clenched.

Arabella raised her eyebrows at him. 'Oh, you disagree?' she said, enjoying herself hugely. 'You think that having grown up as a street sweeper's son you would be nothing more than a street-sweeper yourself, a vulgar creature with no thought beyond where your next ha'penny is coming from? How delightful! We're of the same opinion!'

'There's no need to be offensive, Miss Knightley,' St Just said stiffly.

'Offensive?' She tried to look as wounded as Revelstoke had. 'I thought I was making a point. Look around you, Mr St Just. This ballroom is full of people—like yourself—who've done nothing to earn their wealth. Are they better than the street sweepers and coal haulers of this world, or merely luckier?'

She waited for his reply as they made a final circuit of the ballroom. St Just's grip on her hand was iron-hard, as was the set of his jaw. He was clearly deeply insulted. That moment of shared amusement was lost.

Arabella felt a pang of regret. She pushed it ruthlessly aside. It was better this way—the jerky steps, the painful grip of his hand. There was nothing in this waltz to disturb her, no dangerous *frisson* of awareness. She was conscious of his dislike of her, not his maleness.

The waltz ground to its halt. St Just released her hand. His bow was stiff.

Arabella flexed her fingers surreptitiously. They ached from his hard grip. 'Thank you,' she said, with a bright smile. 'That was delightful.'

St Just made no reply. It seemed impossible that she'd seen friendliness in his eyes only a short time ago; they were cold, totally devoid of warmth. He held his arm stiffly out to her. It was clear he wasn't going to answer the question she'd posed him. He bristled with silent outrage as he escorted her from the dance floor.

'Good evening, Miss Knightley.' St Just bowed again, a wooden movement.

The urge to tease him further was overwhelming. 'My grandmother and I are going to supper soon,' she said. 'Would you care to join us?'

She watched as the muscles in his jaw clenched. 'Thank you,' he said after a brief moment, 'but no. I must take my leave of our hostess.'

'Oh? You're leaving?' It didn't surprise her; his anger was palpable.

'I'm going to my club,' he said, a hint of challenge in his voice.

'Do enjoy your evening, Mr St Just,' Arabella said warmly. 'I hope your losses aren't too heavy.'

She had the impression that St Just almost snarled at her. He turned on his heel and strode away as if he wanted to put as much distance between them as possible.

Her amusement lasted a few minutes, then contrition set in. It had been extremely rude of her to bait him like that, and—if she was honest with herself—it had also been completely unfair.

If she'd had the upbringing her parents had intended, she would be just like everyone else in this ballroom: she'd believe herself superior by virtue of her birth—and she'd be as insulted as St Just had been if anyone suggested otherwise.

Her conduct had been vulgar and wholly unjustified. It wasn't St Just's fault that waltzing with him made her feel so uncomfortable.

Arabella pulled a face. *I owe him an apology.*

A light drizzle was falling, but Adam barely noticed. He ignored the offer of a hackney and strode down Clarges Street. Fury vibrated inside him. How *dared* Arabella Knightley imply that he—a St Just—was no better than a street sweeper!

The walk did nothing to improve his temper. The doorman at White's took one look at his face and confined his welcome to a mere, 'Good evening, sir.'

Adam strode into the card room. 'Brandy,' he said curtly, stripping off his gloves. 'A bottle.'

The hour was early and only a few tables were occupied. Lord Alvanley and a number of gentlemen were seated at a green baize faro table lit by a branching candelabrum. 'St Just!' Alvanley called out, waving his hand expansively. 'Join us.'

Adam drew up a chair and grunted in response to the greetings. Alvanley was holding the bank; a pile of gold coins, bank notes, and vowels lay scattered before him. 'The stakes?'

It wasn't until his third glass of brandy that Adam began to relax. To his annoyance, his luck was in. He imagined the satisfaction it would have given him to tell Miss Knightley tomorrow that he'd lost several thousand pounds at faro.

Revelstoke joined the table an hour later. 'You left the ball early,' he said as he pulled up a chair.

Adam grunted.

'How was your waltz with the delectable Miss Knightley?'

Adam glanced at him. 'If you value our friendship,' he said flatly, 'you won't *ever* do that to me again.'

Jeremy blinked. For once he didn't offer a joke in reply. 'Sorry. Didn't mean to upset you.'

Adam grunted again.

As if the marquis's arrival had signalled a change, his luck turned. He began to lose steadily.

Alvanley tallied up the losses at two o'clock. 'Three hundred guineas,' he said, glancing at him.

Adam could almost hear Miss Knightley's voice in his ear, *I wonder how many families you could feed with that money, Mr St Just?*

He gritted his teeth, poured himself another glass of brandy, and settled more deeply into his chair, determined to enjoy himself. But he found that he couldn't. Each turn of the cards represented money. Families' worth of money.

At three o'clock, with another hundred guineas lost, he pushed back his chair in disgust. 'That's me for the night.'

His announcement was greeted by startled expressions. 'So soon?' Alvanley said.

'Are you all right?' Jeremy asked quietly.

'Fine,' Adam said, pulling on his gloves. *That damned girl has merely ruined any pleasure I might have in playing faro.*

The drizzle had become a light rain. 'Shall I order a hackney, sir?' the doorman asked.

'No.' The walk, the rain, would clear his head.

Adam scowled as he strode down St James's Street. It was his own money, damn it. Why shouldn't he throw it away on the turn of a card?

'Light your way, guv'nor?' a shrill voice cried behind him. He heard the soft patter of feet and turned his head. A link boy.

Adam opened his mouth to refuse, but a glance at the boy's face— thin, eager—made him bite back the words. 'I'm going to Berkeley Square,' he said instead.

He walked along St James's Street with the link boy trotting ahead, the torch casting a flickering light. The boy's feet were bare and filthy, his clothing ragged. Damp hair clung to his skull.

The devil take Arabella Knightley! If it wasn't for her he'd still be at White's, deep in a game of faro. Instead he was looking at a link boy's bare feet and feeling guilty.

'What's your name, boy?' he asked curtly.

The link boy glanced back at him, his eyes large in a too-thin face. 'Sir?'

'Your name?'

'Ned.'

Adam walked another street in silence, then he asked, 'How old are you, Ned?'

The boy shrugged. 'I dunno, guv'nor.'

About nine years old, Adam guessed. Perhaps ten. The same age as his cousin the Duke of Frew's son, Gervase. For a moment he saw Gervase in his mind's eye: sturdy and fair-haired.

Gervase was touring the Continent with his parents; Ned was running barefoot through wet London streets. *Better, or merely luckier?* Arabella Knightley's voice asked him.

He knew what answer his father would have given, what answer the Duke of Frew would give, if asked: *Better.*

Ned was an unprepossessing child, skinny and grubby, his accent straight from the slums—but would Gervase be any better under the same circumstances? Duke's son or not, without regular meals and clean clothes, Gervase would be just as thin, just as dirty, and his language would be as coarse as Ned's.

It was past three o'clock in the morning. It was raining. The boy's torch was in danger of guttering. He should be tucked up in bed, warm and dry, not trying to earn a farthing or two.

They turned into Berkeley Square. 'Which 'ouse, guv'nor?'

'The one on the corner,' Adam said. He'd lost four hundred guineas at faro. What would that money have meant to Ned? Food, a warm bed, dry clothes. Not for one day or one week, or even a month—but for years.

Ned took him to the foot of the steps. A lamp hung beside the door. Rain fell steadily into the bright circle of light.

The boy waited, shivering, while Adam felt in his pocket. It was almost empty. He found a couple of ha'pennies, a farthing and a guinea. 'Go home, Ned,' he said gruffly, holding out the guinea.

Ned's face lit with awe. 'A yellow boy? Thank you, guv'nor!'

'Buy yourself some food—' Adam started to say, but the boy was already running back in the direction of St James's Street. 'And some shoes,' he said quietly, only to himself. *And some warm clothes.*

He watched until Ned had disappeared from sight, then walked up the steps and let himself into the house with his latch key.

For a moment he stood in the entrance hall. There was a sour taste in his mouth that had nothing to do with the brandy he'd drunk. The hush of the sleeping house settled over him, the scent of beeswax polish and flowers. Giltwood gleamed in the light of the lamp left out for him.

He knew the answer to Arabella Knightley's question: *Not better, merely luckier.*

The day dawned grey. Adam, feeling equally grey, decided to visit Jackson's Saloon. A bout with the Champion usually improved his mood; today it didn't. Thought of the four hundred guineas he'd lost at play— and the one he'd given Ned—kept intruding. He wanted to *hit* something, and yet it was frustratingly hard to land a blow.

Gentleman Jack threw him a cross-buttock. Adam hit the floor so hard it jarred his teeth. For a moment he lay where he'd fallen, winded.

'Your mind's not on it today, sir, if I may be so bold as to say so.'

'No, it's not,' Adam said, when he'd caught his breath. He pushed up on to one elbow. 'Maybe I'll try a round with the staves.'

'Might be better, sir.'

Adam accepted Gentleman Jack's hand and climbed to his feet.

He was right: single-stick fighting suited his mood better. The clash of wood, the bone-rattling blows, were a more effective outlet for his frustration. By the end of the bout he was panting and sweating—but his frame of mind was much improved.

He strolled around to White's. 'Afternoon, guv'nor,' a street sweeper cried, hurrying out into the road to clear horse manure from the crossing.

Adam had walked past the street sweeper a hundred times; this was the first time he actually *seen* him: the spikes of sandy hair, the gap-toothed grin, the blue eyes. The boy was older than Ned by a number of years, but his clothes were just as ragged, his feet just as bare and filthy, his face just as thin.

Arabella Knightley's words of last night came forcibly to mind.

Adam dug in his pocket. 'What's your name?'

The boy gaped at him in surprise. 'Sir?'

'Your name,' Adam repeated. He sorted through his coins and selected a guinea.

The boy swallowed audibly. 'Billy Crabtree,' he said, his eyes fixed on the guinea.

Adam held it out to him. 'Buy yourself some shoes,' he said.

Billy Crabtree snatched the guinea. 'Yes, sir,' he said. 'Thank you, sir!' He tugged his forelock and scurried back across the street.

Adam stood for a moment on the pavement. He'd given away two guineas. That left three hundred and ninety eight to go.

Alvanley and Revelstoke were at the table in the bow window, sharing the day's newspapers and a bottle of claret. Both men looked up as Adam lowered himself into a chair. 'Where've you been?' Alvanley asked, with a wide yawn.

'Gentleman Jack's,' Adam said, tenderly feeling his ribs.

Jeremy folded his newspaper and put it aside. 'Throw you, did he?'

Adam nodded.

'Claret?'

'Please,' he said, stretching out his legs. He was feeling almost cheerful. It wasn't the bout of single stick or the glass of wine Jeremy was holding out to him; it was the guinea he'd given Billy Crabtree.

No, it wasn't that. It was the decision he'd made. *Three hundred and ninety eight guineas to go.*

Adam sipped the claret. 'What's new?'

'We hear you gave Gorrie a direct cut last night,' Jeremy said, leaning forwards in his chair. 'Why?'

Adam paused, the wine glass halfway to his mouth. 'Er…what?'

'What did Gorrie do? We're agog with curiosity.'

That was an exaggeration; Alvanley looked half-asleep. Only Jeremy was agog, his eyes bright with interest.

Adam sipped the claret meditatively. If he told Jeremy, within a day the whole *ton* would know. And if the *ton* knew, then Tom would hear of it—and perhaps pay Sir Arnold Gorrie a visit.

Which is precisely what the man deserves.

'Very well,' Adam said, straightening in his chair. 'What happened was this.'

Chapter Nine

Sir Arnold Gorrie had a house in Russell Square in Bloomsbury, an address on the fringe of what was respectable. It was decorated with the same garish ostentation that characterised his appearance. Arabella tiptoed along the first-floor corridor. Crimson and gold predominated, and every nook and cranny bristled with statuary. He was clearly aping the Prince Regent.

Sir Arnold's bedchamber was the second door she tried. It was illuminated only by a fire dying in the grate. A four-poster bed dominated the room, looming huge in the shadows.

Quietly, quickly, she locked the door and unlatched a window in case she needed to leave hastily. Only then did she take a candle from the bedside table and light it from the fire.

The four-poster bed was even more monstrous in candlelight than it was in darkness. The crimson canopy was heavy with golden tassels. Arabella bit her lip. *How truly vulgar.*

Gorrie's jewellery wasn't obvious in the bedchamber, but the shelves in the dressing room held a number of lacquered boxes of promising size.

The first box Arabella opened contained buckles in a variety of shapes and sizes, all set with diamonds. The second box contained tiepins, the third held fobs. That, she shut and put back in its place on the shelf.

Arabella looked at the two open boxes. Tiepins, or buckles?

The tiepins were as vulgar as everything else she'd seen in this house. She examined them closely. The stones were large and gaudy. Sapphires and emeralds, rubies, diamonds, garnets and amethysts. And one elegant tiepin set with a single perfect pearl.

It was the pearl that decided her.

Swiftly she scooped up the other tiepins. They made a large handful, almost too many to hold. The pouch tied around her waist could barely take them all.

Arabella looked with satisfaction at the lone tiepin, lying on its bed of red satin. The pearl gleamed softly. The tiepin was the one elegant thing she'd seen in Sir Arnold's house. Let him be forced to wear it.

She closed the box of buckles and replaced it on the shelf.

She'd drawn a number of cards for Gorrie, but brought only one. Carefully she propped it alongside the pearl tiepin. She looked at it for a moment, satisfied—red satin, the creamy square of card, the stark black words: *Should payment be made for dishonourable behaviour? Tom thinks so.*

There was so much she wanted to say to Sir Arnold. She'd written half a dozen messages, but in the end this was the one she'd brought with her. Like the tiepin, it was simple. She'd expressed her contempt of Sir Arnold, not in words, but in the drawing at the bottom of the message. The black cat had caught a cockerel. It lay at the cat's feet, belly up, its plumage bedraggled—and unmistakeably Gorrie.

Back in the bedchamber, she stared at the four-poster bed with distaste. Sir Arnold hadn't seduced Eliza, nor had he resorted to physical force. He'd used words, veiled threats of dismissal, to woo her into his bed. And Eliza, young and newly come from the country, without family or friends in London, had taken the only course she'd thought open to her.

Arabella thinned her lips. The tiepins weren't enough. She turned on her heel, heading back for the dressing room and the diamond-encrusted buckles, when the bedside cabinet caught her eye.

It was vulgar, like everything else she'd seen in the house. Mahogany, in the form of a fluted column, with gilded Ionic scrolling.

Arabella changed direction. She crossed to the bedside cabinet and lifted the hinged top. She saw a handkerchief, some smelling salts, a bottle of laudanum, two sovereigns, a tin of lozenges, and—

For a moment she stood frozen, then she reached out and touched a cautious finger to the roll of banknotes nestling in the corner.

The first bank note was for one pound. The second was for—

Carefully she counted the banknotes on to the crimson and gold bed-spread. Three hundred and twenty-seven pounds.

Arabella blew out a breath. She glanced at the locked door to the bedroom. Her heart began to beat faster.

The smaller banknotes—the twos and ones—went back into the cabinet. The larger ones went into her pouch, crammed in beside the jewelled tiepins. Three hundred and twenty pounds' worth of bank notes. Enough money to give Eliza and her child a future.

Arabella glanced around for paper and ink. She had to leave a note from Tom, or else a servant could be blamed for this theft.

In a drawer in Sir Arnold's dresser she found some bills from his tailor. In another drawer was a clutter of cosmetics: rouge, powder, eyebrow pencils.

The note was much rougher than any she'd left before, but Arabella felt it made its point nicely. *An honourable man provides for his children,* she wrote in brown eyebrow pencil on the back of a bill for waistcoats. Underneath the words she sketched a cat lying stretched out on its side, watching a kitten play with a ball of string.

She left the message inside the gilded mahogany plinth, curled into the diminished roll of bank notes.

Arabella rode in Hyde Park the following morning. Her spirits were high, despite the greyness of the sky. Merrylegs caught her mood. The mare's canter stretched into a gallop. For a moment Arabella let her have her head, then she reined Merrylegs back. Much as she'd love to gallop, Hyde Park wasn't the place for it.

It was always like this, after a night as Tom: the exultation, the silent laughter bubbling inside her. The exultation would drain away, but until it did she'd hug it to herself—and hold Merrylegs back from a high-spirited gallop.

On her third circuit Arabella saw a familiar horse and rider. Her good mood faltered slightly. She slowed Merrylegs to a trot.

The dappled grey gelding was a magnificent beast, powerful and well muscled, with an easy gait and a proud way of looking down its nose. *Rather like its owner.*

Arabella grimaced. 'Well,' she said to Merrylegs, 'I may as well get this over with.'

She urged the mare into a canter again and came up alongside the rider on the grey gelding. 'Mr St Just.'

Adam St Just glanced at her. His face seemed to tighten. He hesitated for a fraction of a second, and then inclined his head politely.

'May I have a word?'

The grey gelding slowed to a trot, and a walk. 'Yes, Miss Knightley?' Neither St Just's expression nor his voice was encouraging.

'I wish to apologise for sharpening my claws on you at the Mallorys' ball. It was extremely rude of me.'

St Just blinked. Something approaching surprise showed on his face. 'Consider it forgotten, Miss Knightley. I more than deserve any…er, sharpening of claws.'

Arabella lifted her eyebrows, not understanding.

'For my words six years ago.'

Words for which he'd apologised.

'I hope I'm not that ungracious!' she said, insulted.

St Just opened his mouth, and then closed it again. She saw a glimmer of curiosity in his grey eyes. He wanted to know why she'd behaved as she had—but was too polite to ask.

Arabella focused her attention on Merrylegs's ears. She couldn't tell St Just the truth: that the intimacy of waltzing with him made her deeply uncomfortable, that the sensations it engendered were frightening. 'The waltz brings out the worst in me,' she said.

'Oh.' St Just's voice told her nothing, but his expression—when she glanced at him—was faintly perplexed.

Arabella smiled brightly to forestall any questions. 'Good day, Mr St Just.'

He hesitated slightly, then inclined his head. 'Good day, Miss Knightley.'

That afternoon Adam walked around to Bond Street, but instead of entering Jackson's Boxing Saloon, he turned into the neighbouring establishment: Angelo's Fencing Academy.

Jeremy strolled in several minutes after him. 'Ready to lose?' he asked cheerfully.

'I have no intention of losing,' Adam said, peeling out of his coat.

Jeremy grinned, showing his teeth. 'Neither have I.'

Adam removed his boots. He cast a glance at Jeremy's clothing. 'You make a nice target in that waistcoat.'

Jeremy smoothed a hand over the crimson satin. 'Beautiful, ain't it?'

Adam snorted.

He tested the foils while Jeremy removed his coat and boots. Henry Angelo, grandson of the original Angelo, was their referee. 'Ready, gentlemen?' he called. 'On guard!'

The weight of the foil in his hand, the slide of his stockinged feet across the floorboards, Jeremy's grin as they fought, were familiar; they'd fenced together since they were boys. Adam paid no attention to the spectators gathering around the edges of the high-ceilinged chamber. If he was to win, he needed all his concentration. For all his foppishness, Jeremy possessed a wiry strength and lightning-quick reflexes.

The chamber echoed with the soft pad of their feet, the clash of blades, their panting breaths. Parry and riposte and—

'Damn!' Adam said.

Jeremy merely grinned more broadly.

'First point to Revelstoke,' Henry Angelo said. 'On guard!'

They started slowly, circling, parrying and riposting, testing each other. Adam knew Jeremy's style, his strengths and weaknesses, as well as Jeremy knew his. Sometimes it was an advantage, sometimes a drawback.

He won the next two points, and Jeremy the one after that.

'Last point,' Jeremy said, flexing his foil. 'Want to bet on it?'

Adam wiped sweat from his face. He thought of the three hundred and ninety-eight guineas he had yet to give away. 'No.'

Jeremy's eyebrows rose in exaggerated surprise. 'Afraid you'll lose?'

Adam ignored the teasing. He brought the point of his foil up.

'Have you heard about Gorrie?' Jeremy asked, moving into position again.

Adam shook his head.

'Tom paid him a visit last night.'

'What?' Adam half-lowered his foil. How in the blazes had Tom found out about Gorrie so quickly?

'On guard!' Henry Angelo called.

Adam brought the foil up again. He tried to focus his attention on the match, but his concentration was broken. Jeremy took the fifth point swiftly with a *redoublement*. 'Tut-tut,' he said, grinning broadly. 'Someone wasn't paying attention.'

Adam grunted.

'Well done, gentlemen,' Henry Angelo said.

Together they walked off the floor. 'Tell me about Gorrie,' Adam said, as they shrugged into their coats.

'I thought that might catch your attention,' Jeremy said, straightening his cuffs.

Adam glanced at him swiftly.

Jeremy met his look with an innocence that could only be suspicious.

Adam narrowed his eyes. 'You were trying to distract me.'

Jeremy looked deeply wounded. 'Me?' he said. 'Would I do such a thing?'

Adam snorted. He pulled on one of his boots.

Jeremy shrugged. 'It worked, didn't it?' he said with a grin.

'You are an unprincipled rogue!'

'No,' Jeremy said. 'That would be Gorrie. And our dear Tom has punished him for it.'

Adam picked up his second boot. 'Do you know what was taken?'

'Quite a haul, or so I understand. Jewellery, and several hundred pounds in bank notes.'

'Bank notes?' Adam said, astonished. 'He's never done that before, has he?'

Jeremy shrugged. 'Who knows?'

Adam paused, his second boot held in one hand. 'Did you tell anyone about Gorrie yesterday?'

'Lord, yes!' Jeremy said cheerfully. 'Dozens of people.'

'When?'

Jeremy shrugged again. 'At the opera. At White's afterward.'

Adam frowned at the boot he was holding. If Tom had found out about Gorrie yesterday evening...would he have burgled the man that very night?

Somehow he doubted it.

He pulled on his boot slowly.

* * *

Arabella took the carriage to Kensington Gardens that afternoon—and then a hackney to Rosemary Lane. She glanced at the sky as she and Polly hurried through the filthy streets of Whitechapel. The clouds were low and dark.

In the little house on Berner Street, she handed her haul over to Harry and Tess: the money for Eliza, and Sir Arnold's contribution to the school for girls.

The four of them discussed Eliza. 'I want her out of London as soon as possible,' Arabella said. 'In case Gorrie decides to look for his money.'

'It's a lot o' blunt,' Harry said, grinning as he fanned the bills out. 'I'm sure 'e'd like it back.'

Arabella watched as he tapped the bills against his palm and laid them neatly on the scarred wooden table. 'I'd send Polly, but someone's looking for Tom. I don't want any connection between Eliza's disappearance and me.'

Harry looked up sharply. 'What d'you mean, lookin' for Tom?'

Arabella shrugged. 'Someone wants to find out who Tom is. He's been asking questions.'

'Does he suspect you?' Tess asked.

Arabella laughed. 'No. He's looking for a man. But…' her amusement faded '…he's worked out Tom's a member of the *ton*.'

'Should we be worried?' Harry asked, turning a tiepin over in his fingers. The emerald glinted dully in the unlit room.

'No.' Arabella shook her head. 'But we need to be careful. Which is another reason why I'd like Eliza out of London as soon as possible.'

'I'll get 'er tomorrow mornin',' Harry said. 'Take 'er out to Swanley, settle 'er in at the school.'

'I'll come too,' Tess said, with a glance at her husband. 'It'll be less frightening for her.' Her hand rested briefly on her own rounded belly.

'Thank you.' Arabella cast a glance at the window and stood. 'We'd better leave. It's going to rain soon.'

Instead of accompanying Jeremy to White's, Adam went home. He found his sister in the blue parlour, going through the latest issue of *La*

Belle Assemblée with Letty Wootton. The girls' heads were bent close together, fair and dark. '…puffings of reverse satin,' he heard Grace say.

Adam backed quietly out of the room. He went to his study, poured himself a glass of brandy, and sat at his desk, a clean sheet of paper in front of him. He dipped his quill in ink and began to write.

Grace
Miss Knightley
Miss Knightley's maid
Myself

The four of them had witnessed the incident outside Hatchard's on Tuesday afternoon. On Wednesday afternoon, he'd told Jeremy and Alvanley about it. That evening, Tom had paid Sir Arnold Gorrie a visit.

Adam rolled the quill between his fingers. He didn't think Tom had heard about Gorrie from either Jeremy or Alvanley. The timing was too tight.

Somehow Tom had found out from one of the other witnesses.

Which one?

Adam was aware of excitement building inside him. He was getting close.

He swallowed a large mouthful of brandy, then pulled another sheet of paper towards him. He began to list the men he'd seen at Almack's last night. Each name was someone Tom couldn't be.

An hour later, Adam went back to the parlour. Letty Wootton was gone. Grace was curled up on the sofa, absorbed in *La Belle Assemblée*.

'Grace?'

She looked up and smiled.

'I'd like to ask you something.'

Grace closed the magazine, marking her place with one finger. Her expression was expectant.

Adam walked across to the sofa and sat down alongside her. 'Did you tell anyone about what happened on Piccadilly Street? With Sir Arnold Gorrie?'

'That poor girl.' Grace's smile faded. 'No, I didn't.'

'No one at all?'

Grace shook her head. 'Only Aunt Seraphina.'

'Aunt Seraphina?' Adam nodded and stood. 'Thank you.'

Aunt Seraphina was in the morning room, dozing on the *chaise longue* with a cashmere shawl draped over her.

'Oh!' she said, groping for her lace cap, which had slipped over one ear. 'Adam, you startled me.'

'I apologise.' He waited while she composed herself and then asked his question, 'I understand Grace told you what happened with Sir Arnold Gorrie and the young housemaid.'

'Such a dreadful thing for her to have witnessed! What was the man thinking of, behaving like that on a public street?' Aunt Seraphina felt around her, turning back the cashmere shawl. 'Have you seen a book of poems?'

It lay on the floor beneath the *chaise longue.* Adam bent and picked it up. 'Did you tell anyone, Aunt?'

'About what?'

'About Sir Arnold and the housemaid,' he said patiently. One of the pages was creased. He smoothed it and closed the book. Byron's *The Corsair,* he saw, glancing at the spine.

Aunt Seraphina looked affronted. 'Of course not! Such appalling behaviour! And the girl was pregnant. It's not the sort of thing one talks about with one's friends!'

'I beg your pardon,' he said meekly, handing her the book.

Adam went back to his study and poured himself another glass of brandy. He stood at the window, warming the glass in his hand. Outside, it was beginning to rain. Fat drops struck the windowpanes.

He sipped the brandy meditatively, listening to the rain hitting the glass, watching the pavement darken with water. If Tom had heard about Gorrie on Tuesday, it hadn't been from Grace or himself. Which left Arabella Knightley and her maid.

If he was right about the timing. Perhaps he was wrong. Perhaps Tom had acted on the spur of the moment?

If Miss Knightley was at the Foxes' ball tonight, he'd ask her. But not during a waltz.

Adam shook his head and took another sip of brandy. The taste lingered on his tongue, smoky. Outside, the rain began to fall more heavily.

Miss Knightley's apology this morning had been as bizarre as it was unexpected. Sharpening her claws on him? Because the waltz brought out the worst in her?

What a very *odd* young lady she was.

Adam raised the glass and sipped again. He held the brandy in his mouth for a moment, savouring the flavour.

Presumably she'd been sharpening her claws when she'd extolled Miss Wootton's fortune. And when she'd encouraged him to have a stream flowing down the centre of the table at his wedding breakfast.

Adam chuckled in memory of her artless, enthusiastic vulgarity—and almost choked on the brandy in his mouth. He swallowed, coughing.

Yes, sharpening her claws was an accurate description of what Miss Knightley had done.

'Minx,' he said, under his breath. He turned away from the window. A very strange young woman, Miss Arabella Knightley. An enigma. As irritating as she was beautiful.

For a moment he saw her in his mind's eye: the elegant bones of her face, the dark, expressive eyes, the soft mouth.

Desire clenched in his belly.

Adam took hurried gulp of brandy. He strode across to his desk, opened the drawer that held his business correspondence, and pushed Miss Knightley firmly from his mind. But she crept back into his thoughts as he read the latest letter from his steward. The blackness of the ink reminded him of her eyes, the paper brought the pale creaminess of her complexion to mind, and the looping tails of each *f* and *g* and *y* made him think of dark ringlets nestling against smooth skin.

Adam squeezed his eyes shut. *Get out of my head,* he told Arabella Knightley.

It was raining heavily by the time they reached her grandmother's house in Belgravia. Arabella climbed the marble staircase with Polly one step behind, playing the role of servant. She was conscious of a sense of relief. By this time tomorrow, Eliza would be safe at the school in

Swanley—and neither Sir Arnold Gorrie nor Adam St Just would be able to find her.

She pulled off her gloves. The kid leather was slightly damp.

'Arabella.'

She turned. 'Yes, Grandmother?'

Lady Westcote stood in the doorway of her parlour. A lace cap covered her white hair. She wore a lilac gown with vertical pleating on the bodice. The late earl's painted eye stared out from the brooch on her bosom.

'I see you got wet,' her grandmother said, faint disapproval in her voice.

'Yes,' Arabella said, conscious of the distance between them, the pretending they both did. *She wants me in her house as little as I want to be here.*

'I thought you'd like to know…your friend Helen Dysart—her husband has died.'

'What?' Arabella exclaimed. 'George Dysart? When?'

'Last night, if the gossips are to be believed.'

'Oh, poor Helen!' Arabella turned and began to head downstairs again. Her grandmother's voice stopped her. 'Where are you going?'

'To see Helen,' Arabella said, looking back at her.

'It's nearly five o'clock.'

'She's my friend, Grandmother.' *The only friend I have in the* ton, *other than Grace St Just.* 'I'll be back in time for dinner.'

Lady Westcote's mouth pinched slightly. 'Very well.' She stepped back into her parlour and closed the door.

Arabella hurried down the stairs, pulling on her gloves. 'Call back the carriage, Clough. I need to go out again.'

A wreath hung on the door at Number 34, Curzon Street. The black ribbons were dripping.

Arabella watched as the footman jumped down from the carriage. Water splashed from beneath his feet. *Poor man,* she thought, as he plied the door knocker. He looked as wet and bedraggled as the wreath.

The door of Number 34 opened. She saw the footman say something and Helen's butler reply. Rain drummed on the roof of the carriage, drowning their words.

The footman splashed back down the steps. The door to Helen's house stayed open.

'She'll receive me,' Arabella said, turning to Polly. 'Quickly, the umbrella!'

They scrambled down from the carriage, hurried through the downpour, up the steps and inside. The door closed behind them, shutting out the rain.

Helen was upstairs, seated beside a fire in her parlour. She rose as Arabella entered. 'Bella,' she said. 'Thank you for coming.' She wore a gown of black bombazine. Her face was pale and composed.

Arabella hurried across the room. She hugged Helen. 'I came as soon as I heard. How are you?'

Helen gave a shaky laugh. She returned the embrace tightly, then stepped back. 'I'm fine.'

'What happened?' Arabella asked. 'Is there anything I can do to help?'

Helen smiled faintly. 'Thank you, but no. Everything is under control. Do sit, please.' She gestured to the sofa.

Arabella sat.

Helen stayed standing. She stirred the fire with a poker. After a moment she gave a sigh. 'George died last night. He was at a…at a—' She bit her lip and met Arabella's eyes. 'A brothel. His heart gave out.'

Arabella stared at her.

Helen smiled, a twisted movement of her mouth. 'Please don't tell anyone.'

'Of course not!' Arabella exclaimed.

Helen sighed again. She laid down the poker and came to sit beside Arabella. 'George's lawyer has taken care of everything. He seems to think that the circumstances of…of George's death can be kept quiet.'

Arabella reached out and took hold of Helen's hand. She tried to imagine what her friend was feeling. Not grief, after the way her husband had treated her. Relief?

'Would you like to stay with us? You'd be more than welcome.'

'Thank you.' Helen returned the clasp of her hand. 'But I'd rather be here. I know it sounds foolish, but…it's nice to be alone.'

'It doesn't sound foolish at all.'

Helen was silent for several seconds, staring at the fire. 'I loved George so much at first. And then I…I grew to hate him.' She looked at Arabella.

'I used to wish him dead. And now that he's gone—' Tears filled her eyes. Shame was clearly visible on her face. 'I can't tell you how relieved I am.'

Arabella hugged her. 'Anyone would be. It's only natural.'

They drew apart as the door opened. Helen wiped her eyes while a housemaid placed a tray on the table beside the fireplace.

Where did the sympathies of the household staff lie? With their dead master, or their mistress? Their mistress, Arabella guessed, from the expression on the maid's face as she glanced at Helen.

The maid curtsied and left the room.

'Tea, or hot chocolate?'

'Hot chocolate, please.'

What scenes had the staff in this house witnessed? George hadn't limited his abuse of Helen to words; he'd struck her, too. The way Helen had flinched from his upraised hand at the Fothergills' ball told her that.

Arabella accepted a cup of hot chocolate.

'Helen,' she said, hesitantly. 'Forgive me for asking, but...will you be all right financially?'

Helen glanced at her. 'Yes.'

'Are you certain? Because I come into my inheritance next month and I can give—'

'Thank you.' Helen put down the chocolate pot and smiled at Arabella. 'That's very kind of you, but quite unnecessary. A significant portion of my fortune still remains.'

Arabella nodded.

It was cosy in the parlour, with the rain hitting the window panes and the fire burning in the hearth. She sipped her chocolate and hoped Polly had found a warm fire and a hot drink below stairs.

She was aware of a lifting of her spirits. The last five years of Helen's life had been miserable. *But now she's free.*

As I shall be soon.

Arabella came to an abrupt decision. 'Helen… When I come of age next month I'll be leaving town.'

Helen's eyebrows rose. 'Oh?'

'I intend to buy a property in the country. Away from all of this.' She indicated London with a wave of her hand. 'You'd be more than welcome to stay with me—for as long as you like.'

'Thank you,' Helen said. 'What does your grandmother think of your plans?'

'She doesn't know.' Arabella looked down at her cup. She turned it around in its saucer.

'But surely—'

Arabella looked up, meeting Helen's eyes. 'We have guest for dinner. My grandmother will be glad to see the back of me,' she said, with a tight smile.

Helen's brow creased. 'Are you certain—?'

'Yes,' Arabella said, flatly. She placed her cup and saucer on the table. 'I intend to set up schools. For children from the slums. That's not something my grandmother would approve of.'

'Schools?' Enthusiasm lit Helen's face. She put her cup down and leaned forwards. 'Where? How many? May I help?'

Arabella blinked. 'You want to help?'

'Very much! I'm extremely fond of children.'

'Even children from the slums?'

'A child is a child, regardless of its birth,' Helen said.

Arabella smiled warmly at her. 'You may certainly help, if you wish.'

'Thank you.' Helen picked up her cup again, but didn't drink from it. 'My biggest sorrow is that George and I had no children.' Her smile was crooked. 'I should have liked for…for something good to have come from my marriage.'

'But if you marry again—'

Helen shuddered. 'I have no intention of remarrying. But I should very much like to help with your project.'

They talked for more than an hour, while the rain drummed down and the fire burned in the grate and the chocolate became cold in its pot. Finally Arabella stood. 'I must be going. My grandmother will be wondering what's become of me.'

'I'm so glad you came,' Helen said. Despite the dull black of the bombazine gown, she looked happy. There was a flush of colour in her cheeks and a smile in her eyes.

Arabella embraced her. 'If I can help in any way, if you need anything—anything at all—please tell me.'

'Thank you,' Helen said, returning her embrace. 'But everything will be fine.'

* * *

The rain was still coming down heavily the next morning, but by early afternoon it was a mere drizzle. Arabella, restless from a morning spent indoors, decided to go to the British Museum. She went downstairs to ask her grandmother's permission.

'The museum?' Lady Westcote repeated, looking doubtfully at the rain-streaked window panes.

'Yes. To sketch some of the marbles.' She stood quietly, waiting for her grandmother's decision. In her ears she heard her mother's voice: *I want no tears, no tantrums, no sulking. You will always be obedient. You'll be the perfect granddaughter,* ma chère. *Promise me.*

Lady Westcote sighed. 'If you must,' she said. She reached for the bell pull. 'I'll tell Clough to have the carriage brought round.'

Arabella ran lightly back up the stairs. 'We can go!' she told Polly.

It was the work of a few minutes to don a pelisse of cherry-red sarcenet, tie the ribbons of a bonnet decorated with clusters of cherries beneath her chin and pull on gloves.

She gathered her sketchbook and pencils and went downstairs with Polly.

The butler, Clough, opened the door. Outside, the carriage was drawing up at the foot of the steps. A footman, his face perfectly expressionless, stepped out into the drizzle. He raised an umbrella.

Arabella bit her lip. It was the same footman who'd been drenched yesterday. 'Thank you,' she said, and trod down the steps under the shelter of the umbrella.

She was about to climb into the carriage when she heard her name. 'Miss Knightley?'

Arabella turned her head. Adam St Just stood on the pavement, holding an umbrella. She blinked, taking in the rain-splashed topboots, the box coat with its numerous shoulder capes, and the beaver hat with its curved crown and slender brim. 'Mr St Just?'

'I wondered if I might ask a question.'

Arabella blinked again. 'Of course.' She turned towards the house. 'Would you like to come inside?'

'No, thank you,' St Just said. 'My question won't take a moment.'

Arabella shrugged. If he wanted to stand out in the rain, she didn't care. Although the poor footman probably did. 'Ask your question, Mr St Just.'

She had the impression that he hesitated slightly, that beneath the non-chalance he felt a little foolish. 'Er…did you tell anyone about the incident we witnessed on Piccadilly? With Sir Arnold Gorrie?'

Arabella managed not to tense. She raised her eyebrows. 'Still looking for Tom, Mr St Just?' she asked in a light, amused voice.

His jaw tightened. 'Did you tell anyone?' he repeated.

Arabella pretended to ponder the question. She was aware of the footman standing stoically in the drizzle, holding the umbrella over her head. 'No,' she said. 'I spoke to no one about it.'

St Just frowned. He glanced at Polly, standing beside Arabella on the pavement. 'And your maid? Did she tell anyone?'

Arabella turned to Polly. 'Highsmith? Did you tell anyone about Sir Arnold's behaviour on Piccadilly?'

'No, ma'am,' Polly said, in her expressionless servant's voice.

It clearly wasn't the answer Adam St Just had wanted to hear; his frown deepened. 'Thank you,' he said. 'I apologise for delaying you.'

'Not at all,' Arabella said. 'I wish you luck in your search.' Both her smile and her voice were slightly mocking.

She had the impression that St Just gritted his teeth. He inclined his head stiffly and stepped back.

Arabella climbed into the carriage. Polly followed her. The door closed behind them and a few seconds later the carriage moved forwards.

Arabella clutched her sketchbook on her lap. She looked at Polly.

Polly looked back at her, frowning. 'Should we be worried?'

Arabella considered this question for a moment. 'No. There's no way he can find out.'

Polly nodded. She settled back comfortably on the seat.

Arabella chewed her lower lip. There *was* no way Adam St Just could discover who Tom was, was there? She turned the question over in her mind, looking at it from various angles, and then shook her head.

No, her secret was safe.

Adam watched the carriage turn out of Mount Street. He gripped the handle of the umbrella tightly and headed in the direction of White's.

So Tom hadn't found out about Gorrie on Tuesday; he'd found out on Wednesday afternoon—and he'd acted quickly. A spur-of-the-moment thief.

'Hell and damnation,' he said. It was going to be much harder to find Tom now. He'd have to trace him through the men Jeremy and Alvanley had told.

Adam grimaced, imagining the amusement his questions would cause. Arabella Knightley wasn't going to be the only person laughing at him.

He splashed across the street, cursing beneath his breath. He'd been so *certain* Tom had found out from Grace or Miss Knightley or her maid. There'd been no other witnesses. Just the four of them, standing outside Hatchard's, and Sir Arnold himself—

Adam halted abruptly.

The four of them, and Sir Arnold Gorrie—and Eliza, the housemaid.

A hundred yards ahead of him, a hackney was drawn up. Adam furled his umbrella and broke into a run. 'Bayham Street in Camden Town,' he told the jarvey. 'As fast as you can!'

Chapter Ten

Adam fidgeted on the narrow seat while the hackney traversed London. What reason could Tom have had for taking bank notes from Sir Arnold Gorrie—other than to give the money to Eliza? The water drained from his umbrella, making a dark puddle on the floor.

Finally the hackney drew up in Bayham Street. Adam didn't wait for the jarvey to open the door. He jumped down and thrust some coins at the man. 'Wait here for me!'

The boarding house was a plain brick building with narrow windows. Adam hammered on the door and waited impatiently for the landlady to answer. What was the woman's name? Pink? Penny? Pound?

It came to him as she opened the door. 'Mrs Peet,' he said, taking off his hat and making her a shallow bow. 'We met earlier this week.'

Mrs Peet remembered him. She curtsied and invited him in.

'I'd like to see Eliza,' Adam said, wiping his feet on the mat in the hallway. The interior of Mrs Peet's establishment was cosier than the exterior. The floor was polished and neatly stitched samplers hung on the walls.

'Oh,' Mrs Peet said, a look of consternation crossing her plump face. 'I'm sorry, sir, but Miss Eliza has gone. She left this morning.'

Too late. God damn it! His fingers tightened on the brim of his hat. 'Where did she go?' he demanded.

Mrs Peet gave a helpless shrug. 'I'm sorry, sir, I don't know where they went.'

'They?' Adam fastened eagerly on the word. 'Did she leave with a man? What did he look like?'

'There was a man, sir. He was tall, as tall as you.'

He felt a surge of excitement. 'A gentleman? What colour was his hair?'

'Oh, no, sir.' Mrs Peet shook her head. 'He weren't a gentleman. He was a commoner.'

Adam stared at her. 'A commoner?'

Mrs Peet nodded emphatically.

'A servant?' he asked, feeling slightly deflated. 'In livery, perhaps?'

'No, sir,' Mrs Peet said.

Adam frowned at her. 'Did Eliza know him? What was his name?'

It took him nearly twenty minutes to pry the details from Mrs Peet. Eliza had received two visitors, a man and a woman. Mrs Peet wasn't certain, but she thought their name might have been Smith. The man was large and fair-haired, the woman dark and pretty, but missing several teeth. She'd been as pregnant as Eliza.

'Pregnant?' Adam said, baffled. 'Are you certain?'

Mrs Peet was certain. She was also certain Eliza hadn't known her visitors—and that she'd been overjoyed by the news they brought.

'So 'appy she was cryin',' Mrs Peet said. 'Said she'd come into some money.'

Tom, Adam thought. Whoever the man and woman were, commoners or not, they were agents of the burglar.

'And then they left. All three of 'em.' Mrs Peet lifted her shoulders in a shrug. 'I don't know where they went.'

'What time was this?'

'About eleven o'clock, sir.'

Adam thanked her and took his leave. For a moment he stood on the doorstep, staring at the buildings across the street. *Three hours too late.* His hands clenched. 'God *damn* it,' he said aloud. And then he put his hat on and splashed over to the waiting hackney.

He was still annoyed when he escorted his aunt and Grace to the Henworths' musical evening. Three hours too late. The error had been his—and he'd been stupid to make it, stupid to forget about Eliza, utterly and incredibly *stupid*.

The star of the evening was an Italian tenor, a short, stout man with the voice of an angel—or so his companions declared. Adam was too annoyed with himself to enjoy the performance. *Three hours, damn it.*

Miss Knightley was also present. She sat alongside her grandmother, slightly in front of Adam and to his left. He could see her out of the corner of his eye: the dark hair, the elegant cheekbones. She appeared to be enjoying the music.

At the end of the performance, refreshments were served. Adam fetched claret-cup for his sister and ratafia for Aunt Seraphina, and then went to find something stronger for himself.

The punch was quite potent. He stood for a moment, savouring the taste of rum and spices, looking around him. Was Tom one of the guests? His gaze flicked from face to face, and fastened on one: Miss Knightley, sipping from a goblet of lemonade, only a few yards distant.

His pulse gave its familiar, treacherous kick.

Adam's mouth tightened. He looked at her for a moment, at the soft indentation in her chin, at the dark, expressive eyes. What was it about her that attracted him so?

Not her personality, that was certain.

Miss Knightley's expression changed suddenly. She turned her head and stared at the two ladies standing in front of him.

'Miss St Just,' he heard one of them say.

Adam turned his head abruptly, forgetting Miss Knightley.

'…ran away with her music tutor.' The young lady had an unfortunate resemblance to a pug dog. Miss Brook, he thought her name was.

Adam's jaw hardened. He took a step forwards.

'Oh, no. That was merely a rumour. The truth was *much* more interesting.' The voice was Miss Knightley's.

Adam halted.

Both ladies turned their heads. 'I beg your pardon?' Miss Brook said.

'The truth about Miss St Just's music tutor,' Arabella Knightley said. Her smile was open and friendly—and to Adam's eyes, wholly suspicious.

Miss Brook and her companion didn't seem to notice anything wrong with Miss Knightley's smile. 'Oh?' Miss Brook said.

Arabella Knightley stepped closer. 'He went mad.'

'Mad?'

Miss Knightley nodded, her eyes innocently wide. 'The music tutor.

Apparently he'd been suffering from delusions for several months, but when the princess died, he went mad.'

'No!' Miss Brook said.

Miss Knightley nodded. 'He believed he was married to a number of students, but it wasn't until the princess died that his delusions became…*persistent*. Miss St Just was the object of his attention at that time, which was very distressing for her. She asked to be removed from the school.'

'So she didn't elope…?'

'No. She left Bath to escape his advances.'

'Oh.' Miss Brook looked disappointed.

'The tutor was turned off, of course,' Miss Knightley continued. 'Mr Plunkett was his name. Reginald Plunkett. But when it came time for him to leave, no one could find him.' Her voice lowered. 'You'll never guess where he was found!'

'Where?' Miss Brook breathed.

Adam stepped closer to hear.

'At a farm down the lane from the school, in a goat pen. He swore the nanny goat was his married wife.'

'A nanny goat?' There was horrified delight in Miss Brook's voice.

Arabella Knightley nodded solemnly. 'The poor man was sent back to his wife in Birmingham, but he refused to be parted from the goat. I've heard…' she lowered her voice a fraction more '…I've heard that he lives in a goat pen behind his wife's house.'

'Not…with the nanny goat?'

Miss Knightley nodded. Her expression of demure innocence was worthy of Jeremy.

Miss Brook shuddered. 'How shocking!'

'Isn't it just?' Miss Knightley said, looking as if butter wouldn't melt in her mouth.

Adam snorted, and turned away hurriedly. He gulped a mouthful of punch. When he turned back, Miss Brook and her companion were moving away, arm in arm, their heads bent closely together. 'Nanny goat!' he heard one of them say in a low, excited voice.

Arabella Knightley was sipping her lemonade. The demure innocence was gone. He saw contempt in the curl of her upper lip as she watched the young ladies depart.

Adam waited until Miss Brook and her friend had moved out of earshot. Then he stepped up behind Miss Knightley. 'Nanny goat?' he said quietly in her ear.

Miss Knightley started violently. Lemonade slopped over the side of the goblet. 'Mr St Just!'

'I beg your pardon.'

'You startled me!' Miss Knightley said, stating the obvious. Her glove was damp, and there was a small splash of lemonade on her gown.

'I apologise,' Adam said. He held out his hand for the goblet.

Miss Knightley gave it to him. It was sticky.

Adam watched as she pulled a lace-edged handkerchief from her reticule and dabbed at the spot on her gown. 'Nanny goat?' he said again.

Miss Knightley glanced up. 'How much did you hear?'

'All of it.' He almost laughed aloud at memory of Miss Brook's face, the delicious horror in her voice. *A nanny goat?* 'It was pure genius,' he said, grinning.

To his astonishment, Arabella Knightley grinned back at him. There was laughter in the dark eyes, mischief in the curve of her mouth.

God, she's beautiful.

Desire clenched painfully in his chest. For a moment he couldn't speak, couldn't breathe, couldn't do anything but look at her.

Adam wrenched his gaze from her face. He cleared his throat and looked down at the lemonade. A slice of lemon floated in it.

'It made a more interesting tale than a student eloping with her music tutor.'

Desire vanished at her words. He glanced up sharply. 'Grace did *not* elope with Mr Plunkett.'

'Of course she didn't.' Arabella Knightley folded her handkerchief and placed it back in her reticule. 'But what have rumours to do with the truth? Very little!' She held out her hand for the goblet.

Adam gave it to her.

'I hope I've given the gossips something else to talk about.' Miss Knightley's smile was cat-like, sharp and satisfied. She sipped the lemonade.

'I think you can be very certain you have!' he said drily.

Miss Knightley's gaze fastened on something past his shoulder. 'If you'll excuse me, Mr St Just. My grandmother wants me.'

Adam turned and watched as she walked across the room. Her hair gleamed with a dark, rich lustre. It was dressed in the French style, high on her head, leaving her nape bare. Her neck was pale, slender, elegant.

His fingers curled into the palm of his hand. *I want her.*

Adam turned abruptly away and gulped the rest of his punch. Then he went back to the refreshment room and refilled his glass.

It wasn't until Adam stepped into the cool, marble-paved entrance hall of his house on Berkeley Square that he thought to wonder about the facts Miss Knightley had included in her scurrilous little tale. How had she known Reginald Plunkett's name? Or that he lived in Birmingham? How had she known *when* to set her tale?

He pondered these questions as he climbed the stairs. In the corridor outside their bedchambers, he bid his aunt goodnight and detained Grace with a light touch on her arm.

She looked at him enquiringly. 'Yes?'

Adam waited until Aunt Seraphina had closed her bedroom door. 'Grace, have you told anyone in London about Reginald Plunkett?'

Grace flinched. She shook her head. 'No.'

'Not even Miss Knightley?'

Grace shook her head again, and then hesitated. 'I told her a little bit about what happened.' Distress creased her forehead. 'Why? Has she…' her voice trembled '…been talking about me?'

Adam put his arm around Grace. 'Not in a bad way,' he said, hugging her. 'I overheard her telling someone that Reginald Plunkett suffered from delusions and that he thought himself married to a nanny goat.'

'A nanny goat?' Grace's tension eased slightly. She uttered a choke of laughter. 'Truly?'

'Truly,' Adam said. He grinned in memory of Miss Brook's wide-eyed gullibility, her breathless questions—and the expression of extreme innocence on Arabella Knightley's face.

A fluent liar, Miss Knightley.

'But why would Bella say such a thing—?'

'As gossip, it's much more interesting than an elopement that may or may not have taken place.'

Grace stiffened. 'Yes,' she said in a subdued voice.

Adam hugged her again. 'According to Miss Knightley, Reginald Plunkett lives in a goat pen behind his wife's house in Birmingham. With the nanny goat.'

Grace gave a faint giggle.

'I merely wondered how Miss Knightley knew his name. Did you tell her?'

Grace shook her head against his shoulder. 'No. I haven't said his name to anyone since...since *then.*'

'Did you tell her where he lived? Or that it was in November that—'

Grace shook her head again. 'I told Bella he was my music tutor, and that he was married. That's all.' She inhaled a shaky breath. 'When are people going to stop talking about me?'

She was close to tears; he heard it in her voice.

Adam hugged her more tightly. 'I don't know.'

Grace sniffed against the lapel of his coat. 'I deserve it,' she said in a watery voice. 'For being so stupid.'

'It wasn't your fault. He chose you, Grace, because you were more wealthy than any of the other students.' She'd been the perfect victim for the man's scheme: shy and lonely, and desperate for love. 'Here.' He released her and gave her his handkerchief.

Grace wiped her eyes.

'If anyone's to blame, it's me. I shouldn't have sent you away.' Guilt was bitter on his tongue. 'I thought you'd be happier in Bath. I didn't realise you were so miserable there.'

Grace glanced up at him. 'I was happy there, sometimes.'

'But you would have been happier at home.'

Her gaze dropped to the handkerchief, a silent *yes.*

Adam cleared his throat. He reached out and touched Grace's cheek lightly. 'Go to bed.'

Grace nodded and turned away. She hesitated, her hand on the door knob, then turned back and hugged him.

Adam held her tightly. *For heaven's sake, boy,* he heard his father say. *Try to behave as a St Just! It's vulgar to display emotion.*

He pushed the old man's words aside and pressed a kiss into Grace's soft hair. 'Sleep well,' he said, releasing her.

'Goodnight, Adam.' She smiled at him, opened the door, and slipped into her room.

Adam cleared his throat again, and then he walked down the corridor to his own room.

After his morning ride in Hyde Park, Adam went in search of his aunt. He found her in the morning room.

'Aunt Seraphina?'

'Yes, dear?' His aunt looked up from her embroidery.

Her placid smile made him think involuntarily of a Jersey cow. Adam pushed the comparison out of his mind, closed the door and advanced into the room. 'Aunt, I wondered if you'd spoken of Mr Plunkett to anyone in London.'

His aunt looked at him in gentle surprise. 'Spoken of him? Why on earth should I do such a thing?'

Adam shrugged. 'Have you?'

'Of course not!' Aunt Seraphina said, putting down her embroidery.

'Not even to Miss Knightley?'

His aunt looked perplexed. 'No. Why?'

Adam smiled at her. 'No reason.' He bowed and let himself out of the morning room.

He went down the stairs two at a time, whistling under his breath. In his study he pulled out the bundle of papers Grace had received from Tom. He read the first blackmail letter again.

~~My dear~~ Miss St Just, ~~I have~~ a letter ~~of yours~~ you wrote to a Mr Reginald Plunkett of Birmingham has come into my possession.

He gave a satisfied grunt, placed the piece of paper aside, and reached for Grace's love letter. The date was at the top. November 6th, 1817. The day Princess Charlotte had died.

Adam laid both letters on his desk, side by side. They had come from Tom—and they contained information Miss Knightley had known.

The conclusion was obvious: Arabella Knightley was in league with the burglar, Tom.

Chapter Eleven

The Giffords' ballroom was a forest of greenery. Potted palms sprouted in the corners, ferns uncurled delicate fronds, and ivy spilled from various torchères and jardinières. Arabella looked around as she entered. A *contredanse* was in progress, the dancers advancing across the floor in time with the music.

'How delightful,' her grandmother said, glancing around. 'So verdant.'

'Yes, Grandmother.' Arabella suppressed a sigh. Two and a half more weeks of this.

With her grandmother happily ensconced in the card room with a glass of champagne at her elbow and a pile of guineas in front of her, Arabella was free—in her grandmother's words—to enjoy herself. *I'd rather be at home.* She glanced back at her grandmother. Lady Westcote was avidly examining her first hand of cards.

Arabella suppressed another sigh. She touched her fingertips lightly to her bodice—spider-gauze embroidered with tiny rosebuds over a gown of rose-coloured satin. *Armour,* she told herself.

She squared her shoulders and stepped into the ballroom, a smile on her face.

'Miss Knightley,' a voice said to her right.

Arabella turned. The smooth baritone belonged to Adam St Just.

There was nothing in his polite bow to give her cause for alarm, and yet there was an intentness in his gaze, an edge to his smile, that made her skin prickle with unease.

'I wonder if I might request a dance?'

Arabella stiffened. *Not the waltz.*

'The next quadrille, perhaps?'

She relaxed. 'It would be my pleasure, Mr St Just.'

Half an hour later, Arabella took her place alongside him. 'That was a marvellous tale you told last night,' St Just said, as the head couple began to dance the first figure. 'About the nanny goat.'

Arabella glanced at him.

'I don't recall if I thanked you.'

'There's no need to thank me, Mr St Just.'

'No,' he said, with a smile that turned up only one side of his mouth. 'You didn't do it for me, did you? You did it for Grace.'

Arabella looked at him uncertainly. Was that bitterness she heard in his voice, regret that she saw in that lopsided smile? *Of course not. Why would he want me to like him?*

They accomplished their first figure, *le pantalon,* with ease. Arabella discovered that she was enjoying herself. Adam St Just was as skilful a dancer as his friend the Marquis of Revelstoke. There was no fear of him forgetting his place in the figure. He made the quadrille—a dance that had been the downfall of many an unwary gentleman or lady—look easy.

While they waited for their turn at the second figure, he spoke to her again. 'I wonder, Miss Knightley, how you came to know the name of Grace's music tutor?'

He asked the question so affably, with such cordiality, that for a moment she didn't realise how dangerous it was—and then his words registered.

Arabella turned her head sharply. 'I beg your pardon?'

'Mr Reginald Plunkett,' St Just said, his gaze intent on her face. 'How did you know his name?'

Because it was in the blackmail letter.

Arabella was aware of a tiny spike of panic in her chest. *He suspects something.* She grabbed the first lie she thought of. 'Grace told me.'

His eyebrows lifted slightly. 'Grace?'

'Yes.'

St Just smiled at her. 'Grace assures me that she hasn't mentioned Plunkett's name to anyone in London.'

'Oh,' Arabella said.

There was something disturbing in St Just's eyes, in his smile. He reminded her of someone—

Not someone: something. Adam St Just reminded her of a cat stalking its prey: the way his eyes were focused on her face, the sharp-edged smile. 'So I wonder, Miss Knightley…how did you discover his name?'

Arabella stared at him. Her mind was utterly blank. She could think of no credible lie, no convincing explanation.

'Miss Knightley?'

Arabella swallowed.

'Our turn, I believe,' St Just said. He held out his hand to her.

For a moment she had no idea what figure they were to dance, no idea what step to take. His fingers closed around hers. Panic flared inside her—and then her pulse steadied. This was the second figure, *l'été*.

Arabella danced with what she hoped was an outward appearance of calm. Inwardly, she castigated herself. She was a fool to have been overset by St Just's words, a fool to panic. The answer to his question was easy.

'If it wasn't Grace who told me,' she said, once they'd completed the figure and were standing side by side again, 'then I must have heard it from someone else.' She shrugged lightly. 'There's been so much gossip lately. One quite forgets where one first hears things.'

St Just's expression told her clearly that he didn't believe her. 'I thought you disliked gossip, Miss Knightley.'

'I do. But one can't help overhearing things.' She opened her eyes at him, wide and innocent.

His own eyes narrowed. 'How did you know Mr Plunkett came from Birmingham?'

Arabella shrugged again. 'Gossip,' she said airily.

His jaw tightened. 'And the date? How did you know when it happened?'

'The week Princess Charlotte died? I remember someone mentioning that. It stuck in my mind. Such a memorable week!' Arabella creased her brow thoughtfully and tapped a finger against her cheek. 'Now, who was it..?' she mused. 'Mrs Harpenden, perhaps?'

St Just's look was disgusted, and wholly disbelieving.

Arabella smiled widely. She turned her attention to the other dancers, pretending to watch them. St Just suspected a connection with Tom— that was obvious—but he knew nothing. *And he never will.*

She bit her lip, imagining his astonishment if he were to learn the truth. A female thief? Preposterous!

Arabella decided to take the offensive while she danced the third figure, *la poule*. When they were standing quietly again, she turned to St Just. 'Miss Wootton is in good looks this evening, don't you agree? Such an attractive young lady. And such a lovely fortune. Have you had the opportunity to press your suit yet?'

St Just looked at her blandly. 'Sharpening your claws, Miss Knightley?'

His prescience was unsettling. Her smile faltered slightly.

'On that subject, I've had the opportunity to consider your suggestion,' he said in a genial tone. 'Of a stream running down the centre of the table at my wedding breakfast. I believe you're correct; nothing could be more elegant, more tasteful.'

Arabella stared at him.

He returned her gaze with perfect blandness.

Was Adam St Just teasing her?

Arabella was so disconcerted that she almost missed the cue for the fourth figure, *la pastourelle*.

After a lively *finale,* Adam escorted Miss Knightley to where his aunt and Mrs Wootton stood. Exhilaration hummed in his veins. Miss Knightley knew something about Tom. He'd seen it in her face—the sharp glance, the brief freezing of her smile—just as he'd felt her faint hesitation when he'd led her into the second figure. She'd been off balance and alarmed.

He fetched lemonade for Miss Knightley and champagne for himself, returning to find Grace and Letty had joined them. Adam listened idly to the girls' chatter, his eyes on Miss Knightley. She paid him absolutely no attention, seemingly immersed in conversation with his aunt, but he thought there was tension in the way she stood, a stiffness to her shoulders.

She knows who Tom is.

He needed proof, not supposition. He needed handwriting to match with Tom's. He needed drawings—

His mind supplied him with a memory: Miss Knightley standing outside her grandmother's house on Mount Street, about to step into a

carriage. A footman held an umbrella over her head, and in her hands
she carried—

A sketchbook.

I have to see that sketchbook.

Adam sipped his champagne thoughtfully, and then said, 'Grace?'

His sister turned her head. 'Yes?'

'If the weather's fine tomorrow, would you like to take the barouche
out to Richmond? Have a picnic and sketch the views.'

Grace's face brightened. 'What a marvellous idea! Letty, would you
like to come?'

Miss Wootton expressed great pleasure in the invitation.

'Bella?' Grace said, turning to Miss Knightley. 'Will you come with us?'

Miss Knightley looked around. 'Come where?'

'To Richmond tomorrow, to have a picnic and sketch the views!'

Arabella Knightley glanced sharply at him. 'Will you be joining the
expedition, Mr St Just?'

'No,' Adam said. 'Unfortunately I have business in town.'

Grace looked disappointed; Miss Knightley looked relieved. 'I should
be delighted to come,' she said.

Adam sipped his champagne and hid a smile.

The expedition set out from Berkeley Square early the next morning,
under the aegis of Aunt Seraphina. The sun shone brightly in a cloudless
sky; there was no need to raise the folding hood of the barouche. Adam
watched them depart from the window of the upstairs parlour: the team
of grey horses, the coachman and a footman sitting erect on the high
driving seat, the ladies with their bonnets and parasols and sketchbooks.

He let his eyes rest on Miss Knightley as the barouche pulled out of
the square. She wore a bonnet of chip straw, trimmed with flowers and
twists of ribbon. The broad brim hid her face.

Adam turned away from the window, very satisfied with himself. Last
night's exhilaration still hummed inside him. This afternoon, once he'd
gone over matters with his man of business, he'd ride out to Richmond.
And take a look at Arabella Knightley's sketchbook.

He strolled downstairs. 'Has Mr Herbert arrived?' he asked the butler.

'Yes, sir.'

'Tell him I'm ready to see him,' Adam said, and walked down the corridor to his study.

The business with Mr Herbert—including an assignment that concerned Grace's blackmailer, Lady Bicknell—took longer than Adam had anticipated. It was mid-afternoon by the time he rode through the gate into Richmond Park. King Henry's Mound seemed the logical choice of picnic spot, but he found only a party of children and two harassed nursemaids in possession of the view.

Adam stood in the stirrups and looked around in frustration. He saw woodland and meadows and a herd of deer grazing on a hillside. Four riders cantered along one of the bridleways and a landau with a coat of arms on the door panel made its stately way towards the gate and London—but of the barouche and its party of ladies, there was no sign.

'Damn,' he said under his breath, conscious of how large Richmond Park was.

It took him more than half an hour to find them. It was the carriage he spotted first, half-hidden behind a copse of trees at the foot of a low, wooded hillside. Adam squinted. Was that his barouche? He cantered closer. Yes, it was his barouche, with the blue silk lining and the smart leather trim. And behind the carriage, beneath the shade of the trees, his greys quietly cropped the grass.

He felt a surge of anticipation.

Adam handed Goliath to the care of the coachman and trod quietly up the slope. Birds sang in the canopy above him and a squirrel scolded from a high branch.

He paused at the top. The view wasn't as expansive as the one from King Henry's Mound, but it was charming: a grassy hillside, stands of trees.

To his right, beneath the shade of an oak tree, a rug was spread on the ground. Aunt Seraphina was its sole occupant. She lay dozing.

He heard the drowsy hum of bees, the soft whisper of long grass in the breeze, his aunt's gentle snores—and girlish laughter.

Adam walked quietly past Aunt Seraphina. On the other side of the oak tree a second rug had been spread, overlooking the meadow. The girls knelt on it, their heads bent together. They had removed their bonnets.

Their curls mingled—golden and nut-brown and dark sable—as they looked at something Miss Knightley held. He heard a squeal of laughter, a delighted giggle.

'Do another one!' Grace begged.

'Oh, yes!' cried Letty Wootton. 'Do! Please!'

'Another what?' Adam asked.

Three heads turned towards him.

For a moment he couldn't breathe. He'd never seen anything more beautiful, more perfect, than the laughing curve of Arabella Knightley's lips, the dimple in her cheek, the mischief brimming in her dark eyes.

Desire clenched in his chest. He wanted her more than he'd wanted any woman in his life.

Equally intense, and far more disturbing, was a tenderness that made his throat tighten. *I want to make her look this happy. I want to make her smile, to make her laugh.*

Miss Knightley's expression sobered. The dimple vanished. She closed her sketchbook.

'Oh, do show him!' Grace begged. 'Adam, you have to see this! Bella's so clever!'

Adam cleared his throat. He tried to remember his purpose: to find Tom. He stepped on to the rug. 'May I?' He held out his hand.

After a moment's hesitation, Miss Knightley gave him her sketchbook. It was almost full. Only a few pages at the end were still blank. Adam flicked to the last sketch: a cow standing in a paddock. He looked at it, perplexed. The paddock bore no resemblance to Richmond Park.

He blinked—and looked more closely at the cow. It was Aunt Seraphina. 'Good God,' he said.

Grace clapped her hands and gave a choke of laughter.

Adam looked at Miss Knightley. 'That's incredible,' he said. 'How did you do it?'

She shrugged lightly.

Adam examined the sketch again. The paddock, the wooden fence, the distant trees, had been drawn using the minimum of pencil strokes—and yet they were vividly real. He could almost see the leaves turning in the breeze, almost smell the grass. The cow had been sketched quickly—and yet in a few deft lines, she'd made it alive. It was about to breathe, about to blink its large eyes.

He studied it, frowning. How could the cow be a cow, and yet also a person?

It was the eyes, he decided. And something in the curve of cheek, in the mouth, in the way it held its head.

There was no meanness in the sketch. Mischief, yes—but no malice. The cow gazed at him, placid, benign, beautiful—and unmistakably Aunt Seraphina.

'Look at the other ones!' Grace urged.

Obediently, he turned the page—and found himself staring at a ballroom in which were a peacock, a cockerel and a toad. He laughed involuntarily. 'Revelstoke?' he said, glancing at Miss Knightley.

Her lips quirked slightly in a smile. He saw a glimmer of laughter in her eyes.

Adam examined the sketch. The peacock was unmistakably the Marquis of Revelstoke, just as the cow had been unmistakably Aunt Seraphina. It was a resplendent creature, its tail outspread in magnificent display, the crest sitting atop its head like an absurd little crown. He recognised Jeremy in the impish gleam in the peacock's eye, in the sly amusement of its beak.

The peacock had been drawn with a kindly hand; the toad and the cockerel had not. The toad sat to one side of page. It had Lady Bicknell's broad, flat face, Lady Bicknell's wide mouth. It was squat and… Adam searched for the word. Malevolent. The toad was squat and malevolent. Just like Lady Bicknell.

He glanced at Arabella Knightley. If nothing else told him she was in league with Tom, this caricature did. She knew Lady Bicknell was a blackmailer.

The cockerel wasn't malevolent, but it was foolish and strutting and conceited, with a puffed-out chest and absurdly scrawny legs. Its plumage was gaudy and tasteless. Adam studied the sketch with pleasure. She'd captured Sir Arnold Gorrie's inflated ego, his crassness, perfectly. *I would love Gorrie to see this.*

He turned the page—and found himself staring at a stag atop a hill.

Adam glanced sharply at Miss Knightley. She was examining her fingernails.

He looked back at the stag. It was definitely him.

The stag was a handsome creature, magnificently built. It stood on top of the hill, holding its head proudly and looking haughtily down its nose.

Adam stared at the stag. It gazed back at him, certain of its superiority.

He knew exactly what Miss Knightley thought of him.

Arrogant.

Adam felt himself flush. He hurriedly turned the page.

This sketch was of a familiar view. Here was the oak tree, the rug spread on the ground, the picnic basket.

On the rug sat a fluffy white kitten. He recognised it instantly: Grace. It was quite the most beautiful kitten he'd ever seen. Such wide, innocent eyes, such sweetness in its face.

Perched on the handle of the picnic basket was a plump, cheerful robin. Its head was cocked to one side. He saw bright intelligence and curiosity in its eyes. Letty Wootton.

He turned the page again. Here was the same view, but drawn without caricature. Two girls sat on the rug, their heads bent over their sketchbooks. The scene was drawn with a deft, unerring hand. She'd used the barest of detail, and yet he could see the grass heads nodding in the breeze, the pattern on the rug, the crisp ruffles of lace trimming the dresses.

On the next page—

Adam held his breath for a moment, and then touched the sketch lightly. It was a portrait of Grace. She was glancing at him, a smile in her eyes, and she was so real, so *alive,* that he almost expected the curls to stir against her cheek, almost expected her to inhale.

He looked at Miss Knightley. She was regarding him, her face expressionless, almost wary.

'This sketch of Grace… It's beautiful.' He tried to find the words to express his admiration. 'You're an extraordinarily gifted artist, Miss Knightley.'

She coloured faintly and looked down at the rug.

'Isn't she?' Grace exclaimed, and alongside her Letty Wootton nodded, her eyes as bright as the robin's had been.

Adam flicked through the rest of the sketchbook. He saw the marbles at the British Museum and botanical studies from Kensington Gardens, labelled and dated. He examined the writing closely. Had Tom looped his letters so neatly?

The book was a medley of sketches: gardens, museums, street scenes. There were no more caricatures, but several studies of animals. One page was devoted to a mongrel dog. He saw it sleeping, scratching, sniffing a lamp post, and finally trotting off down a street.

On another page was a lean adolescent cat. Adam examined that page with particular interest, studying the cat as it slept, sat and played in various poses. He looked at its tail, its paws, its whiskers. How did she create such a lifelike creature with so few strokes of the pencil?

Adam touched the cat lightly. It was so real he almost expected to feel fur beneath his fingertip, not paper. He glanced at Arabella Knightley and knew, without any doubt, that it was she who'd drawn the cat at the bottom of Tom's note.

He felt a profound admiration of her skill—and a fierce envy of the unknown Tom. *I wish I was him.*

Adam cleared his throat. He turned back through the pages until he came to the portrait of Grace. Its beauty almost took his breath away.

'May I…have this drawing of Grace, Miss Knightley?'

She blinked, and then said, 'Of course.'

'And may I have the one of me as a kitten?' Grace asked eagerly.

'Certainly.'

Miss Knightley labelled both sketches in a neat hand and cut the pages from the book with a small pair of scissors from her reticule.

'Thank you,' Adam said, taking the portrait. *Grace St Just in Richmond Park,* Miss Knightley had written at the bottom of the page. *May 16th, 1818. By Arabella Knightley.*

'This is better than anything Sir Thomas Lawrence could do,' he said, meaning it. It was so *alive.*

The praise seemed to embarrass Miss Knightley. She glanced away, blushing faintly.

'Bella's father was an artist,' Grace said, as proudly as if she'd announced he was the King of England. 'Show him the locket, Bella.'

Miss Knightley hesitated, and then raised her hands to her throat. From beneath her muslin fichu, she pulled a small locket on a golden chain. She unfastened the chain and handed it to him.

The locket was warm from her skin. Adam held it in his palm for a moment, aware an almost erotic sense of connection with her. He gave himself a mental shake and examined the locket more closely.

It was a simple oval, unembellished by curlicues, fashioned of gold and with the smooth, glowing patina of long use. He opened it carefully with his thumbnail. The locket held two portraits inside. On the left was a smiling young lady, with the same dark hair and eyes as Miss Knightley. The portrait was astonishingly detailed. He saw rosy lips and pearl-white teeth and a faint blush tinting the lady's cheeks.

On the right, was the portrait of a young man. He had curling brown hair and a handsome, good-humoured face. He was clearly a Knightley: pressed into his chin was the same indentation Arabella Knightley had.

'Your father painted these?' He glanced at her.

Miss Knightley nodded.

Adam studied the portraits again. Arabella Knightley's parents had been a handsome couple. *And happy, too,* he thought, closing the locket. He turned it over. On the back was an inscription. *Arabella Eloise de Martigny Knightley,* born June 5th 1793. 'Your birthday is next month.'

'Yes.'

Adam handed back the locket and chain. Their fingers brushed briefly. 'I can see where you get your talent from, Miss Knightley. Your father was extremely gifted.'

'He supported us by painting.' Her eyes challenged him.

Adam studied her face. Did she expect him to look down on her father for needing to work for a living?

He didn't feel disdain; he felt sadness—and a surge of anger towards the late Earl of Westcote. The man had had a son, a daughter-in-law, a granddaughter, and he'd thrown them away for the sake of what—pride? 'Your grandfather was a fool.'

The comment appeared to startle Miss Knightley. She blinked. Her fingers closed tightly around the locket. 'Yes. He was.'

While Arabella Knightley fastened the chain about her throat, Grace and Letty Wootton showed him their sketches. They were perfectly competent—and alongside Miss Knightley's, quite lifeless.

'I thought you had business in town all day,' Grace said, sorting through her sketches. Unlike Miss Knightley, she'd drawn on unbound sheets of paper. Their edges fluttered in the breeze.

'It took less time than I expected.' He studied at the portrait of Grace. She smiled up at him, youthful, happy, alive. 'Is there room for this in your portfolio? I don't want to crease it.'

'Of course.' She laid the portrait on top of her sketches.

A gust of wind flipped back the edge of the rug, sent the leaves in the oak tree above them spinning madly—and took the sketches from the open portfolio. The sheets of paper scattered.

'Oh!' Grace cried, starting to her feet.

Adam caught a glimpse of Miss Knightley's portrait—the smile in Grace's eyes, the soft ringlets lying against her cheek—before the page spun out across the meadow.

He abandoned his hat and set off in pursuit. The portrait danced lightly ahead of him, turning cartwheels, leading him halfway down the hill before coming to rest against a tuft of grass.

Adam picked it up reverently. He turned and looked back up the hillside.

The rug was empty. Grace and Miss Wootton and Miss Knightley were chasing pieces of paper across the sloping meadow.

He paused, catching his breath. Arabella Knightley had easily outstripped the others. She was as light-footed, as fleet, as a boy.

Adam climbed back up the hill, holding the portrait carefully by the corners, listening to the shrieks and giggles Grace and Letty Wootton made as they pounced on the scattered pieces of paper.

Back at the rug, Grace gathered the sketches together. A number of them were dog-eared and grass-stained. 'The kitten and the robin,' she said, a note of worry in her voice. 'I don't see it.'

'I have it,' Arabella Knightley said, last to arrive back.

Adam glanced at her face—alight with laughter, flushed with exertion—and looked hastily away. He was aware of a surge of heat inside him that had nothing to do with climbing up the hill.

Grace laid the sketches in the leather-bound portfolio again, closed it and tied the ribbons tightly.

Back at his town house in Berkeley Square, Adam laid the evidence on his desk: the note from Tom, and Arabella Knightley's sketch of Grace.

I believe these belong to you, Tom had written. *I found them in Lady Bicknell's possession.* And then he'd drawn a black cat at the bottom.

Adam examined the cat. It had been drawn with an unerring hand. Miss Knightley's work, surely?

He turned his attention to the writing. The only word in common between the Tom's note and Miss Knightley's label on the portrait was 'in'. He grimaced. Not helpful.

But wasn't the y the same? And the neat curves and loops of the *ell* in Bicknell and the *ell* in Arabella?

The longer he stared at the words—pencil and black ink—the more he was convinced. The handwriting was Miss Knightley's, just as the cat was.

Adam pushed back his chair. He poured himself a glass of brandy and walked over to the window. *What next?* he asked himself as he swirled the brandy in the glass, warming it.

The answer was easy: the next time he saw Arabella Knightley he'd confront her with his evidence.

And then what? Dare he hope that Miss Knightley would confide in him? That she'd reveal Tom's identity?

He strongly doubted it.

And just who was Tom?

Adam sipped the brandy slowly, staring out the window, not seeing anything. He'd thought Tom a gentleman; he knew now he was wrong. Miss Knightley had few friends among the *ton*. Tom had to be the large man who'd collected Eliza from the boarding house. A commoner, the landlady had said. Someone Miss Knightley had known as a child. A friend. Someone she trusted.

He felt a strong surge of envy. The brandy tasted suddenly bitter in his mouth.

Adam turned away from the window and went back to his desk. He stood, staring down at the portrait of Grace, at the black cat.

Such a gifted artist.

He touched Tom's note, brushing the cat with a light fingertip. The next time he saw Miss Knightley, he'd have the truth from her.

That evening, Adam escorted his sister and aunt to the Riddifords' masked ball. Grace, wearing a domino of palest blue, was almost beside herself with excitement; this was her first masquerade. She quivered on the seat beside him in the carriage, her hands in their long white kid gloves clasped tightly together. 'I'm so glad Letty's coming,' she said, as the carriage turned into St James's Square. 'And Bella.'

'Miss Knightley?' Adam said, his interest sharpening. 'She's coming?'

Grace nodded, and peered out the window as the carriage slowed. She clutched his arm. 'We're here!'

The Riddifords' ballroom was at the back of their house on St James's Square, along with a conservatory. Adam entered the ballroom with almost as much eagerness as Grace. He surveyed the assembled guests, looking for dark hair and a softly cleft chin. *Where are you, Miss Knightley?*

'Can you see Letty?' Grace asked. 'Or Bella?'

'No.'

He danced the cotillion and the quadrille without seeing Miss Knightley. The fact that everyone was wearing dominos and loo masks was extremely unhelpful. Frustration built inside him as he scanned the ballroom. A considerable number of ladies were as diminutive as Arabella Knightley, but none had her poise and her slender figure, her graceful way of dancing.

Two country dances later, he still couldn't see her. Some of the ladies had pushed their hoods back to reveal dark ringlets, but they were all too short, too tall, too buxom, too thin.

Adam stood out the waltz, resolutely ignoring those ladies whose hands were unclaimed. He strolled around the ballroom, sipping a glass of champagne, looking for dark eyes hidden behind a loo mask, for a chin with the faintest of indentations.

Adjoining the ballroom was the conservatory. Adam trod down the short flight of marble stairs, but he found only greenery and more refreshments laid out on a table. Two dowagers were sipping punch from crystal glasses, and a young lady in a domino of jonquil yellow was conducting a mild flirtation with a gentleman dressed in green.

Back in the ballroom, Adam frowned across the dance floor. Where the devil was she?

A thought occurred to him. He headed for the door, pushing through the throng of masked guests. 'The card room?' he asked a liveried footman, and was directed to an adjoining salon.

There, seated at one of the tables, was Lady Westcote. The hood of her lilac satin domino was pushed back and she'd dispensed with her loo mask. Her white hair gleamed, as did the pile of guineas in front of her.

Adam turned back to the ballroom. Anticipation hummed beneath his skin. If Lady Westcote was here, then so was her granddaughter.

'Miss Knightley?'

Arabella glanced up. The gentleman standing in front of her wore a black domino. A mask hid his upper face. His hair was brown streaked with gold, his eyes behind the mask were grey, and his jaw was what could be described as chiselled. But even without those features, the man's height, the fine shape of his legs in the black satin breeches and white silk stockings, would have told her who he was.

'Good evening, Mr St Just.'

He bowed. 'You're not dancing the waltz.'

'Neither are you.'

Adam St Just looked at her for a moment. There was something vaguely unsettling about his smile. 'Are you engaged for the next dance, Miss Knightley?'

'No.'

'Then may I have the pleasure?'

'Certainly.'

St Just's smile widened. 'Have you seen the conservatory? It's quite delightful.' He extended his arm to her. 'Shall we?'

Arabella stood, reluctantly. There really was something rather disconcerting about Adam St Just's smile. She placed her hand lightly on his sleeve.

Their pace was slow, strolling. Music and conversations eddied around them. She heard snatches of gossip, of laughter, the swirl of satin dominos and the rustle of petticoats and flounces as the dancers swung past. St Just led her to the back of the ballroom and down a short flight of stairs to a conservatory. Two dowagers sat comfortably in one corner, their heads bent together as they gossiped, but otherwise it was empty except for statuary and ferns and a table of refreshments.

'Would you like something to drink?'

Arabella shook her head. Up the stairs in the ballroom, the waltz came to its end. 'Our dance will be starting shortly.'

'I thought we could sit it out.'

Arabella glanced at him sharply. 'Sit it out?'

He inclined his head in a nod. 'If you're agreeable.'

She considered it a moment.

St Just watched her silently. Unlike Lord Dalrymple, he didn't appear to have taken her aside to make an improper advance. There was nothing suggestive in his voice, nothing flirtatious his manner. Even so, she felt a prickle of alarm.

She glanced at the gossiping dowagers. St Just would hardly play one of Lord Dalrymple's tricks with such an audience. She tried to imagine him leering at her, sneaking an arm around her waist, attempting to snatch a kiss.

It was an impossible scenario to imagine. Adam St Just looked down his nose at people; he didn't grope them.

'Very well,' she said.

His smile seemed to sharpen.

The prickle of alarm strengthened. *Have I made a mistake?* But it was too late to draw back. St Just was leading her to a grouping of gilded chairs at some distance from the dowagers. 'Please,' he said, indicating a chair.

Arabella sat. She clasped her hands in her lap. 'You wish to speak with me?'

'Yes.' St Just sat so that he was facing her. He crossed his legs casually and stretched one arm along the back of the chair next to him.

Arabella eyed him. There was nothing intimidating about his posture. 'What about?' But even as she asked the question, she realised the answer: he wanted her to draw another portrait of Grace.

She relaxed.

'About Tom,' St Just said. 'You know who he is, don't you?'

His voice was so affable that for a moment Arabella didn't realise what he'd said. And then the import of his words sank in. She tensed. 'I beg your pardon?'

In the ballroom a *contredanse* was starting. The music drifted down to them. Adam St Just swung his toe in time to it. 'You know who Tom is,' he said again, softly. 'Don't you, Miss Knightley?' His eyes glittered behind the black mask. His smile was that of a hunter.

Arabella took refuge in affront. 'How dare you suggest such a thing!' She made as if to rise.

St Just abandoned his nonchalant pose. One moment he was lounging in the chair, swinging one foot, the next his hand was at her wrist, a firm, strong grip that held her in her place. The speed with which he moved made the breath catch in her throat. For a moment she sat frozen. Her heart seemed to stop beating. She stared into his eyes.

'You know who he is.' St Just spoke in a whisper, soft, audible to only the two of them.

Arabella swallowed. She twisted her wrist in his grasp. 'You're being perfectly ridiculous, Mr St Just.'

He loosened his grip, but didn't release her. 'You choose the victims,' he said softly. 'You write the notes. You draw the cat. Don't you, Miss Knightley?'

'I have no idea what you are talking about!'

Adam St Just shook his head. 'You forget, I've seen your sketchbook. And I have a specimen of your handwriting.'

'You have a very fanciful imagination!' she said tartly, twisting her wrist again.

He didn't release her. 'You witnessed the incident on Piccadilly with Sir Arnold Gorrie, and by your own admission you heard Mrs Harpenden start the rumour about Letty Wootton. You were present when Lady Bicknell reduced poor Mrs Findley to tears.' His voice was low and matter of fact.

'So?' Arabella said, haughtily. 'Any number of people were present.'

'You were in the Park last year, when Lord Randall beat his horse,' St Just continued. 'I remember the expression on your face. And you were at the Chapel Royal when Miss Smidley pushed Miss Wrexham down the steps.'

'Do you think so?' she said with haughty scorn. 'That was a year ago, Mr St Just. I doubt you can recall who attended that particular service!'

'You were there,' he said quietly. 'I remember you went to aid Miss Wrexham.'

Arabella swallowed. Her pulse was beating fast. She stared at him through narrow eyes, feigning anger. 'And because of that, you deduce I know Tom? Mr St Just, you've read far too many novels!'

He grinned. 'Nice try, Miss Knightley.'

The note of approval made her flush. She was abruptly as angry as she pretended to be.

'Tom paid no visits during the Season of 1816,' St Just said. 'The year you were in mourning for your grandfather and didn't come to London. A coincidence, Miss Knightley?' He shook his head. 'I don't think so.'

His grip on her wrist tightened slightly. He leaned forwards. His eyes glittered fiercely behind the black mask. 'I know you're in league with Tom, Miss Knightley. I assure you I have no desire to expose either of you—but I do want to know who Tom is.'

Arabella looked at him contemptuously. St Just credited her with choosing Tom's victims and writing his notes—but he thought her incapable of carrying out the actual deeds. *I'm not so weak and helpless as you think, Mr St Just.*

She gathered her outrage. 'How *dare* you!' she said, wrenching her wrist from his grasp. She pushed back her chair and stood. The scrape of the chair legs on the marble flagstones was harsh, but the dowagers in the far corner were deep in conversation and didn't notice. 'I find your insinuations and your behaviour grossly impertinent!'

St Just flushed. He stood and put out a hand to detain her. 'Miss Knightley—'

'For your knowledge, I am *not* in league with Tom.' Arabella brushed past his outstretched hand and ran across the conservatory and up the marble steps to the ballroom.

Chapter Twelve

Miss Knightley's words still rang in Adam's ears several hours later, as he unbuttoned his shirt. *How dare you!*

He pulled the shirt over his head and held it for a moment, balled in his hand. *I find your insinuations and your behaviour grossly impertinent!* As an accusation, it stung. It still did. Arabella Knightley was correct: his behaviour hadn't been that of a gentleman.

Adam flexed his fingers around the balled linen, remembering the slenderness of her wrist. Yes, grossly impertinent. *I owe her an apology.*

'Dirty, sir?' his valet, Perkins, asked, plucking the shirt from his hand.

Adam watched the man bustle into the dressing room, but it wasn't Perkins he saw. His memory replayed the scene in the conservatory and halted at her scornful utterance: *Mr St Just, you've read far too many novels!*

Her outrage, her avowal of innocence, had been perfect. Too perfect. The great Mrs Siddons herself couldn't have done better.

Adam shook his head in rueful admiration and turned towards the bed. *How do I get her to admit the truth?*

Because despite her vehement denial, her appearance of innocence, he knew he was right: Arabella Knightley was in league with Tom.

Miss Knightley wrenched her wrist free from his grasp. She turned and ran from him, across the conservatory and up the marble steps to the ballroom.

Adam ran after her.

The masquerade had finished. The ballroom was empty and dark, lit only by moonlight coming in through the tall windows. It stretched into the distance, vast and shadowed. At the far end he saw the fluttering hem of a domino. The slam of a door came faintly to his ears.

Adam ran. He reached the door, opened it, and plunged through—not into a carpeted corridor, but into St James's Square. He stumbled slightly on the cobblestones and swung around, looking for Miss Knightley.

She stood beneath a gas lamp.

For a long moment they stared at each other. He saw the rise and fall of her chest, saw the soft lips part—and then Miss Knightley uttered a laugh, a challenge. She spun on her heel and vanished into the darkness, her domino flaring behind her.

Adam charged after her.

The speed with which Miss Knightley ran was startling. She was as swift as a deer, swifter. Piccadilly Street, Berkeley Square, Mount Street—they flashed past so rapidly it was dizzying. Adam ran faster than he'd ever run in his life—until it felt as if his heart would burst—and yet still Miss Knightley drew ahead of him. At the gate into Hyde Park she paused for a moment, looking back over her shoulder. A gas lamp illuminated her face— the softly cleft chin, the scornful curl of her lip—and then she was gone.

Adam burst into Hyde Park. He slowed to a halt, his lungs burning, and swung around, searching for her. The park stretched out in all directions, vast, utterly empty. 'Miss Knightley?' he called. 'Where are you?'

A soft, mocking laugh was his answer.

Adam spun around again. Miss Knightley stood behind him.

He stared at her, panting.

Somewhere, he'd lost his mask and domino. Arabella Knightley still wore hers. She wasn't out of breath. Indeed, she seemed to find his breathlessness amusing.

He took a step towards her.

Arabella Knightley didn't move. She was completely unafraid of him. Beneath the mask her eyes were darkly luminous. The hood had fallen back from her face. Hair curled about her cheeks, as black as midnight.

'You want the truth, Mr St Just?' The softly indented chin rose, challenging him.

'Yes,' he said.

Her lips parted, they shaped themselves to form a word—

* * *

Adam jerked awake. His heart was pounding as loudly as if he'd run halfway across Mayfair. He knew, with absolute certainty, what Arabella Knightley had been about to say. He heard her voice as loudly, as clearly, as if she stood beside the bed. *I'm Tom.*

He threw back the covers and sat up, dragging air into his lungs. Gradually his racing pulse slowed. His certainty didn't fade; like his heartbeat, it steadied.

Arabella Knightley was Tom.

'Of course she's not.' His voice was loud in the dark.

Adam pushed out of bed, disgusted with himself, and strode to the window. He shoved the curtains back and stared down at Berkeley Square. He'd run past here in his dream.

It was the dream that made him think she was Tom, her agility and strength, the swiftness with which she'd run, the mask hiding her face. She'd been elusive and mysterious—as elusive and mysterious as Tom.

Adam shook his head. Arabella Knightley was no more a burglar than Grace was. She was a *female,* for heaven's sake. A delicately built female.

But not delicately reared. She'd lived among prostitutes and thieves as a child.

Adam leaned his forehead against the glass. If a female was capable of being Tom, it was Arabella Knightley. Her diminutive stature and air of delicacy were deceptive. In the conservatory her wrist had been slender but strong; she'd broken free of his grip with ease. And in Richmond Park she'd run like a deer, light-footed and swift, chasing after the scattered pieces of paper.

He stared across Berkeley Square until dawn crept over the rooftops. With daylight his certainty should evaporate, as the dream had evaporated.

It didn't.

Arabella Knightley *was* Tom.

Adam closed the curtains and went back to bed.

How was he going to get Miss Knightley to admit she was Tom?

Adam wrestled with that question for several hours, sitting in his study with the pieces of paper—of evidence—spread across his desk. He began a list of reason why she *couldn't* be Tom, and stared at the blank page until the ink had dried on his quill.

Finally he threw the quill down with a muttered oath. The only way to make Arabella Knightley admit the truth was to speak with her.

She wasn't going to come to him; therefore he must go to her.

That was easier said than done, Adam discovered half an hour later. He presented his card to Lady Westcote's butler and waited in the entrance hall while the man trod up the staircase. A minute later the butler returned, to inform him that 'Miss Knightley is not at home to callers, sir.'

Adam gritted his teeth and retreated. He surveyed Lady Westcote's house from across the street, frowning as he examined the doorway through which he had been so politely ejected, with its pilasters and ornate entablature. Miss Knightley's London home was a handsome edifice, built in the classical style and crowned with decorative cornice mouldings. It hadn't passed to the sixth Earl of Westcote; he'd received only the title and the ancestral seat in Somerset. This house, and one in Hertfordshire, had gone to the fifth earl's widow, along with a comfortable jointure; the Westcote fortune had gone to Arabella Knightley.

No, Adam corrected himself. The fortune would go to Miss Knightley on her twenty-fifth birthday. In just over two weeks' time she would become an extremely wealthy young lady.

A town carriage clattered over the cobblestones from the mews. The crest on the door panel, within its widow's lozenge, was easily recognisable.

Adam stepped behind a gas lamp and watched as the door to Lady Westcote's house opened. Miss Knightley and her maid walked down the steps and climbed into the carriage. A liveried footman closed the door and sprang up on the box beside the coachman.

Adam glanced around. Further down the street was a hackney. He hurried towards it.

'Follow that carriage!' he told the jarvey, pointing at the disappearing coach, and he wrenched open the door and scrambled inside.

The hackney started forwards with a lurch.

Kensington Gardens were smaller and more formal than Richmond, but Arabella felt her tension begin to ease as soon as she stepped down from the carriage. She looked at green-brown expanse of The Long Water and the willows with their trailing leaves and inhaled deeply. Never mind the smudge of coal smoke across the sky or the clatter of a hackney drawing up behind them, this was what she needed: greenery, water, peace and quiet.

'Where to?' Polly asked.

'The Dutch Garden,' Arabella said, opening her parasol.

The path was dappled with sunlight and shade. The spell of the gardens settled over her, a spell made of small, ordinary things: a blackbird turning over fallen leaves in its search for worms, the scattering of yellow dandelions across the scythed grass, the song of a thrush above her head. Arabella inhaled deeply again. She refused to think about last night, about Adam St Just's accusation—

'Miss Knightley!'

She swung around, gripping the handle of the parasol tightly. She was conscious of Polly stepping closer to her. 'Mr St Just.' She lifted her chin. 'What are you doing here?'

St Just bowed, a courtly movement. 'I would like to apologise for my behaviour last night.'

Arabella blinked. 'You would?'

'It was—as you rightly pointed out—grossly impertinent of me.'

'Oh.' Her grip on the parasol eased slightly.

'And I apologise for suggesting you're in league with Tom. I've thought the matter through—and I believe I was in error.' St Just stepped closer. He was smiling faintly as he looked at her. It wasn't the hunter's smile he'd worn last night, but something quite different. Something warmer, something almost…appreciative?

Arabella didn't return the smile. She eyed him warily.

'I don't believe you're in league with Tom, Miss Knightley. I believe you *are* Tom.'

Her shock was utter. Every muscle in her face seemed to stiffen. For too long she stared at him, while her heartbeat thumped in her ears, then she uttered a laugh that even to her own ears sounded false. 'Me? Tom? You are absurd, Mr St Just!'

He shook his head. 'I don't believe so, Miss Knightley.'

Arabella tried to pretend outrage, but it was fear that gripped her. 'What a preposterous accusation! Every feeling must be offended!'

St Just nodded, as if in approval. 'I've no intention of revealing your…er, activities, Miss Knightley.'

The warmth in his grey eyes, the warmth in that slight smile, shook her even more off balance. 'What activities?' she snapped. 'Mr St Just, you're being so…so *absurd* I must believe you're in your cups!'

At that, he grinned. 'Well done, Miss Knightley,' he said, and made her another bow. Then his expression became serious. 'I know I'm correct,' he said. 'There's no point in you denying it.' He held her eyes. 'Your face tells me, Miss Knightley. As does your maid's.'

Arabella glanced at Polly. Polly was pale beneath the freckles, her expression stiff and wary, afraid. *Yes, if I look like that, he can indeed be certain.* She bit her lip.

St Just extended his arm to her. 'Shall we walk together, Miss Knightley?'

Arabella reluctantly placed her hand on his sleeve.

'I have no intention of exposing you,' St Just said, as they began to walk in the direction of the Round Pond.

Arabella risked a glance at him.

St Just was looking at her. 'Your secret is safe with me. I give you my word of honour.' His voice was quiet, sincere, with an undertone that sounded like—but couldn't possibly be—admiration.

Arabella swallowed. 'Thank you,' she managed to say.

They strolled for several minutes in silence. Her pleasure in the gardens was gone. She felt like a mechanical doll, an automaton, her legs moving stiffly.

At the junction of two paths, St Just paused. 'I'd like to thank you for the service you did my sister. We're in your debt.'

Arabella glanced at him—and couldn't look away. The expression in his eyes was extremely disconcerting. She moistened her lips. 'I could hardly have left the items in Lady Bicknell's care.'

There, an admission, aloud, of my complicity. She felt a surge of panic, of fear.

'I imagine you could have left them, very easily.' His grey eyes smiled at her. 'And yet you chose not to.'

She looked away from those warm, smiling eyes, and swallowed again.

St Just resumed his strolling pace. The Round Pond came into sight between the trees. 'I applaud your choice of…er, victims, Miss Knightley.'

A response to this praise seemed appropriate. 'Thank you,' Arabella said. Her half-boots crunched lightly on the chipped stone, but it felt as if she walked on quicksand, as if the footing was treacherous. She was tense with dread. The warmth in St Just's eyes reminded her of Lord Dalrymple. She repressed a shudder. Was St Just going to demand something in return for his silence?

Panic rose in her throat. *What does he expect from me?*

'I assume that the proceeds of your activities go to the poor,' St Just said.

'Yes,' Arabella said, staring down at the path.

He stopped and turned to her. 'Miss Knightley, excuse my curiosity, but what do you do with the jewels once you have them?'

She raised her gaze. 'I beg your pardon?'

'What do you do with the jewels? How do you sell them?'

'I take them to a friend who knows a…a fence.' She resolutely didn't look at Polly, standing one pace behind them on the path.

'A friend in the *ton?*'

'No. In Whitechapel.'

She expected disdain, contempt even; instead St Just nodded. 'And then you give the money to charity?'

'I give it to a school.'

'Which school?'

Arabella flushed. 'A school that I…founded.'

His eyebrows rose. He stared at her for a moment, and then said, 'Tell me about your school, Miss Knightley.'

She looked at him doubtfully.

'Please, Miss Knightley. I'd like to know.' He was telling the truth; she saw it in his face, heard it in his voice.

Arabella cleared her throat. She fixed her gaze on the Round Pond. 'Several years ago I founded a school, for girls from the slums.'

'Only girls?'

'Yes.'

'Why?'

'So that they don't have to be prostitutes.'

Adam St Just was silent. Above them, a thrush sang.

'Most of them go into service,' Arabella said, staring at the Round

Pond. 'But once I gain my inheritance, I hope to set up a bakery and some other businesses, as well as more schools.'

She glanced at him. He was staring at her. The expression on his face was unreadable. 'That's what I do with the money, Mr St Just.'

He stared at her for several more seconds, his gaze so intent, so direct, that it almost made her step back a pace. It felt as if he was looking inside her. 'Does your grandmother know?'

Arabella almost laughed. 'No.'

He accepted this with a nod. The intensity of his stare didn't waver. 'Where's the school?'

'In Swanley.'

His eyebrows rose. 'So far from town? You go out there?'

'My friend…he goes in my stead, or sometimes…my maid goes.'

St Just glanced at Polly, and then returned his attention to her. 'How do you find the girls for your school? Do you go into the slums yourself?'

'My friend chooses them for me.'

'A big man,' he said. 'With fair hair and a broken nose.'

Arabella looked at him warily. 'Yes.'

St Just answered her unspoken question. 'The landlady at Eliza's boarding house described him to me.'

Arabella returned her attention to the pond. There seemed to be nothing more to say.

'Miss Knightley, may I visit your school?'

The question was entirely unexpected. Her gaze flew to him. 'The school? Why?'

'I'm a wealthy man, Miss Knightley. Your school sounds like something I should like to invest in.'

'Invest?' she said doubtfully. 'But there's no profit—'

'In terms of money, no. But in terms of people, I expect your school turns a great profit.'

Arabella stared at him in astonishment.

'May I visit it?'

Arabella glanced at Polly. *Do I trust him?* Polly looked equally as baffled. She raised her shoulders in a barely perceptible shrug.

Arabella bit her lip, uncertain. 'I've never visited it myself.'

'Never?' Astonishment was visible on his face.

'How can I? It's further out of London than Richmond. I'd need the best part of a day, and my grandmother—'

St Just understood. 'Hard to keep such a visit a secret from her.'

'Yes.'

He frowned slightly. 'But if you've never seen the school, how do you know everything is in order?'

'Harry takes care of that for me.'

'Harry?'

'Harry Higgs. My friend.'

His eyes narrowed slightly. 'The friend who knows a fence?'

'Yes.'

His frown deepened. 'You must trust this Harry Higgs a great deal.'

'I do.'

He looked at her for a moment, still frowning. 'May I meet Mr Higgs?'

Arabella glanced at Polly again, and received another shrug.

She looked back at St Just, studying his face. The grey eyes met hers steadily. He seemed to be entirely in earnest.

Arabella made her decision. 'Very well,' she said, and had the sensation that she'd just plunged off a cliff. Trusting Adam St Just seemed a terribly reckless thing to do. 'We can go now, if you have the time.'

He appeared startled. 'Now?'

'Yes.' *Because otherwise I might lose my courage.*

St Just stepped fastidiously over the open gutter in Rosemary Lane. 'Mr Higgs lives here?'

'No,' Arabella said. 'This is where we change our clothes.'

'Change them?' He raised his eyebrows. 'Is that necessary?'

'You may venture into the slums wearing that—' she gestured at his superbly cut coat of olive green superfine and the glossy hessians with their golden tassels '—but I wouldn't recommend it.'

St Just looked down at himself. 'You think it would be foolish?'

'I think it would be dangerous,' she said frankly.

He glanced sharply at her, and then nodded. 'Very well. A change of clothing, then.'

Arabella watched his face as they stepped into the old-clothes shop, with its racks of used clothing and the dozens of coats hanging from hooks screwed into the ceiling. The smell was nauseating, as if a hundred unwashed people were crammed inside. She thought St Just flinched slightly as he inhaled. His face stiffened. *He's holding his breath.*

St Just glanced at her and swallowed. 'Fragrant.'

The comment was so unexpected that she almost laughed aloud.

Polly entered the shop last and closed the door. 'Sally!' she called. 'It's us.'

Sally, a stout woman missing most of her teeth, squinted at St Just in astonishment.

'This is a friend of mine,' Arabella said. 'He's coming with us today and needs a change of clothes.'

Sally's sparse eyebrows rose as she examined St Just from head to toe. Her gaze lingered on the hat of felted beaver fur with its tall crown and slender brim, the exquisitely tied neck cloth, the ebony-topped cane.

'I want him to look disreputable.'

'Disrepu'ble?' Sally went off into a cackle of laughter. 'He'll never be disrepu'ble, that one.'

'Do your best, Sally,' Arabella said, biting back a grin at the expression on St Just's face.

She and Polly changed quickly in the back room, while Sally selected clothes for Adam St Just. When they emerged he was standing, waiting, a bundle of clothing in his arms and a pair of worn boots held in one hand. He didn't appear to have been offended by Sally; he looked bemused, but not affronted.

'A han'some one, he is,' Sally said once St Just had entered the back room, digging Arabella in the ribs with her elbow.

Ten minutes later St Just emerged. His appearance was entirely altered. He wore trousers that were ragged, frayed, patched, and stained—as well as too wide in the leg and several inches too short. His shirt was of coarse, discoloured cotton; an overlarge and threadbare Benjamin coat with put-out elbows and shiny cuffs hid most of it. A filthy muffler, tied around his neck, and the pair of battered boots with splitting seams completed the ensemble.

Arabella covered her mouth with a hand.

St Just had seen her amusement. His lips twisted wryly. 'Am I disreputable enough?'

Arabella cleared her throat and turned to Polly. 'What do you think?'

'He needs a hat.'

Sally produced one with a low and lopsided crown. The wide brim was visibly greasy.

St Just accepted the hat with a grimace of distaste. He placed it gingerly on his head.

Arabella bit her lip. She felt a pang of sympathy for him—but also a spurt of mirth. Was it wrong of her to find his discomfort so amusing? *Probably.*

She observed him critically. He looked as rough as it was possible for a gentleman to look, but even so… 'Slouch,' she said.

St Just rounded his shoulders.

Arabella nodded. 'And now, if you could walk a little…'

St Just obliged, taking a turn about the shop. Coats dangled about his ears, in danger of swiping the shabby hat from his head. Despite the hunched shoulders, he still moved like a gentleman.

Arabella exchanged a glance with Polly.

'Different boots,' Polly said firmly. *'Much* bigger.'

Wearing boots that were several sizes too large, St Just's walk became shambling and graceless. *Clump, clump, clump* he went down the narrow aisle.

'Perfect!' Arabella said.

His glance was wry. 'I'm glad you approve, madam.'

They left through the back door, stepping out into the dank, noisome alleyway behind the shop. A rat scuttled into the shadows.

'Walk between us,' Arabella said. 'And don't speak to anyone.'

They walked quickly, hurrying through the warren of streets, skirting piles of refuse and splashing through dirty puddles. The noises of the slums filled her ears: shouts, crying children, yelping dogs—and at one point, a lullaby sung by a young woman on a doorstep, holding a baby wrapped in a shawl.

Smells mingled in her nostrils, the fragrance—to use St Just's word— of tanneries and breweries, foundries and slaughterhouses, the fetid odours rising from the piles of refuse, the whiff of open gutters.

Miss Smell O'Gutters, Arabella thought, glancing at St Just.

There was no longer any wryness in his expression. His face, below the greasy brim of his hat, was grim and his arm under her hand was tense.

In Berner Street, Polly knocked on the door of Harry's house.

'Is this where you used to live, Miss Knightley?' St Just asked in a low voice as they waited on the doorstep.

'No. We were in one of the rookeries.' She glanced at him. 'Much worse than this.'

St Just looked around at the soot-stained brick buildings, the boarded-over windows and cracked panes of glass, the rivulet of filthy water running down the middle of the street. His mouth tightened, but he said nothing.

The door opened. Harry stood there, big and fair-haired and broken-nosed, precisely as St Just had described him. 'Pol!' His welcoming smile vanished. 'Who's this?'

'This is Mr St Just,' Arabella said.

'St Just?' Harry subjected Adam St Just to a thorough scrutiny. Arabella had no doubt that he saw the smoothly shaved jaw and the mani-cured hands. 'One o' the nobs?'

'Er, yes.' She wondered if St Just had ever heard himself addressed in quite that way before. 'He knows about Tom.'

Harry glanced sharply at her. 'Told 'im, did you?' She read disapproval in his face, heard it in his voice.

Arabella shook her head. 'He guessed.'

Harry's attention swung sharply back to St Just. 'Did 'e now?'

'May we come in? Mr St Just is interested in the school. He says he would like to contribute.'

Harry's eyes narrowed. 'He sez, does 'e?'

St Just spoke for himself, 'I am quite serious, Mr Higgs.'

The two men matched stares for a long moment, taking measure of each other. Harry was apparently satisfied with what he saw, for he gave a short nod and stepped back from the doorway.

They talked for more than an hour, in the small parlour with its lumpy sofa and scarred wooden furniture. Tess joined them, blushing prettily when St Just rose and bowed to her.

If St Just was uncomfortable in the company of persons of such low class, he hid it well. He asked a lot of questions about the school, and listened intently to the answers. There was no condescension in his manner, no disdain, no contempt. He looked as at ease as if he sat on a giltwood chair surrounded by peers of the realm.

At the end of the visit, Harry and St Just shook hands. It wasn't a polite touch of fingers, but a longer grip, like that between equals.

Arabella blinked, astonished. *They like each other.*

It was an extremely disconcerting realisation.

As before, Adam walked between them, Miss Knightley on his left, her maid on his right. No, not her maid—her friend, Polly. He looked around as they made their way back through Whitechapel. His gaze slid over men lounging in doorways and dirty children playing in the gutters—and a young woman who was clearly a prostitute. Adam observed her obliquely. Her face had been pretty once, now it was ravaged. Her hair was as golden as Grace's. He heard Miss Knightley's voice in his ears: *Better, or merely luckier?*

He looked away.

This was no place for anyone; and most certainly no place for a child—and yet Arabella Knightley had been a child here. The sights, smells, and sounds that assaulted his senses—the piles of rotting refuse, the foul language, the drunkenness, the rats feeding openly in the gutters—were what she'd grown up with. She'd run through these filthy streets, breathed these noisome smells, seen the depths to which people could descend—and instead of turning her back on it, she'd chosen to come back, to help.

His admiration for her, his respect, was beyond words. She was remarkable.

To his right, Adam heard language that made him blanch. He glanced involuntarily at Miss Knightley. She seemed utterly unperturbed. Dressed in the ragged dress and dirty apron, with her sable hair hidden beneath a shawl, she was indistinguishable from the other women on these streets. If she wanted to, she could vanish, blending into the people around them. He'd never find her again.

The thought made alarm surge inside him. He reached for her hand and tucked it firmly into the crook of his arm.

She glanced up at him, her eyebrows raised slightly in enquiry. 'Mr St Just?'

Adam shook his head, and tensed as half-a-dozen boys barrelled out of an alleyway ahead of them. He stepped in front of Miss Knightley, shielding her as the boys jostled past, shouting to one another.

'Oi!' Polly said indignantly, aiming a kick at one of them. 'Clear orf!'

Miss Knightley came out from behind him. 'Mr St Just, you don't have to…to *protect* me.' Her expression was amused.

Yes, I do. It was instinct; he didn't have a choice. Adam stared at her, at the dark eyes and the fine-boned face, and was shaken by the fierceness of his need to keep her safe.

'They're just boys,' Miss Knightley said. 'There's no harm in them.'

'Unless you don't mind your pocket being picked,' Polly said darkly.

Miss Knightley shrugged and smiled. She began walking again.

Adam swallowed. *I have to protect her.* He strode after Miss Knightley, took her hand again and placed it firmly on his arm.

She glanced at him. He clearly saw her amusement.

Adam ignored it. He offered his other arm to Polly.

They stepped over a particularly foul gutter. The stench made him almost gag. How had Arabella Knightley survived this? For that matter, how had Harry Higgs and his wife survived it? How could anyone come from this hell on earth and not be as mean-spirited, as crude, as their surroundings?

And yet Harry Higgs—who'd never left these slums—was an admirable man: intelligent, forthright and, in his own way, honest.

Judge a person by *who* they are, not *what* they are. It was the lesson Miss Knightley had been teaching him the past few weeks. Harry, with his execrable English, was as worthy of respect—if not more worthy—than any member of the *ton*.

Adam looked at Arabella Knightley again, at her dark lashes, the delicate indentation in her chin. His father had been wrong six years ago. *You should have been urging me to marry her, Father. She's more a prize than any duke's daughter.*

Adam sat in the hackney, with Miss Knightley—now dressed in her figured muslin gown and pretty chip bonnet—and her maid opposite. His hair itched and his skin felt as if tiny creatures crawled over it. The odour of the used clothes he'd worn lingered around him. He wanted—most urgently—to bathe.

The emotion rising in him as the hackney rattled through the more genteel parts of London was one he'd never experienced before. Adam let his gaze rest on Arabella Knightley. What he felt for her was more than mere desire, more than respect and admiration—although all three of those things were present. It wasn't a *tendre,* but something much more full-bodied, richer, deeper.

He'd been searching for a bride; he'd found her. The woman he wanted to marry—was *going* to marry—was seated across from him in this shabby hackney. She was beautiful, but more than that she was strong and determined, clever, resourceful, intelligent. In all respects, an exceptional person.

He heard his own voice of six years ago—*Marry Arabella Knightley? Certainly, if one wishes to live with the smell of the gutter*—and grimaced. What a fool he'd been, then and a thousand times since: every time he'd looked down his nose at her, every time he'd disdained her upbringing.

He glanced at the signet ring on his right hand. *Optimus Superbia.* Noble pride.

Blind foolishness, more like.

Adam returned his gaze to Arabella Knightley. Those dark eyes were looking at him. He thought he saw a faint question in them, as if he puzzled her.

Adam cleared his throat. 'Miss Knightley, I...'

He became aware that Polly Highsmith was also observing him. The words dried on his tongue.

'Yes?'

He abandoned his declaration of love and embarked on a different subject. 'Er...you'll stop being Tom, won't you?'

'Stop?'

'Yes.' He might admire Tom's choice of victims and the punishment he meted out—but the risks Miss Knightley took were appalling. 'If you're caught—'

'I'll be leaving London when I come into my inheritance. And when I leave, so does Tom.'

'Leave?' It was an ominous word. He felt a twinge of alarm. 'Leave for ever?'

'That's my intention.'

'But…why?'

'Because I like the *ton* as much as the *ton* likes me,' she said drily. In other words, not at all.

'But…Mr Higgs and the school—'

'I shall, of course, return to Whitechapel if the need arises.'

He heard her unspoken words: *But not Belgravia. Not Mayfair.*

Adam was aware of a sudden sense of urgency. When did she come into her inheritance? In just over two weeks. 'Miss Knightley—'

The hackney came to a halt. He looked out the window. To his astonishment, they were already at Kensington Gardens. It seemed impossible that they'd travelled from a filthy slum to the well-kept gardens of a palace in so short a time.

He handed Miss Knightley down from the hackney. 'You wished to ask me something further, Mr St Just?' she said, once they were standing beside the driveway.

Will you marry me?

Adam felt a surge of recklessness. 'Yes.' He glanced at Polly. 'In private, if I may?'

Arabella Knightley's eyebrows arched in faint surprise. 'Certainly.' She turned to her friend. 'Polly, can you give us a moment, please?'

Polly stepped several paces away and turned so that she faced away from them; a maid, now, protecting her mistress's reputation. Out of earshot, but only just.

His mouth was dry, his pulse suddenly beating twice as fast as normal. He was a St Just, grandson of a duke, related to half the noble houses in England, wealthy beyond most people's dreams—but he was aware that to Arabella Knightley his wealth and his heritage meant nothing.

She might very well refuse me.

Adam swallowed, gripped his cane tightly, and took the plunge. 'Miss Knightley, I wonder whether you would do me the honour of becoming my wife.'

Arabella Knightley blinked. He saw her shock: the widening of her eyes, the paling of her cheeks. 'If this is a jest, Mr St Just—'

'No jest,' he said. 'I've never been more serious.'

She shook her head, her eyes still wide, her lips still slightly parted.

'I realise that this comes as a surprise to you, given my…er, comment on this subject six years ago.' Adam flushed. 'But I'd like to assure you of my admiration and respect for you, and…er, my affection.'

Arabella Knightley blinked again. 'You want to marry *me?*'

'Yes,' Adam said, with complete and utter certainty.

She stared at him. He couldn't tell what she was thinking; her face was expressionless, her dark eyes inscrutable. Finally she moistened her lips. 'Mr St Just, thank you for your…most kind offer, but I—'

A town coach drew up alongside them. The bay horses, the sparkling equipage, the coachman and liveried footman, were familiar; Adam didn't need to look at the coat of arms on the door.

'Mr St Just,' Arabella Knightley said, glancing at the carriage. 'I can't—'

She's going to refuse.

'You needn't give me an answer now,' Adam said hurriedly. 'But please…think about it.'

She looked at him for a long moment, a puzzled crease on her brow. 'Thank you, Mr St Just. I shall.'

Adam stepped back a pace and bowed. He watched as the footman handed Arabella Knightley into the coach. Polly climbed in after her.

The door closed. The carriage drove away.

Chapter Thirteen

The first thing Arabella did when she got home was bathe. She sat in a bath of steaming water scented with orange blossom and scrubbed the smell of the slums off her skin.

Usually a bath relaxed her; today it didn't. She stepped out of the water as agitated as she'd been when she stepped in.

Her thoughts were in turmoil as she dried herself. St Just was the last man—absolutely the *last*—she'd ever thought would offer for her.

Arabella twisted the towel in her hands. *What do I do?*

His offer was astonishingly flattering. Adam St Just, of all people. One of the great prizes on the Marriage Mart, a man who'd had caps past counting set at him… *And he chooses me?*

Why?

He'd said that he admired her, that he respected her, that he had affection for her. She knew what he meant by that last word: affection. St Just didn't leer at her like Lord Dalrymple did, but she recognised the warmth in his eyes. He wanted her, as a man wants a woman.

Arabella shuddered.

'Cold?' Polly asked. 'Here, stand in front of the fire.'

Arabella obeyed. She hugged the towel around her and stared into the flames. Her instinctive response to St Just's offer had been *no*—it still was. Because if she married him, she'd have to share his bed.

Arabella shuddered again.

She dressed automatically in clothes Polly had chosen for her:

chemise, stays, petticoat, stockings, gown. Polly arranged her hair. 'What do you think?' she asked when she'd finished.

Arabella stared at herself in the mirror without seeing anything. She had no idea what colour her gown was or what style her hair was dressed in. 'Lovely,' she said, while at the same time asking herself, *What should I do?*

Her grandmother was hosting a card party, as she did twice a month. Arabella sat through an excruciatingly long dinner without hearing a word that was spoken around the table.

She stared at the grease glistening on the roasted partridges, at the sugar crystals scattering the pastries, at the violets wilting on the syllabub, and asked herself the same question, over and over: *What should I do?*

She chewed, not tasting the food, and laid down her fork at the end of the meal without the faintest idea of what she'd eaten.

They sat down to tables of silver-loo, whist, and rouge-et-noir in the drawing room. Arabella partnered her grandmother at one of the whist tables, but was too distracted to concentrate fully on the cards.

'I must say, Arabella,' her grandmother after they'd been soundly beaten, 'that you're playing remarkably ill tonight!'

Arabella bit her lip. 'Forgive me, Grandmother. I…I have a headache.'

Lady Westcote's expression softened slightly. 'A headache?'

Arabella nodded. 'With your permission, may I retire?'

'Of course, my dear.'

Arabella curtsied, dutifully kissed her grandmother's cheek and left the drawing room.

As she climbed the stairs, she decided to approach her decision in a *rational* manner. Accordingly, once she'd gained the peace and quiet of her bedchamber, she sat at her writing desk. Dipping her quill in ink, she wrote at the top of a blank piece of paper: *For.* And at the top of a second sheet: *Against.*

She tackled *Against* first.

The first item was easy: *Arrogant,* Arabella wrote neatly. Then she stared at the word. Was Adam St Just really arrogant?

She chewed her lower lip. There'd been no arrogance in him today when he'd spoken with Harry and Tess, no arrogance when he'd made his astonishing offer of marriage.

Adam St Just had a way of looking down at people, but was that due to arrogance, or a combination of height and a patrician nose?

Finally, after staring at the word *Arrogant* for several minutes, Arabella dipped her quill in the ink pot again and crossed it out.

She stared irresolutely at the *Against* list. What else could she put down? His statement all those years ago about the smell of gutters? It seemed churlish to, after he'd apologised.

She gnawed on her lower lip. Adam St Just had only articulated what everyone else in the *ton* had been thinking—and still thought.

What a fool he'd look if she accepted his offer. How people would laugh at him!

That decided it; she wouldn't put it on the list.

But that left the *Against* list with nothing on it.

Arabella frowned and rubbed her forehead, and turned to the sheet headed *For.* She would go back to *Against* later.

This list was slightly easier. Her quill scratched lightly across the paper.

He did apologise. Even though it had taken him six years to do so.

Next on the list was: *He rescued me from Dalrymple.*

And then: *He helped Eliza.*

And: *He wants to help with the school.*

Philanthropy was a new venture for Adam St Just, surely? Although his ex-mistress, Lady Mary Vane, ran a charity for indigent soldiers' widows. Presumably he contributed to that?

Ah, that was something for the *Against* list. *In the habit of keeping a mistress,* Arabella wrote. That was a serious entry against him.

She tapped the quill against her chin. St Just chose his mistresses from the *ton,* not the *demi-monde.* Did such fastidiousness make his liaisons better or worse?

It was an unanswerable question.

Arabella chewed thoughtfully on her lower lip. What else had St Just done that could go on the *For* list, or the *Against?*

Memory came: at the Mallorys' ball, after he'd cut Sir Arnold Gorrie, they had almost laughed together.

Sense of humour, she wrote on the *For* list.

And later that evening she'd learned of his propensity to gamble—another item for the *Against* list. *A gambler,* she wrote firmly.

Turning back to the *For* list, she tapped the quill against her chin again, before writing: *Clever.* Adam St Just had worked out Tom's identity, something she hadn't thought anyone could do. He was more intelligent than she'd given him credit for.

What else? There were a number of other things that could go on the *For* list—his splendid physique, his skill on horseback, the lack of ostentation in his dress, his handsome face—but they could all be summarised in one short phrase.

Arabella bit her lip. At the bottom of both lists she wrote: *I find him attractive.*

She laid down her quill and stared at the lists. That last reason was the most important one of all. Being attracted to him was dangerous; it could tempt her into making a terrible mistake.

She might like Adam St Just's smile, might feel flushed and breathless when he waltzed with her, but the thought of being touched intimately by him, of sharing his bed, was—

Arabella shuddered. She couldn't marry him, simply *could not.*

Therefore, she had to refuse his offer.

She screwed up the pieces of paper and walked over to the fireplace. The lists burned quickly. She watched as they crumbled into ashes. Gone.

Arabella bit her lip, feeling ridiculously close to tears. She turned away from the fireplace.

Only one question now remained: How to refuse St Just's offer without hurting him?

Her chance came the following morning, as she was riding in Hyde Park. On her third circuit, she saw Adam St Just ahead of her, astride his grey gelding.

St Just was easily as handsome as his mount: the ease with which he controlled the horse, the strong shoulders, the muscled length of his thighs—

Arabella averted her eyes. 'Well, Merrylegs…shall we do this?'

The mare tossed her head and snorted. Arabella took that as a *yes.* She blew out an unsteady breath. 'Very well. Let's give him his answer.'

In less than a minute she was alongside St Just. He slowed once he saw her; the great gelding dropped back to a trot, and then a walk.

'Mr St Just.' Arabella inclined her head at him. 'I'd hoped to meet you here.' She took a deep breath and launched into the speech she'd prepared: 'I would like to thank you for your extremely flattering offer, but I must tell you that...that I'm not a suitable wife for you.'

His eyebrows rose. 'Surely I must be the judge of that?' he said, with a slight smile.

The smile was disconcerting. Arabella clutched the reins more tightly. 'Six years ago I put loaded dice in Lord Crowe's pocket. Two of them. Uphills.'

The smile froze on St Just's face.

'When he pulled out his handkerchief, they fell on the floor. I believe you were witness to the event. It happened at White's.'

St Just made no reply. The smile had vanished.

'Lord Crowe was ruined. Society turned its back on him. Two months later he killed himself.' Guilt—and its accompanying nausea—rose in her throat. She swallowed. 'I ruined Lord Crowe, Mr St Just. One might even say I killed him. I think we both agree that I'm not a fitting bride for you.'

Adam St Just made no reply. He stared at her, his face utterly blank. There was no smile in those grey eyes; instead she saw condemnation.

Arabella bit her lip. She inclined her head. 'Good day, Mr St Just.'

Arabella was shaking as she changed from her riding habit into a cambric dress. Absurdly, she found herself wanting to cry.

The shaking and tearfulness were symptoms of relief, she told herself as she went downstairs to eat luncheon with her grandmother. That she was also feeling a pang of regret was natural; St Just's proposal had been extremely flattering. Any lady must regret refusing such an offer.

Her spirits were low as she picked at her plate of cold meats.

'Do you still have the headache, my dear?' her grandmother asked.

Arabella looked up blankly. For a moment she had no idea what her grandmother was talking about; then she remembered. 'No.'

'Did you use Hungary Water? Very beneficial, I find. A dab at the temples, or perhaps a handkerchief soaked...'

Arabella stopped listening. She pushed her food around the plate. She had refused St Just's offer in a manner calculated to cause him the least hurt—but his opinion of her must now be abysmal. Tears pricked her eyes. She blinked them fiercely away.

After luncheon, she found herself unable to concentrate on her needlework or the book she was reading. Even the pianoforte and a piece by Beethoven—a combination she usually found easy to lose herself in— failed to hold her attention. Finally she asked her grandmother for permission to visit the British Museum.

'Again?' Lady Westcote asked.

'There's a horse's head I wish to sketch.'

Her grandmother's face softened into a smile. 'How like your father you are.'

Arabella bit her lip and stared down at the carpet, a particularly fine Kidderminster in blue and red.

The horse's head was one of the marbles brought to England by Lord Elgin. It had staring eyes, flared nostrils and broken ears. A war horse, Arabella decided, opening her sketchbook and extracting a pencil from her reticule.

'Miss Knightley.'

Her heart gave a frightened little skip. She dropped the pencil. 'Mr St Just! What…what are you doing here?'

'I followed you.'

'Followed me?' She glanced around for Polly and found her by the window, studying horsemen galloping across a frieze. 'Why?'

'Because I want to talk with you. That tale you told me this morning— was it true?'

Arabella swallowed. 'Yes.'

A frown creased between St Just's eyebrows. 'Why did you place those dice in Lord Crowe's pocket?'

'I thought that was obvious. To ruin him.'

'But *why?*'

'Does the reason matter?' Arabella asked, holding her sketchbook tightly. 'I was responsible for Lord Crowe's ruin, and his death. Isn't that enough?'

His frown deepened. 'I want to know why.'

Arabella looked at the pencil lying on the floor. She bit her lip.

'As Tom, I've always approved of your victims. So I want to know...why Lord Crowe? Why so harsh a punishment?'

Memory came rushing back: her mother's cries rang in her ears, the smell of blood filled her nostrils.

'Crowe was one of your mother's...protectors, wasn't he? After your father's death.' St Just's voice was low. 'What did he do, Miss Knightley?'

Arabella cleared her throat. 'I don't want to talk about it.'

'Miss Knightley, you can hardly tell me that you ruined Lord Crowe and then refuse to tell me why!'

Yes, I can. She blinked back tears.

'I should inform you, Miss Knightley,' St Just said in an affable voice, 'that I'm a stubborn man. If you don't tell me today, then I shall ask the same question of you tomorrow, and the day after that. It will be easier for us both if you tell me now.'

His hand cupped her elbow, drawing her towards a window embrasure. Arabella glanced around for Polly. She was still studying the horsemen.

St Just released her elbow. He removed the sketchbook from her grasp and placed it on the windowsill. 'Now, Miss Knightley—tell me. What did Crowe do?'

The undertone of kindness in his low voice brought more tears to her eyes. Arabella groped in her reticule for a handkerchief. St Just handed her his own, a neatly folded square of white linen. 'I beg your pardon—'

'I am perfectly fine,' Arabella said, annoyed with herself. She wiped her eyes and blew her nose defiantly. She found it impossible, though, to look him in the face. She folded the handkerchief. 'Lord Crowe was the last of my mother's protectors—as you called it. He...had a very violent temper. My mother was afraid of him, but...he was generous with his gifts. She hoped to save enough money to buy a house, so...we stayed.'

'And?' St Just prompted, after she'd been silent for several seconds.

Arabella gripped the handkerchief tightly. 'And one day he hurt her. Very badly.'

'Why?'

Arabella shuddered. 'Because...he touched me.'

She wasn't looking at Adam St Just, but she was aware of him stiffening. 'He *what?*'

She glanced at him fleetingly; his face was as grim as his voice.

'He came early to my mother's rooms and…and he was drunk, and my mother wasn't ready…and—' She could still feel Lord Crowe's clumsy caress, still smell the brandy on his breath. 'My mother came in and told him to take his hands off me and…he lost his temper.'

'You were right to punish him!' St Just said. 'By God, if Crowe was still alive—'

Arabella glanced at him again. 'I didn't punish Lord Crowe for touching me; I punished him for what he did to my mother.'

St Just observed her for several seconds. 'What did he do?'

She looked down at the handkerchief. 'He beat her and kicked her—' The smell of blood was in her nostrils, nauseating. 'There was so much blood. I thought she was dead.' Arabella no longer saw the handkerchief; instead she saw her mother's face: broken, unrecognisable. 'She lost a lot of her teeth. Her arm was broken and her ribs, and…she was blind in one eye afterwards.'

'Dear God,' St Just said, half under his breath. 'But she recovered?'

Arabella lifted one shoulder in a shrug. 'She was half-senseless for weeks. It took months before she was well enough to get out of bed, and by that time her savings were gone—' She turned the handkerchief over in her fingers. 'That was my fault. I paid too much for everything. I thought— My mother's maid, the woman Crowe had hired for her, took us in. She told me how much it cost for the room, how much for the doctor each time he came and I … I believed her. I gave most of Mother's jewellery to her and all of the guineas. Everything she'd saved—' She stopped and took a shallow breath, squeezing her eyes shut against useless tears.

'How old were you?'

'Eight.'

'Your mother couldn't have blamed you,' St Just said softly.

Arabella opened her eyes. She looked down at the handkerchief. 'No, but…her beauty was the only thing my mother had to sell. Without it…'

'She could no longer be a rich man's mistress.'

Arabella nodded. *Only a poor man's prostitute.*

'I understand why you ruined Crowe.' St Just's hands clenched. 'It's well he's dead, for I'd have to kill him myself!'

She looked at him. 'No, you wouldn't. It's a terrible thing to have a death on your conscience.'

His hands unclenched. The fierceness of his brow, the hardness of his mouth, softened. For several long seconds he studied her face. 'Do you regret it?' he asked finally, quietly.

Arabella looked away from that compassion. She cleared her throat. 'Yes.'

'Then I wish you had let me kill him.' St Just reached a hand towards her, and checked the motion as a governess shepherding two girls entered the room. He stepped back a pace. 'I think we need to talk further,' he said, picking up the sketchbook. 'Shall we go to Kensington Gardens?'

'What?' she said, startled. 'Now?'

'We can talk here, if you wish. Personally, I'd prefer a little more privacy.'

Talk? Arabella bit her lip. *But what if he proposes again?*

If he did, she'd have to refuse him. She'd have to tell him, to his face, that she didn't want to marry him—however much she shrank from doing it.

Arabella took a deep breath. 'Very well,' she said, clutching the handkerchief tightly. 'Kensington Gardens.'

Chapter Fourteen

They walked along one of the more wooded paths. Polly was several paces behind—within sight, but not within hearing. Arabella hoped her nervousness wasn't apparent. There were a hundred places she would rather be right now.

Coward, she castigated herself.

'Miss Knightley, I should like to know why you told me about Lord Crowe this morning—and why you chose to portray yourself in such a villainous light.' St Just's pace was strolling, yet she thought he wasn't quite as at ease as he pretended.

Was he nervous too?

Arabella had a sudden flash of insight. *Of course he's nervous.* If St Just still wanted to marry her, he'd be dreading a refusal; and if he'd changed his mind, if he wanted *not* to marry her, he'd be dreading an acceptance.

'Why did you tell me, Miss Knightley?'

She took a deep breath and blurted out the truth: 'Because I thought it would make you withdraw your offer.'

St Just glanced at her. 'I thought that must be your reason. But I confess, I don't understand *why.* If you don't wish to marry me, then you may tell me. I promise you I shan't enact a Cheltenham tragedy.'

'I was hoping to spare you from…from any hurt,' she said, and felt a blush rise in her cheeks.

She had the impression that St Just relaxed slightly, as if an underlying tension eased. 'So you chose to make me angry with you instead?'

'Yes.' She looked away from those keen grey eyes. Her gloves were fastened at the wrist with tiny buttons. She studied them. Mother-of-pearl, glinting in the sunlight.

'May I ask why you wish me to withdraw my offer?'

'Because…because I think we're not compatible,' Arabella said, studying the buttons intently.

'You do?'

'Yes,' she said firmly. 'For a number of reasons.'

'Very well,' St Just said in an agreeable tone. 'Let's discuss these reasons.'

'Discuss them?' She glanced at him.

'I realise, Miss Knightley, that this is a conversation you had hoped to avoid.' Amusement glinted briefly in his eyes, and then vanished. 'But I would be grateful if you could bring yourself to discuss the reasons you believe make us incompatible.'

Arabella bit her lip.

'For my own part, there are a couple of…er, things, that I would like to discuss with you myself.'

'There are?'

He nodded, and then opened his hand to her. 'Please, you first, Miss Knightley.'

Arabella took firm grip of her reticule. She transferred her gaze from St Just to the path on which they walked, the border of grass, the over-shading trees. 'By your own confession you're a gambler, Mr St Just, and I'm very sorry, but I couldn't bring myself to marry a gambler.'

St Just was silent.

'The money, you see,' she explained, glancing at him. 'I know you can afford it, but when I think of the *waste,* when I think of what a difference it could make to people's lives—'

He grimaced wryly. 'You need have no fears on that score, Miss Knightley. You've successfully destroyed any pleasure I had in gambling.'

Arabella stared at him. 'I have?'

'Yes.' St Just looked at her, his expression one of exasperation tinged with humour. 'I used to *enjoy* gambling, you know.'

Arabella bit her lip.

'Thanks to your…er, remarks, at the Mallorys' ball, I no longer do. In fact, I still have three hundred and sixty-four guineas to give away.'

His brow creased slightly, as if he'd had a sudden thought. 'Have you ever considered a school for boys from the slums?'

'No,' Arabella said. 'I'm more concerned with the plight of girls. But perhaps you'd like to start one?'

St Just looked at her for a long moment, his expression startled, and then gave a sudden smile. 'Perhaps I shall.'

Adam St Just was a very handsome man when he smiled like that, his eyes creasing at the corners. Arabella returned her attention to the path. She cleared her throat.

'You had another reason to believe us incompatible, Miss Knightley?'

'Er…yes.' She could see the *Against* list in her mind's eye. She hesitated, unsure of what words to use. Bluntness seemed best. 'Your habit of keeping mistresses.'

St Just's stride seemed to falter. 'My what?'

Arabella looked at him. 'Your habit of keeping mistresses,' she said firmly.

'How did you…? I thought I was very discreet!'

'You are.'

'Then how…?' His eyebrows drew together. 'Did someone tell you?'

Arabella shook her head. 'I'm by nature an observer. I see a lot of things people would like to keep hidden.'

He stared at her, his expression taken aback. After a moment he said stiffly, 'My relationship with Lady Mary is over.'

'I'm aware of that. But it is your habit to have a mistress, and I couldn't tolerate that in a husband.'

'Good,' he said drily, 'because I couldn't tolerate it in a wife!'

'The situations aren't the same. It's quite accepted for a man—'

'I give you my word of honour, Miss Knightley,' St Just said, holding her gaze, 'that if we marry I'll be faithful to you. And I would expect the same undertaking from you!'

Arabella looked at him doubtfully. He radiated sincerity, but… 'It's hard to break the habit of a lifetime, Mr St Just.'

'Hardly a lifetime,' he said, a hint of humour coming into his voice. 'When I was in my boyhood, I don't believe I had a mistress. Although there was a serving maid at Eton, with whom I was quite besotted…' His voice became musing. 'I wonder what became of her?'

He was teasing her. Arabella flushed. 'The habit of your adult years—'

'Miss Knightley,' St Just said, all humour falling away from him. 'My habit as an *unmarried* man has been to have a mistress; my habit as a *married* man will be quite different! That, you may be quite certain of.'

'Oh,' Arabella said, taken aback by the vehemence of his voice, his expression.

Adam St Just held her eyes for a long moment, and then nodded, as if satisfied she'd understood him. 'Do you have any more reasons?'

The last item on the *Against* list had been: *I find him attractive.* Arabella found herself unable to articulate this. 'Er…you had some things you wished to discuss?' she said politely.

'That was the last of your reasons?'

'Er…no. But I should like to discuss yours first.'

Adam St Just looked at her thoughtfully for several seconds, and then said, 'Very well. The first thing is a condition I must place upon our marriage.'

A condition? That sounded ominous.

'If you accept my offer, then you must cease to be Tom. As of today.'

Arabella blinked. 'Oh.'

'Much as I…er, admire your career as Tom, I'm appalled by the risks you've taken. As my wife, I couldn't allow you to take such risks.'

'I intend to retire Tom upon my twenty-fifth birthday—'

St Just shook his head. 'You'd have to retire him now.'

'But—it's less than three weeks away! What if I see something—'

'It must be now, Miss Knightley.' His expression was stern. 'Three weeks is ample time for disaster to happen.'

Arabella set her chin stubbornly.

'Miss Knightley, if anything should happen—' Adam St Just swallowed and looked away. 'By your own admission, you intend to retire Tom. What is three weeks?'

Three weeks was nothing. But even so, the *principle* of the matter was—

St Just turned his head and looked at her. 'Please,' he said simply.

The expression in his eyes, the quiet plea in his voice, were things she had no defences against. Arabella felt a sudden rush of emotion, a tightening in her throat. She dropped her gaze. 'Very well.' Her voice was a little gruff.

'Thank you.'

Arabella concentrated on the path, on the tiny chips of stone, the fringe of grass, the dappling of light and shade. She cleared her throat. 'You had a second condition?'

'Not a condition—more…a question.'

She glanced at him.

'When I waltz with you, why do you…er, sharpen your claws on me?' His smile was wry. 'You see, I'd like to be able to waltz with my wife in…er, harmony.'

Heat rose in Arabella's cheeks. She looked hastily away.

St Just strolled alongside her, apparently at ease. 'I know you must have a reason, but I confess that I'm unable to decipher it.'

Arabella studied the mother-of-pearl button on her glove again.

'Do you sharpen your claws on Revelstoke?'

'No,' she said, as heat mounted higher in her cheeks.

'On Dalrymple, perhaps?'

'No.'

'Then why me?' St Just's tone was good-humoured, plaintive, curious.

Arabella twisted the button between her fingers. 'To…to distract me.'

St Just halted. 'To distract you? From what?'

Arabella stared down at the button. 'I find it uncomfortable,' she said. 'Waltzing with you.'

St Just appeared to digest this statement for a few seconds. 'But waltzing with Revelstoke isn't uncomfortable.'

Arabella twisted the button back and forth between her fingers. 'Not as much, no.'

'Or Dalrymple?'

She grimaced. 'I dislike waltzing with him, but…'

'Not as much as with me.' St Just's voice was wooden.

I've offended him. Arabella nodded, unable to meet his eyes.

'Forgive me, Miss Knightley,' he said stiffly. 'I must assure you that it's never been my intention to make you uncomfortable.'

'I know,' Arabella said. 'It's my fault, not yours.' She clutched the little button tightly. 'I don't…I don't like it when men hold me.'

St Just took a step closer to her. His voice was harsh. 'Miss Knightley, has anything happened to you that I should know about? Has any man other than Lord Crowe tried to harm you?'

'Oh, no!' she hastened to assure him, glancing up at his face. He wore a fierce frown. 'I mean, once in the slums… But my mother hit him over the head with a skillet and he bled everywhere and—'

His eyebrows had risen, although his expression was still fierce. 'You intrigue me, Miss Knightley. I should like to hear more about the skillet.'

'Oh…well…' She fiddled with the little mother-of-pearl button. 'It's rather a long story.'

St Just bowed slightly. He held out his arm to her. 'I have ample time.'

Arabella bit her lip. She released the button and laid her hand on his arm. They began to stroll again.

'The skillet…' St Just prompted.

Where to start? He'd be appalled if she told him the truth about her life in the slums.

Appalled enough to withdraw his offer?

Arabella took a deep breath. 'We had a room in one of the rookeries. Mother… At first she used to work on the streets, but something bad happened to her… She never told me what, but after that she brought her…her clients back to our room.' Arabella glanced at St Just. His expression was stiff, slightly shocked. 'My mattress was in one corner and Mother hung a blanket so that I couldn't see anything.'

She looked away from him and continued, 'Mother was always very particular that I do things *properly*. She said that one day I'd take my place in society—and it was essential I talk like a lady and eat like a lady and move like a lady. That I speak French and Italian, that I sew beautifully, that I…' Arabella shrugged. 'She was determined that I become a lady.'

So many lessons: how to sit, how to stand, how to walk gracefully, how to sip from a glass, how to eat politely.

'Mother had a set of cutlery that she laid out every night. She used to pretend we had lots of courses to choose from.' She could see the room in her mind's eye, the stained walls, the mattresses on the floor, the tiny fireplace with its broken grate—and the miscellany of knives and forks and spoons laid out on the lopsided table. 'I had to use the right ones.' She glanced at St Just. 'It was a game, you see.'

His expression was faintly bemused. He nodded.

'One night, while I was eating, one of Mother's clients came. He wanted— Well, you can guess what he wanted. But my mother was *very particular* about dinner, and she told him to go away.'

She fell silent. After a moment, St Just said, 'I take it he didn't?'

Arabella shook her head. 'He pushed his way in…the door was quite flimsy…and Mother lost her temper. She told him—' She bit her lip. The things her mother had said were unrepeatable. 'And…and *he* said that if Mother wasn't willing, then he'd have me instead, and he grabbed me and…Mother hit him with the skillet.'

'What happened next?' St Just asked, his voice grim.

'He fell over. There was…a lot of blood.' The smell of it came to her nostrils, as strong now as it had been thirteen years ago. Arabella shuddered. 'He was too big for us to move, so I went to get Harry, and he carried him outside.'

'Did this man give you any more trouble?'

'We never saw him again.' She glanced at St Just and saw his expression sharpen.

'Do you think that Harry—?'

'I don't know.' She looked away. After a moment she said, 'I think it far more likely that my mother killed him. It was a very heavy skillet.'

St Just said nothing. His expression—when she darted a glance at him—was sober, thoughtful.

He caught her glance. 'I must applaud your mother's defence of you, Miss Knightley, but her manner of living…your exposure to her choice of occupation—'

'Her choice of occupation?' Arabella removed her hand from his arm. 'Her *choice?*'

St Just had the grace to look ashamed. 'I beg your pardon,' he said. 'What I meant was—'

Arabella was too angry to listen to his apology. 'My mother took in washing, Mr St Just. She sewed. She cleaned and dressed the dead. She did everything, *anything,* to earn money. Whoring was never her choice; it was always a last resort. She *hated* it! Absolutely hated it.' Her anger died, as abruptly as it had kindled. She looked away from him. 'She could only do it if she was drunk, and she always cried afterwards.'

'I apologise,' St Just said again, quietly. 'What I meant was that it's terrible that you, or your mother—or indeed any female!—should be forced to live in such circumstances. I deeply regret—as your mother must have—that you were witness to such things.'

Arabella fiddled with the mother-of-pearl button on her glove. 'You think she should have given me to my grandparents?'

St Just hesitated. 'I can't be a judge of that. Do you think she should have?'

Arabella twisted the button. *I don't know.* 'It would have broken her heart.' The button came off in her fingers. She stared at it for a moment, at the snapped threads. 'If she'd let me go, I would never have known her. I'd have no memories of her.' *As it is, I have thousands. As many bad as good.* She clenched the button in her hand. 'My mother was a very brave woman.'

'Yes,' St Just said. 'She must have been.'

She glanced at him. He was looking down at the path. As she watched, he scuffed a stone aside with the toe of his boot. 'I remind you of Lord Crowe and the man in the slums, don't I?' he said, raising his head. His face was bleak. 'That's why you dislike waltzing with me.'

Arabella shuddered. 'No, Lord Dalrymple reminds me of them.'

St Just's forehead creased. 'Then why—?'

'It makes me feel uncomfortable.'

'More uncomfortable than waltzing with Dalrymple,' St Just persisted.

Arabella looked down at the button. 'Yes.'

'May I ask why?'

She flushed. 'Because…because it feels dangerous.'

'Dangerous, how?'

'I…I find it hard to breathe, and…and my skin prickles and…I feel too hot.'

'Those symptoms, Miss Knightley, sound rather like the symptoms of, er…desire.'

'Oh, no!' she said, her gaze flying to him. 'It couldn't possibly be!'

St Just smiled, his eyes creasing at the corners. 'You sound very certain.'

'I am,' Arabella said emphatically. 'I will never have physical congress with a man!'

His eyebrows rose. 'Never?'

She shuddered again, remembering the ugliness of the noises, the rank male smell, her mother's distress afterwards. 'Never!'

'Ah…' His smile faded. 'This is why you wished me to withdraw my offer.'

Her gaze fell. 'Yes.'

St Just was silent for several seconds. 'You're quite determined never to…er, have physical congress with a man?'

'Yes.'

After several more seconds of silence, he held his arm out to her. 'Shall we walk further?'

Arabella glanced at him from beneath the brim of her bonnet. His face was unsmiling. After a moment's hesitation she laid her hand on his arm.

They strolled slowly in an awkward silence. Above them, birds sang, and from beneath their feet came the gentle crunch of gravel. Arabella was aware of a pang of regret.

'Tell me about your friend Harry Higgs,' St Just said.

'Harry?' she said, relieved to have a subject to converse about. 'He and Polly were my greatest friends in Whitechapel. They taught me how to—' She bit her lip and glanced at him. 'How to steal. And I taught them to read and write.'

'Polly?' St Just looked sharply at her. 'You mean…Miss Highsmith?'

'She's Harry's sister.'

'His sister?' He glanced behind them, to where Polly maintained her distance. 'But her name—'

'She changed her surname.' Polly had wanted to leave her past behind. The Polly Higgs who'd sold her body on the streets of Whitechapel was someone entirely different from Miss Polly Highsmith, lady's maid.

St Just accepted this with a nod. 'How did she come to be your maid?'

'The school began with Polly.'

'It did?'

Arabella nodded. How much should she tell him? 'During my first Season, one day I went to Whitechapel without anyone knowing, to see if I could find Harry and Polly. It was…' It had been shocking—and it had put her own miseries into perspective. 'It was a good thing I did. Harry had broken his arm. He couldn't work, and Polly was trying to earn money by—' She bit her lip, and then hurried on. 'I gave them everything I had, and Polly was able to…to stop. And we decided that the best thing would be a school where girls could learn how to work as servants, instead of…prostitutes.'

'A most admirable plan.'

'Yes. At first it was just Polly, and then Tess.' She glanced at him. 'Harry's wife.' Who'd been a prostitute alongside Polly. 'I'm hoping they can move out to Swanley, Harry and Tess, before the baby's born. Whitechapel is no place for an infant.'

'No.' St Just walked in silence for several paces. 'Harry taught you to steal? Was it necessary that you...er, do that?'

Arabella nodded. 'In the beginning...it meant that Mother didn't have to take so many clients. And at the end, when she was ill, we had no other income.' Her thieving had paid for their food, for the tiny room in the rookery—and it had paid for the stagecoach and that final journey to Kent—where her mother had died and been buried alongside her husband—and her own onward journey to Somerset and her grandparents.

Adam St Just said nothing. She glanced at him and read censure in his frown. 'Mother didn't know I was doing it. She would never have allowed me! I told her...' she flushed '...I told her I'd earned the money, begging. I'm...a good liar.'

'I know,' St Just said. His expression became wry. 'The nanny goat.'

They walked in silence for several minutes, their feet crunching on the gravel. 'Does the school have a name?' St Just asked, as they neared a junction in the paths.

'Not yet. But once I have my inheritance and can formalise everything, it will.'

'What will you call it?'

'The Thérèse de Martigny School for Girls,' Arabella said. 'After my mother.'

'She would be very proud of you,' St Just said quietly.

Sudden tears rushed to Arabella's eyes. She blinked them away. 'I hope so.'

They reached the junction. St Just stopped. 'I should return you to the museum.'

'Yes.'

They stood for a moment, looking at each other. Arabella took hold of her courage. 'Mr St Just, do you...do you *truly* wish to marry me?'

'Yes, Miss Knightley. I truly do.'

'I'm very sorry,' she said.

His smile didn't reach his eyes. 'So am I.'

That evening, Adam attended the Elphinstones' ball with his sister and aunt. He was in no mood to dance. He stood out the first dance, a drink in his hand, searching the ballroom for Arabella Knightley.

She was the daughter of a whore. Common wisdom painted her as impure, little better than a lightskirt herself, when instead, the opposite was true. She was afraid of sex—

'Darling,' a familiar voice said.

He turned his head. Lady Mary Vane stood beside him, smiling her sleepy smile. 'I have that letter you wanted. I'll send it around tomorrow.'

For a moment Adam had no idea what she was talking about—then he remembered. The letter from Grace's blackmailer, Lady Bicknell. 'Thank you. I'm more grateful than you can imagine.'

'For you, darling, anything.'

'Mary, if anyone should ask…you never received the letter.'

Her eyebrows arched slightly. 'If that's what you want?'

'It is.'

Mary nodded. She moved on, leisurely, beautiful.

Adam sipped his champagne. He scanned the ballroom for Lady Bicknell. Once he'd finished with her she wouldn't be blackmailing anyone else.

He saw dowagers with turbans on their crimped grey curls, stout matrons wearing caps of white satin from which ostrich feathers sprouted, dashing young ladies with diamond tiaras atop their heads, débutantes with jewelled combs in their hair—

A face snagged his gaze; dark curls, dark eyes, high cheekbones, and a softly indented chin.

'Lovely, isn't she?' a smooth voice said at his elbow.

Adam grunted, and swallowed another mouthful of champagne.

'Do I hear the sound of wedding bells?' Jeremy asked sweetly.

No. His hand clenched around the glass. 'Were you present when Crowe was ruined?'

'Crowe?' Jeremy blinked. 'Lord, yes. Never forget a scene like that!'

'No,' Adam said, and drank another mouthful of champagne. It tasted bitter in his mouth. He'd turned away from Crowe, as had every man in the room, while Crowe had blustered his innocence. *I should have killed him.* Or better yet, castrated the man and *then* killed him.

'Why do you ask?'

'No reason,' Adam said.

He returned his attention to Arabella Knightley. She was afraid of sex—the kind of sex her mother had been forced to endure, *not* the kind of sex he hoped to share with her. If he could only make her understand the difference—

An idea bloomed in his head. It was shocking, scandalous, perfect.

Dare I? Adam asked himself, as he sipped the champagne.

Given the alternative, he most definitely did.

'D'you like my waistcoat? Matches my eyes, don't you think?'

Adam glanced at him. 'You are a fribble and a coxcomb!' he said, severely.

Jeremy looked gratified. 'One does one's poor best.'

Adam couldn't help it; he laughed.

He made his way around the ballroom to where Arabella Knightley stood. She watched him come, her eyes wary.

'Are you engaged for the waltz?' Adam asked, bowing.

'No, but—'

'Then shall we sit it out together?'

She hesitated a moment. 'If you wish.'

Adam offered her his arm. 'What do you think of Revelstoke's waist-coat?' he asked as he led her towards an unoccupied sofa. It was tucked into an alcove, quiet and out of the way.

'Very pretty,' she said. 'But Revelstoke is always pretty!'

They sat. Miss Knightley smoothed her gown over her lap in a nervous gesture. She was wearing ivory-white satin stitched with pearls.

Adam glanced at her throat. 'You're not wearing the locket.'

She raised gloved fingertips to touch the strand of pearls. 'No.'

A pity. It would have helped his purpose. Adam cleared his throat. 'Miss Knightley, your parents had a love match.'

She eyed him warily. 'Yes.'

'Would you say that they were happy together?'

'I have no memory of it, but my mother always said they were very happy.'

'Miss Knightley...do you think they would have wished you to marry?'

She stiffened. 'That is none of your business.'

'I think they would have wished it,' Adam said quietly. 'I think they would have wanted you to have a marriage like theirs: happy.'

Her mouth tightened. She looked away from him.

On the dance floor, couples made their bows to each other. The strains of the waltz rose, mingling with the perfume and the candlelight.

Adam lowered his voice. 'Miss Knightley, I know your mother found herself in distressing circumstances, that she was forced to do things that were extremely distasteful, but I believe—I *know*—that when she was with your father she enjoyed the...er, the marital act of—'

Her head lifted. Her glare was fierce. 'You are presumptuous, Mr St Just! No one can know that! Least of all you! You never met them!'

'I do know it,' Adam said quietly. 'One merely has to look at the portrait your father painted of her. He adored your mother. And when a man adores his wife, Miss Knightley, he takes great care that she enjoys the physical side of marriage.'

She looked at him stonily.

'I know that you're disgusted by the thought of physical congress with a man—and quite rightly so, given your experiences. But I believe your mother would have wanted you to marry. I believe she would have wanted you to find pleasure in sharing your husband's bed.'

He saw her shudder, and hurried on. 'The act of congress can be many things for a woman. For some, it's a duty; for others, a pleasure; for still others...it's something terrible.' He held her gaze. 'You must believe, Miss Knightley, that I'd ensure you found only pleasure.'

She flushed and looked away from him. 'This is an extremely improper conversation, Mr St Just!'

'Yes,' Adam said. 'Isn't it?' *And it is about to get even more improper.* He took a deep breath. 'What I propose, Miss Knightley, is that you...er, try me out.'

Her head jerked around. The dark eyes were wide with shock. 'That I *what?*'

'You're afraid of something, disgusted by it—without having any personal experience of it. Let me show you how it *should* be between a husband and his wife.'

Arabella Knightley shrank back on the sofa. The flush was gone from her cheeks; she was quite pale. She shook her head.

Adam tried to let no hint of desperation enter his voice. 'You are correct, of course,' he said, smiling affably. 'It is a shockingly improper suggestion! But consider this, Miss Knightley: no one but you and I would ever know. In the eyes of the world your virtue would be intact. And I give you my word of honour you wouldn't be with child.'

She swallowed. 'It's quite impossible, Mr St Just. I *couldn't*—'

'You are the most courageous person of my acquaintance,' he said softly. 'If any woman dares do this, it is you.'

She swallowed again and looked away from him.

'Answer me truly, Miss Knightley—would your mother have wished you to marry?'

Arabella Knightley closed her eyes. 'Yes,' she whispered. Her hands were clenched around her ivory fan.

'Then please…accept my offer.' Adam lowered his voice until it matched hers, a whisper. 'Try it. Try me.'

She sat for a long time with the fan clenched in her hands. Adam watched her, scarcely daring to hope, scarcely daring to breathe. He listened to the waltz, to the soft rustle of fabric, the low hum of voices, the shuffle of feet dancing across the polished floorboards.

At last Arabella Knightley raised her head and looked at him. He saw how afraid she was. She moistened her lips. 'Very well.'

His relief was so intense that he felt almost dizzy. Adam took a deep breath and smiled at her.

She didn't return the smile; instead she seemed to shrink into herself. 'How shall we arrange it?' she asked, her voice as pale and colourless as her face.

Adam wanted to place his hand on her arm, but thought it would scare rather than reassure her. 'I'll go down to my estate for a week—on business, you understand. Grace shall accompany me; and as company for her, you'll be invited.'

'A *week?*' She looked appalled.

'I'd visit you only twice,' he hastened to assure her. 'The first time may hurt slightly, but the second…should only be pleasurable.'

Arabella Knightley didn't look reassured; she looked ill.

Chapter Fifteen

Arabella travelled down to Roseneath Priory four days later, with Grace and her aunt, Mrs Seraphina Mexted—and Lady Westcote.

Her grandmother had unexpectedly refused to allow her go alone. 'I mistrust Adam St Just!' she had declared. 'And after what he said six years ago, I wonder that you should care to visit his home!'

In a second carriage, behind them, were their four maids. Adam St Just had gone down a day ahead, under the guise of attending to business.

Arabella sat and stared out of the window, her hands clenched inside the swansdown muff. Memories churned in her mind: the ugly, animal sounds of sex, the rank smell of unwashed male, her mother gulping gin, her mother weeping.

There were nicer memories too, twisted into the mess: her mother singing, her voice sweet and true, her mother teaching her the steps of the minuet and laughing, her mother's voice: *ma chère, ma joie.*

Her spirits should have lightened as they left London and the *ton* behind; instead, with each mile they travelled, dread grew inside her until she wanted to vomit from it.

The only reason she was in the carriage, the only reason she held her tongue between her teeth instead of crying out *Stop! I can't do this! I have to go back to London!* was another memory.

It had been near the end, when her mother was ill, hollow-eyed and coughing up blood. *You are my princess, ma belle princesse,* her mother had said, and then she'd smiled, a trembling, beautiful smile. *One day you'll find your prince.*

The words turned over in her head with each revolution of the wheels. Arabella stared blindly out the window, seeing her mother's smile, hearing her words: *One day you'll find your prince.*

Her mother had wanted her to marry—and that was the only reason she was sitting in this carriage.

St Just's home was near Haslemere in Sussex, a distance of some fifty miles from London. It was nearing four o'clock when the coach slowed and turned, passing from the lane into private parkland. Arabella began to pay attention to her surroundings.

A vista opened between the stands of trees. 'That's Blackdown,' Grace said, pointing.

Arabella blinked, surprised to see a hill of such height and wild beauty.

'The ridge overlooks the Weald,' Grace said. 'The view is magnificent. I'll take you up there, if you like.'

Arabella nodded. 'Please.'

Woodland closed around them again, the trees almost meeting overhead—and then came another vista: rolling parkland, wooded slopes, and, nestled in a sun-drenched hollow, Roseneath Priory.

'Beautiful, isn't it?' Grace said proudly.

The Priory was a low, rambling building that looked a cross between a small castle and an abbey. It was very Gothic, with gracefully arched windows and a tower, but there was nothing dark or forbidding about it; rather, it looked friendly and welcoming. In the warm, late afternoon light, the honey-coloured stone glowed, as if Roseneath Priory was smiling at them.

The coach swept to a halt in front of the Priory. The two footmen leapt down from the rumble seat at the back, their feet crunching on the gravel. They opened the carriage door, let down the steps and stood to attention, magnificent despite their dusty livery.

Arabella stayed where she was on the velvet-upholstered seat, her hands clenched inside the muff. *I can't.*

The great brass-studded door opened, revealing a butler and a phalanx of servants.

Arabella swallowed. *I think I'm going to be ill.* And then she took a deep breath and stepped down from the carriage.

* * *

Adam didn't meet his guests until dinner. They gathered in the round drawing room. He observed Miss Knightley as she examined the tall windows. Did she like the traceried stonework? The pointed arches? The quatrefoils of coloured glass?

He discovered he was holding his breath. He turned away. He wanted her to like it. She *had* to like it.

Adam gave Lady Westcote his arm into the dining room. Dinner was an informal affair, with conversation across the table. Miss Knightley spoke little and ate even less.

The first course was removed and the second laid on the table. Adam took advantage of the quiet bustle of the servants to lean over to her. 'Don't be afraid,' he whispered.

She glanced at him. He saw the strain in her pale face, in her dark eyes. Her smile was fleeting and perfunctory. It didn't reach her eyes.

She looked more than afraid—she looked terrified.

The ladies retired to the drawing room after dinner. Adam lingered over a glass of port.

He was feeling distinctly nervous. Everything rested on his ability to prove to Arabella Knightley that there could be pleasure in sex.

He fiddled with his glass, turning the stem around between his fingers. What if he hurt her? What if he couldn't make it pleasurable for her?

That's why you asked her for a week, he reminded himself as he poured another glass of port. Tonight he'd take her virginity as painlessly as he could—and then, at the end of the week, he'd show her pleasure.

There should be a hum of anticipation inside him; instead there was apprehension. How did one arouse passion in a woman who was afraid of sex?

He picked up his glass and sipped the port slowly, thinking. Arabella Knightley feared sex because of what she'd witnessed in Whitechapel— therefore he had to give her an experience that was as far removed from those scenes as possible. Which meant…what?

He had to come to her clean. He had to gentle. He had to be sober.

Adam put down the half-empty glass and pushed it away. Sober. Clean. Gentle. She mustn't feel threatened. She mustn't feel dirty. She mustn't feel that he could harm her in any way.

But it is going to hurt her; she's a virgin.
He rubbed his face, blew out a breath and pushed back his chair.

Piano music was coming from the drawing room. Adam opened the door quietly so as not to disturb the performance. He hadn't realised Grace could play so well.

But it wasn't Grace who was playing, it was Arabella Knightley.

He stood in the doorway, not wanting to move, not wanting to miss one note, one chord, while seconds stretched into minutes. Miss Knightley wasn't just good—she was superb. The music that came from beneath her fingertips wasn't flat and emotionless, it was *alive,* it lived and breathed, it sang.

He realised that his lips were parted, as if he was trying to inhale the music.

Adam shut his mouth. He stepped into the room and closed the door silently and stood with his back to it, watching Miss Knightley's face as she played. She seemed lost in the music, her expression almost serene.

She was so lovely, so untouchably beautiful, that his throat tightened and he had to look away. Adam swallowed. He focused his gaze on the room's other occupants.

Grace and Aunt Seraphina were listening with rapt expressions, Lady Westcote was—

Adam blinked, and looked more closely at Lady Westcote. There was raw emotion on her face as she listened to her granddaughter play. He saw longing, regret, love.

She loves her granddaughter.

He didn't know why he was astonished, but he was. He glanced at Arabella Knightley. Did she know her grandmother loved her?

The piece came to its end. Lady Westcote dabbed at her eyes with a handkerchief. Adam stepped away from the door. 'Miss Knightley, that was incredible,' he said, as sincerely as he'd ever said anything in his life.

'Wasn't it!' Grace cried, clapping her hands. 'I've never heard anyone play so well!'

Arabella Knightley accepted their praise with a small smile. The serenity had disappeared from her face. Adam glanced at her grandmother. Lady Westcote's expression was politely approving. The handkerchief was gone.

* * *

'Sleep well, Miss Knightley,' St Just had said loudly when he'd bowed goodnight over her hand. And then, too low for anyone to overhear, 'I shall see you in an hour.'

Arabella had undressed numbly and donned a nightgown. She'd washed her face and cleaned her teeth and brushed and braided her hair. She had bid Polly goodnight. Now she sat curled up in an armchair beside the fire, trying to read the book she'd brought with her, *Northanger Abbey*. It was written with a light, humorous hand. The parallels should have been amusing—the Gothic Abbey, the Gothic Priory—but instead of being diverted, she found it almost impossible to concentrate. She bent her attention to the page and reread, for the third time, the same sentences. *A lamp could not have expired with more awful effect. Catherine, for a few moments, was motionless with horror.*

Arabella stiffened. Was that a footstep outside her door? She listened for several seconds, and then wrenched her attention back to the novel.

Darkness impenetrable and immovable filled the room. A violent gust of wind, rising with sudden fury, added fresh horror to the moment.

Arabella glanced at the clock on the mantelpiece. An hour, St Just had said. Which was now.

She shuddered and gripped the book more tightly. *In the pause which succeeded, a sound like receding footsteps and the closing of the door struck on her affrighted ear.*

Arabella leapt in the chair as the door to her bedchamber opened. Adam St Just stood in the doorway, wearing a dressing gown of gold-and-red brocade. It looked like something the Marquis of Revelstoke would own, she thought. And then her attention focused on his feet. They were bare.

Her throat tightened. She couldn't breathe.

St Just closed the door. 'Good evening,' he said.

Miss Knightley didn't return his greeting. She closed her book and watched as he crossed the room.

Adam halted at the edge of the rug and stood looking down at her. Her face was as white as her high-necked nightgown. Even her lips seemed to have no colour. Her eyes were black in the firelight.

He took a deep breath and held out the glass of port. 'Here. I brought this for you.'

Miss Knightley looked at it warily. 'What is it?'

'Port.'

She shrank back in the armchair and shook her head. 'No, thank you.'

'Just a few mouthfuls,' Adam said patiently. 'It'll help you relax.'

'I don't drink alcohol,' she said. 'Ever.'

'Why not?' he asked, perplexed.

'My mother drank,' Miss Knightley said in a flat voice. 'In the end, she couldn't live without it. She needed alcohol more than food, more than air itself.'

'I see.' Adam placed the glass on the mantelpiece. 'I beg your pardon.' He was at a loss. *Now what?*

He looked around him. The bedchamber was filled with candlelight and firelight and shadows. The four-poster bed with its heavy canopy of damask silk looked vaguely tomb-like.

Adam turned his back to it. *How to get her to relax?* Standing over her certainly wasn't going to accomplish that. He sat down on the rug beside the fire, leaned back against the footstool, stretched his legs out, and tried to look comfortable. 'What are you reading?'

Miss Knightley moistened her lips. *'Northanger Abbey.'*

'Is it good?'

She nodded. 'You may read it if you like.' She politely held out the book.

Adam accepted it. *Now what?* he asked himself, turning the book over in his hands. He needed a subject that would get her talking. 'You play the piano extraordinary well.'

'Thank you.'

For a moment there was an awkward little silence. Adam looked at her in frustration. Firelight gilded her hair and played across her pale cheek. *Talk to me, Miss Knightley.*

As if she had heard him, Miss Knightley said, 'My mother taught me how to play. Music was her passion. She played much better than I do.'

Adam placed the book on the floor. 'She must have been very gifted.'

Arabella Knightley nodded. She looked at fire. 'Mother insisted there was always a piano in the houses we were in, and after…after Lord Crowe, when we were in Whitechapel, she found one in a church.' She glanced at him. 'Every week we'd clean the church, and afterwards my mother was allowed to play the piano.' She smiled faintly. 'And after she'd played, she taught me. We had two pieces of music: a prelude by Bach, and one of Handel's airs.' The smile faded. 'I still have them.'

'The piece you played tonight, is that one of them?'

Miss Knightley shook her head. 'That was Beethoven. I like Beethoven. His music has been…a very good friend to me.'

'How?'

'Oh…' She grimaced. 'My mother made me promise, before she sent me to Westcote Hall, that I'd never lose my temper, or sulk or cry or behave badly in any way. Sometimes it was a difficult promise to keep.'

'I can imagine it was.'

Miss Knightley nodded. 'When it was particularly hard, I played Beethoven.' She glanced at him, with almost a hint of mischief in her eyes. 'Beethoven is very good to play when one is angry.'

'Is it?' he said, amused.

Miss Knightley nodded again. She smoothed her nightgown over her knees and fingered a fold of cambric. 'Beethoven is also why my grandfather made me heir to his fortune.'

Adam's eyebrows rose. 'Beethoven? How?'

She pleated the fold of fabric between her fingers. 'When I was sixteen, my cousin Frederick Knightley came to visit.' She glanced at him. 'The one who inherited the earldom.'

'The ill-bred buffoon.'

Arabella Knightley smiled faintly. 'Yes. That one.' She looked back at the pleated folds of cambric. 'Frederick and his wife are like Sir Arnold Gorrie: vulgar and puffed-up and full of consequence. They're quite stout, too.' She glanced at him. 'My grandfather disliked stout people. He said it was a sign of weak character.'

'Spoken like a thin man,' he said, drily, and won another fleeting smile.

'Mrs Knightley went around the Hall, fingering the curtains and asking how much the furnishings cost and Mr Knightley was full of the changes he would make. Everything was going to be newer, bigger, finer. My grandfather got crosser and crosser. It was very amusing to watch.'

'I imagine it was.'

Her attention returned to the cambric. She unpleated the fold of fabric.

'And then one day, while we were taking afternoon tea, Mr Knightley began talking about my mother. He called her a French whore and said it was well she was dead…and…and I was sitting *right there* in the parlour.' Her hand clenched around a fistful of cambric. 'I was so angry I wanted to hit him. Except that my mother had made me promise—' She inhaled a jerky breath. 'So I asked to be excused, and I went to the drawing room and I played Beethoven.'

She smoothed the crumpled cambric. 'I played Beethoven all afternoon, and when I finally stopped I found that my grandfather was listening.' Her mouth twisted into a smile. 'He said that…' Her voice changed; she was quoting verbatim: '"That whatever my mother had been, my behaviour was impeccable and that he was settling the bulk of his fortune and his properties on me, that his…his fat ill-bred buffoon of a cousin would get nothing except the title and the Hall—and much use either would be to him without any money!"'

Adam grunted a laugh.

'And so you see, Beethoven has been my friend.'

'I do see.' He smiled at her. 'Your mother would have been proud of you. Of your behaviour.'

She raised a hand and touched the high-necked collar of her nightgown. 'I hope so.'

Adam's gaze sharpened. Was her mother's portrait hidden beneath that fine, white cambric? 'Are you wearing the locket?'

She nodded.

'May I see it again?'

Miss Knightley hesitated for a second, and then unfastened the buttons at her throat. She drew out the locket, opened the clasp on the gold chain, and held it out to him.

Their fingers brushed as he took the locket. The metal was as warm and smooth as he remembered. Adam opened the catch with his thumbnail and studied the portraits again. The faces smiled at him, so alive he almost expected to see them breathe. 'You're very lucky to have this,' he said, closing the locket. He looked across at her, seeing the dark eyes, the dark braid of hair, the pale skin exposed at her throat. 'Come down here,' he said softly. 'Let me put this back on you.'

She became very still, staring at him, and then did as he bid, uncurling her legs, climbing down from the armchair. She sat gingerly beside him on the rug and bent her head forwards.

Adam placed the chain around her neck. 'It's the only thing I have from my parents,' Miss Knightley said, as he fastened the catch, his fingers lightly brushing over the nape of her neck. Her voice was faint and slightly breathless. He thought she shivered as his fingers touched her skin. Arousal, or fear? 'That, and my mother's books and music.'

He released the necklace, letting the locket fall back into its place. 'Books?'

She raised her head and nodded, looking at the fireplace and not at him.

Adam examined her nightgown. It concealed her from throat to toe, yards of fabric trimmed with ruffles and twisting of ribbon. Long, full sleeves were fastened at each wrist. Adam reached out and touched the ruffled cuff of one sleeve. 'May I unbutton this?'

He saw her swallow. She glanced at him, and then swiftly away again. 'If…if you wish to.'

'Tell me about your mother's books,' Adam said, taking light hold of her wrist and unfastening the first button.

Arabella Knightley moistened her lips. 'My mother taught me to read from them. English and French and Italian.'

The second button slipped free of its buttonhole, the third. The cuff was fully undone.

'The Italian was *Novelle* by Matteo Bandello…' Her voice faltered as he began to roll the sleeve up her arm. 'And the French one was…was *Fables de La Fontaine.*'

Adam rolled the sleeve up as far as it would go. 'And the English one?' Her forearm was bare, the firelight burnishing her pale skin.

'The English was…was—' She shivered as he lifted her hand to his mouth and laid a light kiss on it. 'The English was Defoe's *Robinson Crusoe.*'

'Defoe?' Adam turned her hand over and pressed a kiss into her palm.

'Yes,' she whispered.

He stroked his fingertips up her arm, from wrist to the hollow of her elbow. So slender, so smooth. 'How does this feel?'

'It feels…dangerous,' she whispered, not looking at him.

'Dangerous?' He trailed his fingertips up her arm again, and then bent his head to follow that same path with his mouth. He thought she caught her breath when his lips touched her skin. He felt her tremble.

Adam kissed his way from her wrist to the sensitive inner hollow of her elbow. There he tasted her skin with his tongue, and felt her tremble again.

Adam raised his head. Miss Knightley's face was averted, her head slightly bowed. He saw the curve of her cheek and line of her jaw above the ruffled collar of her nightgown. As he watched she moistened her lips. 'Mr St Just—'

'Adam,' he said, still lightly holding her wrist. Her pulse was tumultuous beneath his fingers. 'And if you have no objection, I'm going to call you Bella.'

She swallowed. 'No…no, I don't mind.'

'Look at me, Bella,' he said softly.

She did, lifting her head, glancing at him. Her face was no longer as pale as it had been. A flush tinted her skin.

'I need you to trust me,' he said quietly, holding her eyes. 'I need you to know that I'm not going to harm you in any way.'

Bella swallowed, and then nodded. 'I trust you,' she whispered, and then she blushed and looked away from him.

Adam stroked the inside of her wrist and felt her shiver again. 'Good,' he said. 'Because it's going to feel a lot more dangerous than this.' And then he proceeded to show her, unbuttoning her other cuff, rolling the sleeve up, trailing his fingers up her arm and then doing the same with his mouth, making her shiver, making her blush. Then he peeled back the ruffled collar and lightly teased her throat with his fingertips, with his lips. He didn't kiss her mouth, didn't touch her breasts, didn't try to remove her nightgown—nothing that might frighten her, nothing that might make her feel threatened.

Arousal began to build in him. The warmth rising inside him had nothing to do with the fire, and everything to do with the smooth texture of Bella's skin, the taste of her on his tongue. *Take it slowly,* Adam told himself. He kissed her temple, smelling the orange-blossom scent of her hair—and then lightly touched her ankle, lightly skimmed his hand up her leg. She stiffened.

'Does this feel dangerous?' Adam whispered against her temple, and stroked again, ankle, calf, the sensitive hollow of her knee.

Bella shivered. 'Yes.'

He pressed a kiss into her hair. 'Good,' he said, and pushed the foot-stool away. 'Lie down here, alongside me.'

'Adam…' He heard nervousness in her voice.

Adam kissed her cheek lightly. It was warm, flushed. 'Trust me,' he whispered.

He watched her face as he lightly explored beneath the nightgown, his fingers tracing paths from her ankles to her knees. Her cheeks grew pinker and her eyes even darker. His own arousal began to spiral inside him, not urgent yet, but building, tightening. When he judged her ready, he slid his hand higher, exploring the silky skin of her inner thigh with light finger-tips, stroking, teasing, until she was breathless and trembling. 'Adam…'

'Mmm?' He slid his hand higher, touching soft curls.

Bella gasped.

'Dangerous?' he asked in her ear.

'Very.' It was a low, breathless whisper.

Adam smiled, and began to stroke her teasingly, rhythmically.

She gasped again and stiffened. Her fingers gripped his dressing gown. 'Adam.'

'Relax,' he whispered into her ear. 'Enjoy.'

He could feel her arousal beneath his hand, warm and damp, he could hear it in her ragged breathing, see it in her heated cheeks, could smell it—a faint, tantalising fragrance that made the muscles in his groin tighten fiercely.

Adam slid his fingers inside her. She was tight, hot, wet. His erection surged against his dressing gown. He gritted his teeth and concentrated on what he was doing: teasing, drawing pleasure from her, making her pant, making her clutch the lapel of his dressing gown more tightly.

The helpless movement of Bella's body beneath his hand almost pushed him over the edge. When the waves of pleasure surged through her, he felt an answering surge in his own body and nearly climaxed too. He squeezed his eyes shut for a moment and held tightly to his control.

She let out a long, shuddering breath. He felt her body relax.

Adam chuckled. He opened his eyes. 'Dangerous.'

'Very,' she whispered. Her face was turned to him, her eyes huge and dark, her cheeks flushed. Her braided hair was tumbled on the floor behind her.

Adam stared at her. *I love you.*

He swallowed, and glanced at the bed. From this angle it loomed even larger, was even more tomb-like, with its heavy frame and ample canopy.

It would be an easy matter to pick her up, to carry her across to the bed and lay her gently on it, but he couldn't bring himself to push up from the floor. The bed had *intent;* here on the rug there was nothing but firelight and warmth, nothing to scare her, nothing to intimidate her.

Adam turned back to her. 'This next bit will probably hurt. I'll try to…to be quick.'

He was trembling as he slid the nightgown up her legs, trembling as he untied his belt, as the dressing gown fell open. His hand shook as he gently parted her legs. 'I'm sorry,' he said as he positioned himself over her. 'I'll try—'

Bella's eyes were dark and grave, but her mouth smiled faintly at him. 'Don't apologise,' she whispered.

Adam bowed his head. *God give me strength.* He took a deep breath and entered her in one, swift movement.

Bella flinched. He felt her stiffen, heard her gasp with pain. He froze, fully sheathed in her. *I'm hurting her.*

His body urged him to move, to thrust into her again, to find release. Adam held himself still, his head bowed and his eyelids clenched shut. Bella lay tense and unmoving beneath him. He couldn't hear her breathe. 'I'm sorry,' he said hoarsely against her cheek.

Bella released her breath. 'Don't be.'

Adam felt a surge of tenderness—intense, shocking—and almost lost his control. His hips moved once, thrusting, and he withdrew hastily, groping for the handkerchief in his pocket. He came swiftly and quietly into it. The force of his release left him shaking.

Adam belted his dressing gown with trembling fingers and helped Bella to pull down her nightgown, smoothing it over her legs. Then he drew her into his arms, hugging her into the curve of his body.

Bella didn't nestle into him, but nor did she pull away. She lay quietly. *She trusts me.*

The realisation brought tightness to Adam's throat. It was frightening to love Bella this much—frightening to know she could still refuse his offer.

Gradually his pulse slowed and his breathing steadied. When he was certain he had control of his voice, he asked, 'Was that…too dreadful?'

Bella shook her head.

Adam pressed his face into her hair. 'Next time it won't hurt,' he said. 'I promise.'

Chapter Sixteen

Arabella set up her easel and gazed at the scene in front of her. The estate was spread out at her feet: the parkland and woodland in their different shades of green, the mellow honey-coloured Priory tucked in its sunny hollow, the lazy glint of the brook, the broad windswept hump of Blackdown. And above, a blue sky with a few wisps of white cloud.

She hummed as she prepared her paints. Such a beautiful place, this. Magically beautiful. The days ran together, full of sunshine and beauty. Even when it rained, the Priory still felt as if it was bathed in sunlight—the golden stone, the beauty, the sense of safety.

There was so much peace here: in the cloister where roses unfurled their petals and filled the air with their scent, in the walled gardens behind the Priory where fruit trees and vegetables grew in tidy, cheerful rows, in the long stone-flagged passageways with their high-arched ceilings, even in the cool, fan-vaulted cellars. Everywhere, there was peace.

Roseneath Priory felt apart from the world. It felt safe. It felt *home*.

Arabella stopped humming. Roseneath Priory wasn't her home; it was Adam St Just's.

But I want it to be mine.

She glanced at the scene it front of her: meadows and stands of trees, the Priory. This would be hers if she married Adam.

Arabella frowned as she selected a brush. Was it the Priory she wanted, or Adam St Just, or both?

It was an important question; one she needed to know the answer to.

To marry Adam because she wanted his home would be a terrible mistake to make.

Arabella tested the brush between her fingertips. The tuft was soft and flexible. *Do I want to marry him?*

That first night—the rug, the firelight, the candlelight—seemed almost a dream. She had spent most of the past three days in Grace's company. Adam, when she'd seen him, had played the host, not the lover—but she could vividly remember the lover: his gentle touch, his murmured words. Her skin shivered in memory.

Arabella cleared her throat. She focused on the easel, on the sheet of paper. She had pencilled in the outlines yesterday, very faintly. Today she would make a start on the painting.

The Priory was painted, in warm tones of yellow and brown, and the sky with its wisps of clouds, when she heard a horse approaching.

Arabella turned her head.

Adam St Just was coming along the hillside towards her astride a big bay gelding.

Her fingers tightened around the paint brush. Her heart began to beat faster.

The big bay came up to the blanket she'd spread on the grass and halted. Adam bowed in the saddle. 'Miss Knightley,' he said. 'Bella.'

Arabella swallowed nervously. 'Good afternoon.'

He wore the clothes of a country gentleman: dun-coloured coat, plain waistcoat, breeches and topboots. He looked much more approachable than he did in London.

She put down the paintbrush.

'Don't stop,' Adam said.

'The paint needs to dry before I start the next section.'

'Then perhaps you'll have a glass of lemonade with me?'

She glanced at him in query, and saw the small basket tied to the saddle.

Arabella slowly cleaned the brush while he laid the contents of the basket on the blanket: a flask of lemonade, macaroons, plates and glasses and napkins. Where should she sit? Close to him? At a distance? For a long moment she hesitated, and then chose a spot that was close to him, but not too close. A friendly distance.

Adam poured a glass of lemonade and handed it to her. 'Grace didn't want to paint?'

'She had letters to write.' Arabella tasted the lemonade. It was cool and tart, delicious.

Adam politely offered her a macaroon. It was still warm from the oven. She took one and bit into it, tasting sugar and coconut. She watched as he poured himself lemonade and selected a macaroon. He'd taken off his hat and riding gloves. He had strong, long-fingered hands.

Arabella remembered how his hands had felt on her skin, and looked hastily away. She felt suddenly awkward. Adam had touched her so intimately—

She stared down at the glass in her hand. Condensation beaded on it.

'May I?'

She glanced at him. He gestured to her sketchbook, lying closed on the blanket.

'Of course.'

She sipped the lemonade and watched as he turned the pages. The book was one she'd started since coming here. The first few pages were filled with sketches of the windows, the Gothic tracery, the trefoils and quatrefoils. Then she'd drawn the cloister and its roses, the library with its canopied alcoves, the walled kitchen gardens.

Next came the little chapel, where she'd sat in an oak pew with the rest of the household while Adam had given a reading that was simple and sincere and had made her grandmother murmur with approval. After that came various views of the estate, of the ridge of Blackdown with its pines and wild heather.

Above them, a skylark sang. She heard the drowsy hum of bees, the sound of Adam's horse cropping grass, the rustle of paper as he turned each page. Her memory of that marvellous, frightening hour on the rug faded; her awkwardness became that of an artist. What did Adam think of each sketch? Did he see the mistakes she'd made—or the greater picture? Could he see her love for his home?

He gave a snort of laughter.

Arabella put down her glass. 'What?' she said, shifting closer to him on the blanket.

'This.'

She looked over his arm. Ah, he'd come to the caricatures she'd drawn for Grace: the butler, Fiscus, and the housekeeper, Mrs Bidwell.

She bit her lip and glanced at Adam. Laughter creased the corners of his eyes.

Arabella was conscious of a flush of pleasure. He liked the caricatures.

She returned her gaze to the drawings, examining them. Fiscus was a stork, with his height, his thin arms and legs, his long face and jutting beak of a nose. Mrs Bidwell was a bustling hen, round-cheeked and plump and cheerful. Arabella had taken the time to add clothing and a few touches of colour. Fiscus had a tall hat and black tailcoat and grey plumage; Mrs Bidwell, a crisp apron and rosy cheeks and brown feathers.

Adam brushed a fingertip over the drawings. 'Very clever,' he said.

Arabella blushed. She became aware of their closeness, the way their arms almost touched, and drew back.

'No,' Adam said, putting down the sketchbook. He reached for her wrist, lightly clasped it. 'Stay here, beside me.'

Her cheeks became hotter.

Adam smiled at her, with his eyes, with his mouth. 'Please?'

Arabella hesitated, and then allowed him to draw her back to where she'd been sitting. She looked at him shyly from beneath the brim of her bonnet. This was different from the rug and the firelight. She could see him clearly: the grey of his eyes, the glints of gold in his brown hair.

One of his fingers stroked her wrist, drawing a shiver of pleasure from her. 'Do you mind if I do this?' he asked softly, leaning towards her, touching his lips to the corner of her mouth, drawing back to look at her.

Her cheeks became even hotter. 'No,' she whispered.

Adam smiled. He leaned forwards and kissed her again, lightly, softly.

Arabella trembled and closed her eyes.

'The brim of your bonnet is in the way,' Adam whispered against her cheek.

She opened her eyes. 'It…it is?'

Adam untied the ribbons of her bonnet and laid it aside. 'That's better.' He smiled at her and touched his fingertips to her cheek, her jaw. She shivered. Such a *dangerous* way he had of touching her, causing pleasure to prickle over her skin.

His head dipped again, his lips touched hers.

This time Adam didn't stop. His mouth was gentle, coaxing, teasing. Arabella closed her eyes. Her awareness of their surroundings faded. The lemonade and the macaroons, the horse, the hillside, no longer existed. The world narrowed to Adam's hand lightly at the nape of her neck, to his mouth, to the heat rising inside her—

His tongue touched her lower lip, his teeth gently nipped: a question.

Arabella answered by shyly opening her mouth to him.

Adam kissed her slowly, gently. He tasted of sugar and coconut, of lemon. Delicious. Heady. Heat flooded her body. She leaned towards him and clutched the lapel of his coat.

Seconds, minutes, hours…she had no idea how long the kiss lasted before Adam finally broke it.

Arabella opened her eyes. His hand was gone from the nape of her neck; her skin felt cold where it had been, bereft. *Come back.* She blinked and stared at him. Her breathing was ragged, her pulse tumultuous.

Adam stared back at her. His eyes were more black than grey, the pupils dilated. Beneath her hand, his heart beat rapidly. 'I think we'd better stop,' he said in an unsteady voice.

Arabella swallowed and nodded, unable to speak. Her awareness of their surroundings returned abruptly: the blanket, the picnic, the horse. She lowered her hand and drew back.

Adam cleared his throat. He refilled her glass. The flask clunked against the little goblet, as if his hand shook.

Arabella sipped the lemonade. Her fingers trembled. Slowly the heat faded, her pulse slowed, her breathing steadied. Kissing, she realised, was a very *dangerous* pastime.

That evening they attended a dinner hosted by a neighbour of Adam's. Arabella wore her ivory-white silk, with a golden fillet threaded through her hair. She touched her fingers lightly to the silk as the carriage drew up at their destination. *Armour.*

But she had no need of armour that evening; the other guests were pleasant and friendly and eager to make a new acquaintance. Some thirty people sat down to dinner at the long table. She encountered no snubs from the gentlemen seated on either side of her, no disapproving stares from the ladies opposite. *I'm not Miss Smell O'Gutters here.*

Afterwards, the carpet was rolled back in the drawing room and an impromptu ball announced for the younger members of the party.

There were more young ladies than men, but nobody seemed to mind. Lines were formed for a country dance and the next two hours passed with gaiety and none of the aloofness that characterised town manners. Sometimes Arabella's partner was a gentleman, sometimes a young lady—but male or female, all were disposed to enjoy themselves. The last dance was called after midnight. 'A waltz!' someone cried, and was eagerly seconded. From across the room, she saw Adam look at her.

Arabella held her breath as he walked towards her. 'Would you like to dance?' he asked quietly. 'Or would you prefer to sit it out?'

She blushed. 'Dance.'

The pianist played the opening chords. Adam smiled at her and held out his hand.

They began to waltz. The way Adam held her was almost an embrace—his hand at her waist, their bodies so close—but for the first time in her life, Arabella didn't feel uncomfortable being held by a man; instead she was aware of a *frisson* of pleasure. She shivered slightly.

Adam's eyes seemed to darken.

Arabella felt heat mount in her cheeks. She looked hastily away, fastening her gaze on his neckcloth, on the crisp folds of muslin, on the pearl tiepin. It didn't help. The movement of their bodies reminded her of that dream-like hour on the rug—the firelight, the candlelight, the low murmur of Adam's voice. It made her think of this afternoon's kiss: the lemon and coconut taste of his mouth.

Tendrils of desire began to unfurl inside her. She wanted him to hold her closer.

This was why the more straitlaced members of Society disapproved of waltzing: the intimacy, the proximity. It made her think of things she shouldn't. It made her *want* them.

She glanced up at Adam's face. Would he come to her tonight?

I hope so.

Adam's gaze sharpened. 'What is it?'

Arabella swallowed. 'Nothing.'

They danced another circuit of the drawing room. She was intensely aware of his hand at her waist. It seemed to burn through the fabric of her gown. More memories intruded: the soft stroke of his fingers across her skin, the touch of his mouth, the clean, male scent of him. Her pulse quickened and she began to feel uncomfortably warm. She wished that the waltz would finish—such a *dangerous* dance—and yet, when the final chord was played, she was intensely disappointed.

Adam sat alongside her in the intimate darkness of the carriage. After several minutes his hand found hers. Their fingers interlaced.

Arabella sat bolt upright on the swaying seat while conversations drifted around her: Grace discussing the dancing, her grandmother discussing the cards. It would be easy to lean against Adam, easy to nestle into his warmth. Heat built inside her. She wanted more than this hidden handclasp. She wanted his mouth, his bare hands, she wanted his skin against hers.

It was shocking to want such things. *Am I so wanton?*

If they were married, she could have those things without being thought wanton: Adam's mouth, his hands, his skin against hers. If they were married, he could put his arm around her while they sat in the carriage, he could dip his head and kiss her, and when they reached the Priory they could do more than that—and she could be rid of all this heat, all this *wanting*.

They entered the Priory in a flurry of noise and movement: the clatter of heels on the flagstones, the swirl of petticoats and long dresses and cloaks, Grace's laughter, her aunt's amused response. Shadows and candlelight chased each other across the walls, and the high ceiling resonated with the sound of voices and footsteps.

On the oak table in the entrance hall were five candles in silver-gilt holders and a lamp.

Arabella watched while Adam lit the candles one by one. Anticipation built inside her as each small flame flared to life. She was trembling by the time he turned to her. *Say you'll come to me tonight.*

Adam handed her a candle. 'Goodnight, Miss Knightley.'

'Goodnight, Mr St Just.' *Say it.*

But Adam didn't. He merely smiled and said, 'Sleep well.'

Adam whistled beneath his breath as he strolled into the library the next afternoon. Tonight he'd visit Arabella again. And after he'd made love to her, he'd ask her to marry him.

A love match? How very bourgeois. The voice was his father's, cold with scorn.

His cousin, the new duke, would echo the sentiment. *To hell with Frew,* Adam thought. There was such a thing as carrying familial pride too far.

He walked across to one of the tall, arched windows and stood for a moment, staring out. He could see the hillside where he'd kissed Arabella yesterday. Memory intruded: her flushed cheeks, her soft mouth.

Muscles clenched in his belly. Adam turned away from the window. Tonight he'd finish what he'd started that first night. There'd be no pain for her, only pleasure.

He flicked through the newspapers lying on the table. Arabella wasn't the bold lover who'd invaded his dreams; she was shy and inexperienced—which made her kisses infinitely more precious. Her London face, the bravado and the amused contempt, was a mask. Beneath it was the real Bella: lonely, brave, vulnerable—

A slight movement made him turn his head. A lady was seated on the sofa, diminutive, bird-like, white-haired. 'Lady Westcote. I beg your pardon.' Adam bowed. 'I didn't realise you were here.'

Lady Westcote lowered the book she was reading and inclined her head. Adam retreated a pace. 'Don't let me disturb you.'

But Lady Westcote put the book aside. 'You're not disturbing me, Mr St Just. In fact, I had hoped to have the opportunity to speak with you.'

'Oh?' he said, politely.

'Yes.' She nodded at the sofa alongside her, an imperious gesture. 'Please, sit.'

Adam walked across to the sofa and sat, amused.

Lady Westcote surveyed him for a moment, a scrutiny that made him feel like a slightly grubby schoolboy. He resisted the urge to check that his neckcloth was still perfectly creased.

'What are your intentions towards my granddaughter?'

Adam blinked. 'I beg your pardon?'

Lady Westcote leaned closer. Her blue eyes were fierce, her voice sharp. 'Your intentions, Mr St Just.'

'I intend to marry her,' Adam replied mildly.

Lady Westcote's lips tightened. 'Why?'

Because I love her. 'Because I hold your granddaughter in great esteem.'

'You?' Her voice was contemptuous.

Adam flushed. 'Madam, I deeply regret any distress I may have caused your granddaughter six years ago—'

'Smell of gutters.' Lady Westcote's mouth twisted.

Adam shifted uncomfortably on the sofa. 'An error on my part. I have apologised to her—'

'Do you have any idea how much you hurt Arabella? *Do you?*' There were tears in those blue eyes now, fierce, angry tears. 'The Season was difficult enough for her before you said that. Afterwards, it was terrible!'

'Yes,' he said quietly. 'I know. I'm very sorry for what happened.'

'You weren't there,' she said bitterly. 'You didn't have to face the laughter, the whispers—'

Adam looked down at his hands.

'You're the last person I should choose for her. The last!'

Adam looked up. 'Madam, believe me when I say that I truly esteem your granddaughter. If she agrees to marry me, I'll do everything in my power to make her happy.'

'Easily said, Mr St Just.'

He felt a stir of anger, and suppressed it. *I'd be suspicious, too, if I was her.* 'Madam, your granddaughter is an extraordinary young lady, unlike anyone I know. She's beautiful, clever, talented—and very brave.'

Lady Westcote stared at him, her eyes narrow, her expression hostile.

'She is also very lonely.'

Lady Westcote looked away abruptly. Adam watched as she blinked back tears.

'Believe me, madam, when I say that I want her to be happy.'

Lady Westcote groped in her reticule. 'So do I.'

Adam handed her his handkerchief. 'Madam,' he said, 'forgive me, but your relationship with your granddaughter—'

'She hates me,' Lady Westcote said, and wiped her eyes. 'She always has.'

'Why?' he asked quietly.

Lady Westcote was silent for a long moment, then she blew her nose. 'The day she arrived…she was standing in the entrance hall, so small, so alone. She looked so much like Edward—her face, that chin.' Her lips quivered. 'And William—my husband—he looked at her and said: "Where's that mother of hers? I won't have that woman in this house!"'

As if Arabella wasn't standing in front of him.' Her mouth twisted. 'She was dressed in black—he must have known…'

A tear spilled down her wrinkled cheek. She wiped it with the handkerchief, not looking at him. 'And Arabella said…"My mother is dead." Just like that. Politely. There was nothing in her face, but when she looked at William—I could see in her eyes how much she hated him.' Lady Westcote screwed the handkerchief up in her hand. 'William didn't notice. He only ever saw what he wanted to see.' Her voice was bitter, contemptuous.

Lady Westcote smoothed the creased handkerchief with trembling fingers. 'I embraced her. I told her she was my darling. I told her she had a home with us and we'd look after her always—and I held her so *tightly*—and…and Arabella just stood there, and when I looked at her I could see in her eyes that she hated me too.' Her face crumpled.

'I'm very sorry, madam.'

Lady Westcote sniffed into the handkerchief. On her bosom an eye stared balefully at him from a jet-and-pearl mourning brooch. Adam averted his gaze from it. 'Madam…forgive me for asking, but…if you care so deeply for Arabella, why don't you chaperon her more closely at balls? Why do you seek the card rooms?'

'She's happier without my presence,' Lady Westcote said, wiping her eyes.

'She needs your protection,' Adam said, unable to keep censure from his voice. 'From men like Dalrymple—'

Lady Westcote looked at him sharply. 'Lord Dalrymple has been constant in his affection for Arabella—'

'Constant, perhaps—but he doesn't respect her.'

Her mouth tightened. He saw that she didn't believe him.

'Lady Westcote…we both want the same thing: for Arabella to be happy.' Adam held her eyes. 'For her to have a home, a family, a husband who…' *Who loves her* '…who cares deeply for her.'

Her gaze dropped. She pleated the handkerchief between her fingers. 'You think you can make her happy?'

'Yes.'

'That's all I want for her.' Lady Westcote's mouth tightened. She looked at him. Hostility glittered in her eyes. 'My husband wanted a man of consequence and wealth—which is precisely what you are, Mr St Just—but let me tell you that he would *never* have allowed Arabella to marry you!'

'Madam—'

'William never forgave you for what you said,' Lady Westcote said fiercely, the handkerchief clenched in her hand. 'And neither have I.'

Adam sat silently for a long moment, looking at her, then he stood and bowed. 'Good day, madam.'

Chapter Seventeen

After dinner, Arabella played one of her favourite sonatas by Beethoven. Adam came to stand beside her afterwards. 'An excellent performance, Miss Knightley,' he said in a loud voice, and then, more quietly, so that she scarcely heard him, 'May I visit you tonight?'

Heat rushed to her cheeks. She busied herself tidying the sheets of music. 'Yes.'

The long-case clock in the hall struck ten as Arabella climbed the stairs to her bedchamber. She glanced back from the half-landing. Adam stood in the hallway, watching her.

Arabella blushed, and almost tripped over a step.

In her bedroom, a fire burned in the grate and the coverlet had carefully been turned back. Polly chattered cheerfully as she helped her prepare for the night. Arabella scarcely heard a word; her attention was on the little ormolu clock on the mantelpiece, on the movement of the hands around the engraved dial. She couldn't decide whether time was moving too fast or too slowly.

She heard the long-case clock strike the quarter-hour downstairs, and then the half-hour. She washed her face and brushed her teeth and braided her hair, aware of the minutes ticking inexorably past.

Polly left when the hour was three-quarters gone.

Arabella stood for a moment in the middle of the bedchamber, staring at the ormolu clock. The minute hand seemed hardly to be moving. Should she sit in the armchair and read or…or—?

Not, not the bed.

Arabella resolutely averted her gaze from the four-poster with its turned-back coverlet. She walked across to the armchair and sat with her feet tucked under her, trying to pretend to herself that everything was normal. She opened the second volume of *Northanger Abbey* and turned to the page she'd marked, but her thoughts were too disordered to make sense of the words. Anticipation and apprehension churned inside her in equal measure, making the words jerk about on the page. Finally she laid the book aside and hugged her knees, staring at the fire, wanting Adam to come, shrinking from it. If only he'd chosen last night, when she'd been so eager for his touch—

A faint sound drew her attention. She turned her head. The door was open. Adam stood on the threshold.

Arabella's heart began to beat faster.

Adam closed the door. He walked over to the fireplace, bare-footed, silent, and stood looking down at her, his eyes dark and a faint smile on his lips. 'Not reading?'

Arabella shook her head mutely.

Adam extended his hand to her. After a moment's hesitation, she took it. His fingers closed over hers. He drew her to her feet.

Arabella moistened her lips. She was aware of the four-poster behind them. *Not the bed. Not yet.* 'Adam?'

He smiled at her. 'Sit here on the rug, beside me.'

She felt a surge of relief.

Adam released her hand. He seated himself on the rug. Arabella sat alongside him. She hugged her knees and glanced at his face.

Adam caught the glance and smiled at her, firelight and shadows flickering in his eyes. He reached out and lightly touched her face. She shivered as his fingers trailed down her cheek and along her jaw. He traced the cleft in her chin with a fingertip, so lightly that it drew another shiver from her, and then he tilted her face up and kissed her.

Arabella closed her eyes. Heat washed through her. This was what she'd wanted in the carriage last night: his mouth on hers, his hand at the nape of her neck.

He kissed her lips, her chin, the curve of jaw and cheek, her temple, featherlight kisses, kisses that made her tremble at his gentleness, and then he returned to her mouth, nipping her lower lip lightly with his teeth.

Arabella opened her mouth to him.

He tasted her with his tongue, fleetingly, and then withdrew and whispered 'Kiss me,' against her lips.

Her eyelids fluttered open. Adam drew back slightly, watching her, his eyes dark. For a moment she hesitated, and then she did as he asked, sliding a hand around his neck, pulling him closer, lifting her mouth to him, kissing him.

She learned the shape of his lips, and then his mouth opened for her and she tasted him shyly. She felt him shudder, and shuddered herself.

Time ceased to have any meaning. Their kisses grew slowly more intimate. Arabella lost all sense of where she was, sinking deeper into heat, into pleasure. When Adam finally drew back, she opened her eyes and stared at him, dazed.

'The bed this time,' he said, and stood. He drew her to her feet and picked her up as if she weighed no more than thistledown.

'Adam!' she said, clutching him.

He carried her across the room and laid her on the bed. 'Don't be afraid,' he said. 'It won't hurt this time.'

She wanted to tell him that she wasn't afraid, but he was kissing her again and she had no breath for speech, no thought of anything but Adam's mouth, his hands, his long body stretched alongside her on the bed.

He peeled the nightgown from her and touched her far more intimately than he had the first time, running his hands over her breasts, her belly, and then following that path with his mouth. The pleasure she felt shocked her. She was wanton, *wanting*. Heat and urgency built inside her until she was almost mad from it. Her body had never felt so alive. This was what it was made for: to be touched like this, to *want* like this.

She was dimly aware that Adam's dressing gown was gone, that her braid was undone and her hair spread across the pillow. 'Adam...'

He lifted his mouth from her breast and looked at her. His eyes glittered blackly in the candlelight. His face was flushed, his hair tousled, and there was a sheen of sweat on his skin. Arabella had never seen anything more beautiful. She reached out and touched his cheek. His skin was hot beneath her hand.

'Now?' he asked, his voice hoarse, and she nodded, and suddenly his weight was pressing down on her. Her hips rocked at the exquisite pleasure of it.

Adam moved, thrusting into her. Her body responded helplessly. Time blurred, and then fragmented into a long moment of intense pleasure, when the world seemed to splinter around her.

Arabella spiralled slowly down, aware of a sense of completion, as if for the first time in her life she was whole—and then abruptly Adam was gone, and her body felt bereft.

She opened her eyes, looking for him. He was alongside her on the bed, turned away from her. She felt him shudder, heard him gasp, and reached out and touched his shoulder blade lightly. Such a strong, beautiful body. Such a strong, beautiful man. *I love him.*

With that thought came panic and a terrifying sense of vulnerability. Love meant grief, it meant loss.

Adam turned. He gathered her in his arms and held her pressed to him. Arabella closed her eyes. She inhaled the scent of his skin, drank in the heat and strength of his body. This is what her mother had had, what her mother had lost: being held in someone's arms, being safe, being loved, knowing you were precious to them.

She listened as Adam's heartbeat slowed.

'Bella,' he said softly.

She tensed. *Don't ask me.*

'Please…marry me.'

There could only be one answer, even though it terrified her to utter it. 'Yes,' she whispered.

Adam pressed a kiss into her hair. 'Thank you.'

Her throat closed. Tears filled her eyes. She had no defences against this: Adam's love, his tenderness.

I love you, she told him silently, and felt an almost overwhelming sense of panic.

The panic didn't fade overnight—if anything, it strengthened. Arabella picked at her breakfast, pushing the food around her plate, while Grace talked cheerfully beside her.

If Adam was afflicted by the same panic, it wasn't apparent; he ate a hearty breakfast. His eyes, when he caught hers, held a warm smile.

She rose early from the breakfast table and walked in the cloister, hoping that the fragrance of the roses and the hum of bees, the peace, would calm her.

Adam found her there. 'Are you all right?' he asked, looking closely at her.

I'm afraid. Loving Adam was more terrifying than anything she'd done in her life.

Arabella tried to smile. 'I…I was…I was thinking about how it will be in London, once people know.'

Adam pulled a face. 'That comment of mine.'

'Yes.' Their engagement would afford the *ton* considerable amusement.

'I'm proud to be marrying you,' Adam said softly, holding her gaze. 'But if you prefer, we shan't announce it yet.'

Arabella bit her lip. 'Would you mind?'

'I want whatever makes you happy.'

The words, the warmth in his eyes, brought a feeling almost like pain to her chest, as if her heart had turned over. She felt a fresh surge of panic.

Adam captured her hand. 'Why did Tom never pay me a visit? I know I deserved it.'

Arabella looked away from those smiling grey eyes. 'After Lord Crowe, I never took revenge for myself.' She shuddered.

Adam's grip on her hand tightened. 'Crowe deserved what you did to him.'

'Perhaps.'

Adam was silent for a moment. 'Were there others who deserved it?'

'Mr Foliffe,' she said, glancing at him. 'And Miss Greene.'

'Foliffe? The man who…er, gave your mother shelter after she was widowed?'

'Yes.' Arabella turned her head away and stared at the rosebushes, at the delicately tinted petals, at the sharp thorns. 'He opened his house under the guise of friendship, and then he…he told my mother that he expected payment for his generosity.'

'Didn't he die? Didn't his curricle overturn—?'

'He's not dead. He broke his back.' She glanced at him again. 'He's bedridden.'

'That's justice for you.' Adam grimaced. 'Who was Miss Greene?'

'Greene? She was my mother's maid.'

His face hardened. 'The one who made off with your money?'

Arabella looked away. 'I gave it to her.'

'Of course you did.' Adam's grip on her hand tightened. 'You were a child! You trusted her.'

Arabella said nothing.

'If you're not going to pursue revenge on her, I shall,' he said grimly. 'She deserves to hang for what she did!'

'I thought so, too.' She looked at him. 'A few years ago, I had Polly hire a runner to find her.'

Adam frowned. 'And did he?'

'He found her grave. She died not long after my mother. Of the pox.'

'The pox?' His eyebrows rose. 'Syphilis?'

Arabella nodded. 'An unpleasant way to die, I understand.'

Adam grimaced again. 'Very.'

They strolled in the cloister and its rose garden for several minutes. She tried to feel comforted by his hand holding hers; instead, the panic began to rise in her again.

'We should tell your grandmother,' Adam said. 'I warn you, she won't be pleased. She doesn't like me.'

'My grandmother's opinion is of no weight.'

Adam hesitated, and then said, 'She loves you.'

'No, she doesn't. She didn't love her son. She doesn't love me.'

'Are you certain she didn't love him?'

'If she'd loved him, she wouldn't have turned away from him,' she said fiercely.

'But your grandfather—'

She pulled her hand free. 'A mother doesn't abandon her children. Not if she loves them.'

Adam looked at her silently. His face, his eyes, were grave. 'Did you take revenge on your grandparents?' he asked softly.

Arabella bit her lip and looked down. Adam was dressed for riding, in top-boots and breeches.

'Bella, you didn't…you didn't steal from them, did you?'

'Of course I didn't!' she said, looking up, flushing.

Adam studied her. His eyes were narrow, thoughtful. 'But you did something, didn't you?'

Arabella bit her lip again. She turned her head and stared at the roses.

'What did you do, Bella?'

She gripped her hands together. 'I told them I didn't know where my father is buried.'

Adam was silent.

'They disowned him. They didn't deserve to know!' She looked at him, expecting to see condemnation; instead she saw compassion. She swallowed. 'My mother's buried there, too. Alongside him. I thought…I was afraid they'd move him, and then she'd be alone—'

'I understand why you didn't tell them.' He reached out and took her hand again. 'But your grandmother has lost all her children. Three sons! Don't you think she should have the chance to mourn at your father's grave?'

Arabella shook her head. 'No.'

Adam put his arms around her and pulled her close. He pressed a kiss into her hair and then sighed and released her. 'Come,' he said. 'Let's tell your grandmother.'

They found Lady Westcote in the round drawing room, standing at one of the windows. The sunlight was cruel on her face, illuminating every wrinkle, every hollow. She looked elderly, and tired.

'Madam,' Adam said, bowing, 'your granddaughter and I have something to tell you.'

Lady Westcote stiffened. She moved away from the window.

They sat. Lady Westcote perched on a rosewood chair, and Adam took a place alongside Arabella on the sofa.

'Arabella?' Lady Westcote said, her voice a trifle sharp. 'What's this about?'

'Your grandaughter has done me the very great honour of agreeing to be my wife,' Adam said. He reached out and touched Arabella's hand with his fingertips. *Mine.*

Lady Westcote shook her head.. 'Arabella, is this…are you certain this is what you want?'

Arabella didn't reply immediately. Her pause was long enough that, for a few seconds, Adam was afraid of her answer. 'Yes,' she said.

Lady Westcote shook her head again. He thought he saw grief in her eyes.

Adam leaned forwards. 'Madam,' he said. 'I know I'm not the husband you would choose for your granddaughter, but believe me when I say that I'll do everything in my power to make her happy.'

Lady Westcote didn't appear to hear him. She stared at Arabella, her face etched with loss.

Adam looked from Lady Westcote to Arabella. They sat so stiffly, with such a gulf between them. *It shouldn't be this way.* He hesitated, and then said, 'Madam…why did you allow your son to be cast off?'

He was aware of Arabella swiftly turning her head. 'Adam!' she said in a low, fierce voice.

Adam didn't look at her; he watched Lady Westcote. Her face stiffened, and then the stiffness crumbled and he saw her pain. 'It was William's decision. I had no say in it.'

Arabella moved slightly. Adam glanced at her. He saw contempt on her face. Lady Westcote saw it too. 'I tried to persuade him,' she said, leaning forwards on the rosewood chair. 'I got down on my knees and begged—but your grandfather said…' Tears filled her eyes. 'He said that two sons were ample…as if Edward were something he could just discard, like a…a piece of furniture!'

Lady Westcote fumbled for a handkerchief. 'I told him he was wrong, but he…he hit me. And I was too much a coward to argue further.' A tear slid down her cheek. She wiped it away. 'I should have fought harder. I should have stood up to William.' Her hand clenched around the handkerchief. 'Edward died, and then Arthur, and then Henry. I lost all three of them. That was my punishment.'

Adam shifted uncomfortably on the sofa.

'I loved Edward,' Lady Westcote said. 'And I loved your mother. She was such a lovely girl.' She wiped another tear away. 'But your grandfather refused to see any good in the marriage. He was such a stubborn, foolish man!'

Adam glanced at Arabella again. She was staring at her grandmother as if she'd never seen her before.

'Every year I bought your mother a birthday gift,' Lady Westcote said. 'I kept hoping Edward would write, that he'd send his address—' Tears glistened in her eyes. 'And then he did write, to tell us you were born, and I was so delighted, so overjoyed! But your grandfather burned the letter, and I had no address.' The tears spilled from her eyes. She made no move to wipe them away, just let them fall. 'I bought gifts for you, too, and I put them carefully aside because I knew that one day I should meet you—' Grief twisted her face. 'And then your mother came and told us that Edward was dead and…and William refused to…to allow her to stay. I ran upstairs, to get my money, but your mother— She was gone, and you with her. I sent my maid—I thought you might be putting up in the village, but they said the carriage had driven straight through—'

Lady Westcote's hand clenched around the handkerchief. Anguish was fresh on her face, as if the events she was relating had happened yesterday, not twenty years ago. 'After that, I had my maid sell all the gifts I'd bought, because I knew your mother would need money, not jewellery. I saved every penny I could spare from my pin money, I sold what trinkets I thought William wouldn't miss, and I kept hoping and praying that your mother would write, that she'd come back one more time…' Lady Westcote's voice trembled and broke. Her face crumpled.

Adam glanced sideways. Arabella was sitting stiff and motionless beside him on the sofa. Her expression was shocked.

Lady Westcote blew her nose. 'By the time your mother died, I had over five thousand pounds put aside for her.'

'Five *thousand?*' Arabella swallowed. 'I didn't know…'

Adam reached out and took hold of Arabella's hand. 'What did you do with it, madam?' he asked quietly.

Lady Westcote didn't look at him. Her eyes were fixed on her grand-daughter. 'Some of it I spent on music and drawing lessons—although once William saw how gifted you were, he insisted on paying for those himself, so that your talents could then be his.' Her mouth twisted contemptuously. 'As for the rest…I kept saving, even after William had settled his fortune on you. He had such an uncertain temper. I was always afraid he'd fly into a rage and change his mind. I only stopped putting money aside when he died.'

Arabella said nothing. She didn't move, she scarcely seemed to be breathing.

'I know you don't need my money, Arabella, but…I should like to give you a…a gift that would make you happy.'

Arabella shook her head.

'How much is there, madam?' Adam asked quietly.

'Nearly twenty thousand pounds.'

It was a huge sum, a fortune. Enough for several schools. He glanced at Arabella.

She was very pale. 'Why didn't you tell me?'

'Because I know you hate me.' Tears filled Lady Westcote's eyes. 'And I know I deserve it. I failed your father, and I failed your mother, and I failed you.' She looked down at the handkerchief, smoothed it with trembling hands, folded it. 'I know I can't buy your love.'

Arabella moistened her lips. 'Grandmother…'

Adam cleared his throat. He squeezed Arabella's hand and then released it. 'I'll give you some privacy,' he said, standing.

Arabella looked up at him. He saw tears in her eyes, shock on her face, confusion. 'Adam…'

He bent and lightly kissed her cheek. 'Talk with your grandmother.' *Learn to know her. To perhaps love her.* And then he bowed to Lady Westcote and left the room.

Chapter Eighteen

Arabella hoped the panic would subside; it didn't. It sat beneath her breastbone during that last day at the Priory, it kept her awake at night, it accompanied her in the carriage back to London, it climbed the stairs with her to her bedchamber in the house on Mount Street. It stayed with her overnight and was there when she woke.

Arabella hugged herself, shivering beneath the covers, and stared at the light leaking through the drawn curtains. *This is all a mistake, a terrible mistake.*

A ride in Hyde Park and an hour spent at the piano did nothing to calm her agitation. She played mechanically, not hearing the music. Her attention was focused not on her fingers, but on the growing conviction it would be better if she *didn't* love Adam St Just, if she'd said *no* instead of *yes*.

To love someone meant being vulnerable, it meant handing them your heart and soul, trusting them, giving them the power to hurt you.

When her agitation grew too much, Arabella pushed away from the pianoforte. She paced the room. She loved Adam St Just. It was him, or no one. But—

I should have said no.

Lunch was a welcome distraction. Finding her way through the new, careful relationship with her grandmother gave her something to think about other than Adam.

Arabella chewed slowly. She'd planned to sever the tie with her grandmother when she came into her inheritance; looking at Lady Westcote's hopeful, tremulous smile, she knew she couldn't. *It would break her heart.*

A week ago she would have thought it fitting punishment.

Arabella laid down her knife and fork. In the past fortnight her world had turned upside down. Everything was frightening and new.

I'm going to marry Adam.

She felt a surge of panic. Her chest tightened. It was suddenly difficult to breathe.

Arabella reached for her glass. She swallowed a mouthful of water. The tightness in her chest eased slightly. 'I need some…some time alone, Grandmother. May I go to Kensington Gardens?'

Her grandmother's face fell. 'Of course, my dear.'

Arabella felt a pang of guilt. 'Thank you.'

She walked from the Long Water to the Round Pond to the sunken Dutch Garden, hoping that the fresh air, the sunshine, the exercise would ease her agitation. Polly, in her guise of lady's maid, followed silently.

A number of people were wandering in the Dutch Garden, with its hedges and flower beds and geometrical paths. A lady in mourning dress on the other side of the pond caught Arabella's attention. Was that Helen Dysart?

The lady glanced around in a manner that was almost surreptitious, then bent and placed something in a stone urn in which a palm grew.

Arabella halted in the middle of the path. Memory flooded her. She saw a sheet of paper covered in Lady Bicknell's scrawled handwriting. *You may leave the bracelet in the Dutch Garden in the Kensington Palace Gardens. Hide it in the urn at the north-eastern corner of the pond.*

The lady in mourning began to walk briskly away. She wore a veil, but her figure, her style of walking—

It was Helen Dysart.

Arabella hurried around the pond. She bent over the urn and felt among the palm fronds. Her fingers found a package.

'What's wrong?' Polly asked, behind her.

'This.' Arabella pulled out the package. It was about the size of a small book, wrapped in black cloth and tied with ribbon.

'What is it?'

'Blackmail,' she said grimly. 'Lady Bicknell. Quickly! We have to find Helen.' She saw Polly's bafflement, but spared no time to explain. Instead, she caught up her skirts and hurried in the direction Helen had taken, almost running along the path, up the shallow steps, past the hedge—

'Helen!'

The lady in black turned swiftly. She hesitated, and then raised her veil. 'Arabella?' Helen's smile was strained. 'What are you doing here?'

Arabella held out the package. 'You left this behind.'

Helen's face whitened.

'You're being blackmailed, aren't you?'

Helen made no answer. She took the package with a trembling black-gloved hand.

'I know who's doing it,' Arabella said. 'Lady Bicknell. She's done it before. And I can promise that she won't be content with one payment. She'll want more.'

'I don't care.' Helen pushed past her. 'I have to put it back!'

Arabella caught her elbow, halting her. 'Helen, let me help. Please.'

Helen shook her hand off. 'I can't,' she said, not meeting Arabella's eyes.

'That's money, isn't it? Bank notes.'

Helen bit her lip.

'How much?' Arabella asked quietly.

Helen swallowed. She turned the package over in her hands. 'Five thousand pounds.'

Arabella stared at her, appalled. 'Helen, nothing you can have done is worth that much!'

'It's not something I did,' Helen said bitterly. 'It was George.'

'Then don't pay!'

Helen clutched the package to her breast. 'I have to.'

Arabella was silent for a moment, looking at her friend. 'What did George do?'

'I can't tell you.'

'Helen, nothing you can say will shock me. I grew up in the slums. Remember?'

Helen glanced at her.

'What did George do?' Arabella said softly, holding her friend's eyes.

Helen's face twisted. She looked down at the ground. 'It's how he died.'

'In a brothel, you said.'

'Not…not an ordinary brothel. He wasn't with a woman. He was with a…a young boy. A child.'

Arabella briefly closed her eyes. She understood Helen's horror.

'I didn't know until I received the letter,' Helen said. 'I thought…I thought it was a lie! I asked George's lawyer and he said…it was true. They'd decided not to tell anyone because it was so…so unpalatable.'

Yes, very unpalatable.

Helen clutched the package tightly. Tears shone in her eyes. 'Arabella, I couldn't bear it if the truth came out. I simply couldn't.'

'But it's not your name that will be besmirched, it's George's—'

'And mine with it!' There was an edge of hysteria in Helen's voice. 'Of all the things George did, this is…this is—' She swallowed convulsively. 'I have to keep it secret!'

Arabella touched her friend's arm lightly. 'Helen—'

'I know you want to help,' Helen said in a trembling voice. 'But please…let me deal with this.'

Arabella looked at her for a long moment, then withdrew her hand and stepped back.

'Thank you,' Helen said. She hurried back towards the sunken garden and the pond.

Arabella watched until she was gone, then she turned to Polly. 'Lady Bicknell needs another lesson,' she said grimly.

'I'll go to Lady Bicknell's tonight,' Arabella said as they walked back to the Long Water. 'Before she has a chance to spend the money.'

Polly nodded. 'Do you think she'll use the same hiding place?'

'Probably not. I wouldn't, if—' Her attention was caught by a man walking towards them. His height, his easy, athletic stride, the austere elegance of his clothing, told her who it was before she saw his face. Her heart began to beat more loudly.

'Handsome, isn't he?' Polly said, her tone ingenuous.

'Shh!'

Polly grinned and fell back a pace, becoming a demure lady's maid.

Adam lifted his hat and bowed. 'Good afternoon. I hoped I might meet you here.'

'You did?' When he looked at her like that, with such warmth in his eyes, it caused something in her chest to ache.

'I called in at your grandmother's house,' Adam said, offering her his arm. 'She said you were here.'

Arabella laid her hand on his sleeve. Delight and panic mingled inside her. *I've agreed to marry this man.*

The panic surged and she knew, with sudden and absolute certainty, that marrying Adam was a mistake—but when she glanced up at his face, the certainty fled and the panic twisted into joy. She saw the smile on his mouth, the warmth in his eyes, and knew that she loved him.

What am I to do?

'Would you like to drive out to the school with me tomorrow?' Adam asked.

'Oh!' Her eyes widened. 'Oh, yes!' She'd imagined it so many times: the neat rows of beds in the dormitory, the school room with its desks and bookshelves, the long tables and benches in the dining room, the tall oak tree in the front and the vegetable garden out the back—

She clutched his arm. 'Oh, Adam, you'll never guess—! Lady Bicknell is blackmailing someone else!'

'What?' The smile vanished. His face was suddenly stern.

Arabella told him what she'd witnessed in the Dutch Garden. 'Something must be done!'

'Something will be done,' Adam said. His voice was hard, and his expression made her shiver. 'I've proof that Lady Bicknell was Grace's blackmailer—'

Arabella opened her mouth to ask what, but Adam forestalled her question. 'A letter in her own hand,' he said. 'Signed by her. To go with the drafts you sent me.' He smiled; there was no warmth in it. 'I'll pay Lady Bicknell a visit tomorrow and inform her that her career as a blackmailer is over.'

'That would be perfect!' said Arabella, relieved. 'And tonight I'll go as Tom and get Helen's money—'

'No,' Adam said.

'But…we have to get back Helen's money!'

'I'll do that tomorrow.'

Arabella shook her head. 'It needs to be done today! What if Lady Bicknell spends it or…or *says* she has spent it! Helen will never get it back!'

'I'll get it tomorrow,' Adam repeated. 'Don't worry.' He laid his hand on hers and gave it a reassuring squeeze.

'Can't you go today?' she pleaded.

'No,' Adam said. 'It's almost four o'clock, and I'm promised to dinner before the Yarmouths' ball. Tomorrow is soon enough.' He smiled at her. 'Don't worry, she shan't blackmail any more people.'

'We need to get Helen's money back tonight,' Arabella said, pulling her hand free. 'It may not be there tomorrow!'

'And it may not be there tonight,' Adam countered. 'What's to stop Lady Bicknell taking it to the Yarmouths' ball and losing it all in the card room?'

'Nothing. But I have to try. Helen's my friend!'

'Bella…' There was a note of warning in his voice. 'You promised you'd cease to be Tom.'

'I know. But don't you see—?'

'No,' Adam said. 'I don't! We'll deal with Lady Bicknell tomorrow. Isn't that soon enough?'

'I have to do it tonight,' Arabella said stubbornly. 'Come, Polly, I see our carriage waiting.' She began walking towards the drive.

Adam caught her elbow. 'You gave me your word.'

'Well, now I'm taking it back!'

'Arabella,' Adam said, his voice low and fierce, 'if you're caught you could hang!'

'I won't be caught.' She wrenched her elbow free. 'I know what I'm doing.'

Adam caught hold of her elbow again. This time his fingers were tighter. 'Arabella, I forbid you to—'

Anger blossomed inside her. 'Forbid?'

Adam released her arm. His jaw clenched briefly. 'You're to be my wife,' he said stiffly. 'And as your husband, I have the right to forbid—'

'I'm not your wife yet. And nor am I your dog or your child, to be told what to do!'

Adam's jaw clenched again. He looked down his nose at her. 'If you behave like a child, then you may expect to be treated like one!'

Arabella felt a surge of relief, eclipsing her anger. 'If this is how you intend to treat your wife, Mr St Just, then allow me to inform you that I shall not marry you!'

Behind her she heard Polly gasp. Adam's face stiffened, as if she'd struck him. 'Arabella,' he said. 'Bella—'

'Our engagement is over!'

She saw his dismay. 'Bella,' he said, 'please—'

'Good day, Mr St Just.' Arabella turned on her heel. She was trembling. 'Come, Polly.'

The trembling grew stronger as she marched towards the waiting carriage. Once inside, she burst into tears.

Polly fussed over her, clucking with concern.

'It's nothing,' Arabella said, between sobs. 'I'm just relieved. I knew it was a mistake.'

At dinner, Arabella told her grandmother she was feeling unwell and not equal to the Yarmouths' ball. It wasn't a lie; her head ached and her hands still shook.

Lady Westcote expressed concern and declared that she'd stay home too, but allowed herself to be persuaded not to, Mrs Yarmouth being such a close friend of hers.

'Go straight to bed,' she said, pulling on her gloves in the entrance hall.

'Yes, Grandmother.'

'Would you like some laudanum? My maid—'

'I'll be fine, Grandmother.'

Lady Westcote kissed her cheek fondly and hastened out the door in a rustle of silk and lace.

Arabella climbed the stairs slowly. 'Ready, Polly?' she asked, as she entered her bedroom.

They changed from cambric gowns into coarse brown shirts and trousers. Arabella pulled a knitted woollen hat over her hair and made sure that not one curl escaped.

They'd done this many times before. Each time there'd been a thrill; tonight there wasn't. She felt dull and weary as she fastened the pouch around her waist, as she tucked Tom's message inside.

'Here,' Polly said, handing her a piece of charcoal.

Arabella carefully blackened her face. When she was finished, a stranger stared back from the mirror. The cleft in her chin was the only thing she recognised of herself.

'Ready?' Polly asked.

'Yes.'

Arabella placed her foot in Polly's cupped hands. 'Now.'

A grunt, a scramble and she was up on the small balcony with its wrought-iron railing. She crouched for a moment, aware of a strong sense of *déjà vu*. She'd been in this exact spot only three weeks ago.

She looked down and waved.

Polly nodded. She stepped back into the shadows.

The *déjà vu* became stronger; the broken latch was still broken, the window opened with the same faint creak it had last time, the room had the same stale, musty smell. Arabella closed the window behind her. She blinked and let her eyes adjust to the dimness. The shapes of the furniture were the same: a desk, an armchair, two low bookcases. A clock ticked on the mantelpiece.

She walked across to the door and opened it quietly. This time she knew where she was going; there was no need to peer into darkened rooms. She went swiftly and silently up one flight of stairs and turned right.

Arabella laid her hand on the door of Lady Bicknell's bedchamber. For a long moment she stood, listening for movement on the other side of the wooden panel, then she turned the handle and pushed the door slightly open.

She listened, and heard only silence.

Arabella slipped inside and closed the door behind her. There was no key in the door; that, too, was the same as last time.

She didn't like being unable to lock the door. It made the skin prickle between her shoulder blades. She hurried across to the window, opened it, and snatched a glance outside: a drop to a jutting stone window canopy, and then another drop to the pavement. Her escape route—if she should need it.

Arabella turned back to the room. It was overly warm and thick with the scent of perfume. A fire lay dying in the grate. She took the candle from the bedside table, lit it from the coals, and looked around. The room was no tidier than it had been last time.

She ignored the dressing table, with its litter of objects, and trod quickly across to the mahogany dresser. She pulled out the drawer of stockings, and then the hidden drawer behind that. It was empty.

Damn.

Arabella replaced the drawers. She drew in a deep breath and released it. She'd have to search the entire room.

Adam stared grimly across the ballroom. Fury swirled inside him. He'd had a *right* to forbid Arabella. He'd been trying to *protect* her—and she'd reacted as if he was the worst kind of tyrant!

His fingers tightened around his glass. He gulped a mouthful of wine. *She didn't mean it,* he told himself. *She was angry. Once she calms down she'll change her mind.*

But beneath the fury was a tight coil of anxiety. *What if she doesn't?*

'Not dancing tonight?'

'No,' Adam said, not turning his head. He swallowed another mouthful of wine and avoided looking at the faces on the dance floor, because if he saw Arabella, by God, he'd be hard-pressed not to stride across and shake her—

Jeremy stepped up alongside him. 'Looking for the delightful Miss Knightley?'

Adam's jaw clenched.

'Alas.' Jeremy sighed theatrically. 'She's not here.'

Not here? Adam's rage, his sense of ill usage, faltered slightly. He scanned the ballroom, frowning, looking for a slim figure, a head of dark hair.

'How was your week in the country?' Jeremy asked. His voice was light, sly, teasing. 'One wonders…does one hear wedding bells—?'

'What do you mean she's not here?' Adam demanded.

'Who?'

Adam swung round to face him. 'You know damned well who I mean! What do you mean she's not here? Her grandmother is!' He'd seen that perfectly coiffed white hair and abruptly turned away, too consumed by rage to want to see Arabella.

Jeremy abandoned his teasing. 'You're in a filthy mood,' he remarked.

Adam scowled. 'Damn it, Jeremy—'

'Lady Westcote arrived alone.'

Adam's mouth was suddenly dry. *Arabella isn't here.*

Dear God...she wouldn't be such a fool as to burgle Lady Bicknell—would she?

He thrust the glass at Jeremy. 'Here.'

'I say,' Jeremy protested. 'Where are you going?'

But Adam was already striding away.

He set out for Lady Westcote's house, almost running, but several streets short of his destination he halted. He stared at a street sign, dimly visible in the light cast by a gas lamp. Charles Street, where Lady Bicknell had hired a house.

He turned down the street, walking briskly, counting off the numbers in his head. Lady Bicknell's house was on the corner.

Clouds had covered the moon. The street was dark except for pools of light around each lamp post. Adam squinted up at Lady Bicknell's house. Was one of the windows on the second floor open?

It was too dark for him to be certain.

He hurried down the alleyway to the mews. It was darker here, thick with shadows. He looked up at the house and saw nothing out of place.

Adam turned on his heel. 'Polly?' he said in a low voice. 'Are you here?' And then, more urgently, 'Polly!'

One of the shadows broke free from a neighbouring house: a figure dressed in men's clothing, too tall to be Arabella.

Adam strode to her. 'Is she inside?'

'Yes.'

'Dear God.' Adam closed his eyes. Then he opened them and reached for Polly, gripping her arm. 'How long has she been in there?'

Polly didn't pull away. 'More than an hour,' she said, in a troubled voice.

Adam's heart seemed to stop beating. 'You think...she's been caught?'

Polly shook her head. 'No. There'd have been a ruckus.'

Adam tried to breathe calmly. 'Then why—?'

'I think she can't find the money.'

Adam swung around and stared at the house. A package of bank notes would be damnably easy to hide. There must be a thousand places it could be hidden—if it was even there. Lady Bicknell had been at the Yarmouths' ball. He tried to remember if she'd been carrying a reticule, and if so, how large it had been. 'How do we get Bella out?'

'We don't,' Polly said. 'We wait.'

Adam shook his head. 'I'll go in and get her.' Urgency thrummed inside him. If Bella was caught—

'How?'

'The same way Bella got in.'

Polly looked at him for a long moment, her face a pale oval in the dark, then shook her head. 'You'll get caught. It's best to wait.'

'But—'

'Bella always makes sure she's got two ways out. She'll be all right.'

'She's been in there over an hour!' Adam said fiercely.

'Then she'll be out soon.'

Every muscle in his body vibrated with urgency. Dear God, if Bella was caught—

Adam glanced at his watch. Eleven o'clock. 'Another half-hour,' he said. 'And then I'm going in.'

He stood in the shadows, staring up at the window Polly said was Lady Bicknell's. The curtains were drawn. It was impossible to tell whether there was anyone inside, whether a candle was lit.

With each passing minute, more dread gathered inside him, twisting, churning. Adam glanced at his watch. The hands had crawled another three minutes.

A carriage turned into Charles Street with a clatter of iron wheels and hooves. Adam tensed. *Please, don't let it be—*

The carriage drove past.

He found he'd been holding his breath. He blew it out and looked up at the window. *Damn it, Arabella! Get out of there!*

He tried to imagine what she was doing, but his thoughts slid sideways, to Kensington Gardens, to her voice, the anger blazing in her eyes. *I'm not your dog or your child, to be told what to do!*

Adam shifted his weight uncomfortably. He looked away from the window. Arabella's voice continued relentlessly in his head: *If this is how you intend to treat your wife, Mr St Just, then allow me to inform you that I shall not marry you!*

Adam grimaced. He'd been as peremptory as his father, as dictatorial. *I'd have been angry, too, if I were her.*

His head jerked around as another carriage turned into Charles Street. The horses slowed to a walk. The carriage halted outside Lady Bicknell's house.

Arabella sat back on her heels. She wiped her forehead with the back of her hand. She'd searched every inch of Lady Bicknell's bedchamber and dressing room, examined every drawer, inspected every item of clothing, turned up the rugs, checked the mattress, looked behind the mirrors and underneath the chair seats. The banknotes weren't slipped down the back of a painting or hidden inside a vase, they hadn't been stitched into a cushion or stuffed down the toe of a shoe. If they were somewhere in the house, it wasn't here.

She swore beneath her breath and glanced at the clock on the mantelpiece. She'd been here too long. Any moment now—

Arabella looked at the clock more intently. It was made of lacquered mahogany and gilt. It was large enough…

She pushed to her feet and hurried across the room.

The clock was surprisingly heavy. She took it down and unfastened the catch. The back sprang open.

Yes! Breath hissed silently between her teeth.

The clock contained the package of banknotes, still wrapped in black cloth. Crammed in with it was a folded piece of paper. Arabella smoothed the creases and read swiftly.

Dear Mrs Dysart,

It has come to my ~~knowledge~~ attention that your husband was at a ~~Molly House~~ brothel when he ~~died~~ met his untimely end. ~~I wonder whether you knew~~ Were you aware that his choice of ~~prostitute~~ companion that night was male? Further, ~~were you aware~~ did you know that ~~he~~ your husband was with a young boy?

I feel certain that you ~~do~~ will not wish to ~~make~~ have these details made ~~known~~ public. In exchange for my silence on this matter, I ~~would like~~ am willing to accept the sum of ~~three~~ five thousand pounds. ~~You may place~~ Leave the money in the Dutch garden at Kensington…

Arabella grimaced. She refolded the paper and hurriedly stuffed both it and the package into the pouch beneath her shirt. She placed the clock back on the mantelpiece and reached up to balance Tom's message on top. *Among the foulest of God's creatures is the blackmailer.* The black cat sat underneath, his gaze contemptuous.

Behind her, the door opened. '—shoes pinch my toes,' a peevish voice said.

Arabella swung around.

Lady Bicknell stood in the doorway, massive in a gown of lilac satin with deep flounces. On her head was a cornette of tulle and lace.

Time seemed to halt as they stared at each other. Arabella's heart stopped beating, the clock stopped ticking. Everything froze—

Lady Bicknell uttered a shriek.

Arabella dropped Tom's note. She ran for the window, thrust aside the curtains and hooked her leg over the sill.

'Thief!' screamed Lady Bicknell. 'Thief!'

Arabella scrambled out the window. She hung for a moment, gripping the sill, her feet desperately scrabbling for a toe hold. There were none. *Just jump!*

A hand clamped around her wrist. 'Got you!' Lady Bicknell cried.

Arabella pushed away from the wall of the house, trying to fall, to jump—

Lady Bicknell grunted and hung on, her fingers digging in. 'Thief!' she screamed again.

Time seemed to stand still. It felt as if her arm was being wrenched from its socket, as if her hand was being torn from her wrist. She could see the triumph in Lady Bicknell's eyes, see the rouge on her cheeks, hear her panted breaths—

The window shattered with a crack of glass.

Lady Bicknell recoiled, shrieking.

Arabella landed on the stone window canopy, tumbled off it, and fell to the pavement, landing hard, knocking the breath out of her lungs.

She lay for a moment, stunned, listening to Lady Bicknell's screams through the broken window two floors up. She couldn't move, couldn't breathe—

Get up! Run!

She lurched to her feet. A sharp pain stabbed up her right ankle. She began to run unsteadily, limping, too dazed to see where she was going.

A figure loomed alongside. Hands grabbed her.

Arabella wrenched free, staggering, falling to one knee.

'It's me,' a male voice said, and then someone picked her up as if she was a sack of potatoes and began to run.

For several minutes everything was hectic, confused, a blur edged with terror—and then the world steadied and came into focus again. She understood what was happening—she had been thrown over Adam's shoulder; Polly ran alongside them.

Adam lowered her to the ground in an alleyway and crouched over her. 'Bella...' he was panting '...are you all right?'

Arabella pushed up to sit. She was shaking, an uncontrollable shuddering that seemed to come from deep inside her. 'I'm fine.'

Adam obviously didn't believe her. He ran his hands over her face, her skull. 'You're not cut? The glass—'

'I'm fine,' she said again, and almost burst into tears.

'Is nothing broken? You fell so *far*—'

Arabella sat shaking, fighting tears, while he felt his way down each arm—shoulder, elbow, wrist—and then each leg. He worked in silence, the touch of his hands firm yet careful. Why didn't he yell at her? Tell her she'd been stupid, foolish, arrogant? That it served her right?

She flinched when he reached her right ankle.

'Painful?' Adam examined the joint carefully, then released her foot and sat back on his heels. 'I don't think it's broken.'

Arabella struggled to her feet, ignoring the stab of pain. She took a limping step.

'Your ankle—'

'It's just a sprain,' she said, trying not to cry.

Adam swung her into his arms.

'This way,' Polly said.

Their route took them via back alleys and mews. Adam carried her like a child, cradled close. Arabella squeezed her eyes shut against tears. The shaking inside her refused to stop.

In the mews behind her grandmother's house, in a dark pool of shadow, Adam lowered her to the ground again. 'You'll take care of her?' he said to Polly.

'Yes.'

'Send for a physician if—'

'I will,' Polly said.

Adam turned to her. 'I'll visit you tomorrow. After I've seen Lady Bicknell. I'll bring back Helen Dysart's money. I promise.'

Arabella blinked back tears. 'I found the money,' she said in a small voice.

Adam looked at her for a moment, his face hidden in shadow. He said nothing.

Arabella twisted her hands together. 'Adam...' Her voice wobbled. 'She saw my face.'

'Then it's just as well you're covered in soot,' he said quietly. 'I'll see you tomorrow.' And then he vanished into the darkness.

Adam walked rapidly in the direction of Berkeley Square. After two streets he stopped and leaned against a shadowy wall. He squeezed his eyes shut. *Dear God, I almost killed her.*

He stood for several minutes, trying to calm his breathing, but memory of that moment kept replaying in his head: the window shattering, Bella falling—

It had been instinct to throw the stone—and it had been an incredibly stupid thing to do. Bella could have broken her neck. She could have died.

She didn't, he told himself. *She didn't break her neck. She didn't break anything.* He knew that, and yet his hands were trembling and he had a tight, sick knot of horror in his belly.

Adam inhaled a shuddering breath. He opened his eyes and pushed away from the wall, heading for his house and a very stiff drink.

Chapter Nineteen

The next morning Arabella's left arm was almost too stiff to move. Her wrist was ringed with bruises where Lady Bicknell's fingers had dug in. She couldn't put any weight on her ankle; it was swollen to twice its normal size.

'Should I send for the physician?' Polly asked anxiously.

Arabella shook her head. 'I need my writing materials. Can you please get them?'

Sitting up in bed with a tray on her knees, she wrote Tom's last message, drew the black cat for the last time. Then she wrapped the message, Lady Bicknell's drafted blackmail note, and the banknotes in brown paper and tied the package with string. 'Can you take this around to Helen Dysart, please? Don't let anyone recognise you.'

Polly departed, wearing a veiled hat.

Left alone, Arabella hugged her knees. The shaking had stopped, but the urge to cry was still strong. Why hadn't Adam yelled at her? Why hadn't he said *I told you so?*

Tears welled in her eyes.

Adam had been right about last night's burglary; she should never have attempted it. It had been the height of arrogance, the height of stupidity.

Arabella blinked back tears. The world was bleak this morning. Her bedroom, with its pretty cream-and-rose wallpaper, the chintz curtains, the rose-embroidered coverlet, was drab and colourless. Even the sunlight streaming in the windows seemed tinged with grey.

The panic of agreeing to marry Adam was nothing compared to today's despair.

She'd thrown Adam's offer of marriage back in his face. Why hadn't she realised how precious his love was until it was too late?

A tear slid down her cheek. She wiped it away with the back of her hand.

In the early afternoon, when Adam might be expected to call, Arabella made her way slowly downstairs, leaning on Polly's arm for support, and sat on the *chaise longue* in the parlour with her foot propped up on a cushion. She made light of her ankle—*Just a slight sprain,* she had told her grandmother with a laugh. *I slipped getting out of bed*—and hid the bruises on her wrist with a long-sleeved dress.

Lady Westcote was inclined to fuss over her.

'I'm fine, Grandmother,' Arabella said, smiling widely. She picked up the latest issue of *Ackermann's Repository.* 'I'll just sit quietly and read.'

Lady Westcote departed to make her social calls. Arabella had done no more than restlessly flick through the fashion plates when the butler announced the arrival of a visitor.

'Mrs Dysart? Yes, I'm at home to her.'

She put aside the magazine and smoothed her gown over her legs. *I must not betray myself.*

The door opened again. The butler bowed Helen Dysart into the parlour.

Arabella held out her hand. 'Forgive me for not standing,' she said with a smile. 'I've been foolish enough to turn my ankle.'

Helen came quickly across the room and clasped her hand. 'What happened?'

Arabella pulled a rueful face. 'I slipped climbing out of bed this morning. Very clumsy of me!'

Helen didn't release her hand. She stood, looking down at her.

'Do have a seat,' Arabella said, unsettled by that intent gaze. 'I'm glad you've come. I was afraid I'd offended you yesterday.'

'Offended me?' Helen released her hand. She chose a pretty giltwood chair, pulled it closer to the *chaise longue,* and sat, holding her reticule. She seemed to be in a state of suppressed excitement. 'No, I'm not offended.' She stared at Arabella again.

That direct, searching gaze was disconcerting. Arabella shifted uncomfortably. 'Would you like something to drink? Tea, perhaps?'

Helen shook her head. 'Bella...' She leaned forwards on the chair.

'Mrs Ingram paid me a visit, not half an hour ago. She said that Lady Bicknell almost captured the burglar Tom last night!'

Arabella feigned surprise. She opened her eyes wide. 'Oh. How…exciting for her.'

'According to Mrs Ingram, Tom is a small man with black eyes and a cleft chin.'

Arabella repressed the impulse to touch her chin. She clasped her hands in her lap. 'Oh?' she said again.

'Yes,' Helen said, looking intently at her. 'Apparently Tom was injured jumping from the window. Lady Bicknell said he was limping as he ran away.'

Arabella could think of nothing to say except 'Oh' again.

Helen clutched the reticule more tightly. Her eyes were very bright. 'Bella…I know it was you!'

Arabella tried to laugh. The sound came out slightly unsteady. 'Me? How absurd—'

'You match the description,' Helen said. 'And look!' She opened the reticule, extracted a piece of paper, and held it out. 'Tom sent me this, this morning.'

Arabella didn't need to look at it; she knew the short message by heart. *Mrs Dysart, with my compliments, Tom.* She pretended to read it anyway, to look at the signature, at the black cat.

'Only you knew I was being blackmailed,' Helen said quietly, putting the note back in her reticule.

Arabella moistened her lips. 'A fluke,' she said. 'Tom just happened to be at Lady Bicknell's last night and he found—'

'It was you,' Helen said, with utter conviction in her voice. 'Lady Bicknell described you perfectly. And you've hurt your leg.'

Arabella tried to laugh again. 'Helen—'

'I came to thank you…and to warn you. Bella, you must be careful!'

Arabella looked away from that direct gaze. 'Helen,' she said, 'indeed, you're wrong—'

'I know I'm not.' Helen stood and bent swiftly, hugging Arabella. 'Thank you so much.' Her grip tightened. 'And for heaven's sake, be careful! If you should be ruined because of me—'

'I won't be,' Arabella said. She bit her lip. They were words she shouldn't have uttered, an acknowledgement that she was Tom.

Helen released her and kissed her cheek. 'Thank you,' she said once more. 'And be careful!' She picked up her reticule and crossed the room. For a moment she paused at the door, looking back, dressed in the severe black of full mourning. She raised her hand, a gesture of thanks, of farewell, and opened the door and was gone.

Arabella stayed where she was, sitting on the *chaise longue,* staring at the door. *A small man with black eyes and a cleft chin. He was limping as he ran away.* She lifted a hand, touched her chin, fingered the indentation. The moment Lady Bicknell saw her, recognition would spark.

Arabella closed her eyes. There was no proof she was Tom, she would never dangle from a hangman's rope—but once the rumours started...

I'm ruined.

A week ago she wouldn't have cared; now she did. If she was ruined, then so too was her grandmother. And as for Adam—

A tear crept down her cheek.

If Adam should renew his offer, she would have to say no.

A glazier was installing a new pane of glass in Lady Bicknell's bedroom window. Adam traced the path of Arabella's fall with his eyes—from the window sill to the projecting stone canopy below, to the pavement—and felt again that stomach-twisting horror. She could easily have broken her neck.

He crossed the road, trod up the steps to Lady Bicknell's door and plied the knocker.

The butler escorted him to a drawing room decorated in an unattractive shade of green. Lady Bicknell was seated on a sofa, a squat, stout figure. Adam glanced at her gown. Someone really should tell her that so many flounces on one gown was unflattering. He made a shallow bow.

'Please be seated, Mr St Just.'

He chose a chair directly opposite her and sat.

Lady Bicknell smiled. 'To what do I owe the pleasure of your visit?'

Adam looked at her broad face and felt a surge of loathing. Such a despicable hobby, blackmail. 'This,' he said, and removed the bundle of papers from his pocket. He unfolded the topmost page and laid it on the low table between them. 'This is the draft of a blackmail letter to my sister. Very ugly, I think you'll agree. And here…' he placed the next piece of paper alongside the first '…is another one.' He glanced at Lady Bicknell. 'I received these in the mail, courtesy of a gentleman named Tom. I believe you're acquainted with him?'

Lady Bicknell stared at the pieces of paper. She made no movement, no sound.

Adam smiled, enjoying her stupefied expression. He unfolded the third and final page and laid it alongside the other two. 'I received this from Tom the week before last. A letter he'd intercepted to…' he squinted and pretended to read the writing '…Lady Mary Vane. Discussing a charity function. I think we'll agree it's in your hand, won't we, Lady Bicknell? Your signature is at the bottom of the page.' He glanced at her again. Her expression was frozen.

'Compare these letters,' he invited her. 'I think you'll clearly see, as I have, that the writing on all three is the same. And here…' he tapped the letter to Mary Vane '…is your signature, Lady Bicknell.'

Adam sat back in his chair. He crossed his legs and swung one foot, at ease. 'I received another message from Tom this morning, informing me that you had had the…er, ill breeding to blackmail Mrs Dysart. He was most unimpressed.'

Lady Bicknell transferred her stare from the pieces of paper to him.

Adam steepled his fingers and looked at her over the top of them. 'Nothing to say?' he asked softly.

Lady Bicknell swallowed, an audible sound. 'This is nonsense! Lies!'

Adam smiled and swung his foot. 'Your signature speaks for itself, Lady Bicknell.'

'How dare you make such an accusation! You're in league with this…this *thief!*'

'Regretfully, I'm not. I should like to be; I approve wholeheartedly of his tactics.' Adam stopped swinging his foot. 'There are certain people in this world, Lady Bicknell, who deserve to be punished. You are one of them.'

Outrage flushed her broad face. 'How dare—'

'No,' Adam said, his voice flat and hard. 'The question is, how dare you? This—' he indicated the blackmail letters with his hand '—is utterly despicable! It's the work of a person of the meanest, basest character!'

The colour deepened on Lady Bicknell's face. Her eyes slid away from his.

Adam re-steepled his hands. He began swinging his foot again. 'You have a choice, Lady Bicknell. I suggest you listen carefully.' He waited until she looked at him. 'Your first option is to leave London tomorrow. You will return to your home in Colne and never set foot outside Lancashire again. Ever.'

'But—!'

'Your reputation will remain intact,' Adam said, overriding her protest. 'However, if you choose the second option, it will not.' He held her gaze and said softly, 'If you choose to remain in London, I will lay charges with a magistrate and tell the world at large you're a blackmailer…and I can guarantee that the *beau monde* will turn their backs on you. You will be outcast, Lady Bicknell.'

Lady Bicknell said nothing. The flush had faded from her face. She looked pallid.

'You may think that I daren't expose you,' Adam said in a conversational tone. 'That I daren't risk my sister's reputation. But I know—and you doubtless do, too—that Grace didn't run off with Reginald Plunkett. She's guilty of writing a love letter, but not of eloping.' He shrugged lightly. 'A young girl's folly. In a year it will be forgotten. My sister is wealthy enough, and well connected enough, that she'll make a good match.'

Adam swung his foot and watched Lady Bicknell over his steepled fingers. 'Your choice, Lady Bicknell? Will you leave, or stay?'

Lady Bicknell wet her lips. There was a sheen of perspiration on her face. 'Leave,' she said, in a hoarse voice. 'But—'

'No buts, Lady Bicknell,' Adam said, smiling. 'You'll leave London tomorrow. If you don't, I shall ruin you so thoroughly that you won't dare show your face in public ever again. If you set foot outside Lancashire, I shall ruin you. If any word about George Dysart's death reaches the ears of the *ton*, if you attempt to blackmail Helen Dysart again, I shall ruin you. Is that clear, Lady Bicknell?'

Lady Bicknell cast him a glance. He saw hatred in her eyes. 'Yes.'

Adam looked at her for a moment, gently swinging his foot. 'Tell me…how did you come to be in possession of Grace's love letter?'

'I don't have to tell you—'

Adam stopped swinging his foot. 'Lady Bicknell, you're not in a position to argue with me.'

Lady Bicknell flushed. 'I was in Birmingham,' she said, her voice sullen. 'In November last year. My abigail made Mr Plunkett's acquaintance after he'd been turned off. He confided his story in her, and…she told me.'

'Knowing you'd make use of it, no doubt.' His voice was contemptuous.

Lady Bicknell said nothing.

'How much did you pay for the letter?'

'Twenty guineas.'

'And George Dysart's death? Was it your maid who discovered the truth of that?'

'Yes,' Lady Bicknell said again, not looking at him. 'I thought there might be more to the story than had been broadcast. I sent her to…to make the acquaintance of Mr Dysart's valet, and from him she learned which brothel he'd been visiting that night.'

'An enterprising woman, this abigail of yours,' Adam said. 'Alas, I fear you'll have to do without her from now on.'

Lady Bicknell glanced at him swiftly.

'Your maid takes the next ship to America,' Adam said, holding her eyes. 'Is that clear?'

'But—'

'Is that clear?' he repeated in a hard voice.

Lady Bicknell lowered her gaze. 'Yes.'

'Good.' Adam stood and walked across to the writing desk beneath the window. A quick search revealed a quill, ink, and paper. He brought them back to the table. 'Your word that you'll do as you have promised, Lady Bicknell. In black and white, so there can be no mistaking it.'

'But surely—'

'Lady Bicknell, given your history, do you think I'm inclined to trust you?'

She was silent as he uncapped the inkpot and handed her the quill.

Adam sat again. 'I, Margaret Anne Bicknell, of Donwick Hall, Colne, Lancashire…' he dictated.

Lady Bicknell glanced at him swiftly.

Adam smiled at her, baring his teeth. 'I had my man of business investigate you, Lady Bicknell. You'd be surprised how much I know about you and your affairs. Donwick Hall needs a new roof, or so I'm told…'

Lady Bicknell pressed her lips together. She began to write. *I, Margaret Anne Bicknell, of Donwick Hall, Colne, Lancashire—*

'Do hereby admit that, in November 1817, I purchased from Mr Reginald Plunkett…'

The quill scratched across the paper.

'…a letter written to him by Miss Grace St Just, and that I subsequently used this letter to obtain a pearl bracelet and pearl earrings from her.'

Lady Bicknell finished one sheet of paper. She put it aside and drew a second sheet towards herself. Her glance was malevolent.

Adam smiled and swung his foot. 'Further, I directed my maid— please write her name, Lady Bicknell—to seek information concerning the death of George Dysart in May 1818, and, by threatening to reveal the particulars of Mr Dysart's death, I extorted five thousand pounds from his widow.' He waited until she'd caught up. 'And a final line, at the bottom of the page: I do freely admit these things.'

Lady Bicknell hesitated, and then dipped her quill in the inkpot. She wrote stiffly: *I do freely admit these things.*

'Another sheet of paper, Lady Bicknell.'

She didn't look at him this time, just pulled another page towards her. Her posture, her whole manner, was eloquent of rage.

'I pledge my secrecy on the aforementioned matters, and give my word not to engage in any further blackmail activities.' Adam watched over his steepled fingers as she wrote. 'Further, I pledge to return to Lancashire tomorrow and to not set foot outside that county for the rest of my life.'

Lady Bicknell dipped her quill again, almost knocking over the inkpot, so violent was the movement. 'Lancashire!' The word burst from her. 'Why can't I—?'

Because you saw Tom's face. 'It is a condition of our agreement,' Adam said coldly. 'Be thankful Lancashire is a moderately large county.'

Her lips pinched together. She wrote, digging the quill into the page, almost tearing the paper.

'In exchange, charges will not be laid against me and my reputation shall remain intact. And now you may sign it, Lady Bicknell. And date it today, May 30th.'

She did.

Adam read the confession while the ink dried. Lady Bicknell had made no attempt to disguise her handwriting; it matched both the letter and the blackmail drafts. 'Excellent,' he said.

Lady Bicknell made no comment.

Adam gathered the pages. 'I'll have my man of business check that your maid leaves for America.' He stood and looked down at Lady Bicknell. 'Remember,' he said softly, 'I have the power to ruin you.'

Lady Bicknell made no reply. Her eyes shone with hatred.

'Good day, Lady Bicknell. It's been a pleasure doing business with you.' At the door he paused and looked back at her, smiling. 'Enjoy your journey to Lancashire.'

Adam arrived half an hour after Helen Dysart had departed. Arabella's chest tightened painfully as he walked across the room towards her. *I was a fool to think I could stop loving him.*

He stood looking down at her, at her stockinged foot propped on the cushion. 'How are you?'

Arabella blinked back tears. 'I'm fine,' she said stoutly.

Adam frowned. 'Your ankle looks swollen. Can you walk?'

Arabella ignored the question. 'Please, Adam, sit down. There are some things I must say to you.'

He transferred his gaze from her ankle to her face. 'Very well.' He took the same chair Helen had vacated. His posture was nonchalant, but she thought he wasn't as relaxed as he pretended; his expression was watchful, rather than open. 'What are these things?'

Arabella swallowed. She twisted her hands together in her lap. 'Firstly,' she said, 'I wish to apologise for what I said to you yesterday in the park. You were right. I shouldn't have gone to Lady Bicknell's. It was very foolish of me, and…and very arrogant.' She took a deep breath. 'And secondly, I'd like to thank you for your help last night. Without it, I would have been caught—'

'I nearly killed you,' Adam said in a flat voice.

Arabella shook her head. 'No. You saved me, and…and you helped me afterwards.' Her throat constricted at the memory of Adam carrying her. 'I'm in your debt.'

'Debt?' His forehead creased. 'Nonsense!'

Arabella bit her lip. 'Adam…why haven't you said that you told me so?'

Adam's frown vanished. He smiled suddenly. 'If you want me to, I will. But I've always found it a particularly unhelpful thing to hear.'

The warmth in his grey eyes, the wryness in his voice, made her throat constrict even further. *I've been such a fool.* Arabella gripped her hands together.

'Was that what you wished to say to me?'

She nodded, unable to speak.

'Good,' Adam said. 'Because there are a number of things I would like to say. Like you, I'd like to start with an apology.'

'Apology? What for?'

'For forbidding you to go to Lady Bicknell's. As you pointed out, you are neither my dog nor my child.' Colour rose in his cheeks. 'I'm trying very hard not to be my father, but sometimes I find myself behaving exactly as he did. It … er, it's something my wife will have to help me with.'

Arabella lowered her gaze. She stared at her clenched hands. Tears swam in her eyes. *Don't cry,* she told herself fiercely.

'Arabella?' His voice was hesitant. 'If…if I asked you again, would you consider marrying me?'

She bowed her head. A tear slid down her cheek. She brushed it away.

'If you don't wish to, I perfectly understand,' Adam said quietly. 'But I'd like to assure you that my feelings for you are unchanged.'

Arabella closed her eyes tightly. 'Adam, I…I can't marry you. Lady Bicknell saw my face. Soon everyone will know I'm Tom.' And although she tried very hard not to, she began to cry.

'Bella—' Adam moved. His arms came around her suddenly. 'It's not as bad as you think.'

'It is,' she sobbed against his shoulder. 'She said Tom is a small man with a…a cleft chin and black eyes. And she saw I was limping—'

'No one will recognise you from that description,' Adam said firmly.

'Helen did. And Lady Bicknell will too, as soon as she sees me. So…so you see…I *can't* marry you.'

Adam relaxed his grip on her slightly. He handed her a handkerchief. 'Here.'

Arabella blew her nose.

'Lady Bicknell isn't going to see you,' Adam said. 'She's leaving town tomorrow, never to return.'

Arabella wiped her face. 'How can you be sure of that?'

'Because I have her word on it.' Adam reached into his pocket, pulled out a sheaf of papers, and extracted three pages. He gave them to her.

The handwriting was familiar: Lady Bicknell's. Arabella read with growing wonder. The confession was more than masterly—it was brilliant. When she'd finished, she stared at him in admiration. 'Adam…'

He smiled at her. 'You don't need to worry about Lady Bicknell recognising you.'

She moistened her lips. 'No, but…people will wonder when they see I'm limping. There'll be rumours— Oh!' She clutched his arm. 'I have an idea! What if London *sees* me sprain my ankle?'

'If you can contrive it, I'm sure it will serve.' Adam took hold of her hand. 'Does this mean you'll marry me?'

Arabella nodded.

Adam's fingers tightened around her hand. His smile was slightly crooked. 'Is there room for me on that *chaise longue?*'

Arabella blushed. 'Yes.'

Adam picked her up and sat down again with her in his lap, taking care not to knock her injured ankle. Arabella rested her cheek against his shoulder, drinking in his warmth, his solid strength, inhaling the clean, male scent of him. *I almost threw this away.*

Adam stroked her hair. 'I apologise for yesterday.'

'It was my fault,' Arabella said. 'I wanted to…to end our engagement.'

His hand stilled. 'May I ask why?'

'Because I was afraid,' she said in a small voice. 'I wanted to stop loving you.' Fresh tears filled her eyes.

'Do you…love me?' he asked softly.

'Yes.'

His hand curved around her head, a protective gesture. 'I love you, too.' He let out a breath. 'I've never said that before. To anyone.'

Arabella closed her eyes. A tear slid down her cheek. Joy this time, not grief.

'What were you afraid of?' Adam asked.

'Everything,' she whispered. 'It's frightening to love someone.'

His arm tightened around her. 'Perhaps. But it's also the most marvellous thing in the world.'

Arabella turned the words over in her mind. Yes, Adam was right. It was the most marvellous thing in the world.

She lay in his arms, listening to his heart beating, feeling safe. There was deep joy inside her.

Adam touched her chin, stroking the indentation. 'I love you, Arabella Knightley.' He tilted her chin with a fingertip. His grey eyes smiled at her. 'I predict that we're going to be very happy.' And then he kissed her.

Chapter Twenty

On the afternoon of June 1st, 1818, Miss Arabella Knightley was observed in Hyde Park, mounted on a black mare. To the consternation of some and amusement of others, the mare shied at an approaching curricle and unseated her. When Miss Knightley scrambled to her feet, she was seen to be limping.

Damsels watched in envy as the driver of the curricle, Mr Adam St Just, one of London's most eligible bachelors, lifted Miss Knightley into his carriage and drove her home.

Three days later, Miss Knightley and her grandmother, Lady Westcote, relict of the fifth Earl of Westcote, visited Mr St Just at his home in Sussex. It was noted by astute observers that this was the ladies' second sojourn to Roseneath Priory. Thus, the announcement of the engagement of Miss Knightley and Mr St Just came as no surprise.

The wedding followed shortly after. The guests included the Marquis of Revelstoke and Mr and Mrs Harry Higgs of Whitechapel, London.

Mr Higgs gave the bride away.

The wedding breakfast was enlivened by an unusual centerpiece: a small stream, complete with lily pads and goldfish, ran down the middle of the table. When the bride saw it, she laughed.

* * * * *

HISTORICAL

Novels coming in October 2010

INNOCENT COURTESAN TO ADVENTURER'S BRIDE
Louise Allen

Wrongly accused of theft, innocent Celina Shelley is cast out of the brothel she calls home and flees to Quinn Ashley, Lord Dreycott. Lina dresses like a nun, looks like an angel, but flirts like a professional – the last thing Quinn expects is to discover she's a virgin! With this revelation, will he wed her before he beds her?

DISGRACE AND DESIRE
Sarah Mallory

With all of London falling at her feet, wagers abound over who will capture the flirtatious Lady Eloise and her fortune. Dashing Major Jack Clifton has vowed to watch over his late comrade's wife, but her beauty and behaviour intrigue him. The lady is not what she seems, and Jack must discover her secret if he is to protect her…

THE VIKING'S CAPTIVE PRINCESS
Michelle Styles

Dangerous warrior Ivar Gunnarson is a man of deeds, not words. With little time for the ideals of love, Ivar seizes what he wants – and Princess Thyre is no exception! But to become king of Thyre's heart, mysterious and enchanting as she is, will entail a battle Ivar has never engaged in before…

 MILLS & BOON

HISTORICAL

Another exciting novel available this month:

REAWAKENING MISS CALVERLEY

Sylvia Andrew

A nameless beauty on his doorstep…

Lord Aldhurst rescues a cold, dazed lady one stormy night – and now the nameless beauty is residing in his home! He'll shelter her until she remembers where she comes from, but James can't deny how much he'd like her to stay – as mistress of his mansion!

London's most sought-after debutante!

Horrified at her growing feelings for her handsome protector, she flees to London, where she regains her status as the *ton*'s most sought-after debutante.

Until she sees James's shocked and stormy face across a ballroom…